SECRETLY SMITTEN

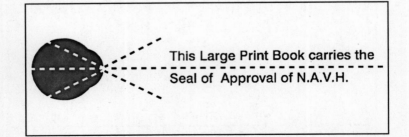

This Large Print Book carries the
Seal of Approval of N.A.V.H.

SECRETLY SMITTEN

COLLEEN COBLE, KRISTEN BILLERBECK, DENISE HUNTER, AND DIANN HUNT

CHRISTIAN LARGE PRINT
A part of Gale, Cengage Learning

GALE
CENGAGE Learning·

Detroit • New York • San Francisco • New Haven, Conn • Waterville, Maine • London

GALE
CENGAGE Learning

THE LIBRARY OF CONGRESS HAS CATALOGED
THE [HARDCOVER IMPRINT] EDITION AS FOLLOWS:

Secretly smitten / by Colleen Coble, Kristin Billerbeck, Denise Hunter, and Diann Hunt. — Large Print edition.
    pages cm. — (Thorndike Press Large Print Christian Fiction)
    ISBN-13: 978-1-4104-5956-5 (hardcover) ISBN-13: 978-1-59415-466-9 (softcover)
    ISBN-10: 1-4104-5956-X (hardcover) ISBN-10: 1-59415-466-X (softcover)
    I. Coble, Colleen. Tess II. Billerbeck, Kristin. Zoe III. Hunter, Denise, 1968– Clare IV. Hunt, Diann. Anna
    PS648.L6S44 2013
    813'.08508—dc23   2013011396

[CIP data for the hardcover edition without any alterations]

Published in 2013 by arrangement with Thomas Nelson, Inc.

Printed in the United States of America
1 2 3 4 5   17 16 15 14 13

CONTENTS

5

LOVE BETWEEN THE LINES
COLLEEN COBLE

CHAPTER ONE

Wrapping paper lay strewn around the floor in a happy crumple of color. Tess Thomas handed her cousin one last gift and suppressed a smile. Nat would blush when she saw the filmy negligee Tess had bought. But Tess knew if anyone would look great in the gown, it was her cousin. It was something Tess would never purchase for herself. But then, what need would she have for a honeymoon gown anyway?

While Natalie began to rip paper with abandon, Tess glanced around the packed parlor of their grandmother's old house. Their friends had all shown up for the bridal shower, and there wasn't space for another chair. A few women even sat on the floor with their backs propped against the wall. That was what Tess loved about the small town of Smitten, Vermont. Neighbors were like family. And they'd all pulled together in amazing ways this past year as they worked to put Smitten on the map as a town based on tourism — a romantic destination, in fact. There were so many new businesses, including a big hotel that had taken over the old lumber mill.

Their great-aunt Violet bustled in with a tray of cookies and tea. "Tess, dear," she whispered. "I'm not sure these gluten-free things are worth eating."

The cookies were as lopsided as Violet's red lipstick. The color of that lipstick had never changed over the years — it was the same orangey red that clashed pitifully with Violet's dyed red hair.

Tess took the crumbliest cookie and took a bite. "They're good, Aunt Violet. And Natalie will appreciate that you went to the trouble."

Her aunt's smile brightened. "I'm so glad, honey. You always were my favorite niece!" She winked dramatically.

Tess's sister Clare took the tray. "Let me help you with that, Aunt Violet." She circled the room with the tray in hand, and to their credit, most guests took a cookie.

Natalie took a break from the gifts to nibble on a cookie and glanced around. "Where's Mia?"

"In the attic," Grandma Rose said. "You

girls always loved to play up there, remember?"

This three-story Victorian was special. Tess, her sisters, and their cousins had loved exploring the attic when they came to visit their grandmother and great-aunts. The grand old home's welcome enveloped visitors the moment they stepped onto the polished walnut floors.

Tess turned toward the hall. "You stay here with your guests. I'll check on her, Natalie."

When Tess reached the bottom of the stairs, Natalie's adopted daughter, Mia, was descending. The six-year-old had a purple boa around her neck and wore a red velvet dress, the hem trailing on the hardwood. She'd found some lipstick from somewhere — probably Violet's, judging by the color — and her small white teeth gleamed behind the smear of orange.

Mia reached the bottom of the staircase and twirled. "Look at me, Tess!"

A wave of love swept over Tess. If only she could have a daughter like Mia someday. "Smashing," she said in genuine admiration. "That's an unusual necklace." She leaned down to examine the tarnished metal and realized it held a pair of dog tags. "Where did you get it?"

Mia looked down at her feet and shuffled. "In the attic."

"Was it in the trunk you were allowed to be in?"

"No." Mia peeked up at her. She held up her arm to show a bracelet. "My bracelet fell off and went down a hole. I put my hand in to get it and found the necklace too." Red stained Mia's cheeks. "Should I put it back?"

Tess put her hand on Mia's soft hair. "No, it's fine, honey. I just wondered where you found it. I've never seen it before."

Natalie appeared in the doorway from the parlor. "Is something wrong?" She glanced at her daughter.

"Not really. I was looking at something Mia found in the attic."

A frown crouched between Natalie's eyes. "Are those dog tags? What on earth . . . There haven't been any soldiers in our family, have there, Tess?" She held out her hand. "Let me see them, Mia."

Mia's lower lip quivered, but she took off the dog tags and handed them over. "I didn't hurt them."

"It's okay, sweetie. I'm sure you didn't." Natalie reached out a reassuring hand to embrace the girl. Lifting the tag to the light, she studied it. "David Hutchins."

Tess's grandmother spoke from behind them. "David Hutchins? Where did you hear that name?"

Tess turned to see the color leave her grandmother's face. "On these dog tags Mia found upstairs in the attic." Beyond Grandma Rose, she saw Aunt Violet turn pale and reach out to steady herself on the wall.

Grandma Rose grabbed the door frame. "With David's name?"

For a moment Tess thought her grandmother might faint. She rushed to her side. "Grandma, are you all right?"

Her grandmother wetted her lips. "I'm fine. I'm just trying to understand this. David died in the Korean conflict. As far as I know, his dog tags were never recovered. Neither was his body."

"See for yourself," Natalie said, joining them, hand outstretched.

Grandma Rose clutched the dog tags, then held them to the light. "Mia, where did you find these?"

"In the attic." Mia's voice wobbled. "I'm sorry."

Tess embraced her. "You're not in trouble, honey. Grandma is just surprised they were there." She stared at her grandmother, who was as pale as the white blouse she wore.

"Who was David Hutchins?"

Her grandmother was staring at the dog tags. She blinked rapidly. "My fiancé."

Natalie frowned. "I'm confused. What about Grandpa Martin?"

Grandma Rose bit her lip. "I loved him, of course, but he wasn't my first love." She hesitated. "First love is special." Her face took on a dreamy expression. "He used to call me his Betty Boop."

Though it hurt even to imagine her grandmother loving another man before her own grandfather, Tess loved a good mystery, and this smelled like the best kind. "If he died in the war, then how did these dog tags get in your attic?"

"I don't know. It makes no sense."

"Could the military have sent them back to you?" Natalie asked.

"They didn't. I would have kept them close. They wouldn't be in the attic."

"You're sure he died?" Tess asked.

"Of course. The army notified his parents. I was there when they told us of his death." She looked down. "It was the darkest day of my life."

Darker than the day Grandpa died? Tess studied her grandmother's face but didn't ask the question.

"Did he live here in Smitten?" Natalie asked.

Grandma Rose nodded. "Over on Green Valley Road. In that big house where Ryan Stevenson lives now."

Tess's pulse kicked at Ryan Stevenson's name. The handsome widower was a Saturday morning patron at her bookstore. Not that he'd ever noticed *her.*

"David's family moved away after his death." Her grandmother's voice broke, then she recovered her composure and managed a smile. "We'd better get back to our guests."

Tess followed her to the parlor, but her brain was whirling. What did it all mean?

The last guests had left and Tess and her sisters were picking up bits of confetti and wrapping paper from the floor. The older women had gone out to practice for Saturday night's concert in the town square. Tess lifted the dog tags from the table and rattled them in her hands. "We have to get to the bottom of this," she said.

Her mother, Anna, shook her head. At fifty, she was still trim and her skin was smooth and pink. Most people thought she was much younger. "It's none of our concern, Tess. We shouldn't be poking our nose

15

into Mother's business."

"Something happened, and even Grandma has no idea what it was. Aren't you the least bit curious?"

Her youngest sister, Zoe, dropped a dust-pan full of confetti into a wastebasket. "I think Grandma deserves to know the truth. How could those tags have gotten there?"

Clare stopped sweeping. "Let's think about this." As the middle child, she was the reflective one, with her feet firmly planted on the ground. "It's very strange."

"Maybe he didn't die in the war," Tess suggested. "Maybe he came to town. What if Grandpa answered the door when he got here and didn't let him see Grandma?"

"Now, Tess, I'm sure it was nothing so unpleasant," Anna said. "I'm sure my mother isn't interested anymore."

"Of course she is! You saw how white she went. She must have loved him very much. And what if he's still alive?" Tess could see it now. A handsome gentleman with white hair stepping out of a restored Roadster. Her grandmother's face bright with happiness. "We could get them together again."

"He's probably married by now, even if he did survive the war," Clare pointed out. "But you're jumping to conclusions. It's more likely that his parents left the tags here or something. Maybe Aunt Violet or Aunt Petunia tucked them away so she wouldn't be upset."

"If that's the case, then there's no real mystery at all," their mother said.

Tess was sure it wasn't something that simple.

Clare's thoughtful frown was back. "We'll need to handle this very carefully. If he's married, we back off without even talking to him, agreed?"

"He should know the truth," Zoe said. "He should know Grandma thinks he died."

"The truth isn't always the best thing," their mother said. "Not if it hurts someone."

Zoe rolled her eyes but said nothing. Clare cut her gaze to the carpet.

Tess picked up more paper from the floor. "I'll do an Internet search. It can't hurt just to poke around a little." Ryan's face flashed into mind. "Maybe Ryan would let me explore his attic, see if there's any information there."

"I'm sure you'd like that," Clare said, her voice teasing. "The most eligible bachelor in town."

Heat flooded Tess's cheeks. "I'm the last person he'd be interested in." She grabbed a cookie from the plate. She'd mooned over Ryan since high school, not that she would

17

admit it to anyone. He had a way of making you feel like he was really listening, really paying attention to you. With two younger sisters, she sometimes felt her needs were forgotten.

"Now, honey, you put yourself down too much," Anna scolded. "You look fine just the way you are." Even as her mother said the words, she stared at the cookie in Tess's hands. "That probably has two hundred calories in it, sweetie."

Tess put the cookie back on the plate. She avoided Clare's sympathetic glance and unbuttoned her too-tight jacket. She'd bought it for the shower with the intention of losing those fifteen pounds. What was it they said about good intentions?

"You're beautiful, Tess. You just don't see it," Zoe said in a matter-of-fact tone. "And Ryan likes you. I can tell."

If only Tess could believe it. "His wife was Miss Vermont. I'm hardly in that league." She resisted reaching for the cookie again. "I'm just thinking that one time at the bookstore, Ryan mentioned that he needed to clean the attic. Evidently the Hutchins family left a ton of boxes up there. Maybe he'd like some help cleaning it out."

"Perfect. It might just take you awhile to go through them," Clare said, grinning.

"Don't go getting any ideas. This is strictly research. I'm not interested in Ryan."

"Whatever you say." Clare stood up straight and stretched. "Looks like we've finished up here. And I need coffee. Anyone want to go with me?"

Zoe got up. "Not me. I spend enough of my life in the coffee shop. I want to go to Ryan's ice cream store."

"I'll go with you, Zoe," Tess said. When her mother lifted a brow, she added, "If Ryan is there, I can ask him about looking through the attic."

She followed her sisters out of the house and told herself their grandmother would thank them in the end.

CHAPTER TWO

"Crème brûlée sundae coming up." Ryan Stevenson smiled at Julia Bourne, who stood waiting with her fiancé, Zak Grant. Zak already had his banana split, complete with coconut and chocolate syrup. The late spring day was unseasonably warm and had brought in a lot of customers.

The bell over the door of the Wind Chill Creamery jingled, and Ryan straightened when he saw Tess Thomas coming in. Her dark hair was pulled back in a ponytail, and her blue eyes crinkled in a smile when he greeted her.

"The usual?" he asked, starting for the Almond Avalanche.

"With coconut topping," she said. "But a small one. Zoe wants to try it too." Her sister moved off to talk to Julia.

"Coming up."

Tess moved closer to the display freezer and studied the flavors. "What are you doing working the counter today? I thought you'd be back in the office crunching numbers or over at the creamery supervising the cheese making. Isn't today the big production day?"

"One of the employees here didn't show up today. The cheese was nearly ready to ship to stores, and I needed a break." He opened the freezer lid and began to scoop out the dark-chocolate ice cream loaded with almonds. "How about you? You're usually at the bookstore on Saturdays." Too late he realized he was revealing the fact that he knew her habits. She'd think he was a stalker.

"Natalie's bridal shower was today," she said, showing no sign of catching his slip.

"Oh yes, that's right. Sophia went with my mother-in-law."

"Right, she was playing with my cousin's daughter, Mia." Tess took the cone he handed her. "Um, listen, I have a favor to ask. Are those boxes that were there when you bought your house still in the attic?"

He began to scoop the ice cream for Zoe. "Yeah. I've been meaning to go through them, but it's a mammoth job and I've been putting it off." He grinned. "Are you needing donations for a garage sale?" He might even face that mountain of work if it would make Tess think more highly of him.

"No." She took a lick of her cone and closed her eyes with a sigh. "This is the best ice cream in the world." She opened her eyes and looked at him again. "This is probably an odd request, but I'd like to find out more about the Hutchins family. Especially David. I wondered if you'd mind letting me go through the attic. I'd even organize things for you and let you know what could be hauled to the dump and what could be donated."

He handed the cone to Zoe and hoped his expression didn't reveal his eagerness. "That sounds like an offer too good to refuse. I'll be glad to help too." When she blushed, he tempered his eagerness. "I mean, if you could use the help."

"I don't want to bother you."

"No bother," he assured her. "What's with the interest in the Hutchins family?"

She glanced around to make sure no one was listening. Zoe had taken her cone and gone to an outside table with Zak and Julia, so the creamery was empty. "I'd appreciate it if you didn't say anything about this to anyone."

He made a zipping motion along his mouth. "My lips are sealed."

"David Hutchins was engaged to my

grandmother. She says he died in Korea and his body was never found. But here's the funny thing. Mia just found his dog tags down a hole in the attic."

"That *is* odd. How did the dog tags get in the Garners' attic?"

"That's what we don't know. I'd like to find a clue about where his family went. You bought the house from them?"

He shook his head. "It was bank owned and had been for ten years. The place was a mess when I moved in. Someone else had owned it for thirty years. I'm not even sure if all the junk up there belonged to them or the Hutchins family."

Tess's face fell. "I hadn't thought of that. But surely there's a clue somewhere up there."

"You and your mysteries," he said, smiling. When her brows rose, he pointed to the book poking out of her bag. "You're always reading one."

Her blush deepened. "While you tend to read biographies." She bit her lip. "I mean, I've called you a dozen times when a book you've ordered has come in."

His surge of elation deflated. Of course she would know his reading habits. It was her business to know what all her customers liked. "When do you want to start?"

"After church tomorrow?"

"Sounds good. I'll be happy to pick you up for church. Then we could go straight to my house."

"You'd have to take me home," she reminded him.

"I don't mind. I'll even spring for pizza."

Her dimple appeared. "I don't expect you to entertain me. It's enough that you're letting me do this. I'll just drive and follow you out to your house. I don't want to be a bother."

Easy. Don't rush her. "Whatever you like."

"I'll bring lunch as a thank-you for the access. Something easy like my spicy enchilada casserole."

He grinned. He hated Mexican food, but he wasn't about to tell her. He reminded himself to have lots of milk on hand so he could choke it down.

It was ridiculous to feel this nervous. It wasn't a date. Tess was going to rummage in his attic, then leave. The aroma of chicken enchiladas wafted up her nose as she stood on the porch of the big old house and pressed the doorbell. She knew better than to moon after someone like Ryan. He was way out of her league.

The door opened, and she caught a

24

glimpse of pale yellow walls and gleaming wood floors. Ryan was dressed in jeans and a Red Sox sweatshirt. Little Sophia hung on to his leg but peeked up at Tess with a shy smile.

"Come in," Ryan said. He swung the door wide. "Here, let me take that." He lifted the bag from her hands. "Smells good."

Tess followed him into the expansive foyer. A flight of open stairs rose to the second floor. The ceilings were at least ten feet high. "Wow, your home is lovely."

"I can't claim any of the credit. Candace did it all." He pointed down the hall. "This way to the kitchen. We can eat there rather than the dining room."

Brown granite topped the cherry cabinets. The slate floors and polished fixtures proclaimed how much the kitchen remodel had cost. Tess eyed the big island. Making bread there would be a dream come true. She couldn't resist touching the smooth surface of the stone. And it was spotless. She'd expected a messy house since he was a single dad. He'd already stacked plates and tableware on the table at the other end of the kitchen. It was a homey wood one that didn't match the cabinets. She wanted to ask if he'd moved it in after Candace died, but the question didn't seem appropriate.

"I baked bread, but I didn't bring butter," she said. "I assumed you'd have some famous creamery butter here."

"You bet." He got it out of the refrigerator.

She scooped up a generous helping of the enchiladas for him. Her serving was half the size of his, but she'd nibbled on M&M's and nuts on the way over. She sliced the bread, then joined him and Sophia at the table. She wanted to believe his expression was anticipation as he eyed his plate, but it seemed more like dismay.

"Did I give you too much?" she asked.

His smile seemed forced. "I had a late breakfast, but I'm sure it will be delicious." He forked a bit into his mouth and chewed. His face reddened. He swallowed, then grabbed for his glass of milk. "Hot," he croaked.

"The peppers were a little spicy," she agreed. "The hotter the better, though, don't you think?"

"My dad hates hot stuff," Sophia said. "I like it, though." Her serving was already a third gone.

Ryan had dispatched half of his glass of milk, and his face had nearly resumed its normal color. "I don't *hate* hot stuff," he said. "I'm trying to build up tolerance to it on my tongue."

"You don't even eat pepper, Daddy," Sophia said.

Tess bit her lip. "Try the bread," she said. "I put some chili powder in it, but it's not hot."

The refrigerator clunked as ice cubes dropped into the tray. Ryan chewed on the bread, and though his eyes widened, he didn't lunge for his milk. Tess laughed and began to relax. He might not kick her out after all.

CHAPTER THREE

Dust motes danced in the air as Ryan stepped onto the attic floorboards. He hadn't been up here since he and Candace first moved in eight years ago. Candace had refused to step foot in the attic after that first time. She said the place gave her the creeps.

It was a perfectly ordinary attic as far as he could tell. Wide floorboards, sloped ceilings, an assortment of boxes, trunks, and discarded furniture. The space was open all around, and a few dormer windows let in more light than the feeble bulb that hung from the middle of the room.

Tess stood under the light and surveyed the area. "All this stuff was here when you moved in?"

"Everything but the Christmas tree and decorations." He pointed them out in the corner.

"Why would they leave so much behind?"

She stepped closer to the wall and opened the drawer on a small desk. "Some of this is really nice. Lots of antiques. Maybe even worth some money."

"Looks like junk to me." It did too. The antique craze wasn't something he understood, let alone was interested in. Why someone would want to dig through dusty old boxes and trunks was beyond him. Old furniture hulked in the shadows, and he had to step over several rolled-up rugs. "Where do you want to start?"

"There's an interesting piece," she said, pointing to a leather trunk under the window. "The trunk alone is beautiful. You should keep it for Sophia's mementos."

"Yeah, Daddy, I want it!" Sophia piped up. She had a doll clutched under her arm and stared around the attic as if some monster were about to pop out.

He put his hand on his daughter's shoulder. "It's just an old trunk," he said. "It looks kind of ratty to me."

Tess knelt in front of it. "The leather is worn, but that gives it character. And the brass will polish right up. It's worth a lot of money."

He opened his mouth to offer it to her, then closed it again. The last thing he wanted was to run her off on her first visit.

"Here, let me open it for you," he said when her struggles failed to lift the lid.

He knelt beside her with Sophia peering over his shoulder. Was that scent of bread from Tess's hair? He leaned in a little closer and sniffed. The aroma made his mouth water. The lid resisted his struggles as well, and he peered at the latch. "I think it's locked."

She slumped back on her heels. "I think we're thwarted unless you don't mind breaking the lock."

"There's a big ring of old keys on a hook by the stairs. Maybe it's on there." He rose and retrieved them. The ring of keys was heavy in his hand and smelled of old metal. The assortment varied from skeleton keys to old house keys.

Tess and Sophia came to stand by him as he flipped through them. "The trunk key will be smaller and probably silver colored," she said.

"How do you know so much about trunks?" He held up a key and walked back to the trunk with Sophia on his heels.

"My grandmother loves antiques. Her house is full of them. She gave each of us girls a trunk for our eighteenth birthday. Mine is smaller than this and not as fancy, but most trunks open the same way."

"Let me, Daddy." Sophia's small hand closed over the key.

He let her take it and helped her guide it into the keyhole. When it clicked, he lifted the lid with ease. The scent of old clothing rose to his nose when he touched the stack of brightly colored fabric inside the trunk. "Nothing much here."

"Fuzzy dice!" Tess swooped past him to lift out a large set of black-and-white dice. "I've seen pictures of these. They used to hang a set from the rearview mirror."

Her elation struck him as funny, and he had to bite his lip to keep from laughing.

She twirled the dice. "They're so cute." She handed them to Sophia and began to riffle through the contents again. "What else is in here? Ooh, look, there're a bunch of old records. And a Betty Boop cookie tin." She glanced up at him. "Grandma said David called her his Betty Boop. I wonder if she brought him homemade cookies in this tin."

"It might be why he kept it. Betty Boop was the Marilyn Monroe of her era, so your grandma must have been really beautiful to him."

She dived in again. "The records are heavy."

"Let me get them." His arm brushed hers

31

as he bent over and lifted the heavy stack of old records. "The Everly Brothers, Elvis, Johnny Horton, Chuck Berry. Someone was collecting all the popular albums of the day."

He looked in again and saw something furry in the bottom of the trunk. "A coonskin cap! My dad had one of these. It belonged to my grandpa."

Her eyes were sparkling. "And you said this stuff was boring."

Tess had a way of lighting up a room with enthusiasm and joy. There was always a smile on her face, and he'd never seen her discouraged or upset. He'd seen the bookstore employees send complaining customers her way, and she always seemed able to calm them and send them home satisfied. That took a special gift. He liked her soft curves and the sheen of her hair. He suspected she had no idea how beautiful she was.

"Look at this," she said.

He realized he'd been staring at her, and her cheeks were pink. The engraved plate she indicated was attached to the inside of the trunk. " 'David Hutchins,' " he said. "So this belonged to him."

"I bet Grandma *did* bring him cookies in that tin."

He grinned. "You're on quite the investigation."

Her face clouded. "But we don't know for sure without asking her."

"Take it and ask her about it. Really, you can have anything up here you want."

"Thanks." She looked around. "These things are worth a lot of money, Ryan. You really should get an antique dealer up here."

"I'll think about it," he said. "Now, what else do you want to look at?"

Even poking through dusty boxes would be fun if she was with him.

The small guest bath was a warm tan. The marble tile was exactly what Tess would have chosen herself if she had unlimited funds and a house this gorgeous. But all it succeeded in doing was making her feel even more inadequate. Not only had Ryan's first wife been beautiful, but she'd possessed a sense of style Tess could never match.

She washed the dust from her hands and arms and scrubbed a black smudge on her cheek. "You are crazy," she told her image in the mirror. "Look at yourself. Hair in a ponytail, no makeup. You are the last person Ryan Stevenson would take a second look at." At least the red top brought out the sheen of her dark hair and lifted a bit of color to her skin.

The towel on the ring was plush tan. She almost let her hands air-dry rather than mar the perfection of the thick terry. But that was silly. She dried her hands, then threw back her shoulders and practiced a smile. Her mother always said that proper carriage could erase five pounds. And if she smiled enough, maybe Ryan would keep his attention on her face.

She found Ryan and Sophia in the living room on beautiful tan leather furniture. A rug that had to cost the earth gleamed with rich shades of blue, gold, and pumpkin atop oak floors. The place was immaculate, with just the right touches of accessories. It made Tess want to run for the comfort of her small cottage with its happily messy rooms.

Ryan's gaze warmed when he saw her. "Sophia was asking for a story, but I guess I'm not the storyteller she wants."

"I want *you* to read me a book," Sophia said. She held up a copy of *Olivia*. "Daddy doesn't do Olivia's voice very well. He makes snorting sounds."

"Well, that's not right. Olivia is much too genteel to snort." Tess took the book and sank into the soft cushion beside the little girl. The book was worn with a few chocolate spots. "Ice cream?"

Sophia nodded. "We always eat ice cream at night when we read."

"Ice cream is good for any time of day," Tess said. "I think your daddy should hire us to be official ice cream tasters so we can tell him the best flavors to make."

"It has to be chocolate," Sophia said. "Anything with chocolate."

"Like maybe chocolate and avocado?"

Sophia wrinkled her nose. "Avocado is for salad."

"What about chocolate and bacon? Or chocolate and chicken?" Tess asked.

"You're being silly," Sophia said reprovingly.

Tess and Ryan both burst out laughing. Warmth spread through her as they sat together almost like a family. Did he feel it too or was it all her imagination?

"I bet you could read this story yourself," Ryan told his daughter.

Sophia folded her hands across her chest. "I like to listen to Tess."

"So do I," Ryan said.

"Well, I'd better read then," Tess said, turning to the first page of the story.

She plunged into the story and put as much animation and emotion into her reading as possible, though having Ryan watch her was a little disconcerting. By the time the story was over, Sophia's head was against her daddy's arm and her eyes were closed. When Tess closed the book, she wasn't sure what to say. The silence should have been uncomfortable but was more companionable than she'd expected.

She cleared her throat. "Well, I suppose I should be going. Thank you for letting me rummage around in the attic."

"When do you want to come back? There's a lot we haven't seen."

His eagerness to have her back was a desire to get the attic organized, she told herself. It had nothing to do with any desire for a friendship with her. "Tuesday after work?"

"Sounds good to me. How about I provide dinner this time?"

His smile put crinkles around his green eyes. Those eyes. She could dive deep into them and search for the meaning. Men shouldn't look that good. If she dared, she would lean over and sniff the spicy scent of his cologne. He would smell as good as he looked, no question.

She rose and picked up the cookie tin he'd given her. "You really didn't like that casserole, did you? Come on 'fess up."

"Okay, I admit Mexican isn't my favorite."

"Why didn't you say something when I

told you what I was bringing?"

"And turn down the only offer of a home-cooked meal I'd had in years? Not happening." He eased Sophia onto the sofa, then stood to walk her to the door. "I enjoyed the day, Tess."

They reached the front door and she put her hand on the doorknob. "So did I." She felt oddly breathless. She pulled open the door and stepped into the fading light of a gorgeous late May day. "Thanks again for the tin."

"Call me later and let me know if you find out anything about it. I'm curious to know how the Hutchinses got it." He fumbled in his pocket and brought out a business card case. "Here's my phone number. My cell too. Call anytime."

She took the card he held out. "You're sure?"

"You bet. I want to help you get to the bottom of the mystery. I'm intrigued too."

Of course, it was all about the mystery. Who wouldn't be enthralled with something this strange?

CHAPTER FOUR

Her sisters' cars were parked in front of the big Victorian house, but Grandma Rose's big old Caddy was conspicuously absent. Tess had thought they would all be gone by now, with Sunday dinner finished and the mess cleaned up. She found her mother and sisters in the sunroom having coffee and cookies — chocolate chip, her favorite. She set the tin on the table and scooped up a cookie. It was still warm, and she savored the melted chocolate on her tongue. Well, as much as she could, with her mother's disapproving stare.

Tess had always loved this room with its soft yellows and comfortable furniture. "Where's Grandma?"

"She stepped out to pick up Aunt Violet. Her car quit on her downtown." Her mother frowned when Tess reached for another cookie.

Zoe lifted a brow. "Dish! We want the

entire scoop. Did he ask you out?"

Tess poured herself a cup of coffee and laced it with cream. "Of course not! I was only there to go through the attic." She reached for the tin. "Look what I found there." She held up the tin where it caught the soft afternoon light.

Clare gasped and touched the tin's embossed figure. "It's darling! But why did you bring it?"

"That's the funny thing." Tess told them where she'd found the tin. "Grandma said David called her his Betty Boop. I wanted to ask her if she took cookies to him. I bet she did, and he kept this as a memento."

Tess set the tin back on the table. "I want to talk to you all before Grandma gets back. How do we find out if this was something she gave David? Just ask her? I'm afraid it might upset her."

"I can tell you." Anna rose and walked to the small woodstove on the west wall. "It's your grandmother's."

"How do you know, Mom?" Zoe asked.

"She had a collection of Betty Boop tins. This one was her favorite. She showed me a picture of it. I asked her what happened to it, and she told me she gave it to a friend."

"I know where Grandma keeps the photo albums," Zoe said.

Their mother shook her head. Her lips were pressed together. "Why are you girls persisting in prying into things that don't concern you?"

Zoe sprang to her feet. "I don't understand why you think Grandma wouldn't care to know the truth."

Clare reached out and grabbed Zoe's hand. She tugged her back onto the sofa. "Let's keep our voices down and discuss this calmly. Mom, wouldn't you want to know if the past was very different from what you'd always thought?"

Anna hesitated. "If it were something good, maybe. But this can only cause heartache. What difference does it make now? Mother married someone else."

"You saw her reaction to his name," Tess said. "I thought she was going to faint. She had very strong feelings for him, and still does. She deserves to know what happened to him. And how did those dog tags get here? It's very puzzling."

"I just don't understand why it matters."

Clare was staring at their mother with a thoughtful expression. "You seem to be taking our interest very personally. Does this threaten you somehow, Mom?"

Anna flushed and turned to stare out the window at the maple trees waving in the wind. "I loved my father. I guess I just wouldn't want anything to sully his name."

"This isn't about Grandpa, Mom," Zoe burst out. "We just want Grandma to know the truth."

Tess patted her youngest sister's hand. "Take it easy, Zoe," she whispered to her. Her mother looked so alone, her shoulders rounded defensively. "I understand, Mom. But I don't think we'll find out anything that will be a detriment to Grandpa. You know Grandma loved him very much. And I promise we'll be discreet."

When her mother turned to face them, tears glimmered in her eyes. "I still don't approve, but you girls are going ahead with it anyway. I can see it on your faces."

"We'll talk to you before we tell Grandma anything, okay?" Clare said, her tone placating.

Zoe frowned and opened her mouth, then closed it again when Tess clamped her hand tighter. "I don't know that we're going to find out anything earth-shattering."

A door slammed and she heard voices. "I think Grandma is back with the aunts." She grabbed the tin and stuck it behind the sofa.

Grandma Rose's two sisters were with her when she joined them in the sunroom. The three were so unalike. Grandma was tall and slim with silver hair and glowing skin that looked younger than her age. She dressed in elegant sweater sets atop modest skirts or pants. She was so sweet, with a servant's heart.

When it came to clothing, Aunt Violet seemed to think the louder, the better. In fact, Tess had always privately wondered if Aunt Violet was colorblind. The outfits she wore never went together. And had no one ever told her that women her age should maybe tone down the hair a bit? You could see Aunt Violet's red hair coming from five hundred yards away.

Aunt Petunia was the oldest of the three but still spry. She was tiny compared to the other women, and she never went out without her favorite earrings, a pair of dangling rhinestones that her husband had bought her in the sixties. Her clothes were all high quality, but they'd been purchased years ago and were a mishmash of styles that she somehow managed to carry off.

Tess rose and hugged each of them. "The cookies are great, Grandma."

"I made them just for you, honey," her grandmother said. "You all look so sober. Is something wrong?"

"Nothing at all. We were just waiting for you."

"Your slippers, your highness." Ryan bowed on one knee in front of his daughter. He'd had a hard time getting the pink princess slippers to balance on the pillow on his knee.

Sophia giggled. "I need help getting them on."

"I shall be honored to assist you." He took one of the slippers and started to slide it onto his daughter's small foot. The doorbell rang. "I'll be right back."

He glanced at his watch as he went to the door. Seven. His pulse skipped when he saw Tess on the porch. Her mouth gaped when she saw him, and he remembered the tiara and netting on his head. The combs holding it in place gripped his thick hair, but he finally managed to wrest it from his head and tossed it to the table in the entry.

"Uh, hi. We were playing princess."

Tess caught her lower lip between perfect white teeth, but a smile lurked at the corners and her eyes sparkled. "I thought I'd misjudged the day and it was Halloween."

"If you tell a soul what you saw today, I'll put mint in your ice cream," he warned.

Her eyes widened. "How'd you know I

hate mint?"

Drat, he'd betrayed himself. "You curled your nose up when I offered to let you try my coconut mint concoction. And coconut is your favorite." He was standing there like some kind of starstruck goof. "Come in. I didn't mean to leave you standing outside."

"It's a beautiful night." She stepped into the foyer. "I tried your phone but just got voice mail. I was driving by and thought I'd pop in for a minute and tell you what I found out. I hope I'm not interrupting something — important." She slanted a definite smirk his direction.

He grinned. "You're about to get that mint in your ice cream, princess."

"*I'm* the princess, Daddy," Sophia said, suddenly appearing at his leg.

"Quite right," Tess said. "You're the perfect princess. I love your dress."

Sophia smoothed the pale blue satin. "Daddy bought it for me at Disney World."

"And you got his tiara there too?"

Sophia nodded. "It matches mine but it's bigger. 'Cause Daddy's bigger."

The snort that came from Tess's pretty face was definitely not ladylike. He could tell she was doing her best not to laugh from the way she clutched the bag in her hand as well as the contorted expression on her face.

Every bit of dignity he thought he possessed was now gone. And he discovered he didn't mind when those blue eyes were looking him over with a hint of mischief in them.

"I brought back your tin," she said, holding the bag out.

"I told you that you could keep it."

She shook her head. "I wouldn't feel right about it. I'm sure it's valuable."

The night air, redolent with the scent of freshly cut grass and roses, drifted in the open doorway. A car rolled past, the *thump-thump* of the speakers' woofers proclaiming the occupant to be a teenager. He reached past her and shut out the world. For a few minutes he was going to have her all to himself.

"Want a milk shake? I was going to make some anyway." His fingers closed around the strings on the bag. Maybe she didn't want to be beholden to him. As far as he knew, she might even be involved with someone. The thought made his gut clench.

"Chocolate?"

"What else, with a girl in the house?" He grinned and took Sophia's hand. "Want to help me make some milk shakes, honey?"

"Can I spray on the whipped cream?" Sophia asked.

"You bet."

Tess followed them. "My kind of milk shake."

He dropped the bag on the sofa as they went past. "The kitchen is a little messy. I never cleaned up after dinner." Spaghetti had splattered on the six-burner stove, and dishes were heaped in the sink.

Tess glanced around. "At least it looks lived in. I was beginning to worry that you had a neatness issue."

"You have something against being neat?"

"It's a sign of a sick mind."

He grinned. "Hey, I resemble that remark."

The blender sat to the right of the stove. He pulled it forward. "Want to get the ice cream out of the freezer?"

"I'll get the cream," Sophia said. She pulled hard on the refrigerator door and retrieved the heavy cream he'd brought home from the creamery. "Can I pour it in the little pitcher?"

"If you're careful." He felt Tess's presence behind him before her arm brushed his. "Got the ice cream?" The question was more casual than the way he felt — every nerve at attention.

"I've got chocolate and vanilla. I wasn't sure how you were making it."

"Yours will be as chocolaty as it can get."

He loaded the blender with chocolate ice cream and added more syrup and cream, then hit the button. The whir that shattered the quiet of the kitchen also added a sense of normalcy. For a minute there, he'd been thinking there was something momentous about the three of them making milk shakes together.

He poured the first milk shake into a frosted glass. When he glanced Tess's way, he found her scrubbing tomato sauce off the stove. He started to tell her not to do that but was caught by the expression on her face — pure joy and focus. A flush highlighted her cheeks, and she looked so darn cute that all he could do was watch.

"Daddy, you're spilling my milk shake!"

He looked down to see the dark liquid overflowing the glass and running down onto the counter. His face burned as he grabbed a paper towel.

The last thing he wanted to do was look ridiculous in Tess's eyes.

CHAPTER FIVE

Fireside Books sat at the corner of Look-away Lane and Main Street, right beside the nineteenth-century firehouse. It had occupied the same Victorian storefront for seventy-five years. Every time Tess stepped onto the wide, uneven floorboards and inhaled the good scent of books, she felt revitalized. Today was her late day because it was story hour time. She maneuvered her upturned clown shoes past the boxes of new stock in the mystery section.

Her employee, Flo Garret, lifted a brow in her direction. Flo was in her fifties and had come to work at the bookstore after her husband died. She was soft and round and appeared to be all fluff and nervous energy, but underneath she had a deep caring for people and a quick mind. Her curly hair was wild today with the humidity, and she wore jeans with a red jacket and pearls.

"I'm reading *If I Ran the Circus,*" Tess

explained. "You know how the children love it when I dress up to match the story." The clown outfit was a bit too big and sagged in the rear end. The pant legs dragged on the floor as well, but it had been the only thing she could find at the costume shop in Burlington.

"I wondered if I could take off early tonight," Flo said. "I have the town meeting."

"Sure, I can close for you tonight. Is it about the train?"

"Yes. We're going to discuss all the reasons we can give that make Smitten a good fit for a stop on RailAmerica." Flo's hazel eyes glowed. "Think of all the tourism it would bring in."

Tess nodded. "We need that train! It would bring in so much business too, and you know how we're struggling to make ends meet."

She would do whatever she had to in order to save the bookstore. It was unthinkable that it would ever close. The place was an icon, a spot for villagers to gather and discuss politics, culture, and good books. And what would she do? She'd worked here since she was sixteen and had saved every nickel until she was able to buy it when the owner moved to New York. It was more than a business to her. It was the one place she belonged, the one place where she fit.

"What can I do to help convince the train executives? Any idea when we'll know?"

Flo's curls bounced as she nodded her head. "It's going to take awhile." She studied Tess's face. "I keep your books, Tess. I know you're barely taking enough of a salary to keep yourself afloat. I want this as much for you as I do for the town. I'll do my best. We can both pray."

"I will." Troubled, Tess walked to the back of the store to her lovely children's book section.

"Miss Tess!" Sophia ran to her and hugged her leg. "You look funny. Your shoes are too big."

"Clowns are supposed to look funny." Tess glanced around for Ryan and found him laughing, so she looked away.

Maybe she did look ridiculous. Candace wouldn't have allowed herself to look so frumpy. The warm sensation that still lingered from yesterday's time with him vanished. Stupid to allow herself to have an ounce of hope that he might look at her with interest.

A group of ten children had assembled on the colorful interlocking mat in the children's area. She had them sit in a circle while she read the story. The kids gasped at the appropriate times and laughed at the right places too. Tess got into the story, acting out parts. Let Ryan snicker. What difference did it make? This was who she was.

When story hour was over, the children drifted off with their parents. But Ryan stayed with Sophia on the mat. Tess pulled off her clown nose and hat. "I need to wash my face," she told Ryan. "It's itchy."

His gaze roamed over her face. "I think you're reacting to that makeup. Looks like you have a rash."

Her fingers flew to her cheeks, and she felt the bumps under the thick layer of greasy makeup. "Oh no!" She rushed for the bathroom in the back and locked the door behind her.

There was nothing in the bathroom except liquid hand soap, but it would have to do. She scrubbed the white and red grease from her face and winced when she saw her skin. Blotchy red patches covered her cheeks and chin. Her forehead had a particularly frightful raised spot, as though angry mosquitoes had attacked her. She wanted to bang her head against the wall.

And Ryan was right outside. Unless he'd had the grace to leave while she was evaluating the damage. But no, she couldn't be that lucky. He was probably browsing the shelves with Sophia as usual. When they came, they usually stayed at least an hour.

She patted cold water on the spots, but it didn't help. And the makeup bag she'd brought was in her purse. Which was under the counter up front. She'd have to walk through the store like this. Sighing, she yanked open the door. Hiding here would do no good, and Flo would be leaving in fifteen minutes.

She spied Ryan at the bookshelves. He hadn't seen her yet. Her heart pounding, she raced past him with her face averted. But in her haste to escape, she didn't watch where she was going. The long, curling toe of her clown shoe caught a chair leg. The next thing she knew, she was flying through the air and landed facedown on the carpet.

Tess looked like she'd been attacked by bees. Even her lips were swollen. Ryan had helped her to the chair behind the counter, and she still sat there nursing a swollen ankle. Tears pooled in the corners of her eyes, and he wasn't sure if it was the pain from her sprain or the humiliation of her fall. Women were hard to read.

"Can I get you anything?" he asked after Flo had finished fussing, then left for her meeting.

"I'm fine," Tess snapped. "I have some work to do." She pulled the keyboard toward her and called up a program.

She seemed mad at him. He tried again. "I can run get you something to eat. Maybe some green tea?" Sophia came to him with two books, and he laid them on the counter.

"I said I'm fine!" She glared at him, but the sight was so funny with her face that he chuckled. "It's not funny, Ryan. You can leave right now if you're going to laugh at me." Her voice was strangled as though she might cry. "I didn't laugh at you in that tiara yesterday."

"You snorted." His comment didn't change the scowl on her face. "I didn't mean to laugh, honey." Too late he realized the endearment had slipped out. "It's just that clown suit and your poor swollen face. Can't you see the humor of the situation?"

"I doubt you'd think it was funny if you were the one who looked like a puffer fish." She sniffled and reached for a tissue.

Oh man. He hated to see a woman cry. Especially if he was the cause — and it was clear he was. "I'm sorry. You're right. I'm a jerk for laughing."

Her eyes were incredibly blue in her red face. When she'd walked in with that clown suit on, he'd been so delighted that he hadn't been able to hide it. How many women were so intent on making other people happy that they were willing to appear just a little ridiculous? In a good way, of course. Candace wouldn't have dreamed of appearing in public like that. She was always conscious of her face and figure. But even if Tess cared about other people, no one wanted to be made fun of, and he wished he could go back and hold that laugh. He wouldn't have hurt her for anything.

"You're forgiven," she said. "But only because I want to get back into your attic." She pointed her pencil at him and narrowed her eyes. "But if you laugh at me again . . ."

"We're through?"

"Exactly." But though she laughed with him, she continued to study him with wide eyes.

Did she feel the pull between them, or was it all on his side? He was used to women who cared about his money and status, and she clearly cared about none of that. If he wanted to impress her — and he did — he had no idea where to start. What did a woman like her care about?

He leaned on the counter. "What time are you finished here?"

"Not until nine. It's Flo's turn to close, but she has a meeting. Then I have to take the money to the bank."

Sophia would need to be in bed by then. He'd hoped he could take Tess out for coffee or ice cream. "I'll see you tomorrow then."

"And dinner, don't forget dinner. It's your turn to cook."

He grinned. "I hope you're not expecting a three-course meal. I'm a pretty plain cook."

"He makes good eggs," Sophia said.

"I'm sure he does," Tess said. "With no salsa, though, right?"

Sophia wrinkled her nose. "On *eggs*?"

"You like hot stuff, Sophia. Try it sometime."

He took out his wallet as Tess rang up the books. "Are you trying to corrupt my daughter?"

"I think it's too late. Face it: you've lost her to Mexican food." Tess handed him the bag. "See you tomorrow?"

"You bet." He took his daughter's hand and exited the store.

On the sidewalk he nearly ran Candace's sister down. He grabbed her arm and steadied her. "Whoa, sorry, Isabelle."

Her face lit with a smile. "Ryan, I had no

idea I might run into you. Where have you been hiding since I got back to town? I've left two messages on your voice mail."

"I'm sorry. It's been crazy at work, and I wasn't sure how long you were going to be around." Not long, he hoped.

Isabelle had made no secret of the fact that she wouldn't mind stepping into her sister's shoes. And he had no intention of being caught in her games. She'd flirted with him even when Candace was still alive, and it had made Candace furious.

"Can we do dinner one night? I'd love to catch up with you and this little darling." She finally deigned to notice Sophia, who was hiding behind Ryan's leg.

"Who is that lady?" Sophia asked in a loud whisper.

Isabelle frowned, then recovered and smiled as she knelt by Sophia. "I'm your Aunt Isabelle, honey. Your mommy's sister."

"I 'member," Sophia said. "You sent me makeup. Daddy put it away until I'm bigger."

Isabelle rose with her smile gone. "Every little girl likes playing with makeup, Ryan."

"There's plenty of time for that later. She's only four."

Isabelle's eyes were sparking. "You're a tough dad. So what do you say about dinner? What's your schedule look like?"

He edged away. "I'll have to check and let you know. When are you leaving?"

"I'm not sure." She was being coy. "I may move back."

He barely managed to hide his dismay. "Oh. Maybe we can have a family dinner. Get your parents too. Sophia would enjoy that."

He made his escape in the wake of her displeasure. It would be like walking a minefield to keep peace in the family.

CHAPTER SIX

The blotches had faded but weren't completely gone by Tuesday night when Tess rang the bell at Ryan's house. She'd covered the rash with makeup, but her eyes were still puffy. She was a little drowsy from the antihistamine she'd taken, so she'd walked the three blocks to his house rather than taking the car.

"No tiara?" she asked when he opened the door. "I'm disappointed."

He looked good dressed in jeans and a red polo that made his dark hair gleam. Men should not have dimples. The one in his left cheek flexed with his brilliant smile. It warmed her all the way to her toes. An aroma rich with garlic and spices was in the air when she stepped inside.

"I hope you like lasagna," he said, closing the door behind her.

"Next to Mexican, it's my favorite." She touched Sophia's soft hair. "Hi, honey. Did you have a good day at preschool?"

"I practiced my tumbling," the little girl said. She took Tess's hand. "I have an Aunt Isabelle. She's going to come to dinner sometime."

"I know you do. I didn't realize she was back in town, though."

The Morgan girls had been intimidating in school. Cheerleaders, class officers, teachers' pets. Perfect faces, perfect figures, and rich enough to maximize their physical attributes. Tess always felt like a brown sparrow next to a bluebird when she was around either one of them. Candace at least had been kind. Isabelle enjoyed her status too much to care about anyone basking in her shadow.

Everyone in Smitten had wondered if Isabelle would eventually take Candace's place. Ryan had dated Isabelle first, and scuttlebutt said Isabelle had never gotten over him. She still hadn't married. Did she think enough time had gone by now? Tess told herself that it made no difference to her. She and Ryan were only friends. That was all it could ever be.

She tugged her top over her hips and let Sophia lead her to the kitchen. A big dish of lasagna was cooling on top of the stove. Romaine lettuce was on a cutting board with a large bowl of salad beside it. He'd even set the table with a red-and-white tablecloth. Real cloth napkins too. A vase held daisies.

"It looks like a restaurant," she said.

"I helped," Sophia said. "Daddy let me set the table."

"You did a very good job."

Her nose detected the scent of something sweet. "What's for dessert? It smells divine."

"It's a surprise. Mostly because I'm not sure it will turn out." His dimple flashed again.

"Anything I can do to help?"

"We're about ready." He deposited lasagna onto plates for them and handed them to her to transfer to the table. "You can put the salad on the table."

She carried the bowl to the table, then slid into the chair he held out for her. "Thanks." His solicitous behavior made her tongue-tied. There had to be some reason for the way he was acting. Was he about to tell her that the attic was now off limits?

The lasagna was good, and she buried her worry by eating every bite. Sophia's chatter helped smooth the awkwardness that seemed to have sprung out of nowhere. Tess listened to the little girl prattle about her new ballet shoes and what she was learning.

"Your face looks like it's healing," Ryan

said. "Or is that topic taboo?"

"Nothing is off limits," she said. "I saw the doctor this morning. It was just an allergic reaction. It will be gone after a few days of taking the steroid pack."

"You're not limping either."

"My ankle is fine."

"You didn't have to cover your rash with makeup. That's one of the things I like about you, Tess. No pretense. You're transparent."

"I don't like people staring." She looked down at her hands, her appetite gone. The compliment felt slightly back-handed to her. Did he mean she had no femininity? She might be slightly overweight, but that didn't mean she gave no thought to her appearance.

He cleared his throat. "Well, I guess we can go to the attic. Dessert needs to cool a bit, and it will make a nice break from the work in about an hour." He flexed his fingers. "I hope you're up to tackling that huge pile under the eaves."

"I'm up to anything," she said, trying to match his light tone. She wasn't about to let him know his words had stung.

She followed him up the back stairs from the kitchen to the second floor. Going this way led down the hall past his bedroom, and she couldn't resist a peek into his private space as they headed to the attic steps. It was more masculine than she'd expected. Had he redecorated after Candace died? She couldn't imagine Candace living with a plain navy coverlet. There was only a picture of Sophia on the nightstand. The bureau was devoid of any decor. A few woodsy pictures were on the pale blue walls.

"Everything all right?" he asked.

Tess realized she hadn't moved beyond the door to his room. "Of course, sorry. Lead on."

Her face burned, but she smiled and followed him to the attic.

Sophia had found a box of old toys, and she played happily while Ryan pulled out boxes and carried them to an old table under the weak glow of the dangling lightbulb. One was a shoe box, and he peeked inside. "There are old pictures in here. They don't seem to be of anyone in my family."

"I love old pictures," she said. "Why wouldn't they take these with them?"

"Maybe they left in a hurry."

"Maybe." She scooped up a handful of photos and began to look at them. She flipped several over and read the inscriptions on the back. "These seem to belong to the Hutchins family. Here is a picture of David's graduation."

He took the yellowed photo and studied the group of fifteen boys and girls assembled in front of the old train station.

"He's the third on the left in the back row," she said. "Grandma is in the front row, first on the right. I recognize her from old pictures I've seen."

"So they graduated together."

"People never forget their childhood sweethearts."

He wanted to ask Tess if she yearned after a lost love. Maybe that's why she'd never married. There had to be some reason a woman like her was still single. She was the perfect package: beautiful, sweet-natured, caring, optimistic. He said nothing, though, not willing to go back to the unease that had developed since last night.

He dug back into the box and pulled out a handful of photos. The one on top was of a man in a uniform in front of the same train station downtown. The woman with him was Rose. They stood with their arms entwined and identical forced smiles. Their linked arms and body language told the real story. The parting would be painful for them both.

Wordlessly Ryan showed it to Tess, and

her eyes welled with tears.

"War stinks," she said. She put it on top of the school picture, then went back to sorting through pictures.

They found nothing more of interest for well over an hour. Ryan was conscious of everything about Tess — the way she tucked a lock of hair behind her ear when she was distracted, the little inhalations she made when she was studying the pictures, the way she crossed her legs, then uncrossed them. He was smitten with her and realized that he had been for a long time. Books weren't the only reason he brought Sophia to the bookstore every week.

Though she seemed to have no interest in him, he was going to do all he could to change that.

"This is odd," she said. "It's a letter from David to his parents." She handed it to him. "It's dated January 19, 1952."

"Why is that odd?"

"It's two years after he was reported missing."

"But it's addressed here. The family would have been gone already."

"And it's never been opened."

He stared at the yellowed envelope. "Should we open it? Is that even legal?"

She bit her lip. "Well, his parents are long

dead. And it might help us get to the bottom of the puzzle."

He didn't like opening mail addressed to someone else, but in this case it seemed the only thing to do. The glue on the flap was only stuck in one place, and the paper separated easily. He pulled out the two sheets inside and began to read. Tess read over his shoulder.

"He's letting them know he's not dead. And they weren't here to get the news! I wonder if he ever found them."

"I sure hope so," he said.

Her breath was sweet as she leaned closer. "Rose married Grandpa on December 16, 1951. So this news came a month after her marriage."

He whistled. "That would have disrupted the honeymoon if she'd heard the news."

"Plus she was pregnant. Mom was born nine months after the wedding."

"He was on his way here to see his parents, not knowing they'd moved. And he asks about Rose. You think he got here and found out she was married?"

"Maybe. But that still doesn't explain how the dog tags ended up in the attic. He had to have been in the house."

"Or else his parents gave them to her."

She shook her head. "No, she'd never seen

them before Mia found them. And his parents had left already, so how could they?"

"Has your grandma said anything else about him?"

"Everyone has carefully avoided talking about the dog tags. No one wants to upset her. I bet she's wondering about it, though."

He grinned. "Your eyes are sparkling, and you're totally engaged in this. You love a good mystery, don't you?"

"Guilty as charged. You have to admit it's intriguing."

"Sure is. So what's next?" he asked. "We know David survived the war and came back here."

"We *assume* he came back here. But why didn't Grandma see him? You would have thought in a town this small that if he'd been in town, someone would have told her, even if she didn't see him personally. But all she knew was that he died in the war."

"We could try to find someone in his family. Or he may even still be alive. How old is Rose?"

Tess's forehead wrinkled as she thought. "Seventy-eight or seventy-nine. I lose track."

"He'd be the same age. So it's possible he's still alive."

Her gaze went dreamy. "Wouldn't it be something if he was still alive and we reunited them?"

"He's probably married too. His wife might still be alive."

Her expression went to crestfallen. "Party pooper. I had a nice daydream going there."

He wanted to hug her. She grew more enchanting to him every day. "Well, you never know. Any ideas how to find his family?"

"We could start with Facebook. Search there and other social network sites."

He stared at her. "Honey, he's nearly eighty. Do you honestly think he's going to be on Facebook?"

She stuck her tongue out at him. "Grandma has a page!"

"You're kidding. I don't even have one."

"A situation I can quickly remedy," she said, lifting one eyebrow.

"I can live without it." He stood and picked up the box of pictures. "You want to take these home and go through them at your leisure? I don't have any use for them. Your grandma might like to see them."

"She probably would. But I'm not going to show them to her yet. She'll know I'm investigating. We're not telling her until we have it all figured out."

He called Sophia and tucked the box under his arm. Now he needed to figure out how to keep Tess there for the rest of the evening.

CHAPTER SEVEN

Several swans floated serenely by on the lake where Tess sat with her mother and sisters. A blue-and-white checked tablecloth covered the rough wood of the picnic table, and Anna had produced her famous fried chicken from the depths of the oversized basket she'd lugged from the car. Tess's contribution to the Sunday feast was home-made herb bread. Zoe had brought a plate of store-bought brownies, and Clare brought mashed potatoes made from scratch. None of it matched the rest of the food, but the mishmash of assorted food was a tradition and gave every Sunday dinner a party atmosphere.

"I saw a sign up for workdays to redo the station," Tess told her family. "A train stop in Smitten would be the salvation of my bookstore."

Clare handed her a plate of food. "It's going to take major workdays to bring that place back. It's filled with mice and spiders."

"Eew!" Zoe shuddered. "Last time I looked, half the floorboards were rotted too."

"Carson is donating new floorboards," Anna said. She was wearing black slacks and a bright pink top that lit her fair skin with color.

Tess had often wondered why she had never remarried after their father left ten years ago. Anna was still lovely and vibrant, and several single men at church had given her more than a passing glance.

"So the train is coming?" Zoe popped a brownie into her mouth.

Anna put a chicken breast on her plate. "We don't know yet. The town is going to put its best foot forward. The decision won't be made for several months, and there will be visits by RailAmerica to evaluate what we could bring to the table. But you have to admit our town would make a perfect backdrop to a scenic journey."

"The train station will look darling when it's restored," Clare said. "Just imagine flower boxes under the windows and the walk lined with purple pansies. We'd have enough tourists coming through that the nursery could stay open year-round. I talked to Mr. Lewis about selling wreaths, holiday decorations, and souvenirs. I wouldn't have to look for a winter job."

"Are you doing the landscaping for the train station?" Tess asked.

"I sure am. I have a ton of plans for the yard." Clare settled beside Tess at the picnic table. "But I'm more interested in what you've found out."

"It's kind of sad." Tess told her family about the letter they'd found.

Anna's eyes filled with tears. "So his family never received it. What if he never found them?"

"He had to have come to town or his dog tags wouldn't be here. So maybe he was able to find out where they'd moved."

"But if he was in town, why didn't someone see him and tell Grandma?" Zoe asked. "I would have thought that kind of news would be trumpeted all over town. It's very odd."

"It's strange for sure," Tess said. She glanced at her younger sister, who seemed unusually distracted today. Ordinarily Zoe would be demanding they get to the bottom of this now. She'd be pushing for them to talk to their grandmother too. "What's up with you, Zoe? I heard you quit your job at the coffee shop."

A smile played around Zoe's lips and her

71

dark eyes snapped with excitement. "I'm starting my own business."

"Doing what?" Anna asked. "Zoe, you never think before you leap. What is it this time?"

Their mother managed not to roll her eyes, but Tess wouldn't have blamed her. Zoe changed jobs like most people changed brands of hand lotion. But maybe this would be what her sister needed.

"Go on," Tess prompted when Zoe's shoulders sagged.

Zoe sat up. "Smitten may be the romance capital, but for those of us who are single here, it's still tough to connect. We see couples wandering the town hand in hand and it makes us feel even worse. So I'm starting a romance club, so to speak. There will be online meetings, but I'll also have parties where people can meet in a safe place in person."

"Where will these 'meetings' take place?" Anna asked.

"There's the community center, for one thing. And I can get restaurants to offer special rates to my group. Natalie has already agreed to host a monthly meeting on the night she's normally closed. So it will be just for my clients." Zoe leaned forward eagerly. "And if we can get the train, imagine the romantic dinner trips!"

"I like it," Clare said. "No big surprises that way. It feels safer than regular online dating. If you don't like the guy you came to meet, you can leave and know your friends are looking out for you."

"Exactly," Zoe said.

Tess tried to imagine herself in a situation like that. She enjoyed meeting new people, but the whole dating scene was scary. Her thoughts flew to Ryan. Would he agree to do something like that? What if he found a girlfriend that way and didn't greet her with that dimpled smile that melted her heart? She told herself she was being silly. Just because there would be a new dating service didn't mean everyone in town was going to rush to join it.

Zoe interrupted her thoughts. "You'll do it, right, Tess?"

Tess stared into her sister's pleading eyes. "You know I hate that kind of thing, Zoe. Clare thinks it's a good idea. She'll join."

Clare swallowed the bite of food in her mouth. "I will not! I don't like meeting strangers. You know that. You talk to different people every day at the bookstore. You're the one who can do something like that and never blink."

"You're both going to join," Anna said. "I

73

will too. We need to be supportive of your sister."

Her mother's inflexible tone ended Tess's objections. She might register, but she wasn't going to e-mail any strange guy. If a man wanted to talk to her, all he had to do was show up at the bookstore.

The entire town turned out for the train station workday on the first day of June. It was important to the residents that everything be ready for the bicentennial. The hope was that the railroad would decide to come through in time to announce it at the big celebration for the town's founding. As he scanned the crowd, Ryan realized he was looking for Tess. Clare was directing people on digging up flower beds for the stacks of shrubs and bulbs she had brought. Natalie was making the rounds with a tray of coffee and gluten-free cookies. A truck with *Carson Lumber* emblazoned on the side was parked in front. The back lift gate was open to reveal oak flooring stacked to the ceiling. But there was no sign of Tess.

Sophia tugged on his hand. "Daddy, what can I do?"

"Maybe Miss Clare could use some help pulling weeds." That should be safe enough. The yard was full of weeds. She wouldn't be able to harm anything.

Clare steered the little girl to where two other children were yanking vegetation from a small patch. She had a smudge of dirt on her cheek. "Looking for Tess?" she said.

Her knowing smile made him squirm, and Ryan decided to be honest. "Yeah. Is she here?"

"I think she's inside." Her smile faded. "Don't hurt her, Ryan."

Her admonition gave him pause. Did that mean Tess had indicated an interest in him? "What exactly do you mean?"

"I mean, you're a rich and handsome widower. And you sell ice cream, which could turn any girl's head."

He laughed at her impish expression. "That's a new one. Think I could win her with enough chocolate almond?"

"Undoubtedly." Clare was still smiling, but her eyes were serious. "You're spending a lot of time with her, and I suspect it's not only because she's helping you go through the attic."

"It's not. I like her. A lot."

"I thought so. And she's not used to male attention."

"Why not? She's beautiful."

"I like hearing you say that. I agree. She *is* beautiful, but she has never taken time for herself. She's always been too busy worrying about making sure the rest of the family has what they need. And . . . well . . . she's not like Candace."

"I'm not looking to replace Candace."

Clare eyed him. "You mean you have no intention of remarrying?"

That wasn't what he meant at all, but maybe it was better to leave it that way. "There's Tess." She was coming toward them with her mother in tow.

The last thing he wanted was for Clare to tell Tess he was interested in her that way. It might make her skittish around him, and he wasn't eager to heighten whatever unease Tess had shown last night. He still didn't know what that was all about.

"Ryan, there you are," Anna said. "I was just asking Tess if you were coming."

Did the entire family think they were a couple now? He found he liked that idea. If he had the nerve, he would move to Tess's side and take her hand. *That* would get the town talking. He sidled a few steps in her direction.

Her hair was up in a ponytail that exposed the long curve of her neck and accentuated her cheekbones. She wore jeans and a royal blue top that made her blue eyes look even bluer. Her smile made his pulse kick.

"So what are we working on today?" he asked, rubbing his hands together.

"I thought I'd paint the trim around the windows," Tess said.

Painting. The chore he hated most. But he'd be spending the day with her, so he'd shovel manure to do that. "Did you bring paintbrushes?"

"Carson did. Paint, brushes, primer, tape. He thought of everything."

Ryan followed her inside where five men were working on flooring. In a back room they found supplies. He picked up some brushes and paint. "Where do you want to start? Inside or outside?"

"Let's do this room before the men come in here to repair the floor."

"Be careful. There are soft spots. I don't want you to go plummeting into the basement."

She pushed a lock of hair out of her eyes that had escaped her ponytail. "I'll be careful." She watched while he popped the lid of the paint can and began to stir the cream-colored paint. "I've been thinking about David. It's odd that everyone in town thought he died. Yet he had to have come to town. His tags were here."

"Maybe he was only here long enough to find out where his parents moved to."

She sprayed the window trim with cleaner and wiped it off. "But someone had to tell him that. Why wouldn't they have told Grandma and everyone else in town? It's very mysterious."

"Maybe he found out where they went and never came here."

"But the tags."

"Maybe he mailed them? Or someone visited and brought them back?" He shook his head. "Lame, I know."

She chewed her lip. "But that still doesn't explain how they ended up in Grandma's attic."

"We may not know until we find someone in the family." He dipped a brush in paint and moved to the window she'd cleaned. "And that might be hard."

"I got to thinking." She rested her chin on her knuckles. "This may sound a little morbid, but if we can discover where David's parents are buried, there should be a next of kin listed."

He had to chuckle at the earnestness on her face. "So you want to go traipsing through some cemeteries? I'm up for it."

"Really? You'd go with me?"

"I wouldn't miss the fun." She looked so adorable that he nearly leaned over and kissed her on the lips. "But first we have to figure out which cemetery to stalk."

"I'll get on it." She put down her cloth and leaned up to brush her lips across his cheek. "You're the best!"

Shoot. He should have moved his head just a fraction and he would have gotten that kiss he'd been dreaming of.

Chapter Eight

The windows looked good. Tess looked around the train station as the workers filtered off for dinner. The trim had been painted and the brick cleaned. Shingles had been repaired, and Clare with her worker bees had laid beds of flowers and shrubs. It would take longer to finish the inside, but they'd made a good start. Sidewalks needed to be redone as well as repointing the brick, so it was no one-day project. She'd loved seeing the entire town out working with one accord.

Only a handful of people remained. Would Ryan ask her to dinner? She was afraid to hope for something like that. He'd dawdled long after Sophia started begging to leave, but he was a man who took responsibilities seriously. Maybe he didn't want to abandon their project until she was ready to leave.

A heavy oriental perfume wafted on the air. Tess recognized the fragrance before she turned, and her smile faded. *Poison.* The name of the perfume matched the wearer. "Hello, Isabelle."

The other woman was perfectly decked out in a linen skirt with a matching jacket over a lacy blue blouse. Her hair was down, a beautiful blond curtain on her shoulders. The pumps she wore were the perfect height to accentuate her legs. Tess put her bitten nails, stained with paint, behind her. If she could have disappeared into the shrubs, she would have.

Isabelle dismissed her with a glance and turned her attention to Ryan. "I thought you'd be here. I've been commissioned to deliver an invitation to dinner tonight with the family. Dad is grilling steaks, and Mother is making her pecan pie. She said to tell you she's making an extra pie for you to take home."

Ryan hesitated and glanced at Sophia, who was smiling up at Isabelle. "I'm a mess. So is Sophia. It's probably not the best time."

"Please, Daddy," Sophia pleaded. "I haven't seen Grandma and Grandpa in a long time."

Ryan shoved his hands in his pockets. "What time?"

"Now." Isabelle's smile was coaxing.

"Not a chance. We both know your mother would faint if she saw me coming toward her white carpet like this. She'd douse me with the hose." There was a tone of unease in his laugh.

Tess had never been inside the Morgan home. It was a lavish estate on the outskirts of Smitten. A tall iron fence surrounded the lush green grounds, and guests had to check in at the gatehouse. Dr. Morgan was a well-known neurosurgeon who practiced in Burlington. His wife was a pediatrician who worked three days a week and spent the rest of her time playing golf. Or so Tess had heard.

Isabelle's smile faltered and she glanced at her watch. "Run home and shower. I'll hold her off as long as I can."

"Good luck with that," he muttered.

Isabelle stiffened. "What does that mean, Ryan? You're still part of the family even when you don't act like it."

He glanced at Sophia, then pressed his lips together. "I don't act like it? See if you can get your parents to pay a little attention where it's needed, and then we'll talk." He held up his hand when she opened her mouth. "Not in front of my daughter. I've said more than I should. We'll be there, but only because it's what Sophia wants."

Isabelle smiled, though it was more of a grimace. "How about I take Sophia with me? You can join us after you've showered."

"Have you looked at her? She's in worse shape than I am."

Sophia's red-and-white shorts outfit was muddy and her hands were filthy. A black smudge ran across her right cheek where she'd swiped her palm. Tess wanted to sweep the child away before Isabelle could wrinkle her nose, but it wasn't her place.

Sophia stared up at her aunt. "I can take a bath at Grandma's house. I don't mind."

"You don't have clean clothes there," Ryan said. "We'll get cleaned up at our house. It won't take long," he said quickly when her face started to pucker. "The sooner we get to it, the sooner we get there."

"Want me to help?" The words had spilled out before Tess could stop them. Her cheeks burned and she wanted to run.

"That would be great," Ryan said even as Isabelle shook her head.

Isabelle's lips flattened and she glared at Tess before recovering her composure. "That's nice of you, Tess, but really, it makes more sense for me to bathe Sophia. I'm her aunt, after all." She put her hand on the little girl's head. "Wouldn't you like me to help you get a bath?"

Sophia's lips quivered and she shook her head. "Tess can help me if we're going to my house. You've never been to my house. Tess knows where my bathroom is."

"Fine," Isabelle snapped. "See you in a little while." She wheeled and rushed to her car, a white Mercedes convertible. The tires squealed as she drove off.

"Sorry," Ryan said. "You sure you want to help Sophia get ready? I can do it."

"I want Tess," Sophia said, grabbing Tess's hand.

"The princess has spoken," Tess said. "I can meet you there."

"No, ride with us. I'll be coming right back past the train station on the way to the Morgans' place."

Tess was dying to know what the situation was between Ryan and his in-laws. It was clear he thought they didn't pay enough attention to Sophia. What a shame. The knowledge made little Sophia even more endearing.

There was nothing more precious than a freshly bathed child with damp hair and skin. Tess toweled off Sophia's hair, then helped her don a frilly lavender dress. She pulled the top and sides of the little girl's hair back and put it in a big matching bow.

The white tights were still in a package, and the patent leather shoes didn't appear to have been worn either.

"You look beautiful," Tess said, standing back to admire Sophia.

Sophia's smile didn't match her somber eyes. "You think Grandma will like me?"

Tess knelt and hugged her. "I'm sure she loves you very much."

"She doesn't like me to get her carpet dirty. But my shoes are new. I'll be careful not to mess up anything. And I need to not be loud."

It was all Tess could do to keep the reassuring smile on her face. What kind of woman wouldn't want to spend as much time as she could with a granddaughter as precious as Sophia? It was clear the child desperately wanted her grandmother's approval. Even though Ryan was a devoted father, a little girl missed a mother's touch and attention.

Tess kissed the smooth cheek scented with soap. "Just be yourself, sweetheart. Anyone would be lucky to have you as a granddaughter. You're kind, loving, and a hard worker. Look at all you got done today."

Sophia's expression was still troubled. "Daddy doesn't like going there."

Tess didn't want to pry. Well, she did, but

she wasn't going to. She released Sophia and rose. "I'm sure you will both have a great time tonight." She glanced at her watch. "Let's go find your dad. It's time to go."

She took Sophia by the hand, and they found Ryan in the hall running a comb through his damp hair. He looked good too. He wore a blazer over tan slacks and his shoes looked freshly shined. No tie, though. She couldn't imagine Ryan in a tie and wished she could peek into his closet and see if he owned one. The spicy cologne he wore made her suppress a sneeze. It was stronger than the usual light scent. Had he put it on for Isabelle?

Tess wanted to believe he had no interest in Candace's sister, but she'd seen the Morgan girls in action for years. They usually got what they wanted. And Tess had no doubt that Isabelle wanted Ryan.

Sophia ran to him. "Daddy, you smell nice."

"Thanks, honey. Shoo-ee, aren't you gorgeous!" He took her hand and twirled her around. "Like a princess." He went down on one knee. "May I escort you to the ball at Grandma's house tonight?"

Sophia giggled. "Okay, Daddy. Can I sit in the front with you?"

Ryan's smile vanished. "Oh, the prince must make sure the princess is safe in the back. She is much too precious to risk. But we'll be to Grandma's in a f lash, and the princess can be escorted with style to the front door."

"Yay!" Sophia glanced at Tess. "I want Miss Tess to come with us."

Ryan glanced at Tess and their eyes locked. His were so warm, almost caressing. For a moment, Tess could almost believe he held tender feelings for her. She told herself it was a trick of the light, but he continued to stare. A shiver played up and down her spine. She couldn't look away, and her mouth went dry at his expression.

Sophia tugged at his hand. "Daddy! Can Miss Tess come?"

"I can't, sweetheart," Tess said, saving him the explanation. "I'm a mess too. There's no time for me to change, and you wouldn't want me to get in trouble with your grandma, would you?"

"No-o." Sophia's expression went from doubt to displeasure. "You should have taken a bath."

"I didn't have clean clothes, and I needed to get the princess ready for the ball."

"Can I take Grandma some of the peanut butter cookies I made?" Without waiting for a reply, Sophia darted down the hall and across the living room toward the kitchen.

"Sorry our evening got derailed," Ryan said.

Tess's pulse pounded in her ears. "Our evening?"

"I'd hoped we'd spend it together. Maybe going through the attic some more."

"Oh. Of course." *Idiot. Of course he was talking about the attic.*

"Want to come over after church tomorrow?"

"I have a family dinner with my mom and sisters at Grandma's house. If I skip out again this soon, I'll be in big trouble."

His expression fell. "Oh."

An invitation to dinner hovered on the tip of her tongue, but she didn't dare speak it. They were friends only, and he might mistake the invitation for more. She couldn't face that embarrassment. "I could come over late afternoon, though, if that's okay."

"We always have popcorn and hot fudge sundaes for Sunday supper."

"Then I'll definitely be here."

"I thought so."

The banter between them lifted her heart. If nothing else came of this search for her grandmother's lost love, at least she had made a friend. And that's *all* he was. A friend. She couldn't compete with the likes of Isabelle Morgan.

He took her hand. "What would you think about going to dinner one night? Just you and me. I can get a sitter, and we could go to Stowe."

Her heart stuttered, then resumed its even thump. His thumb traced a lazy circle in her palm that did something funny to her stomach. "That sounds lovely."

"Friday?"

"I'm free."

"Do you close on Friday?"

"No, I get off at five."

"Six okay, then? Will that give you enough time?"

"Perfect." She was barely able to push the word out with what little breath remained in her lungs.

She told herself not to assume too much. Maybe he just wanted to talk to her as a friend. But if he wanted to ask her advice about Isabelle, she didn't know if she could handle it.

CHAPTER NINE

The atmosphere in the Morgan home was always so formal that Ryan found it easier to watch quietly. Ursula had managed not to shudder when Sophia proudly gave her the cookies. And to be fair, she'd even eaten one after dinner. Owen was warmer than Ursula. Round and bald, he had Sophia on one knee as often as he could. Ryan suspected that he would have had his granddaughter over to visit more often if he had his way. But Ursula ruled the roost.

Ryan had been seated next to Ursula at the table out on the deck, and she had chattered away until his unease dissipated. After Candace died, he'd longed for a closer family. Maybe they were actually going to try now. His own parents had moved to Florida after he took over the creamery, and he'd stopped by his in-laws' several times with Sophia in the weeks and months after his wife's death. Though Ursula had been cordial, he could see her mentally ticking off the minutes. And he'd suspected she blamed him for her daughter's death. Sophia too. If Candace had never given birth, she wouldn't have suffered the brain aneurysm. Ursula had even said as much in the first hours after Candace died. She'd apologized, but now that Ryan knew how she felt, it was difficult to maintain the front of one big happy family.

The sun had set, but they still sat on the deck listening to the music waft over the treetops from the festivities going on downtown. Every Friday and Saturday night the Garner sisters performed. They were excellent too. A couple of them — he forgot which ones — had even played professionally. He thought it might have been Tess's grandmother, Rose. His heart warmed at the thought of her.

And she'd said yes to his invitation. When he got home later, he intended to replay every flicker of her lashes and every smile. Surely she felt a little something for him, didn't she?

He realized Isabelle had been talking to him. "Sorry?"

"You were in a faraway place," she said, smiling.

"I didn't mean to be rude. How are you

91

liking being back in Smitten?"

She wrinkled her nose. "Small-town life is so boring. We don't even have a Macy's. Though the spa in town is topnotch." She twisted a lock of lustrous hair around her finger. "And I found the most unique spa down the road. Mocha Day Spa. Carly Westlake's place in Spring Creek. I had a dark chocolate wrap. The aroma was to die for."

He couldn't imagine anything worse than being wrapped up in sticky chocolate. "Chocolate for your skin?"

"It's a wonderful antioxidant."

Was he seriously having this conversation? "Have you found a job yet?"

She fluttered her lashes his way. "Are you offering me one?"

"No, I've got plenty of workers. And I don't think you'd like dipping ice cream or working on the line to get the cheese out the door. You might chip your nails." He smiled to take the sting out of his words. There would be much wailing in the land if she ever wrapped her long, slim fingers around an ice cream scoop.

Her smile faded and she shrugged. "I've looked around a bit. In a town the size of Smitten, there isn't much demand for a life coach."

"A life coach? That's what you do? What is that?" He knew his tone had been wrong as soon as she tipped her chin up and glared at him. He spread out his hands. "Sorry, I've never heard of it."

"I help people determine and achieve their life goals."

"Sort of like a personal cheerleader?" No wonder she couldn't find a job. It sounded like a lot of psychology mumbo-jumbo. His motto was just to plunge in and do what needed to be done.

"Not exactly." She pressed her lips together. "Let's talk about something else."

The scent of her perfume was overpowering. And not in a good way. Ryan inched away and prayed for the breeze to change direction. "What will you do if you can't find a job?"

"Oh, I don't really need a job. I can live off my trust fund. But I do get bored." Her glance wandered to Sophia, who was kicking a ball in the yard with their little frou-frou dog. "I would be glad to babysit anytime. I just love Sophia. She reminds me of Candace."

The wistful tone of her voice melted him. Candace's death had been hard on everyone. "She looks a lot like her mother. You too. Same shape face and eyes."

Isabelle sighed, a whisper of sound that held yearning. "We're family, Ryan." Her hand touched his. "I want to be closer to her. To you."

He might be dense around women, but warnings began to ricochet in his head. Discreetly, he pulled his hand away. "I know Sophia would like that. She misses her mother."

"What about you?" Isabelle's eyes were pools of mystery and allure. "Don't you need a woman in your life?"

He cleared his throat. "Actually, I, ah, I'm seeing someone."

She bolted upright, and anger replaced the softness in her face. "Who?"

The wrath he glimpsed gave him pause. But surely she wouldn't do anything to Tess. What could she do? The town was going to be talking about them after Friday night anyway. "Tess Thomas."

Isabelle gave an audible gulp. The color washed from her face. "Sh-she isn't your type at all, Ryan. She's nothing like Candace." One elegant hand glittering with rings fluttered in the air.

That hand told him everything. The diamond on her little finger would have fed a family of four for a year. The nails were polished a discreet pink. There were no calluses, no sign she'd ever moved a muscle to do any real work.

He'd loved Candace, had mourned her loss. But Tess was refreshingly different. She laid everything bare — her commitment, her love of family, her faith. There was no pretense in her.

He rose. "Time to go, Sophia."

The kitchen was redolent with the scents of garlic, cheese, and oregano. It mixed with the aroma of mashed potatoes and gravy that Aunt Violet had brought, even though there was no meat to go with them. Clare had brought chicken stir-fry, and Zoe had offered up her favorite Jell-O mixed with cottage cheese and fruit.

Tess lifted the lasagna pan from the oven and placed it on the stove. "Dinner will be ready as soon as the garlic cheese bread is toasted." She slid in a pan of bread she'd brought.

Her mother was frowning as she stared at the lasagna. "Is that low-calorie cheese?" Her gaze went from the bubbling topping to Tess's hips.

Tess shuddered. "Low fat is nasty."

"But, sweetheart, you'll never lose those ten pounds eating all that fattening stuff. And it's bad for you."

"Natural fat is good for you. Don't even *try* to take away my real butter."

Her mother gulped and stepped away. "Well, you know what's best for you, of course. Let's go shopping next week. I saw the cutest sweater at Moose Creek."

That was Mom's usual strategy. Offer motherly advice, then quickly segue to just-us-girls-having-fun mode. Sometimes Tess wanted to shout at her, "Just be a mother!" But she clamped her jaw shut and pulled out the garlic cheese bread. "Food's ready."

She loved Grandma's dining room. The coffered ceiling made the huge room feel cozy. The original plaster walls were painted a muted tan with hints of yellow. An entire wall of windows let sunlight stream into the room to illuminate her grandmother's collection of blue-and-white dishes. This room had been the scene of lots of meals filled with laughter.

Her grandmother sat at the head of the table. Aunt Violet was to her left and Aunt Petunia to her right. "Sit close, Anna," her grandmother said. "I want to talk about Zoe's latest scheme."

The girls exchanged alarmed glances. "How did you hear about it?" Zoe asked.

"This is Smitten, child. Anything you do is public knowledge in twenty-four hours."

Aunt Violet tittered. "A romance business. I think it's a wonderful idea, Zoe."

Zoe eased back in her chair and scooped a helping of Jell-O onto her plate. "You do?"

"Of course. I might join myself."

Zoe glanced at her grandmother. "How about you, Grandma? You have an online account."

"Oh my goodness, no, Zoe. All my romance is behind me."

Perfect opportunity. Tess took the salad bowl from Zoe and put some greens on her plate. "I guess you've had your fair share of romance, Grandma. We had no idea you'd been engaged before Grandpa." She ignored her mother's panicked shake of the head. "I'd like to know more about this David fellow and what happened."

Her grandmother's smile was forced. "That's old history, honey. And rather painful, if you don't mind a little honesty."

"I can only imagine," Clare put in. "To get that kind of news while you're waiting for him to return must have been hard. Who told you? Did someone come from the army?"

"Yes, two nice soldiers showed up at the door. I was visiting his parents when they came, so we all heard the news together." She blinked rapidly, then put her napkin on

97

her lap. "He wasn't the only one to die in that battle. They had his belongings from the barracks, but his dog tags weren't found."

Tess noticed the way her grandmother's hands trembled and the way she was biting her lip. Maybe she should change the subject.

"Then how did they end up here?" Zoe asked.

Tess pinched her sister's thigh and shot her a warning glance. "It's okay if you don't want to talk about it, Grandma," she said.

"It's about time someone changed the subject," Anna said. "This is much too painful for your grandmother."

Grandma shook her head. "I think the girls are right to ask me about it. It's all been hidden too long. What would you like to know about David?"

Clare began to cut squares of lasagna. She exchanged a startled glance with Tess. "What made you fall in love with him? How long did you know him?"

Grandma laughed. "Oh, David was quite the charmer, wasn't he, Violet? All of the girls were crazy about him. Tall and handsome, with light gray eyes that changed color with the weather. And the way he looked in his uniform . . ." She fanned herself. "Oh my."

Tess hadn't thought of passion in the relationship, but she saw it in her grandmother's eyes. If that man walked through the door right now, her grandmother would throw her arms around him and swoon. Tess just knew it. The knowledge made her heart hurt. What kind of love survived that long? Would a man ever love her with that kind of enduring devotion?

Ryan's face came to mind. He liked her — that much she knew. But she could never compete with the memory of Candace.

"You have an odd expression on your face," her mother said. "Are you feeling all right?"

What would her family say if they knew he'd asked her out? She should tell them before they heard about it through the grapevine. "I'm fine." She wetted her lips. "I have a date on Friday."

Her mother clapped her hands. "A date! Oh, that's wonderful. Is it someone you met online?" She glanced at Zoe. "Did you arrange this, Zoe?"

"Not hardly. All I've gotten done so far is install the software I'm going to use." Zoe pointed her fork at Tess. "Give! You've been holding out on us."

"It just happened yesterday."

The corners of Clare's lips lifted, then she laughed. "It's Ryan, isn't it?"

"How did you know?"

"It's written all over you. You're already crazy about him, aren't you?"

Tess stared down at her plate rather than look into her sister's knowing eyes. "I like him." She peeked at Clare from under her lashes. Her sister was chewing on her lip. "What, you don't like him?"

"I like him a lot. All the women in town think he's hot enough to melt bricks." Clare put down her fork. "But, Tess, word is out that Isabelle has plans for him."

Zoe gasped. "She wouldn't! That's just gross. He was married to her sister."

Their mother shrugged and lifted a bite of lasagna. "It happens, girls. Families are close. What better mother for Sophia than her own aunt?"

Tess wished she'd never said a word. Her bright anticipation had tarnished.

CHAPTER TEN

Excitement hummed along Tess's spine as she hurried into the creamery. She hadn't been here often. It was the heart of Ryan's business, where the milk was turned into luscious ice cream and aged cheese.

The receptionist, Bethany Hopkins, saw her hesitation. "Hi, Tess, can I help you?"

"I — I'm looking for Ryan. Mr. Stevenson, I mean."

"Go on back. He won't mind."

Tess thanked her, then rushed to the back room. Stainless freezers lined the concrete floors and block walls. From here the ice cream would go to stores all over the country. She wandered through the maze until she found a hallway that led to a large office area divided by cubicles. A young man directed her to the back where Ryan's office was.

A walnut desk dominated the large room. Files and books covered the top and more stacks were on the floor. Ryan was seated behind the desk. A pair of glasses perched on his nose, and he was so intent on his computer that he didn't notice her until she said his name. The genuine pleasure that rippled across his face warmed her.

"I hope I'm not interrupting," she said.

He leaned back in his chair. "Please, interrupt me. I'm doing payroll. My least favorite job in the world."

"I would have guessed you hired that out."

"I have a bookkeeper who usually does it, but her daughter had a chance to go on a field trip to DC, and she wanted to go along to chaperone. Which means I'm stuck with it this week." He rose and came around the desk. "Sorry this place is such a mess." He lifted a pile of folders from the chair by the door. "Have a seat."

She had to smile. "I think the state of this office disqualifies you from the title neatnik."

His smile widened. "I was trying to impress you on your first visit to the house. I didn't want you to know what a slob I am."

Impress her? Her spirits rose. "I'm not staying. I wanted to tell you what I found out!" If she didn't tell someone soon, she was going to explode. "The cemetery where

David's parents are buried is near Burlington."

"So they didn't go far."

She shook her head. "I thought I'd go over and see what I can find out. I was going to see if you wanted to come with me, but it looks like you're busy."

"I'm finished."

His nearness flooded her with warmth. The musky scent of the cologne she loved filled her senses. If she took his hand, would he jerk away? She didn't have the nerve to find out.

"What about Sophia?"

"We can pick her up from day care on the way out of town. Burlington has a great pizza place if you're game."

"You can probably tell that pizza and I are on a first-name basis."

"I like a woman with curves."

The intensity in his eyes made her gulp. He'd actually looked at her *that way*? She'd spent many nights lately imagining what it would be like to be pressed against that broad chest. She'd wondered how those firm lips would feel against hers, what texture his hair was, how the stubble on his chin in the evening might scrape across her cheeks if he kissed her.

The moment between them seemed to last

an eternity. What did she even say to that remark? She'd had so little experience with men that she didn't know how to play coy.

She finally cleared her throat and gave a nervous laugh. "I've got plenty of those."

"I've noticed," he said softly. His hand reached out and touched the curve of her cheek, trailed down her neck until he twisted a lock of hair in his fingers.

She forgot to breathe. The sensation curling in the pit of her stomach was something she'd never felt before. Then it dawned on her. *Desire.* So this was what she'd heard about but never experienced.

He leaned closer. She lifted her chin an inch and closed her eyes.

"Mr. Stevenson?" The teenage boy's voice behind them sounded nervous.

Tess's eyes flew open and heat flooded her cheeks. What had Ryan thought of that ridiculous pose? He was probably glad they'd been interrupted. But he didn't look happy. In fact, he seemed downright snarly.

"What is it?" he snapped.

"Uh, the ice cream conveyer broke. Sorry to bother you."

"No problem." Ryan's voice sounded normal again. He grabbed the phone and barked an order into it, then turned back to the boy. "Max will be along. Show him what's wrong."

"Yes, sir." The kid gave a nervous glance in Tess's direction, then turned and practically ran from the room.

There was no way to recover the moment. Still, Ryan took her hand as they walked to the front, where the customers would be able to take one glance and see there was something between them. And there *was,* wasn't there? Or was it just how men acted?

"Here we are." Ryan opened the door for her in front of the restaurant. Since they'd wandered through the cemetery the other day, he'd been waiting for this night with eager anticipation.

The new place on Main Street, Logger's Run, was packed, but Ryan had called ahead to reserve a table in the back corner. It had once been an old boardinghouse, but the renovation had taken the rustic character and enhanced it with wide plank floors, chairs and tables from hewn wood, and various axes and other tools from the lumber trade hanging on the walls.

"I hope you don't mind a change of plans," he said as they followed the hostess to their spot. "When I heard this was opening tonight, I thought it would be great to support them. We can always go to Stowe another night." He grinned at her. "And to tell you the truth, I wanted to show you off to everyone here."

Her face went pink. "I don't mind at all." She thanked him when he pulled out her chair.

Man, she did that dress proud. It was red and clung in all the right places and showed off her killer legs. Her hair was up in some kind of twisty hairdo, and the dangly earrings touched her neck in exactly the place he'd like to kiss. Lucky pieces of metal. He was glad he'd worn a sport coat, though maybe a muscle shirt would have been better so he could beat off the other guys he saw glancing her way.

He'd relived every second of that near-kiss the other day, and he had every intention of getting a real smooch tonight.

He nodded out the window. "Look at the view."

She turned and inhaled. "Smitten is like a fairyland now."

That was a good way to put it. From the large windows the town looked spectacular. Twinkling lights were wrapped around antique streetlights on the brick sidewalks. Bright flowers nodded hello to passersby from the window boxes framing the storefronts. Out on the square, people walked hand in hand toward the gazebo to listen to the Garner sisters. It was a place he was proud to call home, and a town he wanted to help others learn to love.

He picked up the menu. "I hear the lobster is terrific."

Her brow furrowed. "That's so expensive."

She was downright adorable. Candace always ordered the most expensive thing on the menu. "I can afford it, honey."

Her gaze came up, then caught and held his own. She was scared. He could see it in the way she bit her lip and how often she shifted in her chair. If only he could tell her he wouldn't hurt her. Her family had probably warned her against him.

He ordered lobster for them, and they both decided to try the raspberry iced tea. After the server brought hot rolls and their drinks, he leaned across the table and took her hand.

She shot a nervous glance around. "I'm so glad we found out where David's sister lives. I wanted to call her, but I wasn't sure what to say."

He cupped her hand with both of his and rubbed his thumb across the top. Her skin was so smooth. He turned it over and touched the roughness on her fingertips. She wasn't afraid of work, though. "Want me to call?"

She gulped and nodded. "You wouldn't mind?"

"Got her number?"

"In my purse." She seemed in no hurry to pull her hand away.

With reluctance, he released her. "I'll call while we're waiting for our food."

She dug a piece of paper from her purse and handed it to him. He tapped in the number, then leaned close so Tess could listen with him. A woman's voice answered. She sounded much too young to be in her seventies. "Mrs. Howard?"

"No, this is her daughter, Stephanie." The woman sounded curious. "Mom passed away twelve years ago."

"I'm sorry." Ryan explained why he was calling. "So there's a bit of a mystery here, and we were wondering if your mother had heard from her brother after the war?"

"Oh yes. He came to her funeral. As far as I know, he's still living."

Tess's head was pressing against his, and he found it hard to think. "That's great! Have you seen him lately?"

"No, I'm sorry. I haven't heard from him since Mom died. There was some mention that he lived in California, but that's all I know."

"Would you have a phone number?"

"Hang on." There was rustling in the phone. "I have an old phone book of my mom's. I'll give you the number that she had."

He jotted down the number she rattled off. "Thanks so much."

"Let me know what you find out. I'd love to hear if there's a happy ending."

"We will," he promised. He ended the call and smiled at Tess. "Might as well call, yes?"

Her eyes were bright. "Oh, I hope he's there!" But a woman with a coarse, raspy voice answered and said she'd never heard of David, and she had rented the place for five years. He hung up and shook his head. "So it's a dead end."

She bit her lip. "We're no further than we were. And for all we know, he could be dead now too."

"We'll find him. Or at least where he's buried. Your grandma might like to visit his grave."

"I think she would. There was real passion between them. Even now I can see it."

Her eyes were so luminous. They let him see right to the heart of her caring nature. "True love never fades with the years. It grows deeper roots and becomes richer."

He wanted to rush into telling her how he

felt, but it was too soon, and she was so fragile. She had no idea of the power she held over him. And maybe he didn't want her to know. It was hard to turn over that kind of control to another person.

"Is that how you felt about Candace?" she whispered.

It wasn't going to be easy to explain the relationship he'd had with his wife. And he'd never spoken to anyone about it before. This probably wasn't the time or place either.

"Not exactly," he said finally when it was clear she was waiting for an answer.

"Oh." Her voice was small and hurt.

"I think I'll go wash my hands," he said. Maybe if he got away by himself, he could figure out the right words.

Why did she assume he wanted another fashion plate, when it was a warm and real woman like Tess who was so much more interesting? A wife wasn't an ornament but a soul mate.

CHAPTER ELEVEN

Her pulse had finally stopped galloping in her chest. Tess leaned back in the chair and let out her breath. What had possessed Ryan tonight? He was acting like a man in love. At least that was how she was interpreting it, but what did she know about love? Or about men, for that matter?

"Well, I wasn't expecting to see you here." Isabelle's smooth voice was laced with something unpleasant.

Jealousy? Malice? Tess couldn't decide. "I think half the town is here tonight."

Without waiting for an invitation, Isabelle slid into Ryan's vacated seat. "I suppose you're here with Ryan?"

Tess eyed her warily. "Yes, I am."

Isabelle was everything Tess was not and wished she were — the kind of woman who attracted the attention of every man between fifteen and a hundred and fifteen. Nearly every guy in the room had glanced their way since she'd sauntered into the room.

She leaned in and whispered, "He told me he was going to woo you."

"H-He did?" Was that what he'd been doing? Wooing?

Isabelle flashed a sultry smile toward a man in a tailored suit. "Of course. We're very close. He tells me everything. And he's right. You would be the perfect mother for Sophia. Between you and me, I don't think Ryan could stand to have another wife who betrayed him. And he knows you would always be faithful." She fluttered her fingers in Tess's direction. "I mean, let's be honest, Tess. You're not the kind of girl who has many options where men are concerned."

Though the words were cruel, Tess barely flinched. Isabelle wasn't telling her anything she didn't already know. *A mother for Sophia.* A month ago Tess would have accepted that job without a qualm. But not now that she knew how that curl of passion in her belly felt. She wanted more.

Isabelle's slim shoulders shrugged. "Don't look so offended, dear. Men are so practical."

Tess could barely move her lips. "I'm not offended. I know I'm not in your league, Isabelle. I've always known that."

Isabelle stood. "Well, I'm glad we had this

chat. It's always good to go into marriage with your eyes wide open."

Tess couldn't muster the will to tell her good-bye. Surely those were pitying glances directed her way. Everyone in town must know why Ryan was seeing her. Everyone but her. Something was crushing her chest, but she couldn't stay here and examine what emotion was squeezing the life out of her. She jumped to her feet and stumbled out the door. That might have been Ryan's voice calling after her, but she didn't pause.

She thrust open the door and rushed into the night air. It was moist and fragrant with flowers. There was a wooden bench half hidden in the flowers and shrubs, and she managed to make it to the seat before her legs gave out on her. Her head swam, and she put her head between her knees. What had she expected? Did she seriously think a man like Ryan Stevenson could find her beautiful? Desirable? She gave a choked laugh. What a fool she was. A total fool.

A shadow moved in the moonlight and Ryan's voice floated out of the darkness. "Tess?"

She scrubbed at her cheeks. "I'm here." How could she escape this situation with her dignity? But no, what difference did it make now? The shrubs rustled as he moved to join her.

"Honey, what's wrong?"

"Wrong? Why, nothing that a little money won't fix, right? You needed a mother for your daughter, so why not pick someone no one else wanted?" By the time she was finished, her voice had risen to nearly a shout.

He tried to take her hand, but she jerked it away. "Tess, I don't know what you're talking about."

"Isabelle told me, okay? You don't have to pretend any longer. I know you're only dating me to find a mother for Sophia."

"Isabelle said that?" He still sounded bewildered.

"I know all about Candace's infidelity. I'm sorry about that, but it's not okay to — to . . ." She ran out of words and out of strength.

He knelt in front of her. His dark curls gleamed in the wash of lamplight. The earnestness of his eyes drew her. "Tess, do you really think everything I've said has been a lie? Have you seen evil in me, Tess, have you?"

Her shoulders sagged. "No," she whispered. "I've seen only goodness and mercy in your life."

His lips smiled, but his eyes were serious.

114

"Part of what Isabelle said is true. It's hard for a man to admit he wasn't enough for his wife. And I wasn't enough for Candace. She was never happy at home. She craved bright lights and adulation." He ran his fingers through his hair and exhaled. "Some of it was my fault. I was working a lot of hours. She told me she wanted a divorce just before Sophia was born. We argued, and she went into labor early. Forty-eight hours later she was gone."

"I'm so sorry." She could hear the heartbreak in his voice and longed to heal his pain.

"So am I." When he smiled again, the humor reached his eyes. "But I'm ready to love again. It sneaked up on me. I finally realized I was going to the bookstore for me, not for Sophia."

She dared to cradle his face in her hands. His cheeks were smooth. He must have shaved tonight before he came to pick her up. "Can you say that one more time? I can't quite grasp it."

His hands circled her shoulders and he drew her close enough that his breath mingled with hers. "How about I make it clear, Miss Tess? I love you. I'm not quite sure when it happened. Maybe when you came into the store in that ridiculous clown suit. I knew then that you were a woman who would always be herself. Good, true, honest. And so very beautiful."

When he pulled her toward him, she went willingly. His lips were everything she'd dreamed of: firm and warm and oh so tender. The feelings that washed over her weren't motherly at all. She wrapped her arms around his neck and kissed him back with all the passion she could muster. Which was quite a lot.

She lost all sense of place and time with his warm breath caressing her face. She could spend the rest of her life in his arms. And she had a suspicion that was exactly what he was planning.

■ ■ ■ ■

MAKE ME A MATCH

KRISTIN BILLERBECK

■ ■ ■ ■

CHAPTER ONE

Zoe Thomas perched herself atop the metal ladder and straightened the wooden sign that read *Cupid's Arrow Matchmaking Services.* She looked down at her older sister, who stood on Main Street's brick walkway. "Better?"

"A little higher on the right," Clare called up. Zoe wondered if it would ever be straight according to Clare's exacting standards.

She pressed upward and peered down again to the brick sidewalk. "Now?"

"Perfect," Clare confirmed.

Zoe breathed a sigh of relief, amazed that Clare hadn't produced a level from the overalls she wore. Clare could survive in the woods for an eternity with all that came out of those gardener pockets of hers. Zoe jumped from the ladder and brushed her hands together. Seeing the hand-painted calligraphy announcing her business made everything so real.

"Can't you just feel the love? Imagine Smitten being bitten by its own love bug. And Nat's marriage to Carson was the perfect kickoff to my new business." Zoe's heart filled with possibilities, seeing the fruits of her labor. The tired storefront looked fresh and inviting with its newly painted wood-paned windows and a gold-framed "services offered" announcement. She'd draped two small crystal chandeliers in jewel tones to bring attention to the services menu, and with a little specialized lighting, the display would emanate romance.

Clare grimaced. "This is still Smitten. If the men here have been bitten by anything, it's something closer to a mosquito carrying malaria."

Zoe's shoulders slumped. Poor Clare, never looking for the spontaneous. "Life is too short to be so serious, Clare. We can't exactly claim to be the romance capital if we don't believe our own slogan. Romance should start here; we shouldn't simply import it." She blew her bangs off her glistening forehead. "It's hot already today. I'm glad we started so early."

Clare wouldn't allow her to change the subject. "The point is, Smitten is a romantic *destination*. The couples bring the love with them. We just warm the embers of the fire they've already built. I'm worried, Zoe. You could lose everything with this."

"We have plenty of single men and women in Smitten. Why shouldn't we start a spark of our own? Remember that song we sang at church camp?" She struck a pose and started to sing. "It only takes a spark to get a fire going . . ."

"Fire, and a bit of dynamite might get things going." Clare's ponytail bobbed as she spoke, which was a lot of passion coming from her serious older sister.

"Now you're just being surly." Zoe knew Clare's words came from a deep need for security. In Clare's mind, one didn't just willy-nilly up and decide to start a business. It took expertise like Clare possessed in gardening, and then accountants with ten-year forecasts for the math skills the sisters hadn't mastered. "If I lose everything, I'll let you be the first to say 'I told you so.' How's that?"

"I'm only saying" — Clare spoke in her soft, motherly tone — "I'd be remiss if I didn't say that I'm worried about you. You've worked so hard for what little you have. Why not forget all this and go to college? Smitten will be here when you get back."

Zoe waited out the recycled warning. Advice that had already come from her cousin Natalie, from her mother, and from most everyone in town whom she'd ever been straight with in her long history of not being able to keep her opinion to herself. People had a nasty way of enjoying telling her their predictions of imminent failure, which only made her want to succeed more. Not to prove them wrong, but because she believed so strongly in what she was doing.

"Not everyone has a big family like we do, Clare. People are lonely. I see it every day when I deliver dinner to the shut-ins. Human contact is what makes life worth living. If I can make that happen for one person, it will be worth it. Okay, I guess it would be two people . . ."

Clare rubbed her head as if the conversation gave her a migraine.

"Smitten needs a matchmaker. Dating in a small town is never a secret, so folks keep to themselves rather than risk public humiliation on a relationship that might fail. This way it's my failure, and no one is the wiser. Do you see?"

"Not really, but somehow the Lord always looks out for you. I'm going to pray he works extra hard this time."

"We have different ideas of success, Clare.

If all it takes for people to be less lonely is a little initiative on my part, that's worth my time and money. Don't you think? The failure is in ignoring my calling."

"Everyone in town already knows each other," Clare protested.

"That's true, but with the neighboring towns, the seasonal employees, and even with the locals, they need encouragement. They need a chance to get to know one another without the pressure of everyone knowing their business. Maybe they think love is not in the cards for them, but it's actually right in front of them if they'll only take this small risk."

"And pay the small membership fee." Clare shook her head. "Zoe, I love how you care for people. I really do. I'm only worried there's no money in this as a business. Your heart is so huge that you never think of details like cash flow. Trust me, it matters."

Clare ran a seasonal plant nursery, and she worried each winter that this was the year she wouldn't make it to spring.

"I know you're good at discerning people who might belong together, but does that mean there's a business in it?"

"Maybe they won't pay," Zoe said. "I'll make you a deal. If I haven't turned a profit within the year, I'll apply for college next fall." She regretted her words the minute they tumbled out of her mouth, but it only meant Cupid's Arrow had to work.

Clare exhaled audibly. "All right, Zoe. I don't understand it. I never have understood that romantic view of life you've got, but if this is what you want, I've got no choice but to support you."

Zoe had heard that her whole life, about her romantic dreams and magical, dreamy way of thinking.

"Why didn't you go to college, Zoe?"

"Smartest girl in town, but you've got no ambition."

"There's an entire world outside of Smitten if you'd only go search it out."

But she wasn't as starry-eyed as everyone thought. She simply had no interest in a world bigger than Smitten. She had everything she needed right here: good friends, people she loved and cared about deeply, a ministry with the town's senior citizens. Now that she'd started her own business, her family should finally feel the same way.

The screech of metal punctuated by an awkward *clank* seized their attention. Zoe rushed to the wobbly ladder and caught it right before it hit her storefront window. She braced the ladder against the clapboard wall and pressed her back against it to hold everything steady, but a spray of nails rained down around her. She glared at the stranger who had mistakenly walked into the obstacle, and tried to make sense of what just happened.

The first thing she noticed was his eyes. They were a color she'd never seen before, a watery mix of gray, blue, and green — like a rare marble she might have fought over as a child. Against the man's tan skin, their intensity was heightened. She searched for something rational to say but kept getting lost in his gaze, which was like a mystery she needed to solve.

She finally snapped out of her dreamy state and realized that he was bleeding.

"I'll call you back." The man, dressed in a fancy dark city suit with a look-at-me sheen, pressed at his ear, and she assumed that he was disconnecting from some type of inner-ear Borg device. He took her hands into his own. "Are you all right? I didn't hurt you, did I?"

He dropped one of her hands and touched her hair — a touch she felt to her toes. He showed her a long silver nail that he'd removed from her hair and smiled in a way that felt so intimate she clutched the collar of her T-shirt to protect herself.

"You've got a small cut," she managed. "C-come in the back and I'll clean it up."

He rubbed his right temple where he'd run into the ladder. She could see the red mark developing. Selfishly she worried she'd have her first lawsuit before she opened the doors for business, but she quelled the thought.

The mystery man pulled a handkerchief from his suit jacket and dabbed the side of his head. "I'll be fine. I'm not sure how I missed that ladder."

She looked at the rusted ladder and pondered the same thing, but she didn't want to say anything to incriminate herself further.

"I'm not sure if you're aware of it, but it's against city policy to obstruct the sidewalk during business hours without a permit. Do you have a permit?"

"I . . . uh, what?"

"A permit. You can obtain them at city hall. Soon you'll be able to download an application off the Internet, but you need to give me at least a month for that."

"And who are you exactly?" She pressed herself farther back against the ladder in a pathetic attempt to hide it. "What I mean is, how would you know what's illegal in Smitten? I've never seen you before."

He raised a brow. "I'm the new city manager. It's my job to know the city codes — and to see that they're implemented."

Zoe shook her head in disbelief that a complete stranger was telling her about Smitten. "I've been in this town my whole life. We don't have a city manager." She looked to her sister for backup, but Clare just shrugged as if none of it concerned her.

"The town board hired me. With all the recent successes after Sawyer Smitten's wedding, this has become a real destination spot. That requires more management than your selectpersons can handle, I'm afraid."

"Yes, I'm afraid too."

"You've heard we've been in contact with RailAmerica to get the railroad to come back to Smitten." He felt his temple, then looked at the tips of his fingers, tinged by his own blood.

"Naturally." Zoe loathed his know-it-all tone, as if she were some kind of weekender to be patted on the head and sent home with a bottle of maple syrup.

"Dealing with the railroad will be one of my primary duties, but safety is priority one. A ladder on the sidewalk of Main Street in the middle of high season is a genuine hazard. I'm glad it was me who walked into it and not an elderly tourist. It's going to take cash to get that railroad here, and a lawsuit is something we can't afford."

Zoe tried to see things from his perspective, but the way he acted, as if he cared more about Smitten than she did, made her want to tell him that elderly people paid attention to where they were going. When she didn't answer, he kept talking.

"With these uneven bricks, a ladder on Main Street is not ideal in any season. This" — he gripped the ladder — "should be secured and surrounded by emergency cones."

She stood at attention and saluted. "Aye aye, captain."

He looked away from her. "I didn't mean to give orders." His hurt expression, combined with the expanding puddle of blood on his temple, made the exchange feel surreal, as if someone else ruled her words — though she knew it was her own dark side afraid of change.

"Come back into the store and I'll clean that up for you." Her fingertips aimed toward the small cut, but she clasped her fingers into a fist and veered at the last moment.

"I should have introduced myself first. I'm William Singer."

"Can you? Sing, I mean. Our choir is

always looking for baritones."

"I can't. Tone deaf as they come, so the name is, I suppose, unfortunate." He pulled the ladder from behind her and fastened it shut. "Can I put this somewhere for you?" He paused. "I assume you're done with it." He looked up at the sign she'd just attached. "You did that yourself?"

She nodded.

"It looks good. Straight."

"Thanks to my sister Clare." She nodded toward her sister, but William never removed his eyes from hers. He set the ladder against the wall again.

"Cupid's Arrow." He stepped back toward the street and crossed his arms over his chest. His jacket stretched and protested against his rounded biceps, and Zoe realized how out of place he looked in a suit. No one wore a suit in Smitten except on Sundays for church; during the week, it meant a funeral service. "A baby shop?"

"Aunt Violet told you it sounded like a baby shop," Clare said.

It was as if they were children again, and Clare had added *neener, neener, neener.*

"It's a *matchmaking* service."

He blinked as though she spoke in a foreign tongue.

"People are so busy these days even in

129

Smitten that they don't make time for connection. Human connection," she added, staring at the phone contraption strapped to his ear.

"Are you married, William Singer?" Clare asked, and Zoe glared at her sister.

"Me?" He pressed his left hand, void of a wedding ring, against his chest. "No, I'm not married."

Zoe wanted to change the subject before Mr. Singer asked about signing up for her services. She intended to discourage short-timers — guys like this who might just want to date someone while they were in Smitten, then vanish into the proverbial sunset alone. She might be desperate to sign people up for the service, but she wasn't willing to compromise her principles. She wouldn't willingly allow hearts to be broken by a traveling man.

He lifted the ladder again, as anxious to finish the uncomfortable conversation as she was. "You want to show me where to put this before someone else walks into it and the city has a lawsuit on its hands?"

"Mr. Singer, you weren't looking where you were going. I'm not a fan of this Star Trek communicator stuff becoming reality, for that reason. If you're going to live here in Smitten, you should know we prefer proper communication. Face-to-face."

He gave a lopsided grin. "I'm grateful you've decided to share that with me." He lifted the ladder a few inches higher. "Where did you want me to put this?" he asked again.

"I'm Clare Thomas," her sister said. "We weren't formally introduced." She scowled at Zoe as if to remind her she was supposed to be a matchmaker. "Follow that alley to the back of the store. That's where Zoe keeps the ladder."

"Pleasure to meet you, Clare," he said, setting the ladder down again to shake her hand. "This country air produces very pretty women."

Clare rolled her eyes, and Zoe veiled a smile with her hand. "You don't have to waste your city talk on us Smitten girls. We appreciate the effort, though, and as long as you don't cite me, that's compliment enough."

"Let me ask you something." William set the ladder down. "Does this personal communication in Smitten get any easier on a guy?"

"You'll have to excuse my sister. She's heavily invested in Cupid's Arrow, and change is not her strong suit anyway. You represent change." Clare narrowed her eyes just like their mother did, and Zoe thought maybe it wouldn't hurt her to be less forthright — as her mother always told her. She could still think her truth without saying it.

Political insincerity may have worked where William Singer came from, but he'd have to sharpen his skills with authenticity if he meant to stay in Smitten. Of course, he wouldn't stay in Smitten. He had short-timer written all over him, so she tried not to muster any sympathy for the way his strong jaw set against the slightly pitiful scrape alongside his eye. Nor would she notice how darling it made him look, even if her heart did soften at the sight of it.

CHAPTER TWO

William Singer wondered how long he'd last in a town like Smitten. So far, no one had exactly rolled out the welcome mat for him, and he'd found the books were like those of most old towns: in the red. Somehow they'd always managed to pull out of deep trouble with some creative community event and last-minute inventive accounting. The town had a long way to go as far as laws, codes, and upholding them went. The place was a lawsuit waiting to happen. If he'd learned anything in his career, it was that playing by the rules never went over well with people used to doing things their own way. He wasn't looking forward to imposing reality on the town of Smitten. Telling Zoe Thomas alone the truth might get him ridden out of town on a rail. He had the feeling she could dish it out but maybe wasn't as adept at receiving truth. Then again, who was? It was always easier to spot the sawdust in someone else's eye than the plank in one's own.

He followed her down the small alley between the two storefronts on the historical Main Street. Little more than a brick tunnel. He had to turn the ladder sideways to fit, and he kept banging it into the brick wall, as he had a hard time looking away from Zoe's small and elegant figure. Even in scruffy jeans and with her blunt haircut, she was the essence of femininity. She turned when he crashed the ladder into the wall for the third time.

"How did you get this out there to the street?" he asked.

Zoe shrugged. "Practice, I guess." She faced him and watched him carefully as though he hid some great secret. "I'll take it from here."

He tightened his grip. "Not a chance. A gentleman —"

"We Smitten women don't need to be taken care of," she interrupted. "We're a tough breed." She smiled, and he noticed her long, graceful fingers as they grasped the cold metal near his own hand. He remembered the feel of them only a few moments prior, and he clutched the ladder tighter rather than reach for her.

"My mama would have my neck if she knew I let a lady carry her own ladder."

She stared at him with her laser focus, as if she could read coordinates of everywhere he'd been in the last ten years. "Your mama didn't grow up here. The women of Smitten have been taking care of things for longer than you've been alive. Women don't make it in a logging town unless they come from tough stock."

He eyed her diminutive, elegant hands again, and something snapped in him. He didn't ever want Zoe Thomas to fend for herself again, though he couldn't understand where such a thought even came from. They passed an open door to the office and he noticed a pot steaming on the stove. "Is that something you need to turn off?"

She stepped back and looked inside. "No, it's on low. It's simmering."

"Do you live here?"

"No, I don't live here. It's my shop. I'm starting a matchmaking and event service. I'll coordinate social events and hopefully make a few romantic matches." She glowed with pride and her enthusiasm was contagious. Unfortunately, his mouth took over.

"How does one make money at that exactly?" He watched as a small spark of light died in her eyes, and he regretted his words before the last one was even out of his mouth.

She glared at him. Apparently he wasn't the first person to ask that question.

"If you don't mind my asking. I mean, it seems like romance just happens here in Smitten."

"There's a small monthly fee, and I'll get a cut from the events I run, but I've already got an active online community. I receive a small income from the ads there and from member fees. There will be sports activities like singles' day at the ski slopes, canoeing at the lake, and a swing dancing class — just to name a few ideas." Her eyes twinkled with excitement, and she absolutely came to life when she talked about her plans.

William didn't think he'd ever witnessed anything so mesmerizing as Zoe's enthusiasm. Her zeal was positively contagious. He found himself thinking maybe *he* needed a dating service. Church certainly hadn't brought him the woman of his dreams, but a ladder and a swollen temple may have.

She led him to a small wooden shed in the back alley, and following her lead, he folded the ladder into the wooden shack and leaned it against the wall.

He couldn't stop worrying about the pot left alone. These old buildings with their notoriously faulty wiring and wooden frames were little more than kindling to a simple spark. "Are you sure that pot is okay?" he asked.

She shrugged. "It's fine."

"What is that you're making?"

"Just dinner," she answered.

"Zoe, I know you've done things a certain way for a long time here in Smitten, but you're killing me with the gas on in that building. I can't leave without taking a look at the wiring."

"You're not with code enforcement. Aren't you a glorified accountant?" She looked down at her feet after she said it. "I'm sorry." She met his gaze again. "I didn't mean that."

He laughed only because it sounded like she did mean it — and she meant it very intently. "Maybe I am a glorified accountant, but I'm also in charge of zoning laws for the city. This street is zoned commercial, but I'm nearly positive you're not zoned for commercial cooking. That means you're most likely not insured for damages if there's a fire. That means the city itself gets sued, and trust me, this is why I have a job." He walked down the alley and entered the building through the side door, propped open by an old logging stump.

"Make yourself at home."

The wafting scent of onions and nutmeg met him, with a hint of sawdust and must. The first thing he noticed in the crumbling building was all the exposed wiring along the wall. It took every ounce of self-control not to rip out the new city manual he was writing and flag her for the myriad electrical issues. "Zoe." He pulled his notebook from his interior suit jacket. "You can't cook in here until you get this exposed wiring covered. You could blow up a city block with one spark." He turned off the burner and the flame died.

She marched beside him and turned it back on. "Do you mind? If that doesn't heat, there will be no dinner for eight seniors, and I'll roll them all to your front door and tell them why they're hungry. I understand I have to fix it, but surely it can wait a week."

"Seniors?" He stared again at the beautiful brunette who barely looked old enough to be out of high school, much less running her own business and cooking for old people. "You mean you're cooking for others?"

"Shut-ins." Her lower lip protruded, and the action caught his attention in a way that made him feel ashamed he hadn't taken her seriously. "Didn't the town you came from have older people who can't get around to the grocery store and such?"

"I was in Hilo, Hawaii. The seniors are pretty robust there, and family does the job."

"I think if you did more careful research, you'd find that even in the paradise of Hawaii there are some older folks on their own. Not everyone has a family, Mr. Singer."

At the sound of his formal name, he felt as if she'd kicked him in the gut.

"During the week I make a small meal and deliver it in the afternoons. Sometimes it's their only meal. It's certainly their only company."

"Miss Thomas, I think that's wonderful, but you can't put yourself and others in danger to do it." He turned the burner off again. "You'll have to find another place. You can't cook in here. Not until this wiring is up to code."

"What do you mean, I can't cook in here? It's my office. I pay the rent here."

"Who rented it to you? It's illegal to rent a place that isn't up to code. You'd need a permit for commercial cooking, and you'd certainly need to make sure all wiring is up to code. What's your landlord's name? There is no way the fire department is go-

139

ing to let you have any kind of event in this office." He drew a pen from his pocket. "Do you have your landlord's number? I can take care of this."

"I think you should leave now."

"I'm trying to help you, Zoe. No one should be renting out retail or business space that isn't safe. Smitten is getting too many visitors to do things the way they've always been done. With tourists comes responsibility, and liability insurance for the city. That's why the town board hired me — so that Smitten can run more efficiently."

She didn't say anything but walked to the ancient pink refrigerator in the corner of the wooden room and opened it. She drew out a silver ice tray and pulled the lever until the encased ice cracked into cubes. She withdrew a few, wrapped them in a terry-cloth kitchen towel, and dabbed the side of his head. Without thinking, he braced her hand, moved by her gentle touch.

"What are you cooking?"

"It's a butternut squash soup. A lot of times what my sister Clare grows in her garden is what I use for ingredients that day. She had a lot of squash today. Probably enough for the whole town." She didn't make an effort to remove her hand, and instead moved it so that the cold ice reached the entire scrape.

"Why can't you cook at home?"

"I live out by the lake. My car's been acting up, so I've been taking the bus into town. It's easier to cook here and run it to the seniors. I keep a bike here." She nodded toward a lime-green beach cruiser with a giant basket leaned against the corner. "It travels well over the gravel roads."

"You live out by the lake? Near the cabins?"

"In one of them, actually." She dropped her hand, and he suddenly felt as though he were missing a limb.

"I live in the cabins too. Just temporarily until I find something in town."

"Do you mean if you stay?"

"Pardon?"

She stepped back and placed the ice pack on a wooden chopping block near the stove. "City people don't usually stay very long in Smitten. The way we do things drives them batty and they're off." She hunched one shoulder. "Like you'll be when something bigger opens up."

His eyes widened at her forthright assessment of him. "I wanted to come to Smitten."

She gave a placating smile as if she didn't believe a word he said. "If you'll excuse me,

141

I have a lot of work to do before Friday."

"What's Friday?" he asked.

"My first event. It's an icebreaker, and we're going to have some food, give people a chance to get to know one another. Zak's going to bring barbecue. Have you met Zak yet? He's the owner of the Smitten Grill."

"I haven't had the pleasure. Zoe, you can't have people gather in this building until that wiring is inspected and covered."

"I can. Did you see that notice out front? The fire department approved me for an occupancy of sixty-seven people, and we won't have nearly that many on our first night."

He said nothing. He couldn't override the fire department. Not until he had the backing of the entire town board and proof that Smitten truly did want to streamline its management and run itself like a genuine town. He felt his jaw twitch at being so powerless. It always felt this way when he started in a new city as it underwent big changes. It just never bothered him so much before. Feeling powerless at first was part of the job. Feeling powerless in front of Zoe made him feel an inch tall.

He drew out his code book. "You're in violation of the current laws. I want to support you in this new venture, but I'm going to have to recommend that the fire department come back out and reinspect the premises. You can't open for business until that electrical is under current code." He wrote the approval number in his book, then closed and pocketed it.

Zoe's mouth gaped open as she watched him. He felt her gaze upon him, and heat rose from his collar. She pointed to the wall, and he followed her slender finger.

"There's the inspection. All signed and accounted for." She shrugged, as if everything was taken care of and there was nothing more to say. Her innocence made him want to burn his code book, but he couldn't do that in good conscience, no matter what she thought of him. But the cost felt high as her wide eyes blinked back at him.

He backed away from her toward the open door. He'd only just started in Smitten, and he had to prove himself worthy, but the cost felt astronomical as Zoe kicked the stump from the threshold and let the door slam between them. He heard the lock click and had no doubt that she'd fired up the stove again and ignored everything he said to her. He looked down the long corridor toward the street and saw Zoe's sister Clare staring back at him. He forced himself to walk toward the street and forget the way Zoe made him feel. For now, for his own sanity . . . that was all he could do.

CHAPTER THREE

Zoe's heart pounded as she stepped up to Mr. Warner's front door with his nightly meal. She felt like a criminal, having cooked dinner in her new commercial building, and found herself looking over her shoulder all day. It shouldn't have made any difference to her — after all, she had the fire department's approval — but a niggling feeling pressed on her. For some unknown reason, she wanted to impress William Singer and for him to take her seriously as a business-woman.

As she looked back at the bike on its kick-stand, she half expected to see William in his car taking notes on her subversive activities. She'd probably just watched too much *CSI.* She knew she didn't have time to prepare for the event, get back to the lake, and have dinner ready on time. Older people liked their schedules, and when she was late she often got an earful. Not only that, but she didn't want to admit to her family that they'd been right about her renting the tired old storefront.

With fall well under way, the day's dwindling light forced her to keep an earlier schedule. She balanced her basket with the last plate inside and rapped on the peeling red front door.

She opened the door a smidgen and peeked inside. "Arnold, it's Zoe. Can I come in?"

"In the kitchen," a gravelly voice called.

She made her way through the small bungalow and found Arnold sitting at his small Formica table with the lower half of his arm slung over its edge. "Where have you been?" He looked at the black numbers on the large wall clock as the minute hand made a loud click.

"I'm sorry. You were last on my route today. I'm having dinner at my mother's, and you're closest to her house."

"Zoe, are you still taking the bus and riding that crazy bike everywhere? Winter is coming, darling. You need to be more practical. I told you to take my Buick. No one uses that thing, and it's just sitting there in the garage. Take it and use it — at least until your car is working again."

"If I don't have a better system by the end

of the week, I will."

"Promise?" Arnold asked.

"Pinky swear," she said, though he probably had no idea what that meant. "Why are you in the kitchen already today? Are you hungry?" She removed the canvas bag from her shoulder and set the basket on the table. She brought out a small covered bowl and a paper plate of cheese and crackers. "Butternut squash soup, fresh from my sister's garden."

"You Thomas girls are a credit to your mother. It smells delicious." He waited patiently for her to grab some silverware, and she gathered up the well-washed plates that rested on the countertop from the day's earlier meal.

"Your TV working okay? It's not like you to be in the kitchen so early," she mentioned again.

Arnold shrugged. "The games were over for the day, and the news—well, I just don't recognize the world any longer. I knew you'd be here soon, so I thought I'd just wait. Here you are late today. What happened?"

"I got held up. It's the first day I cooked at the new office and I have to get used to things, that's all." She set the silverware on the table.

Arnold lifted the bowl closer to his nose and took a whiff. "Smells great."

"It tastes that way too. Has a little cream in it, so it should stick with you tonight. Very hardy for the colder nights."

"I'm glad you've noticed it's getting colder. That beach bike of yours is out of season."

She smiled at his fatherly tone. "Turns out Smitten has a new city manager, and he came by Cupid's Arrow today. He said I shouldn't cook there because the wiring isn't up to code, and if I started a fire the city would be held liable."

"That's secondary. If the wiring isn't up to code, you could be putting yourself in danger, and none of us could forgive ourselves if something happened to you."

She rubbed Arnold's shoulder. "I'll be careful."

He scooped a spoonful of soup into his mouth. "Mmm. He's probably right, you know. This country is nothing but lawyers anymore. You can't trim a hedge in your own backyard without being sued these days, but wiring is nothing to mess with."

Zoe stared into Arnold's pale blue eyes and realized the frantic energy she'd brought with her. She took in a deep breath, sat beside him, and cupped his hand. "I'll figure it out. How's your day going?"

"Same as always. I finished a puzzle. Did you see it when you came in?"

"I didn't. I'll check it out. Is that the one you've been working on? The old truck?"

"Hey, I prefer the term *classic,* thank you. I owned that very model at one time. Now, sit down and eat something. There's plenty here for both of us. Get yourself a bowl."

She squeezed his hand. "Not tonight. My mom is having a family dinner, and I'm running late, as usual." She stood up and went to the refrigerator. "What do you want to drink?"

"If it's not too much trouble, can you make me some coffee? There's decaf in that green canister there."

She glanced at her watch but figured her mother would expect her to be late. It was already past the time where she'd get by without a lecture. "Sure."

Everything in Arnold's kitchen was meticulously kept, and she pulled the Folger's canister from the wall and scooped some into the stained Mr. Coffee machine.

"You usually eat here on Mondays, you know. Smelled so good I forgot to bless it first." Arnold looked at his plate and went silent while he prayed.

She waited for him to finish and look up.

149

"My mom usually does dinners on Sundays, but Aunt Violet and Aunt Rose had a gig for their band and were in a tizzy, so Mom put it off."

"Your Aunt Violet has been in a tizzy about something since 1945. Why should today be different?"

"It's the whole family this time. It turns out my Grandma Rose had a beau before Grandfather. They found the man's dog tags from the Korean War and you would have thought that we were going to war all over again."

Arnold nodded. "I remember."

"You do?"

"Sure. David Hutchins."

"Little Mia found his dog tags in the attic. Grandma Rose said he died in the Korean War, but she has no idea how the dog tags got there. It's added some excitement to the household."

"So the Garner sisters have themselves a mystery, do they?" Arnold giggled like a small child, and she laughed at him.

"I wouldn't say my aunts have a mystery. No, we granddaughters have ourselves a mystery because no one wants to talk about it, so naturally that makes us even more interested. He may not have died in the war after all."

"Sometimes history is best left in the past."

"I agree with you," she said. "But if nothing else, we should get the dog tags back to their rightful owner, don't you think? His family would probably want to have them."

"You girls have no romantic notions about this former beau?"

"We're keeping the aunts and Grandma Rose out of it for now. We know he survived the war, and we've tracked him from California to North Carolina. We're trying to find out for certain if he's still alive. Wouldn't you want your dog tags returned to your family?"

"What's Rose say about this?"

Zoe shook her head. "Not a thing. No use in getting her hopes up."

"And Violet?"

"I don't think she knows a thing about it."

"I'll bet she does." Arnold chuckled as he swallowed another spoonful.

"What's that supposed to mean?"

"Not a thing, Zoe. Don't worry your pretty little head about it. And I'd give up any idea of finding David. If he wanted to be found, I reckon he'd have come back a long time ago."

Zoe wondered if that was true, but the

romantic in her wasn't about to let well enough alone. If her grandmother had another shot at love, there was hope for everyone. Cupid's Arrow was about creating connections between people, and what better way to make it happen than with the public relations firestorm a love story resurrected from the fifties could start?

"Well, thanks for bringing by the dinner, Zoe. It was wonderful, as always."

"You want to come to my mom's with me? I'm sure there'll be some delicious dessert. And you never know if one of those Garner sisters isn't worth a second look." She grinned.

"I've been looking at those Garner sisters since I had the eyesight to see them, and none of them ever looked back in sixty years. Besides, it's almost my bedtime. I never will understand you kids and your late nights."

It was only five o'clock, but in an old logging town the men rose early and were home for supper by four thirty or so. Zoe went back to making coffee and chided herself for not spending more time with the people she fed. They needed more than a hot meal. "The coffee's almost ready. I'd better be off to my mom's before it gets dark."

"Do you have anyone signed up for that dating service of yours yet?"

"I already have thirty people — can you believe it? I think some of them might be doing me a favor, but once I get going, they'll see how believing in me did *them* the favor."

"Paying to meet a mate. It sounds so backwards."

"People don't meet as easily as they once did, Arnold. Everything is all wired now. Face-to-face meetings are more difficult."

"Speaking of wired." Arnold put down his spoon. His bowl was wiped clean. "I don't want you cooking in that old storefront until you get it checked out. The new city manager is right. Electrical is nothing to play with."

She paused. "That's right, you were an electrician at the mill. I'd forgotten." She probably shouldn't have mentioned it. Now Arnold would worry.

"You're not old enough to remember when one of those old buildings went up in flames in the sixties. Zoe, it tore through that building so fast, there was nothing left of it in a matter of minutes. If the new city manager thinks you should get it checked out, you should get it checked out."

"The problem is, I can't afford to fix the

wiring, and I promised Miss Draper that I wouldn't bother her with repairs, so she gave me the rent for a song."

"That woman is as rich as Croesus, and she has a responsibility. Don't let her cry poor and put yourself in danger for something as ridiculous as money. She could buy and sell this town. Do you want me to talk to her?"

"No, Arnold. Don't worry, I'll handle everything."

He shook his head. "I'm coming to check it out tomorrow."

"Arnold, I can't let you do that."

"I'm not going to sleep until I check it out, so you may as well pick me up in the morning. You can get the Buick then."

"Exposed wiring is that big of a deal?"

"Exposed?" Arnold slapped the table. "You didn't say the wiring was exposed. The fire inspector must have missed that. He wouldn't let you gather people in that place."

"The walkway by the store is really uneven. I'd feel terrible if you fell. I'm just going to have to hire an electrician and pray for a way to pay for everything until the income starts." She mentally started calculating where she might come up with the money. Even worse, if Arnold reacted so violently, what must the new city manager think of her?

"I'll bring the walker," Arnold said.

Zoe knew that was a generous gesture on his part. He didn't like to go out, and he didn't like to look feeble.

"I can't ask you to do that. Maybe I'm not fit to run a business." Why did everyone else know these simple details?

"None of us is fit to do anything. It's only with the Lord's help we get by. Life is full of setbacks, Zoe. This town was dead as a doornail, but did we give up? Just put one foot in front of the next and accept the help. Accept the help."

She nodded, but wished she had a better alternative than calling on a ninety-year-old man for help. It was Arnold's turn to rest in life. "All right, I'll pick you up at eight tomorrow."

"Don't be late."

She smiled. "I won't." When the coffee had dripped enough, she filled his cup and set it on the table. "Black, right?"

"You better run home now before one of your aunts calls me looking for you. They'll blame me for talking too much, and I don't want to encounter their wrath."

"I'll see you in the morning." She flung her canvas bag over her shoulder. "I'm turning off the coffee machine. If you want more, you'll have to heat it up in the microwave."

He gave a weary grin. "That's my girl."

"Just once, I wish you'd eat with Miss Evelyn. She's good company, and it would save me a trip."

"I don't want no womenfolk. I want to watch the game when I want to watch the game, and I don't want anyone telling me chocolate is bad for my cholesterol. At my age, you get stuck in your ways. You just focus on yourself — finding you a man and starting a family."

She shook her head. "Not me, Arnold. I may be young, but I'm set in my ways too. I was meant to put people together, not be part of a couple."

"I don't believe that. Anyone who cooks like you must have to beat the men off with a stick. The trouble will be that no man is good enough for our Zoe."

Everyone she cooked for was well advanced in years and preferred soft, strained food. Unless she was planning on setting herself up with an octogenarian, her cooking skills were of little use in "finding herself a man."

"You're just trying to change the subject. Maybe Evelyn likes chocolate. I'll ask her tomorrow."

"Don't ask her anything. You go on about your business and leave the romance to the young, where it belongs." He crossed his arms and sat back in his chair. "That goes for your grandmother too. Don't think I don't know what you girls are up to, trying to track down David Hutchins."

She smiled. "Evelyn might cheer you up."

"Already wore one woman out," he grumbled. "Besides, I've known Evelyn since before your mother was born. Don't you think if we were meant to be, we'd be?"

"Maybe, but I'm a romantic. Maybe romance is different at your age, but it's still nice to think about having someone to talk to, isn't it?"

"You'd best be on your way, Zoe. I'll see you in the morning."

CHAPTER FOUR

Zoe skipped down the stairs of Arnold's house and hurried along the asphalt side-walk, hurtling on her bicycle toward her mother's house. When she approached the modest wood frame house, the sun was dwindling and she realized Arnold was right. She'd need a car soon.

At her mom's, she parked the bike off the pathway and took the stairs two at a time. Anna stood in the door with a hand on her hip. "It's about time you got here. Where have you been, young lady?"

Zoe kissed her cheek and brushed past. "Just running late, as usual. Do you need help in the kitchen?"

"Don't be silly, dinner's on the table. What did you bring?"

The family ate weekly in a potluck format, and though the meals rarely made sense or went together, it had become their way. They might enjoy a meal of Mom's sweet potatoes and marshmallows served alongside Aunt Violet's chicken tikka masala that she'd garnered from some gourmet magazine. Her oldest sister, Tess, always brought her incredible homemade bread, and that went with everything. Clare always brought fresh vegetables.

Aunt Violet, with her haphazard red lipstick and cotton-candy-pink blush, met Zoe as she entered the dining room.

" 'Bout time. Being late conveys the message that you think you're more important than everyone else, Zoe. Keep that in mind."

Zoe kissed her aunt on her sparkly cheek. "I love you, Aunt Violet, and I'll make it on time next week. I promise."

"What did you bring?"

"Orange Jell-O," she answered sheepishly. She often got so overwhelmed cooking for the elders of Smitten, her family paid the price. They got what was left in her, and today that amounted to Jell-O salad set with mandarin oranges. She wished she'd thought to say orange aspic. It sounded better. Not that any of the women ever complained. They simply enjoyed being together.

Most folks said Smitten was a man's town because it had been a logging town for decades, but you'd never know it by Zoe's family. Her mother, Anna Thomas, considered herself an abject failure at romance after the divorce. Zoe disagreed. That was her father's failure, since he'd left them after she and her sisters were grown and had begun another family as if they'd never existed.

Zoe scanned the dining room, which somehow didn't feel right. As her aunts and grandmother parted, she noticed a male figure standing at the head of the table smiling conspiratorially at her. William Singer? Her stomach betrayed her by fluttering at the sight of him.

"What's he doing here?" she whispered to Aunt Petunia.

"Yes!" Aunt Petunia shouted. "We have a man here! Good-looking one too. Did you see the build on that guy? Didn't think they made 'em like that anymore."

Zoe wanted to crawl under the table. Tess, God bless her, tried to salvage the moment.

"Zoe's business must already be working. We have a man at our table." Tess winked at her. "This is William Singer. He's new in town. It appears the success of Smitten has brought the need for a city manager."

"We've met," Zoe said, avoiding the pull of his gaze. She kept her eyes locked on Tess, though everything in her fought the urge to stare at the mystery of William

Singer. Gone was his telltale city suit, and though she'd only caught a glimpse of him, she realized she could name every detail of his presence: dark-washed jeans, nothing that might be purchased in town, and a gray collared shirt, casually unbuttoned at the top. She could picture the outline of how the shirt hugged his muscular chest, and the depth of those sea-colored eyes, and she wondered if that's why the Garner/Thomas women were destined for romantic failure. Perhaps they were programmed to find attractive only dangerous men who couldn't stay put.

She cleared her throat and pulled Clare around the dining room wall. "What is he doing here? Did you know about this?"

Clare, now dressed for dinner in a loose-knit cardigan over an ancient cotton dress that hung like a sack on her, smiled as if she'd done a good deed. "I thought you'd be happy I invited him. Maybe he can give you some advice on what you can do to fix the store. He didn't have anywhere to go, and I know how you hate to see people alone."

"Not him," Zoe hissed. "I don't mind him being alone. He *should* be alone. Clare, I'm trying to stay under the radar with this guy. If he finds out I don't have the money to fix the wiring and open for business on Friday, I could get shut down, and you know I can't afford that. Every penny is accounted for, and I only have so much time to make this work."

Clare raised her brows. "I think you might protest too profusely, if you know what I mean."

Zoe pursed her lips.

"You have to play by the same rules as everyone else with your business. Taxes aren't convenient either, but we have to pay them. Besides, until William's rental house is ready, he's staying in one of Carson's smaller cabins — the ones with no kitchenette. He doesn't have any way to cook for himself. If I were you, I'd make friends with him until that junker of yours is fixed."

"What are you two whispering about?" Grandma Rose asked. "Let's eat. Dinner is getting cold."

"Yes, Grandma." Zoe whispered to Clare again, "Why didn't you send him to Zak's grill if he can't cook for himself?"

Her mother smiled at her and pressed on her shoulder toward the dining room. "William, I'd like you to meet my youngest daughter. This is Zoe, our matchmaker."

William stood and nodded his head in greeting since he couldn't get around the table in the cozy dining room. "We met earlier." He touched the scrape on his forehead absently.

Out of his suit, William Singer still looked just as much the city man. Zoe tried to find any flaw, but the truth was his flaws had to be within, because on the outside he was impeccable.

His face seemed to belong in Smitten, though. He sported a rugged five o'clock shadow, and his hair, if left to grow, would curl at the edges. She wondered if he'd left it to do just that when he'd been in Hawaii, and if the crisp haircut was for Smitten alone. She wondered if he'd stay in Smitten long enough for her to watch those curls grow, or if he'd continue to clip his hair as if he'd attended an all-boys school.

"Zoe," her mom said, "I saved the seat next to William for you. I imagine you'll want to grill him for your dating business."

"Thanks, Mom." She lifted the chairs away from the wall and made her way to the back of the dining room, where William sat trapped by the women of her family. "Aren't you afraid you might not make it out of here alive?"

"I wasn't until you came."

He smiled, and again her stomach flipped. What was up with that?

"You'll be happy to know I found an electrician to help me with the wiring," she said — not adding that the electrician was ninety years of age and unable to walk without assistance. An electrician was an electrician.

"I knew you would. You seem like a capable woman with a strong arm." His eyes twinkled, and her mother seemed to take note.

"Zoe, what did you do to our guest?"

"I didn't do anything. Let's eat, the chicken's getting cold." She pulled the bowl from her canvas bag. A Tupperware bowl of mandarin orange Jell-O. It appeared less than gelled after its trip across Smitten to deliver the rest of the dinners, and she watched William eye how much it jiggled.

What kind of man notices that Jell-O hasn't set right?

"William," her mother said from the other end of the table, where she could easily access the kitchen. "Would you mind leading us in prayer?"

He cleared his throat. "Of course." He reached for her hand and their grandmother's, then bowed his head. Zoe felt a bolt of energy surge through her arm at his touch and forced herself to focus on his prayer.

"Dear heavenly Father, I thank you for the warm welcome to Smitten, and for providing me with these welcoming, beautiful friends for dinner. Thank you for this food that has been provided and for the hands that prepared it. In Jesus' name. Amen."

"Amen," the women said in unison.

Aunt Petunia stood and served their guest a few slices of chicken and mashed potatoes. She poured gravy over the plate, and Zoe rolled her eyes. "Auntie, I think he can serve himself."

Petunia sat back down. "I'm terribly sorry."

William chuckled. "Not a problem. For a moment I was back at my mother's table, and I wanted to hold my palms up to show you I'd washed for dinner."

"Did you?" Anna asked.

He held up his palms. "I did."

Everyone around the table laughed, and Zoe thought how easily he charmed them. She wasn't fooled by his smooth talk and velvet smile. With William Singer as city manager, Smitten would lose control of the way things had always been done. He brought change, and she worried that his kind of change would ruin what made Smitten, Smitten.

"So, Zoe." William seemed so close to her in the cramped dining room that she couldn't look directly at him when he spoke for fear it would prove too intimate. "What is it about matchmaking that intrigues you? Are you a hopeless romantic?"

The way he made her feel light-headed went against all she knew to be true about his kind, and she struggled to keep her dark impression of the stranger.

"Not really," she said. "I just hate to see people alone. I'm so grateful I have my family, but I look around town and I see that it's not that way for everyone. Sure, we all look out for one another here in Smitten, but we're like the rest of the world. Life gets busy, and marriage takes effort."

"So you're focused primarily on marriage, then?"

"I suppose you think that's simple, coming from the big city where everyone dates willy-nilly."

He laughed. "I've been in Hilo, Hawaii, for the last two years. It's not exactly a big city, but I suppose dating there was for the purpose of marriage."

"Which you object to?"

"Zoe!" her mother chastised.

"No, it's fine, Anna." He looked at Zoe again, and she focused on the shifting Jell-O on her plate. "I don't object to marriage by any means. It's just that I specialize in short-term projects for cities on the verge of big changes. It's not a lifestyle that's conducive to marriage."

"I wouldn't think so."

"Zoe, not everyone wants to stay planted in the place they were born. Some women would find that a great adventure," Clare said.

"Would you find that a great adventure?" William asked her in a way that caused Zoe to question her own commitment to stability.

"We have each other," Tess said. "I doubt it's easy for a guy to be brought home to all these women, but when the right one comes along, he'll put up with us." Her cheeks pinked and she looked at her plate, no doubt remembering the way they'd all welcomed Ryan.

"The right man will." William looked at Zoe with soft eyes, and she shifted in her chair.

"I — I should get home."

"You just got here!" Tess said. "You didn't eat a thing!"

"Zoe, you're too antsy for your own good," Violet said. "Finish your meal and make polite conversation with the good-looking man next to you. Maybe you'll learn something."

"I'm having my grand opening this weekend and I've got a ton to do. You don't mind, do you?" She smiled toward William. "I have to take the bus home, and I want to get there before too long. Early morning with the electrician and all that."

"Actually, I do mind," her mother said. "I don't like you taking the bus out to the lake so late at night."

"Mom, it's not even six o'clock."

"Regardless, it's nearly dark out there, so I've asked William to drive you home."

"Of course you did." Zoe slumped in her chair. She may have been the matchmaker, but she supposed she had to have learned it somewhere. He was near her age and gainfully employed, so why wouldn't her mother think he was perfect for her?

CHAPTER FIVE

William waited as Zoe hugged her family good-bye. He grinned at the show of emotion. It was as if it was the last time she'd ever see them. She turned toward him and descended the stairs in slow motion, as if being pulled by a force she couldn't control.

In contrast, his heart raced at her approach. It was like nothing he'd ever experienced before. It wasn't some primal attraction. He wanted her good opinion desperately, and he'd felt that way from the start when he'd made a fool out of himself by walking into her ladder. If there was ever a time to make a good impression, that had been it. And he hadn't.

In her worn blue jeans and faded shirt, Zoe evinced a luminous presence that captured his attention with every subtle movement. She was a rare breed who could sport pixie hair and tomboy clothes, and stream femininity in the process. One thing she didn't hide was her feelings about him and all he represented to her precious town of Smitten. He was eager to prove himself her ally, but the harder he worked at it, the worse the situation became.

"Do we need to get your bike to the lake?"

"I keep it in town to deliver the dinners. Clare will toss it in the back of her truck and get it to me by morning."

"Sounds like you're used to this car of yours not working."

"I simply haven't readjusted my clock to fall yet. That's all."

He raised his hand to the women on the doorstep. "Thank you again, ladies. Dinner was wonderful."

The women all smiled with warmth and waved him good-bye. He wondered how her family could see him in such a different light . . . and why none of their opinions mattered like hers did.

"Your family is incredible," he said as she stepped beside him on the walkway. "I suppose you know that, but it was nice to feel welcomed by them."

She smirked as if there was something more behind his comment. "They are pretty incredible."

He pressed the button to unlock his car, then opened the passenger door for her. She peered at him curiously but climbed into the bucket seat and sat down. The streetlight shined upon the gold flecks in her hazel eyes, so he failed to notice that she'd grabbed the door to pull it closed for herself. She tugged it from his hands and slammed it. He waved again at her family to let them know everything was all right, though he wasn't so confident himself.

He came around to the driver's side and slid inside. "That's the second door you've slammed in my face today. Is this something you're going to make a habit of?"

She stared out the window.

"I just want to know so I can keep an eye on my fingers and limbs."

She faced him, and he dropped his hand from the car keys after inserting them in the ignition.

"Do you care to tell me why you've taken such an immediate disliking to me? Your family doesn't seem to think I'm so bad."

"It's nothing personal."

"So what is it?"

She shrugged her delicate shoulders. "Does it really matter? You'll get the town set to rights and be on your way. There are lots of lovely people here in Smitten. What I think about you hardly matters, and like I said, it's not personal."

"But it does matter to me. For what it's worth, it feels personal."

"Why?" Her eyebrows lifted.

"Because I've heard nothing but wonderful things about you since I got to town. Even Carson told me if I needed anything at all and he wasn't around, to call on you. He said you knew everyone in town and that you could take care of any problem as easily as he could."

"I think Carson sold you a bill of goods. I may know everyone, but so does everyone else in Smitten. That's what makes it Smitten. I'm not special here."

The downturn in her voice concerned him, and he wished he knew what skeleton he'd rattled. He turned over the ignition. The only thing worse than trying to garner Zoe's good opinion was her family's prying eyes watching his epic failure.

"Carson meant I could contact you because the other cabins are all taken up by tourists. He wanted me to know there was someone who lived there year-round who could direct me if he was off on business."

He'd had no idea Zoe would look the way she did; he'd imagined a female lumberjack. Yet as soon as Carson mentioned her name, he just had the feeling they were destined to meet. If he'd known she'd be downtown as he did his first walk-through, he would have practiced his entrance. He certainly wouldn't have walked into a ladder. Nothing said "professional businessman sent to rescue the financial aspects of the town" like a Three Stooges impression.

"Turn left," she said as they got to the corner. "It's not you."

"It feels like me."

"Okay, it is sort of you."

He laughed, and she joined him. Her laughter was infectious. He wanted to hear more of it, but he seriously doubted he'd get the opportunity.

"Care to elaborate?" He could tell by her expression that the answer was no, but to his surprise she continued.

"I've been doing small jobs for people in Smitten since I was thirteen. My family really wanted me to go to college, but I just had no desire."

Soon they were on Main Street.

"I worked in my cousin Natalie's coffee shop there." She pointed out the coffee shop.

"Right. She just married Carson."

"Yes." She nodded and actually smiled.

"I was headed over to Mountain Perks when we . . . when I ran into you."

She laughed again, and he felt warmed by

the sound. "I'm not laughing at you running into my ladder —"

"Yes, you are," he accused playfully.

"Okay, maybe I am, but you know how you were dressed all fancy? The juxtaposition of you running into my rusty ladder . . . and looking like you stepped out of *GQ* . . . I don't know, it just struck me as funny once I knew you weren't hurt."

He pulled up to the stop sign at the end of Main Street and leaned over to point to the Band-Aid on his temple. "I was hurt. Remember?"

"Oh, come on. That's just a scratch."

"Maybe, but some guilt on your part would be appropriate."

"That's Zak and Julia's place." She pointed to a large rustic wood building that reminded him of a covered bridge. "The Smitten Spa & Grill. I worked for Julia part-time in the spa besides the coffee shop. Just odd jobs here and there. This is my first career move." She clasped her hands in her lap. "I suppose that sounds funny to someone like you who has been in business so long."

He didn't think any such thing. He admired her immensely for risking her savings for something she believed in so passionately. He, on the other hand, made all his decisions based on the next promotion, the bigger city.

"I admire your ability to sit back and wait for the perfect moment," he said. He stared at the red door on the restaurant where she'd worked. "The Smitten Spa & Grill?" He waited for an explanation.

"Julia moved back from New York, and Zak wanted to rent out some space since the grill wasn't doing as well with the mill closed down. I guess it was meant to be, because they're in love now, and both businesses are doing fine."

"What did you do at the spa?"

"I was just a receptionist. Julia tried to teach me and encouraged me to get my license as an esthetician, but I took too long to mix things. She said I'd been baking for too long."

"A license to be a what?"

"A facialist. But it wasn't for me. Besides mixing, you have to be quiet when you're giving facials, and I want to talk to people, ask questions, learn about their lives. They want to relax. I'm too social for that. It felt kind of like working in a morgue to me, but Julia loves it. She feels as if she's painting the world to make it more beautiful."

"So matchmaking came into the picture."

Her expression dropped, and he drove

onto the two-lane highway back toward the lake outside of town.

Her voice became softer. "You wouldn't really shut me down before I opened this week, would you?"

He stalled, wondering if he'd been played by her friendly conversation. "I've done this before, Zoe. It's not easy to be the new guy in a town that's been run a certain way, but the way things were doesn't work anymore. If it did, I wouldn't have been called into town in the first place. You forget, I want you to succeed."

"So that's a yes, then." Her pink bottom lip, fresh and full without makeup, pouted.

Was that cherry ChapStick he smelled? His reaction was visceral.

"You'll shut me down even though I've thrown everything I have into this business and rented that very place so I could cook there? It had the kitchen and the stove already."

He heard the desperation in her voice. Though she was more than capable, he wasn't going to let her walk all over him to get her way. "I'm only upholding the law. It's for your own safety. How would you feel if something happened to people inside your store and you knew you could have prevented it?"

"I understand," she said tightly. It was clear she didn't.

He changed the subject. "So knowing what you know now, who would you set me up with in Smitten? Say, for the railroad fund-raiser? Who do you see as my type?"

"No one."

"I'm that detestable?"

"It's not that. You're quite handsome, actually. Successful. I can see that you've got potential."

"But . . ."

"In my business plan it states that I'll help folks build solid, foundational relationships that will last. No offense, but you don't seem like the type to settle down. How many places have you lived in the last ten years?"

He nearly choked at her question, which proved she knew more about him than he cared to admit. "My specialty is acting as interim city manager until a town can find someone permanent. Crisis management, you might say. That way, when towns feel like they can manage, they don't feel guilty about letting my position go. It's designed for that. I sign two-year contracts specifically. Besides, you of all people can hardly fault me for having a lot of jobs."

"So like I said — not the type to settle down."

The way she said so matter-of-factly that he wasn't worthy of her dating service made him want to strive for a reassessment. His mother certainly thought it was time for him to settle down, but the fact was, his contract was for two years. What would he do in a town like Smitten after that?

"You're focused on your career to the point where you don't have time for love," she said pointedly.

"How would you know that?"

"I assume you took this job in Smitten because of all the great press we're getting, which means you don't plan to stay because then, like a great baseball player, you'll get courted away by bigger money. Once you've accomplished whatever goal you've set for Smitten, you'll be on your way, and whoever I set you up with would be heartbroken."

"That's a lot of prophecy for someone who doesn't even know me."

"It's all right," she said softly. "It's a lifestyle choice. And frankly, we don't have to like each other. It's just that I'm a Smitten girl and you're —"

"An interloper?"

She pressed her lips together and didn't reply, so he had his answer.

"No," she finally said. "Not an interloper. I didn't mean it that way."

"What if I were to stay in Smitten? How long does one have to stay in Smitten or the surrounding area to join Broken Arrow?"

"*Cupid's* Arrow," she corrected him. "And longer than one railroad fund-raiser. I'm trying to find couples looking for lifelong companionship who might be too shy to put all their cards on the table in a small town."

"Fair enough. If I took you to dinner, maybe you could make a better assessment about my long-term potential. Do you think?" He raised his brows and waited with bated breath for her answer.

"Are you asking me out to dinner?"

He nodded. "I am. Just to make sure I get a fair shake." He rubbed his temple just in case it would provide any incentive for her.

"I think I could make you a perfectly fine meal in the storefront if you'd let me cook there."

"I didn't make the rules. I only enforce them. I'm a public servant."

"I have to cook anyway," she said. "For the seniors. So there's no sense in wasting money on a meal out."

"A good meal with entrepreneur Zoe does not sound like a waste of any precious resource to me."

She eyed him suspiciously, but her expression softened. "All right. Dinner."

"Tuesday at seven?"

"Why so soon?"

"Let's be honest — I have to get you to dinner before the sharks at Cupid's Arrow get to you."

Her eyes were inquisitive, and he understood she didn't know what to think of him, but she had a faith in all things beautiful that made him want to prove himself to her. Maybe being Smitten's city manager *was* a temporary gig that he'd only taken on because it would look great on a résumé to help a burgeoning town rise to the next level.

One would have to be buried six feet under to have missed all the hype about Smitten as a new place for destination weddings. But with each thought, he only proved that Zoe was right about him. It was merely a stepping-stone for his career. But seeing Zoe interact with her family made him wonder if he knew what he really wanted.

"Honestly, Mr. Singer, my thoughts are on the office space. I thought it could double so that I might cook for the shut-ins. Now I worry how I'll pull it all off and get the business open on time. My mixer is on Friday, and running back and forth to the lake is going to cost me a lot of time. Time that I don't have."

"But you have to eat, and I'd love to hear all the reasons you were never tempted to leave Smitten."

"What about Saturday night, then? It will be less stressful. I'll be more present."

He nodded and fought the urge to shout *Yes!* It wasn't exactly an enthusiastic affirmative, but he'd take it.

CHAPTER SIX

Zoe shifted in her seat and wished that the
eternal ride out to the cabin would end. William made her nervous. He was everything
she wasn't: educated, sophisticated, and
business-savvy. He had a trustworthy air to
him. But then, her father had probably had
that too, or her mother wouldn't have married him and borne three children. The trust
issues went deep. Maybe that's why she
never wanted to move. Smitten, and the
people in it, had proved trustworthy. She
could witness the faithfulness of God in
those around her.

As the church's steeple rose on the horizon, she wondered if her desire for safety
and the familiar was actually a lack of faith.
That's what rubbed her the wrong way
about William. He didn't seem afraid of
anything. He could go where the wind blew
him, and nothing rocked him. She looked at
his handsome profile as he focused on the

road ahead of them. He had a warmth about him, and she felt comfortable in his presence, which was probably the reason her walls rose immediately and actually forced a sense of anxiety.

She told herself to behave and treat him as she would any other stranger in town, but every time she opened her mouth, something ugly came out. Had she ever done that before when she'd been interested in someone?

Zoe placed her hand on the console between them. "I'm scared to death."

He pressed the brake. "Of me? You're scared of me? Zoe, I'll drop you back off at home if you're —"

"No. Not of you. I've set people up before, even had a few friends get married, but I have no idea how to run a business. I have no idea how to do anything." The sting of tears burned behind her eyes, threatening to unleash themselves in front of a man who already saw her as unstable.

William pulled the car to the side of the road and placed his hand on top of hers. His eyes bored into her with a sincerity that she'd never experienced before. He seemed to understand. Without saying a thing, he made her feel safe. She blinked away the tears, and he plucked a tissue from the center console and dabbed underneath her eyes with the most tender of touches.

"It's natural to feel that way when you embark on something new."

"Not if you know what you're doing. People who are educated like you."

He chuckled. "Is that what you think of me? I'm the guy who walked into a ladder this morning."

She laughed through her tears. "It's kind of you to say so. I think I may have misjudged you." She felt his grasp tighten, and with it felt herself relax in his presence.

"I wanted to come off as a person of authority who had the respect of the town. I came off like a jerk."

For a moment they were lost in each other's gaze, full of compassion for one another. He didn't seem like an educated know-it-all who would disappear, but someone like her, a human being with fears and frailties. She stared at the firm lines of his lips and wondered what it would be like to kiss a man like William Singer. The thought woke her, and she broke from her trance.

"You can ask for help, Zoe. If there are any questions you have about running the business or what kind of numbers you need to make it work, that's my specialty. I can help you." He breathed in and exhaled deeply before he pulled the car back onto the road.

She didn't know what to say. She feared if he looked at her business plan, he might think it looked like a creation in color crayons meant for display on the refrigerator.

"You'll ask for my help if you need it?"

She nodded. She wrapped her arms around herself and gripped her upper arms, aware that this handsome stranger now knew more about her fears for Cupid's Arrow than her entire family put together. She felt exposed. "I have plans for the business. I'm — it's —"

"Zoe, show me someone who isn't scared to start their own business and fly on their own without a steady paycheck, and I'll show you a crazy person. Give yourself credit. It takes time and commitment to get a business going. I don't want to take the wind out of your sails, but there's more you'll come up against. The electrical is the start, but you take it one step at a time, and before you know it you have a viable business."

"How many times did you give that pep talk at a Rotary meeting?"

He pointed at her playfully. "You!"

As they took the long road toward the

lake, her pulse quickened and she searched for something more to say so that their time wouldn't come to an end.

"I can't believe that you live out here by yourself and you were going to take the bus home," he said.

"The bus drops me off on the main road and I run this gravel road. That way I don't need to make time for exercise. Sometimes I have extra plates from my visitations, so it's not ideal, but I've learned to wrap them in towels on days I'll be running, or use only plastic. But I worry it's not healthy to eat off of plastic plates, so I try not to do that."

Why did she keep rattling off pointless information? Why did she suddenly want him to like her? What good would it do? He was a short-timer. Rationality overcame emotion and she straightened in the seat.

"You run on this deserted road by yourself? It doesn't worry you?"

"Well, it didn't until you mentioned it!" She smiled at him. "I'm kidding you. It doesn't scare me. I know Smitten so well, and I do carry pepper spray in the event that I ever meet with something less than desirable." She lifted her bag, which rattled like she was a homeless woman with every possession she owned on her person.

"You're telling me that if I attacked you,

you could pull out the pepper spray from that giant bag and still have time to protect yourself? Go ahead. I'll give you a thirty-second head start. Find your pepper spray." Again he pulled the car to the side of the gravel road and lifted his brows in challenge. The lake glistened in the foreground as the sun's last rays sparkled on its waters.

Zoe grew quiet, lost in its beauty. "I never get tired of that view. The pink of the sky against the lush greenery here. I almost have to pinch myself that I get to live here."

William put his car in park and watched Zoe, who was lost in the heavenly view. "I agree," he said.

"Did you know that I plan to run romantic dinner evenings on the train when it gets here?"

"*If* I can get the train back to Smitten."

"I believe you can. We all do."

"It's one of the things that attracted me most to the town. That, and the opportunity for big successes with a small budget."

"I love the train," she said, still staring at the lake. "The romance of it. Someone else is driving, and as a passenger you get to take in the view with someone special. I thought we'd run murder-mystery nights and have everyone dress up from a bygone era.

Doesn't that sound like a fun way to meet people?" She finally turned her gaze back to him.

"You have an old soul, Zoe."

She blinked as she digested his comment. It was perhaps the first compliment to come out of his mouth that she couldn't fling off with ease. She picked up the wooden turtle on his dashboard and ran her fingers across its belly. "What does the turtle mean?"

"My last temporary assignment was in Hilo. I told you that at dinner, right?"

She nodded.

"On my days off I used to go to the coast and take pictures of the turtles. They fascinate me. With all these temp jobs, they remind me that the turtle is always at home wherever he goes."

"I live over there." She pointed to the last cabin on the lake. Her long fingers caught his eye in their elegance, and he thought if any woman could make a man stay put, it was Zoe Thomas. Even in her holey jeans and oversized T-shirt, she possessed a quirky style all her own with a wispy scarf wrapped around her waist and short gray suede boots. She looked like a Hollywood star incognito for a weekend getaway.

He put the car in drive again and pulled up to the side of the gravel road in front of her lonely cabin at the end of the row. The sun was behind the mountain, and the brightness of the moon cast a deep blue hue over the valley.

"Looks like we're out of daylight," he said as she reached for the door handle.

"Yeah."

"The ride goes faster with company. Do you need a lift to town in the morning?"

"No thanks."

"I can come back for you if you're worried I'll leave too early."

She shook her head. "Thanks again for the ride." She looked down in her open palm and handed him back the wooden turtle. "The turtle is at home wherever he goes," she echoed, but he didn't understand what she meant by the remark.

He worried that if she left him now, she'd forget the warmth she'd shown him, and the initial chill would return.

"Zoe." He reached for her. "Please. Let me get the door for you." He clambered out of the car and around to the passenger door. As he opened it, she turned away from him to gather up her belongings. If he didn't make his move, he'd regret it, and she'd go back to remembering why she didn't like him.

He reached for her hand and helped her

out of the car. The movement forced the canvas bag off of her shoulder, and its contents spilled out onto the gravel road. She immediately bent and he followed, grabbing up various cooking utensils and Tupperware boxes. They both stopped at the orange Jell-O salad remnants, which looked a deep violet under the moonlight as they jiggled on the pebbles.

"The one day my Jell-O doesn't set right . . . I may have to turn the refrigerator up at the store." She recovered. "When it's legal to cook there and all."

He lifted her chin away from the mess. "Show me the lake?"

She shook her head, and the last of the sunlight reflected off her dark tresses. "I shouldn't. I have to get things ready for tomorrow."

He felt the tug of her fears speaking for her and watched as she closed her eyes as if thinking on what might happen if she let him into her world. He slid the half-emptied canvas bag from her shoulder. "Let me walk you in."

He plucked the rest of the items from the ground and put what was clean back into the bag.

"You don't have to do that," Zoe said.

He dropped the bag and all its contents

again, then advanced toward her as though she might run. His palms wrapped around her cheeks. She lifted her chin toward him, and he bent to press a kiss on her lips. She returned his kiss and then pulled free and ran to her doorstep, leaving a trail of items on the overgrown lawn underneath the wooden rail fence that surrounded the property.

He collected them all and climbed the three steps to her log cabin, where he left the bag on the stoop under the porch light. "Good night, Zoe," he said to the closed door. As he walked the short gravel path to his car, he stared back at the house, and a smile bloomed from every cell. Hawaii was the sea turtle's home. Smitten was Zoe's home. He wanted to understand what it took to call a woman like Zoe *home*.

CHAPTER SEVEN

Zoe tossed and turned all night. He'd kissed her. Out of the blue. She hadn't done anything to encourage him. Not that she could remember anyway, and she wasn't the sort of girl who had that kind of come-hither look that made a man melt. Which made William Singer even more confounding than he already had been. She couldn't erase the kiss from her mind. It hadn't felt forward and obnoxious. It seemed . . . natural, which confused her to no end. And sweet.

The kiss put her into a kind of trance that lasted all night and well into the bright morning sunlight. She would have forgotten to exit the bus if Rod, the driver, hadn't woken her from her reverie.

"Zoe!" he shouted. She looked up to see the other passengers waiting for her to exit.

"Oh, I'm so sorry." She looked at the faces waiting for her to make a move. "Thanks,

Rod. I'll see you tonight." She hiked her canvas bag with the day's groceries over her shoulder and padded down the steps.

A grin overtook her at the sight of her new business. Her new business, little Zoe Thomas's new business. She saw her bicycle in the window and silently thanked Clare for taking care of the details. For some reason, she felt only lightness and happy thoughts at her vision. The fears had been banished. She'd like to chalk it up to prayer, but truth be told, she hadn't gotten a lot of praying done thinking about that kiss. She crossed the brick street to the white clapboard storefront and headed down the alley to the back door. She unlocked the door and entered, breathing in the familiar musty scent. The interior of Cupid's Arrow looked more like the inside of a barn than a retail space, though in a charming, romantic way. Its rough-hewn plank walls slapped with whitewash and rustic wood floors echoed back to another era when Smitten was a man's town. A few bits of lace and some chandeliers had transformed the place to create an aura of romance for both men and women. Zoe dropped her bag on the counter and examined the open electrical boxes as though she had some idea of what she was looking at, but all she knew was that the exposed wires needed to be covered. With what, she had no idea.

Tess would arrive soon. She'd called the night before to tell Zoe what she'd been able to glean from Grandma Rose about her long-lost beau, and she'd agreed to pick up Arnold that morning. It took everything for Zoe not to blurt out that William Singer had kissed her, but the giddy emotion she felt bubble at the thought of sharing kept her from spouting off. If anyone heard her tone, they'd know her disdain for Mr. William Singer was something she had to work at.

Tess announced her arrival. "We're here!" she shouted.

Zoe was washing her hands, getting ready to prepare the night's dinner before she finished decorating the shop for that day. "Back here!" she shouted as she walked through the doorway to the front.

Arnold scuffled toward her with his walker. Zoe cringed with every step. "Arnold, be careful. I'm worried about you on these old planks. They're not even."

"Quit fussing. You're like an old woman sometimes, Zoe. I may be old, but I'm not an invalid yet."

She crossed her arms and sighed.

"Arnold and I were talking about David

194

Hutchins," Tess said, her eyes shining. "Grandma's first love."

"He served in the Korean War with my nephew." Arnold nodded, still studying the walls and following the wires with his eyes.

"You didn't tell me that," Zoe said, feeling oddly disappointed.

"I'd forgotten. I told my son when he called last night that you girls were stirring up trouble from the past and he reminded me. After that, I called my nephew to see if he kept in touch."

Tess balked. "We're not stirring up trouble. We're trying to solve a mystery. If David didn't die in the war, how did his dog tags get in our grandma's attic?"

"He lived through the war," Arnold stated. "My nephew confirmed it. In fact, James told me he got a Christmas card from him last year."

"A Christmas card!" Tess squealed. "So he's still alive now?"

Arnold shrugged. "He's not that old. Seventy-eight or so."

"Is he married?"

"How would I know if he's married?"

"Where did the Christmas card come from?" Tess probed. "What did the postmark say?"

"Tess," Zoe said calmly. "Arnold doesn't

195

know where the card came from. His nephew got the card."

"This year? Or last year?"

"Tess!"

"All right, but, Mr. Warner, you'll find out for me, won't you? You'll ask your nephew? Or you can give me James's number. I could call him."

It was so like Tess to ignore that which she didn't want to hear.

"Tess, Arnold came to look at the electrical for me." Zoe talked through her teeth. "Maybe we could bring this up later?"

Tess frowned. "Okay. Clare's coming to bring Arnold home in a little while. I've got to get going." She raised her voice. "Bye, Arnold!"

He grunted as he held on to the walker with one hand and ran his other along the wire at eye level. "You're renting this place, right?" he asked.

"I am, but it's owned by Miss Draper, and she specifically told me she had no money for upgrades. If I wanted to rent it, I had to take it as is."

"I'll bet she said that."

Ellie Draper was nobody's fool. She ran the chocolate shop in town, and though she was very sweet, when it came to business she was ruthless. Compared to the rest of

Smitten, at least. Not that Zoe regretted it. The spot on Main Street was worth the effort. She simply had to make it work until her stream of income was constant.

Arnold looked up toward the ceiling, and Zoe held her palms up behind him, worried that he'd lose his balance and topple over. "Here's your problem." He turned his walker around so that the padded seat faced him, then settled into the ready-made chair. Her shoulders relaxed with him safely seated as he pointed toward the wall.

"You'd be grandfathered into code with this old copper wiring, and it looks like it's in good condition. You can't go wrong with copper. Not in electrical, not in plumbing. So that's no trouble. The only thing I see is that this junction box needs to be covered." He pointed a shaky finger toward the metal box on the old wooden wall. "You can go buy a cover for it, screw it in, and you're ready to go."

"That's it?" The tightness in her jaw returned. "The new city manager made it sound like I had major work to do before I open. He said I couldn't cook in here."

"You're cooking in here?" Arnold's fuzzy brows lifted.

"Remember? So I don't have to go back to the cabin when I'm working."

"Roll me back there," Arnold said. "Your problem must be in the kitchen if this guy threatened to shut you down."

She did as she was told and took Arnold near the stove. He rose, wobbled for a moment, then braced himself against the wooden island until he hobbled to the stove area and positioned himself behind the appliance where the wall ended. He groaned. "Oh. Uh-huh." Another grunt. "No, that won't do." He gazed at her. "Do you have a flashlight?"

"Right here." She handed him one. He lit it and manipulated the beam of light behind the stove. He clicked his tongue a few times and moaned again. There were a few disappointed groans, and Zoe knew there was more to her electrical problem than an easy fix.

"The new city manager is right. You're running too many circuits on this panel. It's not really a danger, but it is against the new code, and you won't be grandfathered in for that. These appliances suck a lot of electricity, so you're going to need a new panel if you want to cook. If you unplug the stove, you're fine, but it's still only temporary. I'd cover those wires if I were you. They're legal for now, but they're not ideal."

"How much will a new panel cost?"

"Probably be about five hundred dollars."

"Five hundred! Zoe, you can't afford that." Clare's voice of doom preceded her into the room. She was wearing her work overalls with her leather gardening gloves hanging out of the pocket.

"Relax, Clare. I'll think of something. I can cook at Mom's house until I get it fixed. I only need a few cents to get the place open for Friday's grand opening. I'll tackle this like I'd eat a side of ribs at Zak's place. One bite at a time."

"I think I did a good job with the hanging plants. How many flower arrangements did you want for Friday?" Clare said.

"I'll take whatever you can spare. Honestly, Clare, you have the greenest thumb. It seems like you can grow flowers just by dreaming about them."

"I'll need a number."

"Of course you will." Zoe looked back at Arnold, who was tinkering with the stove. "Arnold, sit down for a minute. I have to check something in the front."

He ignored her and kept right on tinkering.

"I don't think he heard you," Clare said as they went through the doorway to the brighter part of the storefront that faced Main Street.

"He heard me. Arnold hears what he wants to hear."

"I heard that!" Arnold shouted.

"Told you."

"I sure hope this isn't a mistake," Clare said as she pulled a spray bottle from her overall leg pocket and sprayed the plants she'd stationed around the room. "I don't understand where you got your romantic sensibilities from. It's one thing to be a romantic, but to put your life savings on the line for it?" Clare shook her head. "In Smitten of all places!"

"In Smitten more than any place. We're the romance capital now, remember?" Zoe walked to the front table where she'd displayed a myriad of trinkets and antiques that brought to mind romance. "On Friday, I'd like to have a bouquet of red roses with baby's breath here on the antique lace. Between the chandelier and the candelabra." She felt giddy just picturing the end product. "Hey, thanks for dropping off my bike last night."

"I didn't drop off your bike."

"Yes, you did. It's right there."

"I didn't drop off your bike."

"So what do you think of bouquets in Victorian vases?" Zoe continued. "I'm sure Aunt Petunia has some vases lying around."

"Maybe you could set them in an old teapot. That way you wouldn't need as many roses. It would be cheaper and still look just as romantic."

"Sometimes I can't believe we were raised in the same household. You have a scarcity mentality, Clare. God can make more good things, I promise you."

Clare spritzed her with water. "Aren't you worried? You should be worried."

"Why should I be? You're doing all the worrying for me. I worried my bike wouldn't be here and look, there it is." She was worried, but telling Clare wouldn't help. Zoe walked to the table on the opposite side of the room. "I'm thinking yellow roses here. That way I'll know who is really interested in love and who wants friendship."

"By the roses we put out?"

"I'll bet you the men will congregate to the yellow side and the women, the red."

"You really think people are going to show up?"

"I know *you* are going to show up. I've got this great guy for you to meet again. Remember Josh Campbell?"

Clare's face scrunched up. "He played chess in high school. That Josh Campbell?"

"You can't judge someone by high school.

Think about the fashion statements we made."

Clare peered down at her frumpy overalls, cuffed at the ankles. "Your point?"

"My point is, you're my sister and you'll be here."

"Are you inviting the new city manager? I really liked him, and so did Mom."

She wondered if Clare could see the redness in her cheeks. "Absolutely not. If William Singer had his way, he'd find a law on the books from 1837 and shut me down like I'm running a brothel."

"Oh, Zoe. Must you be so crude? I thought William seemed very nice, and he seemed so interested in all you had to say last night while you just thumbed your nose at him. You were actually embarrassing. Mom and Aunt Violet even said something when you left."

Zoe's first thought was that she was glad that Mom and Aunt Violet weren't in the car with them on the way out to the lake. "I didn't do any such thing. You all arranged for him to drive me home without asking me if that would be all right. We don't even know him. He could have been an ax murderer."

Instead, he was worse. He was a world-champion kisser who made her feel alive and full of sunlight and buttercups.

"You know how we feel about you living outside of town."

"Well, showing a perfect stranger where I live and that I live by myself isn't exactly protection, is it? You know, everyone always says about the serial killer, 'He was just so quiet and polite.' "

Arnold shuffled out of the back room, got to the doorway between the rooms, then rested on his walker. "Zoe, I'm tired and ready to go home."

She nodded. "No problem, Arnold. Clare's going to take you. She was just leaving." Zoe kissed her sister's cheek. "Arnold, thanks for letting me know what needs to happen. Now I won't have some electrician from out of town rip me off."

"Before you go," Clare said to him, "Tess asked me to give you this. It's a copy of all the research she's done on David Hutchins, and she wants you to call if your nephew knows any more about him. He can call her directly."

"Wouldn't it be great to bring them together again after all these years?" Zoe said. "I'll bet I could get the story on national television and everything. That would help business around here."

"If you'd let outsiders in, you mean,"

203

Clare quipped.

Zoe had every intention of letting outsiders into her dating club. Just not William Singer. She wanted to believe it was because he was an interloper and an outsider, but a tiny twinge of jealously told her otherwise. She reasoned that she was only helping the women of Smitten. William was a heartbreaker, she could see it in his eyes, and she had a certain responsibility to see that he broke no hearts before he left his temporary position.

"Clare, be honest. Do you think William has any intention of staying in our little town?"

Clare shrugged. "Why not? Smitten is a lovely place to live. Do you think that will go unnoticed by him?" She fiddled with the clip on her overalls. "Besides, I think William isn't so much interested in Cupid's Arrow as he is in its owner."

"I'm sure if there is any interest it's only because I told him no. Something tells me William is used to getting his way."

She really hadn't been able to get William off her mind, so the more she vehemently denied that he had any effect on her, the better. Maybe she'd come to believe it. The truth was, she'd been scanning the door hoping for him to make an appearance, even if it was to bring her a citation.

Clare put her hands on her hips. "Maybe whatever happened between them is best left in the past."

"Between whom? William and someone?"

"Zoe, pay attention. Not William, *David Hutchins*. Maybe they were really bad for one another in some way. Would Grandma's life have been different if she'd known he was alive? Or maybe he met someone else and didn't have the courage to tell her."

"Clare, you always take the path of least resistance. Nothing worth having is easily won." She turned to her old friend. "Is it, Arnold? What's worth risk more than love?"

"You girls have more energy for love than those of my generation do." Arnold's head drooped and his eyes fluttered. "You put too much thought into this. Just ask your grandmother what happened. Honestly, sixty years of being married, and I never will understand women."

Zoe heard the fatigue in Arnold's voice. He wasn't protesting love nearly so much as he was desiring a seat. "We need to get you home. I wish you had let me bring your wheelchair."

"This is a dating service, right? What if the woman of my dreams was here, and I'm sitting like an old codger in a wheelchair

205

when I meet her?" He winked at Clare.

"Grandma had her great love." Clare sprayed a plant with vigor as if she could squeeze risk from life. "Clearly it wasn't meant to be, or she would have married him and not Grandpa. What kind of man doesn't tell his ex that he's alive?"

The question hung in the air like a toxic fume. As much as Zoe loved the truth, no one wanted to believe Grandpa wasn't Grandma Rose's true love. Maybe the past was best left in the past.

Zoe looked up to see William standing on the sidewalk outside her building beside Fire Captain Brand. She felt her legs weaken beneath her. The two men were conferring right in front of her storefront, and she felt betrayal to her toes. Was this how her grandmother felt when David Hutchins was gone?

As the two men parted, heading in separate directions, she scrambled to the window and pressed her fingertips against the glass. Her lungs emptied as William walked away in his crisp suit without a glance. Cupid's Arrow suddenly felt like a very lonely place.

After Clare and Arnold left and Zoe was alone in the office, she checked her books to see if not fixing her car might make way for her to fix the electrical. At least get the exposed wiring covered until she could afford more. Arnold told her that keeping certain lights off would help to keep the electrical charge down and prevent any real danger.

Zoe reasoned such lighting would only make the ambience more romantic, and set to taping certain light switches in the off position. Necessity was the mother of invention. Hadn't her bike been the answer to more seniors needing supper in town?

She heard a small rap on the window and looked up to see Fireman Brand peeking in. She unlatched the front door and pulled it open. "Good morning, Captain Brand. What brings you here?"

As if she didn't know.

He did a quick sweep of the room with his eyes and looked back at her. "Nothing. Just doing a walk-through in town this morning."

"Any particular reason?"

"Nope."

Fireman Brand didn't seem especially nervous about the building, but his eyes stopped on her bicycle. "The meal delivery going okay?"

"I haven't had any complaints yet." She grinned. "That's not true. Last summer a few people begged me for no more zucchini."

He laughed and plucked a sticky note off of her bicycle seat. "You and the new city manager playing nice?"

"Pardon me?"

"William Singer, the new city manager."

"What about him?" She feigned innocence.

"Seems you've already got him wrapped around your finger." He handed her the note.

Zoe, the weather's going to change, and I'm handy with a spark plug. Why don't you let me take a look?

"William brought my bike here?" She crinkled the note in her fist. "How did he get in?"

Fireman Brand made no further notes as Zoe stood red-faced at the discovery of William's offer.

"I'd best be on to the next business. Best of luck this week." He grinned as if he were in on some grand secret.

"There's nothing going on between William and me, if that's what you're implying."

"You're the matchmaker. Far be it from

me to do your job for you." He tipped his cap and exited.

CHAPTER EIGHT

Zoe checked her phone Friday morning and did the math. Twenty people had RSVPed for the grand opening that evening. Fourteen women and six men. She bit her bottom lip. "This isn't good. Smitten is a man's town . . . so where are the men?"

"You rang?"

She looked up from her desk to see William in the doorway in his formal business attire with the telltale cocky smirk on his face. She wanted to be wise to it, but her heart leapt at the sight of him. She stared back at the computer to avoid eye contact.

"You're back."

"Just like I promised."

"They're still making you wear that monkey suit?" Why did she feel the need to criticize him rather than be kind? He looked gorgeous in his suit, but she wasn't about to say that, so she reverted to her lowest self, and now she felt terrible.

He entered the store and closed the squeaky door behind him. Noticing the noise, he manipulated the door back and forth with one arm until the noise grated on her. "I can fix this." He wiggled the door again. "Got any WD-40?"

"I can fix it too. I'm familiar with the miracle of WD-40."

"I was trying to be helpful, not condescending." He stepped over to her, the click of his dress shoes echoing through the building with every step, and her heart pounding the closer he got. He pulled his left arm from behind his back and produced an elegant bouquet of roses. Red, naturally. Smooth characters like William Singer wouldn't have it any other way, she supposed. "I came to apologize."

She gazed at the flowers, then back at him. "Apology accepted." She grasped the proffered bouquet. "Wait. Are you apologizing for the way you ingratiated yourself into a dinner invitation at my mom's house the other night? Or for the kiss?"

"Neither. I can't rightfully apologize for the kiss, because I'm not sorry for that. If there's anything I've heard you dislike more than change, it's dishonesty."

She placed the flowers on her desk and swiveled her antique oak chair around to face him. "Then what are you apologizing for?"

He leaned on her desk, so close that she feared he might hear the pounding of her heart. "I'm apologizing for doing my job. Well, not for doing my job and telling you what the code ordinance is, but for the way I said it. I shouldn't have led with that. Bad form. And as you're the resident matchmaker, I worried you might set me up with the town nag to even the score, so I figured I should come by and let you know you've got a week to make the changes with no citation. That is, as long as you're not still cooking on that fire hazard you call a stove back there."

She grinned, despite her desire to kick him out. "I already told you, I won't be setting you up. You're not staying, which means you're not of the right criteria for the Smitten crowd." She said it in a very affected tone of voice, so that he might know how seriously she took his apology. "But where've you been with this apology?"

"Did you miss me? Absence makes the heart grow fonder and all that?"

"Not quite."

"You don't know I'm not staying. Not unless you can add psychic to your sign out front, and I'm not sure that would go over well with the Smitten town board. Most likely, your application for a business permit would be declined. Truth is, I was in a meeting with the CEO of the railroad. It was time for Smitten's bid to be presented." He reached into his jacket pocket. "Speaking of which, I brought you another gift." He handed her the piece of paper.

She stared at it. "A building permit?" She narrowed her eyes. "You shouldn't have."

"It was no trouble."

"As I'm sure those flowers weren't. Did you pick them out of Carson's garden?" She knew by the wrap that they were from Clare's nursery, but after a gift of a building permit, she definitely wanted to give him a hard time.

"I saved you a trip to city hall. All that red tape and the lines."

"Lines in Smitten?"

"I'm imagining the future." He grinned.

"Speaking of fire hazards and electrical work, you'll be happy to know I brought chicken breasts that I cooked at home. Everyone is having curried chicken salad tonight, so no cooking here. And Zak's place is catering my event." She looked down at the phone. "Speaking of which, I need to call him and make sure he gets some friends here for the party. If they won't show up for the women, they'll definitely show up for the ribs. Smoked meat is the way to a man's heart, you know."

"I did not know that. What else can you tell me about the weaker sex that I might find helpful?"

"If you follow the smoked ribs with my homemade fresh red raspberry pie, men are ready to put a ring on it."

He laughed out loud. "I honestly can't figure you out, Zoe, but I think you like me despite yourself."

"Why doesn't that surprise me? You probably think Angelina Jolie feels the same." She stacked the papers on her desk.

"Nah, we're over. I told her it was me or Brad." He hung his head. "Well, you know how that turned out. She'll be sorry. I imagine one day she'll come slinking back with her six kids in tow."

"I wouldn't hold my breath. So are you here to catch me in the act of running my business with bad electrical?"

"I promise, I am not. I came by to see if you needed any help to get ready for tonight."

She eyed him suspiciously. "Why Smitten anyway? It seems like a step down from the jobs you've had." She looked at the computer. "I Googled you."

"Oh, so that's how you found out about Angelina and me."

She slapped the side of his arm.

"The adventure of it, that's why I'm here in Smitten. I've done a tropical island, a small Texas town, and Los Angeles while I was working my way through USC. Did I tell you anything you didn't read on Google?"

She shook her head. "Not a thing. Facts are just facts. They don't describe a person. Like why he feels he has the right to kiss a perfect stranger or apply for a building permit in her name."

"Nor does it explain why a beautiful woman like yourself doesn't see the possibilities in a guy like me. Look" — he held out the backs of his hands for her to inspect — "my nails are clean." He smiled. "I have excellent dental hygiene, and most importantly, I'm easily persuaded by pie."

"You're also easily persuaded by the next paycheck. The truth is, William Singer" — she slammed her palm on the desk as though they were in a court of law — "you're easily persuaded by a lot of things, aren't you? The call to adventure, your moments of romantic whimsy near the lakeside, the next bigger paycheck . . ."

"Don't forget a beautiful woman."

"Beautiful women," she said with a bad taste in her mouth.

"Not women," he corrected. "Woman."

She walked to the front of the store and moved the floral arrangements about the table rather than face him. She had enough to worry about. There was so much to be done before tonight; she didn't have time to flirt with a cool cucumber like him. It meant nothing to him, while words like that had never been spoken to her before. The way she volleyed back to him, she'd have only herself to blame when her heart lay broken on the court and he flew to the next match.

"If you don't mind, I really have a lot to do. All these tables need to be set up, and I want to get the movie screen up so I can introduce the services during the appetizers."

"No problem." He motioned toward the flowers. "Like I said, I just wanted to apologize." He walked out the door without another word. Only the squeak of her door and a quick breeze from Main Street noted his absence. That, and the empty place in her heart as he walked away.

You're being ridiculous! Love at first sight doesn't exist! Love was a journey, not a destination people found themselves at by pure accident. Love that lasted had to be built.

The door squeaked again and her eyes brightened, then drooped again. "Hi, Mom."

"Don't act so thrilled to see me," Anna said. "I saw that handsome William leaving in a huff. Honey, you've got to quit picking a fight."

"I'm thrilled to see you, Mom. Really." She went over and hugged her mother. "What are you doing here?"

"I came to help, naturally. Your sisters will be over later. Your aunts didn't want to come for fear everyone would think the event is for old ladies and stay home."

"My matchmaking is for all ages, Mom. Most of it will be done online, but the mixers are for the younger set who want to do things like ski in groups, canoe in the summer."

At least her mother was successfully distracted from William.

Clare and Tess walked into the storefront, and Zoe instinctively knew something was amiss. With everyone's busy schedule, they were rarely together except on assigned meal days. "Clare, what's wrong?"

"Nothing's wrong, per se."

"Meaning something's wrong."

"When I drove Arnold home, I noticed that his place needed a bit of weeding. While I was there, he came up with David Hutchins's phone number." Clare held up a scrap of paper.

Zoe grinned. "To help love along. Sometimes it needs a little push."

"We don't even know for certain he's alive," Tess said. "This will tell us for sure."

"Right. We can decide later if we want to tell Grandma. Dial the number, Zoe." Clare handed off the scrap of paper.

Zoe punched in the numbers and pressed the speakerphone button. The ring echoed throughout the old building, and everyone grew stone-faced.

"Yeah," a gruff voice answered.

"M-May I speak to David Hutchins, please?"

"Who's calling?"

Zoe swallowed hard. "It's complicated. He doesn't know me."

"What do you want him for, then?"

"Is he alive?" she asked.

"Zoe!" Clare hissed.

"Yes, he's alive. Who wants to know?"

"This is Zoe Thomas. He doesn't know me, but he knew my grandmother once. Well, I think he knew my grandmother once. Back in his hometown of Smitten,

Vermont. Do I have the right David Hutchins household?"

The line grew quiet, and Zoe began to think she'd lost the connection. "Is anyone there?"

The gruff man on the other end of the line cleared his throat. "What is your grandmother's name?"

"Rose. Rose Garner."

There was an audible gasp from the speaker, and the sisters and their mother all stared at one another. What had they started?

"Is —" The man cleared his throat again. "Is Rose alive?"

"Oh yes, she's alive. We learned about you when our cousin's daughter found your dog tags. From the Korean War." Zoe rolled her eyes. She supposed he knew which war he'd served in.

"Did she explain how the dog tags happened to be there?"

Zoe looked around to her sisters, but everyone shrugged. "No. We just thought it was a fluke, but we were surprised to learn that Grandmother had been engaged once before. We thought, after all these years — well, you know, Smitten's bicentennial is coming up, and we thought —"

"If this has anything to do with the railroad coming to Smitten, I have no comment."

"No, no. This has nothing to do with the railroad!" Zoe stared at the phone. How did he even know about Smitten trying to get the railroad to come? She thought that was a town secret as they vied for its return. "We just thought maybe you'd like to come back to Smitten. To see the town and —"

"Does your grandmother know you're calling?"

"Well, no, but I'm sure —"

"I'm sure she doesn't know. Why don't you ask your Aunt Violet about the dog tags? And tell her not to worry, I won't be returning to Smitten."

The line went dead, and the women looked at one another.

Zoe saw the unanswered questions in her sisters' eyes. This wouldn't be the end of it.

CHAPTER NINE

William hadn't been invited to the opening soirée for Cupid's Arrow, but as Smitten's city manager, it wouldn't have been right to skip such an event. Anytime a business opened, the city wanted to support its prospects. It was purely business. That, and he wasn't about to let anyone hit on Zoe. The event started at eight, which gave him time to finish up business late at the office and change into more casual fare for the mixer.

He'd seen the flyers and read the online ads. Zoe had done a fabulous job of informing everyone what her business was about and making the idea nonthreatening to people. It felt like a fun idea for a group of friends to meet and simply see if there might be something more. Meanwhile, he had no doubt that Zoe was working hard in the background to make romance happen. He doubted it was just like a lightning strike.

Unless a guy met a woman like Zoe . . . and that was exactly why he planned to be there. To ensure that lightning only struck once.

Smitten's downtown was dressed up with year-round Christmas lights, with tourists out for their evening stroll, picking up trinkets, searching for antiques, or tasting the fudge and maple syrup offerings. It was enough to make a man nearly forget the call of the ocean and the feeling of sand beneath the feet.

William checked his watch. Three minutes to go. He wanted to let a few people in first so that he didn't stick out like a sore thumb. A sore, uninvited thumb.

The railroad deal he was counting on to connect Smitten with bigger surrounding cities for a more vibrant economy was far from a sure thing. RailAmerica drove a hard bargain, and the competing towns simply had more money to invest. What the towns could come up with, as well as ticket potential, weighed heavily in their decision. The railroad administrators weren't going to say yes out of the goodness of their hearts — and their decision would probably make or break his permanent status. For once, William felt in over his head. For once, it mattered whether or not he stayed.

Someone patted him roughly on the back.

He turned around to see a muscular, rugged-looking guy. "Hey, you must be the new city manager. Zak Grant."

William breathed a sigh of relief. "Julia's partner at the Spa & Grill."

"And husband."

William held out his hand. "William Singer. Glad to meet you."

Zak held a flat aluminum tray that smelled like heaven — where surely barbecue would be served. "It's great to meet you. On your way to Zoe's grand opening?"

William nodded.

"Me too. I've got a friend coming who runs the local construction company, and he's told his guys they can start late tomorrow if they come."

"Does it need that kind of push?"

"Nah, people love Zoe. She knows everyone from working at Julia's spa and Natalie's coffee shop. Luckily, a lot of those friends are single."

"Oh," William answered through a clenched jaw.

"You married?"

"Nah. Happily single," he said, stretching the truth. Happily single until he'd met a darling brunette with a pixie cut.

"Well, now's your chance," Zak said, and William followed him into the building.

The room, which had once felt so large and empty, was now crammed with people ranging from around twenty to middle-aged. No one looked the least bit uncomfortable in what he would have thought was an awkward situation.

At the sight of Zoe, his mouth dropped. She wore a minidress, black with white details, that hugged every curve. It had a high neckline and a white ruffled skirt on the bottom. Her tiny waist was hugged by a black velvet bow, and her legs, which seemed to go on forever in velvet heels, were bare, tan, and unreal. He wanted to grab an overcoat to cover her up for fear someone else might see what he did — that her beauty was natural and magnetic.

Her eyes were enormous, and it was the first time he'd seen her in lipstick. A fifties siren red. She talked to people as she worked the room, serving punch. He hid behind as many patrons as possible until he felt someone's arm around him.

"She's beautiful, isn't she?"

He turned to see Anna Thomas, Zoe's mother.

"Stunning," he said.

"She never wears lipstick. I suppose she doesn't need to."

"As the city manager, I'd have to vote

against the idea of her wearing makeup. City hazard. Accidents."

"Oh, William, you're such a charmer. No wonder Zoe said to watch out for you."

"She said that?"

"Not in so many words, but —"

"Excuse me, won't you? I'd better get to work and get people away from that wiring." He met as many people as possible while casually pulling them from leaning against the walls. He pulled chairs out for women, and he got too close to the men so they just naturally moved. In fact, he did whatever he could to keep the exposed wiring from being an issue. He knew Zoe hadn't expected so many people, and she had to realize that her sixty-seven capacity had been blown out of the water.

"Let me know if you need anything," Anna told him as he passed.

He ended up with a group of construction workers who were so into the appetizers, they failed to notice any of the women there.

"So the railroad will mean more construction jobs. If you can't make the fund-raiser, join one of the work parties. We're going to redo a rail car and show them what Smitten is capable of." He passed out business cards and asked that they call him to confirm times.

The guys all nodded, anxious to get back to their ribs and conversation. With the crowds and Zoe near the front entrance, William thought he'd make his way to the back room and sneak out the alley. He didn't want her to think he was there in a business sense.

"Excuse me," he said. "Excuse me." The room bulged with people. "Excuse me," he said to a young woman leaning against the wall. "You don't want to lean against that wiring."

The young woman glared at him.

"The wires could catch on your dress," he said awkwardly. "Wouldn't want to get a pull."

A burly man who was obviously from logger stock stood over the young woman with his chest puffed. "She's taken! She's only here to support Zoe."

The woman went right back to leaning against the wires. Maybe he was there on business after all. He had to get across the room to Zoe and let her know there were too many people for safety purposes. He wouldn't be popular, but he had bigger fish to fry.

"Zoe!" he yelled across the room, but with the buzz of conversation and the music, his voice was barely audible even to himself. In the distance, across the room, Zoe shook her short locks as she laughed with those who surrounded her.

He stopped, unsure of how he'd get her alone to tell her that she needed to weed out the people who weren't necessary for her party's success.

"Is there a problem, Will? You look nervous." Zoe's sister Clare came up beside him. "Rib?" she said, holding up a platter.

"No, no thank you. Clare, can you get Zoe to come back here and talk to me? She's got too many people here." He'd no sooner finished the sentence than Zoe appeared, and he wondered how she'd maneuvered through the throng of people so quickly.

"William, you're here! I should be irritated, but I'm in such a good mood, not even you can ruin it." She giggled and touched his temple. "You're healing nicely."

"Zoe. You're over capacity. We need to thin this crowd. Someone could rub up against those wires." He practically had to shout over the noise of the room. "I've seen this before. Take it out on me all you want later, but I'm begging you to clear the room before something terrible happens."

"What?" She leaned in close so that she could hear him, then rose on the tiptoes of her heels and kissed him on the cheek.

227

"Thank you, William. Isn't it wonderful?"

"Zoe!" The wail of a siren drowned him out. The siren got louder, then ceased.

"You called the fire department on me?"

"I —" He tried to explain he hadn't, but the firemen in all their regalia had burst into the building and scared the crowd. William worked the room to keep people calm, and the chatter in the room became louder and more intense.

The fire chief's voice boomed through his bullhorn, instantly changing the mood of the room from something casual and party-like to anxious. "Attention, patrons. This room is over capacity. I must ask you to vacate the property immediately. Please go out only through the front entrance, as we will need to have a count as you exit. Thank you for your immediate cooperation. Once again, this room is over capacity, and for your own safety we ask that you vacate immediately in an orderly fashion."

Zoe gazed back at him, her eyes wide and full of fear as the fire chief led her to the back room. In them William saw an accusation of betrayal. Who could blame her? He'd gone against his own common sense, as well as the law in his new city, to impress a woman. Even if she was Zoe Thomas.

The people filed out, leaving the tables

with their elegant centerpieces strewn with remnants of ribs and half-empty glasses.

"William?"

He turned to see the burly Carson, current town patriarch and for all intents and purposes the man who hired him, standing beside him. "Carson —"

"Did you know about this?"

"The event?" he asked, as if pleading ignorance would help his case. "I knew about the mixer, but as of this morning only twenty people had said they were coming. I'm certain Zoe had no idea of the turnout."

Carson mumbled under his breath, "I don't need to tell you that we can't afford mishaps while RailAmerica is considering Smitten."

"No, sir."

"I'll see you in my office in the morning. Eight o'clock sharp."

"Yes, sir." He'd calmed rougher seas than these in Hawaii, but it had never mattered to him like Smitten did.

He caught one last glimpse of Zoe as Fire Chief Brand handed her a piece of paper. He assumed it was a citation, and judging by the amount of people over capacity, she wasn't going to get off easy. That meant paperwork for the department and automatic closure until she had a chance to meet with the fire department and the town board. He slinked out of the room, wondering how he'd ever face her again.

CHAPTER TEN

Morning at the lake was always postcard-perfect. The shingled cabins across the lake reflected a mirror image of themselves over the water. The soothing image negated everything Zoe was feeling, and she was reminded that when times looked their darkest, God was at work. Cupid's Arrow had been a success, but at what cost? She came away from the window and saw her mother carrying a tea tray.

"What are you looking for?" Anna asked.

Zoe sat down on the small love seat. "I was hoping William might come by, actually."

"I have a feeling William might be done with Smitten and its women."

"Don't make me feel worse, Mom."

"He did try to tell you, Zoe."

"I couldn't have known everyone in Smitten was going to show up!"

"This is a supportive town."

"I've got to come up with the money to fix the wiring. My contract promises that there will be weekly events for members, and I've been warned I can't open the business doors again until I've met with the fire department."

"Zoe, I'm not sure why things happen the way they do, but you did break the law."

"I didn't. Not technically. I had the fire department's approval."

"But didn't William tell you that the building wasn't up to code for a gathering — even a small one?"

"Whose side are you on?"

"There are no sides here, Zoe." Her mother backed down the way she always did. Anna hated conflict.

Zoe looked at the tea tray. Her mom had set out small cookies and linen napkins that Zoe didn't even know she possessed.

"That's all my stuff, from my kitchen?"

Anna nodded. "If you weren't so busy cooking for everyone and using Tupperware, you'd know you have some very nice things from your grandmother and your aunts. You might think about inviting William here to dinner sometime."

Zoe's stomach fluttered at the mention of his name before she remembered his face at the grand opening the night before. And the way Carson spoke to him, and the way he left without a word. William had been right, but she knew Carson — he wasn't the sort of man to accept excuses. And though she barely knew him, something told her William wasn't the type to offer them.

"If I have to refund everyone's money, Cupid's Arrow is dead. Even with the fire department showing up last night and cutting everything short, I had seventy-seven sign-ups." She poured herself a cup of tea. "Maybe they felt sorry for me."

"Or maybe they saw that you can deliver what you promised. You always were the girl who wanted to make sure everyone was having fun at a party. You couldn't stand to see someone alone in a corner. People know that heart, and they want to give back. Maybe find a love of their own."

Zoe sat down on the sofa and poured two cups of tea. Her mother sat beside her. "What if I made a mistake? What if I wasted my time and all my money on this, and last night was it? Then I've lost everything and I might not be able to stay in town, Mom. I might need to go somewhere else to find a job to support myself."

"This is just a setback, Zoe. Don't make it a catastrophe. You've already got members signed up on the website, so it can't be about the parties alone. People want to connect, and that's proof."

"What if it's not just a 'setback' for William? Carson looked pretty intense last night talking to him."

"I'm sure William will simply tell Carson that he told you of the law."

She shook her head. "I don't think he'd do that. I just don't think he'd let me take the blame."

"Well, he's not stupid, Zoe. He wouldn't lose his job over you not doing as you're told."

Zoe wished she could be so sure.

Her mother made it sound so easy, but the setback made Zoe question everything. Maybe Smitten wasn't going to be the same town anymore. Maybe with the addition of William and the new ways of the world, she'd be nobody in the scheme of her beloved town. Made obsolete by the ripe age of twenty-seven.

"What if I misheard God? Maybe he didn't want me to do this, and I rushed into it."

"Maybe," her mother said as she set down her teacup. "If that's the case, God has something for you to learn from it. Look for the lesson. Sometimes the lesson is the gift."

"Mom, you sound like a greeting card.

This is serious!" Zoe sipped her tea and tried to find comfort in the view. The lake was still glass-smooth. All of her internal struggles didn't make one ripple on the lake outside.

"Mom, what really bothers me is that I put all those people in danger last night. That's what William had been trying to tell me. If I really cared about people, I wouldn't have gone through with the event just because it was convenient for me."

Her mother came close and enveloped her with an arm, pulling her into a hug from the side. "Zoe, not everyone in Smitten has been to Shelby's School of Manners. Those people didn't all RSVP. You had no way of knowing you'd have that kind of turnout, and those wires have been there for nearly a century. There was no reason to believe they'd suddenly go up in flames last night. And they didn't go up in flames either. The threat of danger is not danger."

Zoe nodded. "I think it is to a man like William. I thought he just liked rules, but now I think it's because he's seen the darker side of businesses not working safely."

"He probably has. Next time you'll have someone posted at the door, and you'll ensure people let you know they're coming by turning away those who haven't responded. You can always make phone calls the day of an event and ask."

"If there is a next time. I have to come up with the money to fix the wiring, and that's more than everything I made last night."

She heard the slam of a car door and looked out to see Carson walking up the path, a black notebook in hand. A wave of fresh fear washed over her.

"What does Carson want?" Anna asked.

"No doubt to tell me I'm out of business." She opened the door before he knocked.

His eyebrows were raised. "Zoe."

"Good morning, Carson."

"I'm here on business," he said in a stern voice.

"I figured. Come sit down and have some tea."

"No tea for me." He looked around as if to note the condition of his cabin. "Good morning, Anna."

"Carson," her mother said. "Sit down, won't you?"

"I've inspected the building this morning with the fire chief." He took a seat.

"And?"

"Fireman Brand approved you for opening, but the truth is, you never should have been allowed to inhabit the building until the electrical was fixed."

"Ellie Draper rented it to me on the condition that it not cost her any money. I should have made those repairs and checked them out with an electrician." She swallowed the lump in her throat. "It wasn't Fireman Brand's fault."

"Fireman Brand warned Ellie of the conditions. She was told to make the arrangements."

"No, we had an agreement, Ellie and I. I just didn't know about the electrical until —"

"Wait. You knew about the electrical?"

She nodded but wouldn't look at Carson. "William Singer told me earlier in the week, but I didn't have the money and told him so. He told me it wasn't illegal, but that it wasn't safe. I didn't think he had the guts to go through with shutting me down. Guess I was right."

Carson got that disappointed look on his face. The one her mother gave her when she'd knowingly done something wrong. Shame flooded her face, and she could feel its intense heat.

"I see."

"I listened to Fireman Brand because he gave me the answer I wanted."

"Well, the inspection department will soon be more vigilant in its inspections."

"What do you mean?"

"I mean, Fireman Brand and his cohorts are currently studying the code intensely. There will be a test."

Great. Now she'd sent the firemen back to school. No doubt she wouldn't be signing any hot firemen for her business. "Will William need to approve everything?"

"You misunderstand. William Singer has tendered his resignation, and I've accepted it. Ellie will have to update the space if she intends to rent it at all. I don't think you realize how dangerous that situation could have been, Zoe."

"What?"

"Ellie is responsible as the owner. No matter what kind of deal she made with you, she can't legally rent out an unsafe building."

"No, what did you say about Mr. Singer?"

"He's leaving us. It's a mutual agreement. If he's going to make deals with city business owners, well, that's exactly the problem we've had in the past. We can't have a good ol' boys network and continue to grow the city's tourism revenue. One lawsuit could ruin us all. And if word got back to the railroad . . ."

"A good ol' boys network?" Zoe felt overwhelmed and light-headed. She'd known the law. She'd known what William told her was the truth, and yet she'd relied on Smitten's old ways. She'd taken advantage. "William was fired because of this? I mean, it can't be a good ol' boys network if William was involved. He just got here, and like I said, he told me I wasn't ready to open, but I had so much invested already —"

"As I said, we mutually decided to end his tenure here. I think his services are not what we're looking for. We need a fresh start. Someone who isn't afraid to do the hard tasks."

Zoe shook her head frantically. "No, he wasn't afraid. He told me the law. William shouldn't be fired!"

Carson gave her a look.

"Or let go, or mutually anything. He told me the law. I ignored it."

And worse yet, she'd allowed what could have been William's feelings for her to override his intuition. In fact, if she was honest, she'd been manipulative. She didn't dare tell Carson about their upcoming date, though, or William might be accused of even worse.

"The fact is, Zoe, he could have turned you in and prevented the event. That's the kind of decision we need our new city manager to make."

"But if the event hadn't been so big, no one would have known about the electrical. This is my fault, Carson. You have to allow me to make it right. Please!"

"It's not about whose fault it is, Zoe. It's that we brought Mr. Singer on to uphold the laws and take our city into the black. We wanted him to work with the railroad and bring it here. This is the simplest of his duties. If he can't do this, we can hardly expect him to get the railroad and manage the city budget."

"You can. I took advantage!" She looked out the window and saw that William was packing his car. "Carson, please give William another chance!" She stared at the carpet while she added the truth. "I flirted my way out of the issue."

Her mother smiled proudly. "So you did notice him!"

"Maybe you'd like to be on the search committee for our next city manager."

"No!" she shouted, louder than she'd meant to. "We don't need a new city manager." As she watched out the window, she saw William walking out the door of his cabin with a suitcase. "Oh no, I've got to go."

She swung open the door and bounded

down the steps. She watched as William loaded the suitcase into his trunk and walked around to the driver's side door. "William!" she shouted. "William!"

With the lake in front of her, she was certain her voice carried across the entire area, but he didn't turn. Instead, he glanced back at the cabin, then got into the car.

The lakefront cabins were strung like a necklace of pearls along the water, and the road itself was shaped like a horseshoe. Zoe turned in between the cabins, determined to cut him off as he circled the road. She ran over the grassy knoll and came down the hill before his car appeared.

She approached the small, white picket fence that surrounded the property and took a running leap over it — and landed with a slide on her backside on the gravel roadway. William's car appeared suddenly, and he slammed on the brakes, skidding over the rocky path so that his car stopped mere inches from her.

He jumped out of his car and came toward her. "Zoe?"

She nodded. "It's me."

"Zoe, I almost killed you. What on earth are you doing? You scared the daylights out of me."

She took his offered hand and allowed him

to help her up. His arms wrapped around her waist, and she rested her head against his chest. It felt solid against her ear, and the rapid, consistent thump of his heart confirmed his words.

"You were fired?"

"Mutually resigned, if you don't mind." He cupped her cheek in his hand. "Are you sure you're all right? You took quite a leap."

She waited breathlessly as he touched her, hopeful that he'd kiss her again. But once she nodded that she was okay, he dropped his hand and stepped away. She stepped toward him again. "You were just going to leave without saying good-bye? We have a date tonight. Were you going to stand me up?"

He chuckled. "I didn't think you'd miss me all that much."

"You tried to prove to me that you were a man of character. Good enough for Cupid's Arrow — and yet you were going to leave town while we had a date set up. That does not bode well for your character."

"No, it doesn't, but I wasn't really trying to join Cupid's Arrow. I was only trying to get on the owner's good side."

"I'm sorry I took advantage of that."

He smiled and cupped his hand along her jaw. "I'm not. If you didn't feel guilty about it, you wouldn't be here. You wouldn't be you, Zoe."

She tugged at his hand. "Please come talk to Carson with me."

"You really want our date that badly?"

She nodded. "I do, actually."

"Even if it means you're wrong?"

"What do you mean?"

"You predicted that I wouldn't make it to the railroad fund-raiser, much less the bicentennial celebration. My leaving would make you right."

"Then I'd prefer to be wrong. I was so obnoxious. Will you forgive me? Smitten is a town that welcomes everyone, and I tried to let you know right from the beginning that you weren't welcome. I'm ashamed of myself." She looked into his eyes. "Wait a minute." She dashed to the car, opened the passenger door, and reached inside to grab the small wooden turtle that William kept on his dashboard.

"The turtle?"

"You told me the turtle is always home because he brings his home with him wherever he goes." She wrapped her fingers around the turtle's shell. "I think your turtle should stay here."

"You're stealing my turtle?"

She shrugged. "It's not stealing. Not if

you give it to me. Anyway, I'm thinking you need to put down roots somewhere. Mr. Turtle can't be your mascot anymore, so I'm going to keep him here with me. If you want him back, I suggest you go talk to Carson with me."

He grinned. "Will giving you my turtle help me get back into your good graces?"

"Definitely."

"Does that mean you'll accept my application to Cupid's Arrow?"

She shook her head. "I'm the jealous sort."

"I'll bet you are."

"Carson's at my house right now. Please come talk to him with me. You owe it to me to help me make this right."

"I owe you?"

"If you hadn't been telling me the rules right off the bat, I might have listened to your warning and none of this would have happened."

"Ah, so this is all my fault."

She giggled. "Maybe not all your fault, but I know I can convince Carson if you'll give me the chance."

"I have no doubt you can convince Carson, but there's still the matter of this being a temporary position."

She held up the wooden turtle. "And if it's not temporary?"

"Then maybe you'll have to teach me what it's like to put down roots."

"Maybe you'll have to teach me what it's like to go on an adventure." Her heart hammered in her chest as they talked. For the first time in her life, leaving Smitten didn't seem so outrageous. Like the turtle, she carried her home with her.

William bent to kiss her, and she returned his kiss passionately. Cupid's arrow had struck with exacting precision.

KNIT ONE, LOVE TWO

DIANN HUNT

CHAPTER ONE

The Sit 'n Knit was Anna Thomas's world. Her definition of family had widened to embrace the women who came into her yarn shop — especially the regulars.

Some days that was enough.

Anna inhaled the scent of coffee that always perked on the counter behind her. She tore open her UPS package — a high-grade merino-nylon blend of yarn — and smiled. Warm and versatile, the yarn was a great choice for sock knitting. Some people grabbed cheap yarns off the shelf of a department store with no idea of the difference quality yarn could make in a project. She looked around her shop at the bins filled with colored textiles, some bulky, some intricate and thin for lace projects, and gave a contented sigh. She offered quality — and a piece of herself — with every sale. The women in her shop, there for the lesson on picking up stitches, milled around, commenting to one another on their projects, laughing together. Anna's business also offered a place where women could encourage one another in their creativity and in life in general. Who could ask for more?

The bell on the shop door jangled as someone stepped inside. Anna gathered her ball of cotton yarn, knitting needles, and half-finished peach-colored dishcloth, then bent over and tossed them into the bulging bag where she kept her current projects. She stood upright and stretched a bit. It was then she spotted a man of about fifty. He had a firm, strong jaw; a trim, fit body; and salt-and-pepper hair that looked good on him. His smile was warm and welcoming, and his blue eyes sparkled.

He looked familiar. The lopsided grin on his face told her he knew she was trying to place him. Her heart gave a funny leap as he walked toward her and stretched out his hand. "Michael Conners," he said. "That's my mom, Emma." He pointed her way.

His hand was strong and warm. It shamed Anna that she didn't want to let go.

"Oh, Emma is one of my best customers. A lovely lady." She'd spoken of her newly-retired-from-the-marines son often and fondly. "Nice to meet you. I'm Anna

Thomas."

"Yes, I know." He paused. "We're neighbors." There was a teasing glint in his eyes that caught her a little off guard.

"Oh, so that's where I've seen you. Sorry, I —"

"No need to apologize. I've only lived there about six months. But we also go to the same church." He winked.

Emma had cancer. Her body grew more fragile with every passing day, but she still managed to come to the Sit 'n Knit. When Michael looked away, Anna studied him. It was noble of him to come to his mother's side. Still, Anna would be careful. Clearly, he didn't plan to settle down in Smitten. Not that she wanted him to. So why was her hand still tingling?

She nodded, trying to calm the unsettled feeling in her stomach.

"Well, good to see you." He walked over to his mom. Anna watched his every step, her heart pounding as though she'd been running. What was the matter with her?

When the knitting class was over, the ladies spilled into the other rooms, pouring cups of coffee from the brewing pot, browsing through knitting books, touching cashmere yarns. Anna walked around the chairs and scooped up yarn debris, then dropped

251

it into the trash can. Arms elbow-deep into the sofa, then the chair cushions, she dug around for lost hooks and needles. Her efforts were always rewarded. She found several crochet hooks and threw them into a large plastic container with other strays.

Michael, who had suddenly appeared beside her, winced.

"Something wrong?" she asked.

"Would you like a rubber band for those hooks? That would keep them all together so you wouldn't have to dig around for them."

"I — well, uh, yeah, I guess." Embarrassment warmed her cheeks. Did he think her incompetent?

Michael walked over to her counter, picked up a rubber band, then playfully stretched it in front of him, acting as though he would snap her with it. She smiled in spite of herself.

He picked the hooks up one by one from the container in her hand, bunched them together in a single bouquet, wrapped the rubber band tightly around it, and offered it to Anna with a slight bow. "For you, ma'am."

Was that supposed to make her feel better? Was he hitting on her? Did this work with other women? Was that what they taught him in the military? Please. Her husband had been a military man. She wasn't going back there.

"Thanks," she said, tossing the bundled hooks back into the container and snapping it shut. She forced a grin, then picked up her load.

"Can I help you carry that?" Michael asked.

"No, I'm fine, thank you." She was a woman, not a weakling. Her feet moved faster than the rest of her and she nearly lost her balance. What was wrong with her? She turned for one last glance at Michael and saw him helping his mother out of the shop.

Once inside the sanctity of her office, Anna closed the door and tried to calm her pounding heart. She couldn't imagine why Michael had unnerved her so. Maybe because he was a man of uniform — or had been. She'd been there, done that.

When she regained her composure, she went back into the store and walked over to Sally Sanderson. Sally was one of Anna's dearest customers and friends. "I'm going to the bakery, Sally. I'll be right back. Will you watch the shop?"

"Will do," the older woman said.

Anna would rather walk down to Mountain Perks, say hello to her niece Natalie, and grab a mocha, but she thought her customers might enjoy some cookies.

After a quick trip to the bakery, Anna stepped back inside the Sit 'n Knit, brushed the snow from her shoulders, and pulled off her coat. "I'm back." She hung her coat on the wooden rack, then walked over to the group of knitters sitting in the circle, needles clacking away. She waved her bag through the air. "I got some cookies from next door." Oohs and aahs followed.

"You're too good to us," Sally said. "But I like it." Her needles paused long enough for her to pluck a cookie from the bag. "Mm, they're still warm."

"Count yourself lucky," Anna said, straightening her checkout station. "It's getting colder outside. Wind gusts up to thirty miles an hour."

"Brr," Debbie Matney said with a shiver. "That's why I love being in here where it's warm, knitting with my favorite people."

The others nodded while munching on their cookies. Anna smiled and counted herself blessed. How many people could say they had a job they could hardly wait to get to in the mornings? When Joe left her ten years ago, she didn't know if she'd ever be able to smile again, let alone own a business. But with the encouragement of her girls, she'd invested her divorce settlement money into her dream business: a yarn shop where women of the Smitten community could gather to craft, create, and share life. Anna loved the feel of the yarn between her fingers. It gave her pleasure when a customer brought in a finished masterpiece: a sweater, a hat, a blanket. She rejoiced in their creation. When a customer brought in a project gone bad, Anna enjoyed that too. She loved helping them get their stitches back on track, bringing hope to the project. It had occurred to Anna more than once that God did the same for her when she got off track . . .

The bell on the door jangled. Zoe, Anna's youngest, stepped inside, stomped her feet on the mat, and walked toward her mother. "It's freezing outside."

"I've got some cookies and hot chocolate or coffee, if you have a minute," Anna said.

"No thanks, Mom. I just wanted to pick up another skein of yarn. I underestimated what I would need for Will's sweater."

"Hi, Zoe," the ladies called out.

"Hello, everyone." She bent down to look at Sally's knitting. "Beautiful scarf."

"Thanks, sweetie," Sally said, winding her yarn around the needles.

Anna couldn't be happier that God had brought William Singer into Zoe's life. He was a wonderful young man. The future looked bright for her youngest daughter.

"Let me see. What dye lot have you got there?" Anna took the wrapper from Zoe and matched it with the wool blends in the appropriate wooden bin. "You lucked out. One such animal left." She waved the coveted skein and walked it over to the cash register.

"I love this stuff. It's so soft. It will make a nice sweater. I'm getting Will ready for his first Vermont winter." She leaned in toward her mom and whispered, "Hopefully the first of many."

"How's the dating business coming along?" Sally asked.

"It's a little slow, but I believe it will catch on," Zoe said.

"I still say you need to find romance through the normal course of life. You can't force these things," Anna said, ringing up Zoe's purchase. She tucked it into a pretty bag and closed it with a raffia bow.

"I don't force things at Cupid's Arrow, Mom. People have to fill out information. No one makes them date anyone they don't want to date." Zoe shook her head and smiled at Sally.

"This world, she is a-changin'," said a woman named Betty. "What with the Internet and all, people are finding each other who never would have had the chance otherwise."

"Exactly." Zoe grabbed a cookie after all and nibbled at it. "I just want to spread a little love in Smitten."

Anna poured a cup of hot chocolate and held it out to Zoe.

"Oh, I really don't have time. But how about I take it with me? Thanks, Mom." She pulled on the blue woolen scarf, mittens, and hat that her mom had made her last Christmas. "See you, ladies." Drink in one hand, handbag and purchase dangling from her other arm while she held on to her cookie, Zoe kissed her mother's cheek and sped out the door.

"Kids, they never have time these days to sit and smell the roses." Anna shook her head and threw away a customer's forgotten receipt.

"You still doing Sunday afternoon meals with your girls?" Sally asked.

"Yes, thankfully. I love those days."

"You're lucky to have them. Most kids don't even live around their families anymore. We live in a mobile society."

"So true," Anna said, feeling sorry she had

complained. Sally's boys lived in another state.

Anna didn't know what she would do without her girls, her mom, and her aunties. She loved how they took turns hosting Sunday dinners, the hubbub of family, the chaos and the peace, all of it. She prayed it would never change.

The doorbell jangled again. Anna looked up, and her heart caught in her throat. She couldn't imagine what Michael Conners would be doing back at her yarn shop.

"Well, well, we meet again."

All smiles and brawn. Mr. Confidence himself.

"Michael Conners. Back so soon?" Anna gazed around her station to make sure it looked tidy.

"Yeah, but not for long. I'm headed to Sugarcreek Ski Resort."

"Oh yes, your mom mentioned you worked there part-time."

"I do, but I'm off today. Just want to get in a little skiing."

"I see." Anna knew very little about skiing, so she didn't comment. "So, do you knit?"

His laughter rattled the windows.

"The boys back on the base would have a

good laugh over the thought of me knitting."

"Some men do," she said, her tone a little sharper than she'd intended.

"Some men. Not me." He lifted his calloused palms. "See these hands? They were built for man's work. I'll leave the knitting to you women." He looked toward the circle of women and winked, and they all smiled.

A fire kindled in Anna's belly. "Are you implying a man can't be manly and knit?"

He shrugged. "To each his own, I guess. Just don't expect you'll ever see me doing it."

The fire in her belly grew. Did he think it would be beneath his dignity to knit? That these women were frivolous time-wasters to do such a thing?

"Then what brings you here?" she asked, folding her arms across her chest and tapping her foot.

"Mom wanted some new yarn, and she forgot to get it when she was here." He gave her a smile. "Knitting here with the ladies seems to calm her. I have you to thank for that."

The words humbled Anna. If she could play a small part in encouraging Mrs. Conners, she was privileged to do so.

Suddenly the deafening sound of needles

gone quiet filled the air. Anna looked at the circle of knitters and found they were all staring at her.

She ignored them. Well, she tried to anyway. "What is your mother making?" Anna asked in her most professional voice.

"Uh, I don't know."

"Then how do you know how much yarn to get?"

"I don't know."

"Do you know what type of yarn she wants?"

"The fuzzy kind?" He grinned. When she didn't smile back, he cleared his throat. "I thought you would tell me all that."

"Well, I can hardly do that if I don't know what she's making."

"She finished those tricky slippers she was working on this week," Sally interjected. "Why don't you give him some of those pretty new cotton shades that you have for making dishcloths? That would give her something easy to work on for a change."

There was a definite twinkle in her friend's eye as she spoke. A twinkle that Anna didn't like one little bit.

"That's a good idea." With her chin hiked, Anna walked over to the cotton bin and showed Michael the different colors. She refused to look up at him, but she felt sure he was watching her and not the yarn.

"Yes, these will work," he said, plucking a couple of skeins out of the bin without so much as a second glance.

Did he have any idea the work that went into making these yarns? Did he touch them to get a feel for them? Consider the perfect color? Of course not. What was he doing here anyway?

He tossed the skeins of durable worsted weight yarn in the air and began to juggle them. Anna glanced at the women in the circle and saw that their hands were still quiet. He had them mesmerized. She wanted to bop every single one of them — or at the very least take back her cookies.

She rang up the yarn and announced the price.

His eyes widened. "Wow. Yarn doesn't come cheap."

"You get what you pay for, Mr. Conners," she said.

"Please, call me Michael."

The way he said that made her guard drop a little. She put his purchase into a pretty bag and took great delight in winding the raffia into an especially elegant, feminine bow. He rewarded her with a frown.

"Thank you. I'm sure Mom will enjoy this." He turned to the group and tipped his head. "Ladies." With that he headed out the door, pretty little package dangling softly from his big, manly man hands.

Anna covered her mouth to stop the giggles until the door closed, then let her laughter out.

"Why did you do that?" Debbie asked.

"What?"

"Well, you weren't exactly friendly," Sally piped up.

"That man just irritates me."

"Or not," Sally said.

Her words boiled in Anna's midsection. "He's just so full of himself." She busied herself straightening some of the bins. When she got to the cotton bin, she noticed it was already straightened. "Well, of all the nerve."

"What is it?" Beth wanted to know.

"He straightened this bin."

"Wow. Gorgeous, and he cleans too? Grab him." One look at Anna, and Sally's smile left her face. Without another word she swept her needles into full running motion.

Michael Conners may have these women fooled, but he didn't fool Anna. She knew his type all too well.

"Not the friendliest sort around," Michael said in answer to his mother's question.

"Don't be too hard on her, dear. She's

been through a lot. Her husband up and left her awhile ago. Her three grown daughters all live in town, thankfully. They're a fine family." Emma Conners's soft, age-spotted hand patted Michael's hand the way she had when he was a boy.

"Now, don't you go getting any ideas," Michael said. "I'm just fine living on my own." Though he had to admit, the spark in Anna's gray eyes and her melting smile made this woman a definite consideration.

"Sure you are." Another pat. "That's what all men think. But we women know better." This time she squeezed his palm lightly and Michael laughed.

With his mother settled in her room at the Smitten Assisted Living Center, Michael stopped by the church to see if they needed help with the set for the Christmas program. Pastor Walden assured him they had plenty of helpers, so he headed on to the ski slopes. The snow was sticking to the ground and seemed to be heavy enough to pack. Good news for the slopes.

He turned the wipers on to brush away the falling snow. Try as he might, he couldn't get over Anna Thomas's reaction to him. Not rude exactly, but he obviously had irritated her. He couldn't imagine why. Maybe his presence intimidated her for some reason.

Not that it mattered. He was in Smitten to help his mom. Period. He had no intention of getting involved with a woman. Once his mom was gone, there was still more of the world he wanted to see, and he couldn't do that holed up in a small town.

The turn signal clicked off time while Michael waited for a car to pass, then he maneuvered his car into the Sugarcreek parking lot.

He shook off his mental ramblings. This was going to be a good day. He hefted his skis from the backseat. A very good day indeed.

CHAPTER TWO

Clare, Zoe, and Tess set the dinner table while Anna scooped the last of the mashed potatoes into a serving bowl and added it to the table — but not before placing a dollop of butter on top.

"This looks great, Mom," Clare said, settling into her chair.

"It sure does," Aunt Violet said.

Although the girls had places of their own, and Anna's aunts and mother lived on the family homestead, they made it a point to meet every Sunday afternoon for a meal. With the kids grown and her husband gone, Anna had purchased a quaint little home, but they somehow managed to get everyone around the table.

Everyone held hands, and Anna ushered them into a prayer of thankfulness for their meal and God's many blessings.

While silverware clanked and iced tea glasses were refilled, they talked of work, family, and Smitten news.

"So, Tess, how's that man of yours doing?" Aunt Petunia asked.

Tess grinned. "Ryan is doing well. His new root beer ice cream is a big hit."

Aunt Violet nudged Anna. "Look at the way she just perks right up when she talks about him."

"Zoe's the same way with her man," Anna said with a grin.

Clare chuckled, and Tess turned to her. "Don't you laugh. You've got a man now too."

"That's right. How's your young man, Clare?" Aunt Violet asked, shaking her head. "My, my, we can hardly keep up with you girls and your love lives."

Clare's new young man, Joshua Campbell, was full of compliments of Zoe's dating service.

"Don't discourage them," Anna said. "I've been trying to find them the right men for years."

"Joshua's fine. Don't print the invitations, though. It's not like that."

Anna had heard that line before. Clare struggled with commitment. Anna feared Joshua was on his way out. But maybe she was wrong.

"So, Zoe, do you think that dating business of yours could catch me a man?" Aunt Violet asked.

Suddenly the whole room took a collective breath.

"Well, sure we could. I've told you that before, Aunt Vi. You ought to sign up." Zoe sat up eagerly in her chair and leaned toward her great-aunt.

"You can't be serious," Anna said. It was bad enough that *she* had to apply to the dating service to support her daughter, but Aunt Violet?

Aunt Violet's nose hiked. "Wouldn't hurt you to get back into the dating game." She patted her hair. "Why leave all the fun to the young folks?"

Anna's breath caught in her throat. "I had my time. It didn't work out, and that's that." She placed her linen napkin on the tablecloth and rose. "Now, apple or pumpkin pie?"

Aunt Violet went with Anna to the kitchen.

"You weren't serious about that dating thing, were you?" Anna asked.

"Of course not. Though Zoe loves the idea. I just like to tease about it."

"Well, you nearly gave me a heart attack."

They carried the deep-dish pie plates to the table and cut generous portions before placing them on dessert plates. The air was sweet with the scent of sugar, apples, and pumpkin.

"Speaking of love . . . ," Grandma Rose said.

Clare groaned. "Not that again."

"Bet you girls didn't know your mom met Michael Conners at her shop."

Tess brightened. "You did?"

"She did. And he's a very nice *single* man her age," Rose offered.

Anna rolled her eyes.

"Michael Conners. Is that the fellow who's renting the cottage down the street?" Aunt Violet wanted to know.

"The very same," Aunt Petunia answered.

"He is a nice guy. I bumped into him at the toy store when I picked up something for Sophia. Sometimes she and I go there just to look around for fun. I've seen him there a couple of times, in fact," Tess said.

"Why would he buy toys?" Anna asked. "He doesn't have any small children."

"Who knows?" Clare said before biting into her apple pie. "Maybe he likes kids."

Zoe had been clearing the table of serving dishes and walked into the room to hear Clare's comment. "Who are we talking about?" She scooted back into her chair.

"Michael Conners. The guy down the street," Clare said.

"Oh, right, I heard about that," Zoe said, picking up her fork and taking a bite of pumpkin pie.

Anna looked up. "Heard about what?"

"I heard some people talking about it at church. They said Michael banged his leg up pretty good skiing. Fortunately, it's just a bad sprain."

Anna turned off the car ignition and maneuvered the multiple packages from the store.

Once out of the car, she clicked her remote button. One of these days she'd build a garage. The driveway was slippery from an earlier snowfall, so she walked her path carefully to the door. As troublesome as it was, she loved the feel of snowflakes on her eyelashes and catching them on her tongue. When it came to snow, she was a little kid at heart. If she thought no one was looking, she might even have plunged into the fluffy white mixture and made a snow angel. But of course she was much too dignified for that.

A giggle escaped her. What would Michael Conners think if he looked out his window and saw her making angels in the snow?

The air was cold but not frigid, with a clear sky. The glow of moonlight resembled soft lamplight in a cozy room. The quiet crunch of tires on packed snow from a neighbor's departing car was the only night sound Anna heard. She loved moments like these when Smitten townsfolk had ended their busy days and taken to dinner around the table in the quiet of their homes. A tinge of sadness tugged at her for moments gone so fast, life already lived.

With a contented sigh she unlocked the front door and pushed through. Dropping her keys on the hallstand, she released her bags and fell onto the sofa. "Oh, my aching feet." She kicked her shoes off and decided to fix some hot chocolate and settle in for the night.

The phone rang. With a groan she shoved herself off the sofa and answered the cordless. "Hello?"

"Anna, dear, I hate to bother you, but it's my son," Emma Conners said.

"Oh, hello, Emma. I heard about his accident. Is he doing all right?"

"He says he is, but I'm worried. He lives right down the street from you. Would you mind popping in on him and seeing if he needs anything?"

Anna glanced at her watch. Seven o'clock. She could just call him. There were likely enough pot-roast-slinging widows taking him food, but she couldn't tell his mother no. "I'd be happy to check on him."

"Thank you, my dear. And you'll call me when you get back?"

"Of course." Anna hung up.

Her hot chocolate would have to wait. Good thing she'd left her coat on. That was one less step. Since the air was pleasantly cold, Anna decided to walk. Michael lived at the end of the street, not too far away.

Sinking deeper into her woolen scarf and mittens, she scrunched her cap snug over her ears and eased along the shoveled sidewalk. The last thing she needed was to have a sprained ankle alongside Michael. In the distance Sugarcreek Mountain stood bold and protective around the small valley of Smitten. Stars twinkled overhead as Anna whispered a prayer for guidance. What would she say? How could she help? She took a deep breath and released it in a puff. Why did she worry? God would give her the answers when she needed them.

She arrived at the house and stepped up on the porch. Though the cottage was older, it had plenty of character with strong wooden columns and an inviting porch swing. She knocked, then wondered how he would let her in. Oh dear, she hadn't thought about that. Her visit would only cause him more problems. She should have

271

called instead. Maybe he hadn't heard her and she should just go. But what if he did hear her and he got up, and by the time he answered, she was gone?

Just then she heard uneven footsteps approaching the door.

The door swished open. "Anna, come on in." Michael stood before her with a crutch snug under each arm. He seemed to be managing, but by the looks of his swollen ankle, he wasn't going to get very far. He settled onto the sofa and lifted his leg onto the cushions. "What brings you here on this cold, wintry night?"

Closing the door securely behind her, she walked over to a chair near the sofa. "Your mother was worried and asked me to check on you. I'm sorry about your foot."

"Stupid accident. I wasn't paying attention." He shrugged. "It happens."

She glanced around at the clean hardwood floors, polished stands, simple rugs scattered about, plain boxy furniture, and sparse furnishings. In the corner lay an organized stack of magazines in a holder. Tidy, but sterile. A gas fireplace with flickering flames made the room feel cozy.

"So how are you getting along? I understand meals are being brought in for you." Earlier she had wondered why everyone made such a fuss about a sprain, but she could see for herself that it was a nasty one.

"Yeah, Pastor Walden saw to it. There's some leftover lasagna in the kitchen. Would you like some?"

"No thanks." She tried to swallow the words that were scrambling to get out. "I suppose you could use help with errands and such for a few days. Places you need to go."

"I'll manage." He moved his leg and winced.

"How? You can't drive with that," she said, pointing to his swollen right foot.

"I'll figure it out."

"Listen, we both know you want to do this on your own, but the fact is you need help. We all do from time to time, you know. I've certainly had my turn. It was humbling at first, but that's what we're here for, to help each other." She'd never said that aloud before and wondered why she was confessing it to a virtual stranger.

He shook his head. "I don't want to bother anyone."

"I know. But as I said, you have to learn to let folks help you."

He thought a moment, then seemed to resign himself to his current situation. "That's good of you, Anna." There he went again with that soft, vulnerable voice that knocked her guard right off-kilter.

"So will you call me when you need help for errands?"

He sighed. "I will. Thank you."

He looked miserable, and a pang of compassion hit her. "Hey, anytime you need to get out or be with people, whatever, let me know. I'll take you out." Did she have to say it that way?

"Thanks."

She could tell he thought she was just being nice. Despite her initial reluctance, she decided she would follow through. But once he was better, they would cut ties. Neighbors. That was all they would be.

"So how did your mom like the yarn you bought her?"

He hesitated. "I haven't given it to her yet. Forgot to take it when I went to see her. I'm sure she'll like it fine."

"It's a worsted weight cotton yarn you bought her. Easy to work with, very durable, just right for knitting dishcloths."

He smiled. "You really know your stuff."

"I make it my business to know."

He nodded.

"Well, I'd better get home before it gets too late." She pulled on her coat and fumbled with the buttons.

"Anna?"

She turned around to face him. "Yes?"

"I have a doctor's appointment tomorrow afternoon, three o'clock. Will that work for you?"

CHAPTER THREE

Michael leaned back into his feather pillow on the sofa. Anna had to have some interest in him or she wouldn't have come down to his house, right? She could have just called. His ankle ached, so he shifted his weight. He wasn't sure what intrigued him about her. Maybe the way she spent time with those ladies at her shop, teaching them to knit, making them feel as though they mattered. Which they did, but most people went about their business without paying much notice to others. Not Anna.

He liked that.

Though he didn't want to get involved with anyone while he was in Smitten, it didn't hurt to have a friend. Did it?

For some reason it intrigued him, too, that she kept her distance, as though she was afraid to get to know him. His mom said Anna had been married to a military man. Maybe she didn't like men in uniform. A plump of his pillow and a grin. He was always up for a good challenge. Besides, working on her would give him something to do while he had to lie around with a bad ankle.

He didn't like her waiting on him, though. Made him feel weak. He fumed a minute. Then a thought hit him. With her tending to his needs, they were sure to get to know one another better. Maybe it wasn't such a bad thing. One could always use a good friend.

He reached for a pen and paper. In the meantime, he had a letter to write.

By the time Anna made it home and got ready for bed, she was exhausted. She sat at her vanity and rubbed the cream on her face that guaranteed youthful-looking skin until she was ninety-five. She shook her head. How did she fall for all those commercials?

She leaned into the mirror and scrutinized the laugh lines at the edges of her eyes. After a thorough examination, she picked up her jar of cream and said, "You aren't doing your job."

As much as she hated to admit it, mirrors didn't lie. The naked truth lay in the creases on her face. She screwed the lid back on the jar and with a sigh walked over to her bed and pulled back the covers.

"What is the matter with you, Anna Thomas? There's more to life than worrying about wrinkles."

The wind had picked up outside and gusts of snow pelted the windowpane. Airy, wafer-like flakes floated toward the ground. Frost glistened on the window. Anna reached for her Bible, read in the books of James and Psalms, then talked to the Lord about her day, her love for him, her concern for her loved ones. When she finished, she clicked off her light and snuggled deep beneath her warm comforter, all soft and billowy.

She had so much for which to be thankful. Her girls were safe in their homes. Two of them were seriously in love, one to go. She hoped they would know a love like her mother and father had shared. So many happy years together. Regret filled Anna as she thought about her own marriage and how she had failed. No one else had ever made her feel that way about it; still, she did. Why couldn't she have made it work?

It was useless to think about. Joe Thomas had his dreams and ideas, and they hadn't included Anna for the long haul. His girl-friend — now wife — had proven that. They were living happily in Arizona. Anna's heart hurt for her girls. Their father had little contact with them. Another ache shadowed her heart. Not because she loved Joe; time had eased that pain. But one thing she did remember was that she never wanted to have that pain again.

The doorbell rang, interrupting her troubled thoughts. Who would be coming over this late? She lifted the covers and stepped out of her bed. Grabbing her robe and slippers, she walked down the hall and peeked through the peephole in her door. Zoe.

Anna opened the door. "Are you all right? What are you doing here?"

Zoe stepped inside, shivered, and stomped the snow from her feet on the rug. "I'm sorry to come so late. I should wait and talk to you about this with my sisters, but I can't sleep tonight without telling you."

"Well, come in, honey, so we can talk about it." Anna started to take Zoe's coat, but she refused.

"Thanks, Mom, but I won't stay long. I just needed to see you tonight."

Anna nodded and led the way to her sofa. Once they settled in, she turned to Zoe. "Now, tell me what's on your mind."

Zoe cleared her throat. "You know that David Hutchins guy that Grandma was engaged to, who they thought had died in the Korean War, then found out he didn't?"

Did they really have to have this discussion at nine thirty at night?

"Yes, yes." Anna felt impatient with where this could be heading.

"Well, I talked to him."

Anna swallowed hard. "You what?"

"I wanted to arrange a meeting for him and Grandma. I thought it would be so romantic."

"Zoe, you didn't."

"Well, you can't deny it, Mom. After all these years, to find each other again. But that's not why I'm here. He told me that he came back to meet up with Grandma, but Aunt Violet showed up in her place. She told him Grandma was married. She also told him that she herself was in love with him."

Anna gasped.

"He didn't return that love, and Aunt Violet has lived with this secret all these years. He gave her his dog tags to give to Grandma, but Aunt Violet kept them instead and never told Grandma that David hadn't died. David didn't think he could come back to Smitten with that past between all of them."

"Oh, that's horrible. But why are you telling me now?" Anna straightened the decorative pillow and plumped it behind her.

"We were hoping *you* could tell Grandma. You know, so at least she'd know he was still alive and that he came back for her."

"Oh, Zoe, there goes your romantic heart leading your head again. We can't tell Grandma what Aunt Violet did. Think of how hurt she'd be! I think we're better off leaving things as they are. It doesn't hurt Mom not to know. In fact, after all this time, it's probably better this way."

"Tess said you'd say that." Zoe's voice and expression revealed her obvious disappointment. "Sometimes confrontation is good when the truth can come out."

"Trust me on this," Anna said, patting her daughter's hand. "Some secrets are best kept."

"It's good of you to take my insurance claim to my boss. It saved me having to mail the forms, and he was in a hurry to get them," Michael said.

"No problem," Anna said, clicking her turn signal to pull her car into the parking lot of Sugarcreek Ski Resort. Once she shut off the engine, she turned to look at Michael, who sat in the back with his foot propped. "Now, where did you say the office was?"

"Oh, Rick is working in the coffee shop today, at the top of the mountain. Just take the ski lift up. He's expecting you."

Anna could sense all the saliva leaving her mouth. The pounding of her heart grew in intensity and her palms started to sweat. Dare she tell Mr. Manly Man she was afraid of heights? She looked at him and decided now was as good a time as any to face her fears head-on. She could do this.

"You don't mind, do you?" he asked, looking worried.

"No?" Somehow the word sounded like a question, even to her. She tried to mean it, but failed.

"Great." He grinned, and her insides went soft. "Here it is." He handed her an envelope. "I'll walk out with you. Maybe I'll see some of the guys."

Just what she wanted, an audience when she got sick.

They climbed out of the car and walked toward the ski lift. Snow had been falling for a couple of hours. The air's chill had a bite to it. The sun pushed through the gray clouds and managed to wash the slopes to a dazzling white. Still, its warmth did little to help Anna's shivers. She'd never been on a ski lift in her life. What if she fell off? No, she wouldn't fall. And she would not look down. No matter what, she would not look down.

Michael explained to an employee that Anna was taking papers up to the coffee shop. "I'll see you in a little bit, Anna." Crutches in place, he hobbled over to talk to another friend.

The closer she got to the ski lift, the clammier her hands felt, despite the frosty air. Since it was the middle of a school and work day, there weren't a lot of patrons present. Her heart pounded so hard, a headache started to form.

Anna followed the signs, then waited for the lift to clutch her into its waiting arms. Once she was on it, she lowered the bar, though her faith teetered as to whether or not it could protect her.

When the lift edged out of the building, Anna kept her eyes straight forward, swallowing hard against her rising panic. The lift rose higher and higher, causing her stomach to tilt. What had she been thinking? She'd never make it. Her ex-husband's voice echoed in her head. *"You're weak, Anna. You've always been weak. Always will be."*

Her chin hiked. She was not weak. She was strong. She was courageous. Look at all she'd been through, how far she'd come! The lift took a swing upward, causing her stomach to heave a little. *Oh, God, please help me.*

Joe was right. She was weak. She should have told Michael instead of letting her pride get in the way.

She kept her eyes closed until she felt the lift descend toward the building. To her relief, there were instructions on where to jump off. With one quick leap, she was on solid ground again.

Shaky steps carried her to the coffee shop on the mountain, where she approached the barista. "Hello, can you help me? I need to see Rick."

The young woman looked to be twenty-something, with her dark hair pulled back into a ponytail. "He just left. Went back down the mountain to check on something."

Anna's heart sank. "How can I find him? I don't know what he looks like."

The barista stopped wiping the counter and looked up. "He looks like Dennis Quaid. People tell him that all the time."

Dennis Quaid. That narrowed it down a bit.

"Okay, thanks." Anna shielded her eyes when she stepped back outside into the sunshine. Standing in position, she waited while the lift scooped her into its embrace once again. A worker clicked the latch on the bar, and once more she seemed to float in midair. The ride down was a bit easier, but her stomach grew more timid as the ride went on. If she could just get her feet on the ground, the nausea would leave.

A gust of wind stirred the lift on its descent and her stomach rolled. Perspiration lined her palms, but she didn't dare take off her gloves. Anna told herself she'd be on the ground soon, but it couldn't be soon enough to please her. The world seemed to spin around her. She prayed one of the most fervent, desperate prayers she had prayed in a long time, and soon she came to the end of her journey.

Grabbing the envelope, she jumped off the lift and took a moment to steady herself. The uneasiness she felt grew into increasing anger with every step. All of that for nothing. She should have told Michael she couldn't do it, period. It was none of his business why. He'd probably had a good laugh at her expense, watching her tense, tight body sit rigidly on the lift. Or maybe he hadn't even noticed her suffering. Probably couldn't care less.

She saw him talking to another man nearby and she walked over to him. "Excuse me, could you tell me —" She stopped mid-sentence when she saw that the man who stood in front of her looked to be Dennis Quaid's twin. "Wow, it's true."

"Yes, I know, I look like Dennis Quaid," Rick said with a grin, reaching to shake her hand.

She was overcome with wanting to tell him how much she enjoyed *Soul Surfer.*

"Michael tells me you've been a godsend."

"He–he did?"

Michael shuffled on his good leg and cleared his throat.

"Sure did." By the grin on Rick's face and the discomfort on Michael's, Anna could tell Rick enjoyed the teasing.

Had Michael really said that about her? Her stomach turned over. Must still be upset from the lift ride.

Anna gave Rick the envelope, and the three of them talked a few minutes longer before Anna and Michael got back into her car.

"Why didn't you tell me you were afraid of heights?" Michael said.

Oh, here it was, the moment of reckoning. Anna backed the car out of her parking space and headed onto the road. "What makes you say that?"

"It looked like you were going to be sick on the lift. And when you walked up to us, you were white as a sheet. You're just now starting to get some color back. Are you okay?"

At that moment, heat infused her cheeks, and she knew she had color. "I'm fine."

"I never would've asked you to go up there if you'd told me."

"It's no big deal —"

"Yes, it is a big deal, Anna. We all have things we deal with. That happens to be one of yours."

"I thought you'd tell me to face my fears."

"I have my own weaknesses. I don't have the right to jump on yours."

Well, she hadn't seen that coming. This from the egotistical manly-man? Compassion? Understanding weakness? A gentle giant? She'd always admired that in a man.

Maybe he wasn't the same as Joe.

CHAPTER FOUR

Anna finished her beginners knitting class, then settled in with the established knitters in the room. Business was slow for a Saturday. She had hoped to gain a new following as tourists sauntered through town — especially those who lived in neighboring towns. The influx of tourists had been good for business, but Anna was hoping the new railroad would bring in more shoppers. Her store wasn't in trouble yet, but quality yarn didn't come cheap, and she needed the sales to keep the shelves stocked.

"What's wrong?" Sally asked, throwing a stitch onto her waiting needle.

"What do you mean?" Anna asked, embarrassed that her facial expression must have betrayed her private thoughts.

"You looked upset just now."

"Oh, not upset. Just trying to think of ways to bring more interest to the shop. I love this place, but it's pretty expensive to maintain. It would be nice to bring in some more revenue."

No one said anything for a few minutes, then Debbie broke the silence.

"I was reading an article the other day about a woman who owned a knitting shop, and to do something different she offered spinning classes —" Sally opened her mouth to say something, but Debbie held up her hand. "And she raised her own sheep right behind the shop."

Anna had just taken a drink of coffee and choked on it. Sally's jaw clamped shut.

"I didn't say you had to do it; I just said I read an article about it," Debbie said with a chuckle.

"But where would I put sheep here in town?" Anna said.

"You'd have to move," Maria, a newcomer to their knitting group, said.

Anna was already shaking her head. "I can't afford to move."

More silence.

"I like that idea of spinning classes, though. Just need to figure out where to order wool." Anna offered a weak smile, trembling slightly within at the idea of something new and different. Still, she needed time to think it over, pray about it, see how the Lord would lead.

"Well, I think it's a wonderful idea —" Sally began.

The bell over the door jangled, and Anna looked up to see rosy-cheeked Tess and Zoe bundled in thick woolens and boots. They brushed the snow from their coats, stomped the snow from their boots, and ventured inside.

"— sheep or no sheep," Sally finished.

"Girls, what a nice surprise," Anna said, getting up to hug them.

"We were out doing some Christmas shopping, so we decided to stop in," Tess said, picking up a sugar cookie and pouring a cup of hot coffee.

"What's this about sheep?" Zoe asked, pouring hot apple cider in a cup.

Sally filled them in on the conversation.

"Oh, Mom, that's a great idea," Tess said, getting caught up in the moment.

"Well, maybe the spinning part —"

"No, raising the sheep too! That would be such a novelty for your shop. It would attract kids too, so their mothers could shop for yarn."

"It really is a cool idea, Mom. Never heard of anything like that around here, or even in Stowe and some of the other towns," Zoe added, pulling off her scarf.

Anna felt this conversation was careening

out of control. She didn't want the hype to get ahead of her and muddy her thoughtful consideration of the matter.

She raised her hand and said, "Nothing to get excited about at this point. Just the germ of an idea. I need to pray about it and think it through."

Zoe sagged into an empty chair. "Give it up, ladies. Once she says she has to pray about it, there's no talking her into something."

Sally shrugged. "It's a good idea, that's all I know."

"It's working well for the people in that article," Debbie said.

"I like the idea of sheep," Maria joined in.

The ladies went back to knitting while Tess and Zoe followed Anna into her office. Anna tucked away some shipping receipts in folders and stuck them in a cabinet. She turned to see her girls standing there.

"Something on your minds?" she asked.

"Well, it's that whole thing with Aunt Violet and Grandma and David," Tess said.

Anna sighed. "Now, girls —"

"Come on, Mom. Grandma has the right to know," Zoe said.

"I think so too," Tess chimed in.

"I'll think about it," Anna said, making a full resolve in her spirit to leave things alone. It would be best for everyone.

"Here's your grocery delivery," Anna said, unpacking the food from the sacks onto Michael's kitchen countertop.

He tried to hobble over and help her, but she shooed him away. "I can handle this. I'll make you a sandwich while I'm here."

"I told you I'm much better. You don't need to wait on me." No longer using his crutches, he limped over to the table. "I'm going to drive into town later today."

"You think you're ready?"

"Yeah, I do."

"Well, just be careful and don't push too soon. I'm just down the road if you need me to pick up anything for you."

He watched her as she carefully unpacked the groceries and put them away. She truly had a servant's heart. Unfortunately, from the way he saw it, she had no interest in him other than as a neighbor in need.

She placed the plate with his sandwich and chips on the table, along with a glass of iced tea. "While you eat your lunch, I'll get your mail."

"You're spoiling me."

"Don't get used to it; it's short-lived. You said so yourself." She pulled on her coat. "Be right back."

He was beginning to wish he hadn't said anything. But he couldn't fake it. Maybe he'd bang his foot again so she'd keep coming . . . Something about Anna kept drawing him to her.

"Oh my, it's getting colder out there," she said, brushing the snow from her hair. Taking off her shoes, she walked over and handed Michael the mail as he sat on the sofa in the living room.

"Thanks." He thumbed through the envelopes and spotted one marked RETURN TO SENDER. He sighed.

"Something wrong?"

"What? Uh, oh no, nothing's wrong." Should he tell her? She was a friend and had done so much for him.

"Are you sure?" Anna sat down in the recliner facing him.

Another sigh. "I have a son. I was gone a lot when he was growing up, and he resented me for that. When his mom died, he blamed me for that too. She died of a heart attack, but despite what the medical personnel told us, Christopher couldn't help thinking if I'd been home and we'd gotten her to the hospital sooner . . ."

"I'm so sorry. Relationships can be tricky."

"Yeah. He's twenty-two now. I haven't seen him for five years. I send letters to his last known address, but they always come back."

Compassion filled her eyes, and Michael wondered if he'd revealed something too personal. Anna didn't need to hear about his problems. No doubt she had some of her own.

"Well, that's enough about me —"

"I'm truly sorry, Michael. I'll pray for you and your son. Did you say his name is Christopher?"

"Yes. Thank you." It touched him deeply that Anna offered to pray for them.

A moment of silence hovered between them.

"Now, fair is fair. I've told you the woes of my family. Do you have anything you want to tell me?" he asked.

"As a matter of fact" — she paused and licked her lips — "I do."

Anna relayed the earlier conversation she'd had in her shop about the sheep. She waited a moment. "Of course, I'm praying about it. But it's such a big undertaking. I don't have the facilities for it. While it seems like a good idea, it also seems out of reach."

Michael rubbed his jaw. "Well, now, I don't know about that."

"What do you mean?"

"If you're really interested, I have five

acres of ground with a barn, no house, at the edge of town. I bought it at a good price as an investment before my mom got sick. Thought I'd let the equity build up and then sell it. If the railroad comes to town, it should turn a good profit. Anyway, it's idle for now. You could take your sheep there and care for them. See if you like dealing with them or if it's too much hassle."

Michael couldn't deny his excitement at the possibility. It would give him more time to be with Anna, get to know her without the pressures of dating.

"I've been doing some work out there, so I have electricity in the barn," he continued. "There's a well, so you'd have no trouble with water. You'd just need to get hay, some minerals, whatever it takes to keep sheep healthy, and you're good to go."

"Wow. I didn't see that one coming."

"It might not be a perfect setup, but it would work. And with me working part-time, I'd be happy to help when I got off work."

"No, no," Anna said. "I'll not have you doing my work. And we'd need to settle how much I would owe you, all that." She sighed. "I just don't know."

"Anna Thomas, after all you've done for me, you won't let me offer my land to you.

That's what friends do. And that land is doing nothing for anyone right now."

"But this would be ongoing. I could never take advantage of you that way."

"Look into it," he suggested. "Decide how many sheep you'd need to start with. Research the best kind of sheep for your needs, check out the price for each one. Since it's wintertime, they won't be grazing outside, so you'll need to check into the cost of hay. I'm sure you could learn a lot by talking to some farmers in the area. Once you check on all that, if you're still interested, let me know. I'm sure we can work out something."

"That's a good idea." She grabbed her handbag.

"And check with Phil McCreedy at the farm up the road. Any guy who makes milk deliveries with a horse and buggy for a bit of nostalgia knows how to think outside the box. I'll bet he could give you some pointers."

"That's another good idea. Thanks." She stood. "I guess I'd better be going. Let me know if you need anything else."

"Thank you, Anna," Michael said, standing.

Anna turned back around. "Also, if you could help me pray about this, I'd appreciate it."

"You got it." He waved and closed the door behind her. He would pray about it, all right. Hopefully, his wouldn't be a selfish prayer.

Anna trudged through the melting snow and considered the train depot building. It looked like everyone in town had turned up for the workday. The RailAmerica people would be here soon to evaluate whether Smitten would get one of the stops on the line. And why shouldn't it? It was the most beautiful depot she had ever seen. Clay-colored bricks, green doors. Securing the deal with RailAmerica could change everything for the town. They'd have so much to celebrate at the upcoming bicentennial. Aunt Violet and the committee had been working hard for months to make sure they did the town proud.

The unseasonably warm temperature this weekend hovered in the midforties. It was a far cry from the cold and snow they'd been having. With the bright sunshine and slight heat wave, it seemed a perfect day for another town workday.

Anna joined the other ladies in setting up food on the oak counter at the ticket office in the depot.

"What ya got there?" Clad in jeans, a

warm jacket, a scarf, and gloves, Michael stepped up beside her.

"Michael, what are you doing here?"

"What? I'm a good citizen. I want to help out on workday."

"But your ankle —"

"Is fine. I've been down long enough." He pulled off his jacket, scarf, and gloves and placed them in a pile with others. "Besides, pounding nails on a hardwood floor is not going to hurt my leg — unless, of course, I hit it with a hammer."

His grin caused her heart to somersault — again. "I guess you're right." She held up her pot. "To answer your question, this is chili. I thought we might get hungry while we're working."

"Leave it to you to think of that."

She hoped his comment didn't mean she always thought about food.

"Not just me. My daughter Zoe brought cupcakes, Natalie brought gluten-free cookies and coffee, and Shelby Majors brought hot tea and scones. Oh, and Aunt Violet brought sandwiches, and let's see, Ellie Draper brought some candy from Sweet Surrender. Everything will be laid out buffet style." She pointed toward the counter. "Help yourself when you want something."

"Sounds like you ladies have thought of

everything. Once you put the food out, grab a hammer and come join me — unless you have your heart set on washing walls."

Words stuck in her throat as she watched his back turn to her. He'd asked her to join him? What did that mean? She didn't want the fine community of Smitten to get the wrong idea. Then again, maybe she was assuming too much. They had reached a certain level of friendship.

Once the chili, plastic bowls, spoons, drinks, and cups were set out, Anna grabbed a hammer and scanned the room for Michael. She'd forgotten to ask him if he would be working in the freight room or the waiting room. She spotted him in the waiting room and then hesitated. He was talking to Heather DeMeritt, a young single mother from their church. Heather was thin, with long blond hair and a beautiful smile. She worked hard to provide for her two-year-old son.

"Hi, Mom." Prybar in hand, Zoe stepped up beside her, with William close behind.

"Hi." Anna hugged them both. "Glad you could come. What's your job today?"

"We'll be prying up molding in the ticket office," William said.

Before Anna could respond, the wooden floor creaked as Heather's toddler rolled by in a shiny new wagon that Nick and Shelby Majors's daughter, Willow, was pulling.

They all smiled. "Looks like someone got a new wagon," Anna said.

"Oh yeah, he got it from Parakaleo Pal," William said with a smile.

"Who?"

"Somebody has been anonymously helping single mothers in the area — donating money, food, something for the kids — and leaving a card that says *Parakaleo Pal*," Zoe said.

"I think it means 'encourager,' " William added. "It's pretty cool, if you ask me."

"I would agree," Anna said. "Quite a mystery, though. Kind of fun."

The sound of hammers pounding on wood echoed through the room.

"Yep." Zoe grabbed William's hand. "We'd better get to work before they fire us."

"Slave driver," he said with a laugh.

They waved good-bye to Anna. She took a deep breath and walked over to where Michael sat on the floor, tapping a nail into submission.

"Did you notice Phil McCreedy was here?" Michael asked, running his hand across a nail to make sure it was even with the floor's surface.

Anna eased onto the floor. "Oh?" She

looked around until she spotted him.

"You ought to talk to him while you have him here. Maybe you could set up an appointment to meet with him about your spinning idea."

Anna considered that.

"With sheep of his own, he's bound to be helpful."

"Sheep? Did I hear someone talk about sheep?" Pastor Walden groaned as he dropped to the floor. "Not as young as I used to be," he said with a laugh.

"Hello, Pastor." Anna explained the sheep concept.

"Impressive idea. I've always thought you were a savvy businesswoman, Anna. The way you've built that business from the ground up always impressed me. You're really an inspiration, you know. We could use more creative thinking like that. Especially if that train comes to Smitten like we hope it will!"

Mrs. Walden called him over to help cut plastic to cover the electrical outlets and vents. "Guess I'd better go." He stood, then turned back to Anna. "If you decide to get sheep before Christmas, I could use some for the live nativity the church is planning. Let me know."

The pastor hurried off, and Anna could

feel Michael watching her with something akin to admiration in his eyes. It made her uncomfortable.

"So, another reason to go for it. You'd be helping the church out if you got those sheep," Michael said.

Anna laughed and swatted at him. "You're no help."

"Hey, cut that out or they'll dock your pay."

Anna warmed to the playful bantering. "I think I'll grab a broom and sweep where I can," she said, standing.

"Was it something I said?"

"No, no. I thought I'd work my way over to Mr. McCreedy."

"Good idea," Michael said, but he looked disappointed. She knew she shouldn't get all smug about that, but it did her heart good to have a . . . friend.

As Anna headed toward Mr. McCreedy, Zoe intercepted her. "Did you talk to Grandma yet? She's here if you want to. She's taping plastic around the wall outlet over there."

"I see her," Anna said. She was feeling good and didn't want to engage in what was sure to be a tension-filled conversation with her mother. "I'll talk to her about it later. Right now, I need to talk to Mr. McCreedy."

"Mom, this time is perfect. She's sitting alone."

"This isn't the time or place to deal with family matters, Zoe. I've got business to attend to. I'll talk to her later."

CHAPTER FIVE

Late Sunday afternoon after the family left, Anna stepped into the coffee shop. The heated room and coffee smells wrapped around her like a warm greeting. She bought a mocha and found a seat. She'd gotten hooked on the chocolaty confection when Zoe worked here. She was savoring the heat and the flush from her sip when Michael walked through the door. He spotted her, waved, and went to order his coffee.

Anna tried to quell the unsettled feeling in her stomach. Her body was playing mutiny with her. She had no feelings for this man other than friendship, and that was the way it would stay. Not just because he was military — he was proving himself different from her ex-husband, and she found the gentle giant in him hard to resist. Still, how well did she know him? Before they'd gotten married she thought she knew her husband. Look where that got her.

Besides, she was doing just fine on her own.

"Mind if I join you?" Michael asked, making her heart jump.

"Not at all. Have a seat."

Anna, don't act so eager.

"Please don't think I'm stalking you. I just thought it was a perfect day for some serious espresso."

Anna laughed. "I lean toward the mochas."

He eased into an overstuffed chair beside her. "How did it go with Mr. McCreedy?"

"You won't believe it! He told me he would give me four of his sheep 'on loan' through January to see if I can handle it, if I like it, whatever."

"That's generous of him."

She took a sip of her mocha. "Well, there is a catch. If I decide to buy sheep, I have to buy his."

"If you decide to take them, I can go with you to get them. We can use my truck."

Her heart kicked at his offer. It was almost as if he *wanted* to be with her. "That would be great. I'm going to contact a lady I found online who has taught spinning for years. She has videos you can subscribe to that teach you everything you need to know."

"That sounds like a good idea."

"McCreedy has Shetland sheep, which is the kind I want. I researched it some already. They have soft, warm wool. Makes good yarn. I might add Merino sheep later, if I decide to do this."

"Sounds like you're seriously considering it."

She liked the way he listened intently to her plans. "Crazy as it sounds, I am. It sounds like a fun challenge, and I think it would give the business an edge."

"Hey, why don't I take you out to my acreage and you can look around the barn, all that, to see what you think."

Her stomach tossed again. Was it from anticipation about the sheep or about being alone with Michael? She didn't know. "That would be great."

Anna left her coffee behind and climbed out of Michael's truck. A slight dusting of snow covered the ground as new flakes spilled from the sky. The gray wooden barn in front of her was spotted with peeling paint, but the hardware on the doors was new. It seemed in good enough condition. Cobwebs laced corners and spiders scurried about. A couple of empty stalls had bits of hay debris and earth that had been scooped into a pile. Obviously, Michael had already been out here and started working. He'd have the barn as sterile and tidy as his house in no time. The faint smell of old dirt and manure lingered.

"Isn't it great?" Michael said.

"It would be perfect for the sheep, Michael. Thanks for the offer."

"You're welcome." He looked around the barn. "You know, I always wanted a place out in the country with a barn and some livestock."

"Really? Think of the work."

He shrugged. "A little work never hurt anyone. And I have the time. Remember, I only work part-time at the slopes. I do that for a reason."

"Oh?"

"I have enough money to enjoy a comfortable life with my military pension. Listen, I was a workaholic when my family was here. I won't make that mistake again. I'm trying to make time for what matters."

The way he looked at her then made her feel flushed. Though what he said sounded good, she braced herself against it. Once you gave your heart away, people changed.

Friends. They were just friends.

His gaze on her was intent. "I just wish I had realized all that before I lost my wife and son. But I didn't know the Lord then.

That's made the difference, of course."

"I know all about that. Believe me." The way he stared at her caused a fluttering in her stomach. It meant nothing, though. Nothing.

Michael walked around, checking random tools. Anna stayed close, unsure of what creatures might inhabit the barn. When a mouse scurried across the floor, she grabbed his arm and a scream erupted from her throat. She leaped onto an empty crate.

He chuckled and helped her down as the mouse ran off. "You'll have to get used to that in the country. Comes with the territory."

Anna didn't like the sound of that, but she hoped the sheep would keep the mice away. She felt cold when Michael's hand dropped away from hers.

"I feel better when I'm out here in the country somehow. Sometimes I still get anxious when I'm not busy doing something productive. I have to keep telling myself I don't have to be making money to be valuable."

"Owning my own business, I have to be careful too. With no children at home, work can consume me sometimes. It's a balancing act."

"It's a hard balance. I just know I don't

want to come to the end of my life and realize I didn't do anything but make money. I want to make a life." He looked at her and laughed. "Sounds cheesy, huh?"

She laughed with him. "Maybe a little. But I understand where you're coming from."

"How long have you been in Smitten?" He leaned against a wooden beam.

"Born and raised here. We traveled some when my husband was in the military, but we always knew we'd come back to Smitten to raise our girls." She shrugged. "We had family here. We liked small-town living."

"Was your husband from here too?"

She shook her head. "He came here to visit a friend when he was on leave. We met, had a whirlwind courtship, and got married." Opening herself to conversation about Joe unnerved her. She wanted to change the subject and fast. She glanced around. "I've prayed about it, Michael. And now, seeing your space here, I'm going to give it a trial run."

"That's great," he said. He leaned toward her as though to give her a hug, coughed, and edged back. "I think you'll enjoy the adventure."

"Thank you so much for your help and encouragement. And for bringing me out to the barn this afternoon. It's been fun."

"One good turn deserves another," he said. "You helped me when I couldn't get around much. Now it's my turn."

She smiled and pulled the handle on the truck door to get in, ignoring the disappointment she felt that he'd helped her out of a sense of responsibility.

Friday night Anna joined the other angel choir members on the risers. This was not a singing choir. Music played over the sound system, and the angels merely raised their arms in praise. Their wings, large and feathered, were attached to their arms and backs. It made quite a spectacular sight.

The air was icy, but at least the wind stayed calm. Participating in her church's live nativity was one of the highlights of Anna's Christmas season. This year was especially fun because Mr. McCreedy allowed the four sheep she was borrowing-with-the-option-to-buy to take part. In fact, the bleachers she stood on overlooked the sheep pen where four men, dressed as shepherds, watched over the sheep. They had a fire pit with a strong fire going to keep warm.

Everyone wanted to be a shepherd.

Tires crunched in the snow as cars meandered through the lot and down their street. Some people pulled in and got out of their cars to take pictures or to take their children up close to see Mary, Joseph, and baby Jesus.

Because of the cold weather, participants worked in half-hour shifts. When each shift was done, they'd go inside and eat sandwiches and cookies and drink hot chocolate. It was a festive yet meaningful time for all.

With the sting of winter on her cheeks and the tingle of cold air on her fingers and toes, Anna was looking forward to her break. They were halfway through the "Hallelujah Chorus"; once that was over, she could go inside.

Just as the singers on the CD belted out, "Forever and ever," a car backfired next to them. The sheep bleated, then scattered. One of them jumped the fence.

Anna gasped and pushed her way through the adoring angels, sideswiping a few with her enormous wings.

"Sorry, Shelby. Excuse me, Natalie. Sorry, Julia."

"Ouch!"

"Didn't mean to do that, Reese."

Once she'd made her quick apologies, she ran toward the sheep, wings flapping at her back, feathers flying willy-nilly, halo askew.

She had to get to that sheep before it ran out into traffic.

Onlookers watched as shepherds and angels closed in on the runaway sheep. Joseph peered through a crack in their temporary shelter to see what was happening. The donkey turned and hee-hawed. Other sheep bleated their sympathy to their runaway comrade, and a goat fainted right on the spot, knocking over a bucket and sending it clanging and rolling across the frigid parking lot. An agitated llama — compliments of a llama farm in Stowe — spit toward its llama partner, but the glob landed smack-dab on Anna's chest. She stopped and stared at the gooey mess, then gasped as the sheep reached the corner where the manger stood.

Moving cars were only a few feet away. She had to get him — now. Seeing the sheep round the bend and enter the manger scene, Anna closed in on him. Just as the animal took steps toward moving traffic, Anna threw herself on him, wings and all, and held on for dear life. Once she realized the sheep had stopped moving, she grabbed his halter and stood to her feet. That's when she heard clapping. Turning toward the sound, she spotted Michael and Pastor Walden grinning and clapping.

"I told you she'd make a great shepherd," Michael said to the pastor.

She tugged on the sheep. "Years of mothering three active girls was great practice."

The men laughed, then Michael went to the sheep pen and opened the gate for her.

"Let's go in and eat," he suggested, his hand nudging the small of her back.

The crisp air, the excitement of rounding up the sheep, and Michael's compliment left her practically breathless . . . or was it because of Michael's guiding hand on her back?

With Michael offering his barn for her sheep, Anna had felt compelled to invite him and his mother over to share Christmas Day with her family. It was the least she could do, she had told her girls, though they just grinned at her.

After they had finished their Christmas meal, everyone settled in the family room near the decorated Christmas tree. Beneath the tree, wide ribbons and bows adorned colorful wrapping paper that covered gifts of assorted shapes and sizes.

The wind wailed against the house while the little group snuggled into the warmth of the fireplace and Anna read the Christmas story from the gospel of Luke. A time of sweet prayer followed.

Aunt Violet, Aunt Petunia, and Anna's mother, Rose, got up and played some Christmas carols on their instruments. As "Silent Night" flowed across the strings of their instruments, Anna thought it a perfect moment. She couldn't help looking at Michael, sitting next to his mother, holding her hand. He seemed nothing like Joe, but how could she be sure? Once married, some men changed — at least Joe had. Not that she was thinking of marrying Michael . . .

Just then he met her glance, and she prayed he couldn't read her mind. Marriage, or any kind of relationship for that matter, was most likely the furthest thing from his mind.

The sisters finished their music and received the appropriate applause from the tiny audience. Afterward, Anna asked Michael to pass out the gifts.

The air soon filled with ribbons and scraps of Christmas wrap and the chatter of happy family and friends and glee over each thoughtful gift displayed. Sweaters, makeup, jewelry, and gift cards piled around each individual's small fortress.

"I figured a shawl might keep you warm when your room gets cold," Anna said to Emma when she opened the gift Anna had made for her.

Knobby fingers stroked the soft yarn a time or two. "It's lovely, my dear." Mrs. Conner draped the shawl around her shoulders. "And it feels so nice." She looked over at Anna's mother. "You have a lovely daughter."

Rose smiled. "I happen to agree."

Anna felt her cheeks flush with the attention. "I'm so glad you like it." She turned to Michael. "You missed one," she said, pointing to the lone gift beneath the tree.

Michael pulled it out. A look of surprise came over him, and Anna grinned. "You didn't think I'd invite you over without a gift, did you?"

"Thank you." Michael worked his fingers through the tape while everyone watched.

Zoe tossed a wink at Anna, much to her dismay. Rose smiled. Aunt Petunia clasped her hands together like a little girl about to break out in a clapping frenzy. Aunt Violet looked as though she would reserve her judgment until she saw the gift.

When he opened the box, Michael pulled out a black cashmere scarf. "Did you make this?" he asked, admiring the gift.

"Yes, I did."

The aunts exclaimed over the stitches. Even Aunt Violet.

"This is way too nice." He wrapped it around his neck.

"My, my, I should say that's nice," Michael's mother said, admiring the handiwork.

"Mom, you are so talented," Zoe said.

"That's our mom," Tess said.

"Oh, stop, it's just a scarf." Anna looked at Michael. "You've helped me out with the sheep. It's the least I could do." She picked up the pieces of loose wrapping paper near her and stuffed them into a garbage bag. "Next year I'll be knitting with wool from my very own sheep!"

"Knitting something for me?" Michael asked playfully.

"Who knows? Maybe," Anna said with a grin. She stood to take the trash bag out to the kitchen.

"Wait," Michael said.

Anna turned to him.

"I have something for you as well." He smiled and pulled a box from his pocket.

The entire room went silent. Anna could feel the stares boring into her.

"Michael, you shouldn't have." The wrapping slipped from her fingers as she opened the box to find a sterling silver charm in the form of a sheep.

"I just thought it sort of, um, fit," he said.

Whispered oohs and aahs followed. Obviously Michael had won her girls over. Aunt Petunia and her mother too, by the looks of things. Aunt Violet's expression said she refused to commit one way or the other.

"It's very nice, Michael. Really. Thank you."

"I saw you wearing a charm bracelet one day, right? You do have one?"

"Yes, I have one. This will look perfect on it." Anna tried to swallow the lump in her throat. The gift was so . . . unexpected. It tugged on her emotions more than she cared to admit.

After a moment Clare announced, "Sorry to run." She pulled her coat from the guest closet and tugged it on. "I have to go, Mom. Josh's family gathering is in a half hour."

Anna got up and straightened the new scarf dangling from Clare's neck and kissed her on the cheek. "Don't break his heart."

Clare laughed and waved her off. "You worry too much."

Anna didn't remind Clare of her track record of breaking it off with any young man who got too close.

Clare said her good-byes and headed out the door.

When Anna came back into the room with the others, she noticed Michael had gone into the kitchen for something. Her girls were talking with her mom and aunts near Emma, but Emma wasn't paying attention.

"What are you talking about?" Anna asked when she stepped up beside her girls.

"I asked them if they'd heard of this Par-akaleo Pal thing," Zoe said.

"Yeah, I heard about it," Tess replied. "Don't know who it is, though. Could be a group of people."

"I heard they help people all around town — single mothers, that is," Zoe added.

"I heard about that too," Aunt Petunia said. "It's a nice thing, whoever is doing it."

"What on earth is a parkaloo?" Aunt Vi said.

"Par-a-ka-le-o," Tess corrected. "I think it's Greek or something — at least it sounds like it. I think it means 'encourager,' but I'll look it up on my computer when I get home."

Michael cleared his throat. "Yes, well, Mom is getting tired, so I'd better get her back." He stood. "Anna, I don't suppose you'd want to go with me to check on the sheep later?"

"I'd love to. Everyone is leaving here to go to other celebrations," Anna said. She always hated the quiet of her home after everyone left. This would give her something to do on Christmas afternoon.

"Great. The way that wind is picking up, I think we should make sure they have all that they need in case we can't get to them right away. I have to stop by my house and change clothes after I drop Mom off. Then I'll come by and pick you up."

"I'll be ready."

Michael and his mother left the house with Anna looking on. The cold wind tossed snowflakes about and caused bare tree limbs to creak and groan. She shivered. A layer of frost covered the window on her door. Heavy gray clouds hung from the afternoon sky.

She was glad Michael had thought ahead about the sheep. If they weren't able to reach them before the snow got deep, the poor sheep would starve. It was really more than a one-person job, this sheep-raising thing. Had she been foolish to jump in with both feet so quickly? With a sigh she closed the door, the last blast of wind chilling her to the bone. At least she could be thankful Michael had a barn and that the sheep were inside.

CHAPTER SIX

After the festivities of Christmas Day were over, everyone had gone home except for Anna's mother, Rose.

"That was a lovely Christmas dinner, dear," Rose said. "Are you all right? You look a bit worried about something."

"I'm going out to the barn to check on the sheep with Michael."

"And?"

"And what? I'm just a little nervous about spending time with him like that." *Nervous* was putting it mildly.

"You're just going to a barn, not out to dinner." Rose took her daughter's hand and gave it a pat. "I know it's hard to forget the harsh words Joe said to you."

"Harsh? He told me I looked like a cow in my blue dress." Her throat closed at the memory. "Always said my hair was too short or too thin or too mousy. Of course, he compared me to his latest fling — and she was always at least ten years younger. How could I measure up?"

Rose pulled Anna into a full embrace, then stepped back and with her hands on Anna's shoulders looked her in the eye. "That was Joe. This is Michael. And you know as well as I do Michael isn't anything like that."

"I don't know that at all. I barely know Michael. I thought Joe was special too, and my life was miserable."

"Take your time. Get to know Michael. But don't shut him out without giving him a chance. You have to allow yourself to love again, Anna."

"He's a friend, Mom. That's all he is, and that's all he'll ever be."

Her mother sighed and glanced at her watch. "Well, I should be going. Think about what I said?"

"All right." Closing the door behind her mother, Anna leaned on it and sighed. She knew she was capable of love. But would she ever be able to trust a man again?

Michael leaned in toward the windshield to get a better view as the wiper blades brushed away the falling snow. "Boy, it's really starting to come down. We'll run in, feed and water the sheep, then head back to the truck. Sound good?"

Anna gave a nod, but the thought of facing the snow and cold was daunting.

"Let's go." The truck doors protested, cold steel upon cold steel. The howling wind chased Anna and Michael forward. Long icicles clung to the eaves of the barn. The old building rattled and groaned against the wind. Anna pulled her scarf closer to her neck, then tucked the sides further into the nape of her coat. Cold air nipped at their gloved fingers and the tip of her nose, while snowflakes slipped onto their eyelashes, coating them in lacy white.

Out of breath from running and the cold, they found refuge in the barn.

Anna turned and saw Michael starting up the new wood-burning stove that stood in the middle of the barn.

"Did you install that since we were out here last?"

"Well, I had it installed," he said, reaching into a pile of cut logs and loading a couple into the potbellied stove.

"But why? You don't even live here." Anna handed him another stick of wood.

Michael shrugged. "I thought if it got too cold, I'd come watch over the sheep and turn on the stove to keep us all warm."

A bold and tender gesture. Her resolve

against this man was melting.

They turned around at the same time to find the sheep out of the large stall, bleating and staring at them.

"The latch on that stall doesn't work. I'll have to fix that," Michael said. "In the meantime, we'll put them in individual stalls to keep them out of trouble."

"Michael, there are only three. Where's the fourth?" Anna scanned every nook, cranny, and stall for the lost sheep. It couldn't be out there in that storm.

"It has to be here somewhere," Michael said.

After a thorough look in the barn, Anna pointed out a small back door that was open partway. A paint can blocked it from opening more or the barn would have been North Pole cold.

"What are we going to do? I haven't even paid for those sheep yet."

"Don't worry. I'll go out and look for him. He might have ventured into the woods behind us."

"Not the woods!" Anna straightened her hat and scarf. "I'm going with you. They're my sheep, and I'm responsible."

Michael held her arm as they tromped through the snow and stepped into the cold forest where the wind whined and raced through the frigid trees.

"Here, sheep," Anna called out, wishing she had taken Zoe's advice and named the animals. Not that sheep probably came to their names being called.

"You all right?" Michael assisted her over a fallen log.

If only her fingers weren't so numb from the cold. She nodded, bracing against the chill, praying the little sheep was all right and that they would find him. "Did you hear that?" She tipped her head and listened.

"I hear it!" Michael said. "This way."

They found the sheep caught in a wild bush, and Anna watched as Michael released it from its entrapment.

"Poor thing," Anna said.

They urged the sheep forward. Snowflakes filled the air, making it hard to see. Anna's lungs ached from the piercing cold, and her legs couldn't carry her fast enough. She was certain if someone bumped her, she would break into little frozen bits. Fortunately, they were soon within the warm confines of the barn. Once they got the sheep into their stalls, Michael turned to her.

"You stay here. I'll go start the truck and get it warm before we leave." He went outside.

Anna talked to the sheep, petting their

bulky wool until Michael stepped back into the barn.

"I'm afraid I've got some bad news," he said. "The truck is dead. We'll have to call someone to get us."

Anna took in a quick breath. "My cell phone is out of power. I meant to charge it last night but I forgot."

"No problem, I'll use mine," Michael said, his hands rummaging through his pants and coat pockets. A moment later he looked up. "I don't have it. I'll bet I left it at your house."

Panic fringed Anna's insides. She couldn't stay here. Alone. With Michael Conners.

"What are we going to do?"

"We've got the stove to keep us warm, so we'll be all right until someone notices we're missing. At least the kids heard us make plans to come out here."

"This is like being caught up in an episode of *Little House on the Prairie,*" Anna said.

Michael laughed as he loaded up the woodstove with more kindling and logs. Warmth swept through the room, and Anna could feel her body and her attitude starting to thaw. Michael laid some heavy blankets on the floor for them to sit on near the stove.

"Sitting on the floor isn't all that comfortable, but maybe we'll be all right till some-one gets here," Michael said.

Anna held her cold fingers out to the fire. "I'm so glad you put in this stove or we'd freeze!"

"I have to admit I kind of hoped we'd find ourselves out here like this."

"You mean you planned this? The dead truck and the missing cell phone?"

"No." He laughed. "But I'm not saying I'm above it either. There's no one else I'd rather be trapped in a barn full of sheep with, Anna."

"I'm not sure that's a compliment."

"It is. Hey, you still look cold." Michael got up to load more wood into the fire. "I can't get any more wood in there. Hope-fully you'll warm up soon."

"Is that another blanket over there?" Anna asked, pointing to the slip of red and yellow peeking from a wooden box near the back wall.

"So it is!"

She got up and went to retrieve the blan-ket. It was underneath a heavy toolbox, so she struggled to pull it out, then turned around and came nose to nose with Mi-chael. A half step back was all she could manage because of the box behind her. Mi-chael didn't move.

"I thought you might need help." His eyes held hers.

Without saying another word, Michael leaned his head toward Anna. For one blessed, glorious moment she forgot her reservations and gave herself fully to the kiss, lingering in the smell of wood on his clothes, the taste of peppermint on his soft lips, the strong embrace of his arms. When she pulled away, it took her a moment to focus, caught up as she was in a hazy mist of dreams.

"Thank you," Michael said, his eyes never leaving hers.

"For what?"

"For the kiss. I've wanted to kiss you for quite some time."

Though she didn't realize it until right at that moment, Anna knew she had wanted that too. Emotions swirled within her. She didn't know what to say or do. She went back and settled into her seat on the floor, wrapped in blankets — though she was warmer now.

Much warmer.

Had he been out of line to kiss her? Michael tossed the thought around in his mind while he and Anna sat in the silence, listening to the wood snap and crackle in the stove.

"It's been a great day, a great Christmas," Michael said, studying her.

Anna kept her gaze on the flames in the stove. "It truly has." She turned to him and smiled.

"Haven't seen a snowstorm like this in a while," he said.

Her cheeks were rosy, her eyes dreamy. "Despite the frustrations, I love the snow. It's so beautiful."

This woman captivated him with her appreciation of the little things in life.

"My wife hated the snow. After my retirement, she wanted to head for Florida." He looked up. "Never happened."

"That must've been hard."

"It was hard. So sudden. No time to prepare, you know?"

She nodded.

"Then that thing with my son on top of it all. Well, it took me to my knees."

Anna didn't say anything, and embarrassment flickered up Michael's midsection. He'd said too much. "Oversharing," he'd heard someone call it. Something he never did — until now.

"My husband didn't die, but despite how bad our marriage was, I hadn't expected him to leave."

"Where is he now?"

"Living in Arizona with his girlfriend-turned-wife."

"I'm sorry, Anna. I can't imagine any man doing that to you." He reached out and cupped her soft hand in his own.

She looked up at him. "I'm scared, Michael."

"Me too."

"It's hard to trust again."

"I know," he said. "All I'm asking for is a chance."

The light from a vehicle in the driveway shone inside. Michael frowned. They were being rescued, and there was nothing he could do about it.

After pulling her car into the parking lot of Mountain Perks, Anna parked and headed for the door. When she spotted Michael's car, a blip of excitement ran through her. Last night in the barn their talk had ended too soon. Tess and Ryan had come for them, but she and Michael were having such a lovely talk she wished the rescue could have waited.

Stepping into the shop, she took in the usual smells of rich, dark coffee with a hint of chocolate.

Her eyes scanned the room and landed on Michael — and a young woman next to him.

He beamed at her. "Anna, I'm so glad to see you. Of course, you know Heather from church."

"Yes. Heather, good to see you."

Heather smiled politely, then left the shop with a wave at them both.

"Wish I could stay and have a coffee with you, but I've got to get to work this morning. They're having a problem with one of the ski lifts. Talk to you soon?" Michael said.

She nodded and he touched her arm, smiled, and left.

Anna walked to the counter and ordered her mocha. What was he doing with Heather? Sitting at the table, she tried to make sense of it all. How odd that he didn't offer any explanation. She supposed they could have been having a church meeting of some kind. She turned the napkin between her fingers, then straightened it. Not that he owed her an explanation, of course.

Still, last night had meant something, hadn't it? Besides, Heather was too young for him. Though that didn't seem to stop men these days. She sipped her mocha. She didn't know whether to be mad or confused.

Confusion won over, but a tinge of jealousy was not far behind.

CHAPTER SEVEN

The next evening, a cup of chamomile tea in her hand, Anna settled onto her sofa after a long day at the shop. A few returns on yarn, but mostly shoppers were there for after-Christmas clearance. After work she had checked on the sheep. They were fine. Sheep truly were low-maintenance farm animals. Their coats, thick and bulky, promised a harvest of wool in the spring.

The phone rang.

"I missed you today," Michael said.

"Oh?"

"I went to Mountain Perks and you weren't there."

She chuckled. "I like my mochas, but I don't go there every day. Do you?"

"Only when I think I might see you."

Her heart skipped. Did he really just say that? She wanted to mention Heather while he was in a good mood, but she didn't want to sound like a jealous woman. Surely Michael and Heather were just two friends meeting for coffee.

"Did you hear there's going to be a Valentine's Day dance at the Timber Lake Lodge?" he asked.

"No. How did you find out?"

"Natalie told me at the coffee shop. She's helping organize the event."

"Oh, that must've been why she called and left a message that she needed to talk to me. They probably need help."

"I guess Sawyer Smitten and his wife will be there. He'll emcee and sing for us."

"Oh, that sounds wonderful," Anna said.

"Will you be my date?" His voice was low and uncertain.

A schoolgirl shiver ran through her. "Well, let me see, I'll have to check my calendar," she teased.

"Oh, I see how it is. Playing hard to get. Well, let me know in time so I can get another date if you reject me."

She loved listening to his low laugh. "I'd be happy to be your date," she said quickly, wanting to make sure he heard her and wouldn't run off and ask Heather.

"Great. It's settled then."

Anna heard Michael's doorbell.

"Someone's at the door. Guess I'd better go. I'll call you later."

■ ■ ■ ■

Michael was still smiling as he hung up. Their relationship was developing nicely, and he liked where it was headed. With his mind on Anna, he opened the front door, and all thoughts came to a screeching halt.

"Hi, Dad."

Michael's heart leapt at the sight of his son, tall, rugged, good-looking, dark eyes and hair, strong jaw. His body discipline-strong. "Christopher?" His throat clogged.

"Can I come in?" Christopher asked.

"Of course. What's the matter with me?" Michael stepped aside, clearing the way for his son's entrance.

Christopher walked inside, dragging a small suitcase behind him. He dropped the handle and turned to his dad.

"Let me take your jacket."

Christopher shrugged off his coat, and Michael hung it over a chair.

"So, how have you been?"

"Been fine." Christopher stared down at the floor.

Michael wasn't sure what to say next. "Would you like something to drink?"

"No thanks. I just ate."

"Where are my manners? Let's go sit

down." Michael took three steps, but Christopher wasn't following.

"I'm sorry, Dad."

Michael turned around slowly as though he didn't want to break the miracle that stirred in the room.

"I'm sorry," Christopher said again, his eyes searching for forgiveness.

Two miraculous words that swirled in the air and landed deep in Michael's chest, never to leave. How he had longed for his son to come home. Now here he was. His son was home! *Thank you, Jesus.* Unbidden tears slipped down Michael's face. "I'm sorry too, son."

Michael immediately lapped up the distance between them and pulled his son into an enormous hug. "I'm sorry that I didn't know how to handle things after Mom's death. I should've done something to stop you from leaving." Michael's words were choppy as he spoke through his emotion.

Christopher pulled away and looked at him, his own face flooded with tears. "It's not like you had a parenting book for that sort of thing. It just happened. I was a stupid kid. I know I hurt you. Will you forgive me?"

Michael patted his son on the arm and laughed with relief. "I'll forgive you, and you can forgive me, and we'll call it even. How's that?"

"Works for me."

They stood there for a moment, then Michael said, "Come sit down and tell me what's been going on in your life."

Staring at his calloused hands, Christopher said, "I followed your footsteps and joined the marines."

"No wonder I couldn't find you."

"I'm not retiring there, though," Christopher said. "I served four years and did a stint in Afghanistan. That was enough for me."

"I understand," Michael said. "So what brings you here?"

"After being there, seeing . . . well, war, I realized the importance of life — of family. I'm out of the service now, and I want to make amends." He stopped looking at his hands and lifted tear-filled eyes to his dad. "I missed you, Dad."

"I've missed you too."

Both started talking at once, catching up on one another's lives.

"You'll have to come see Grandma. She's missed you terribly."

"It'll be great to see her again." He paused. "Is Grandma the reason you moved to Smitten?"

Michael nodded. "She's not doing so well."

Christopher gave a solemn nod.

"So what are your plans?" Michael asked.

"I wondered if I could move in with you and try to get established here in Smitten. I remember visiting Grandma here, and I've always liked this town. Since I just got out of the service, I decided to make a fresh start of things."

Michael's plans to leave Smitten one day began to fade. "I'm glad you did. I can't begin to tell you how I've missed you, son. So thankful the Lord brought you back."

Christopher coughed. "Yeah, well, it's good to be here."

The doorbell rang again.

"Oh, that will be Heather. I forgot I told her I'd meet with her this evening," he said, heading for the door. "She's a nice gal. You'll want to meet her."

"Oh, a love interest, eh?"

"No, no, nothing like that." Michael opened the door. "Heather, come on in."

Michael introduced Christopher and Heather, then went to the kitchen to fill some glasses with iced tea. By the time he returned, Christopher and Heather were deep in conversation and barely noticed his arrival.

Michael decided this new friendship had definite possibilities. He smiled to himself and thanked Jesus for bringing his son home.

Anna finished the woolen scarf she'd made for a friend at church. She tucked it into her knitting bag, cleaned off her registry station, and clicked off the lights in her shop.

On her drive home she spotted quite a few ice skaters in the town square. Graceful skaters waltzed across the pond while some not-so-graceful skaters struggled to stay upright.

Michael would love to get out there and skate, she knew that much. It seemed hard for him to sit still for very long. Though he loved to stay active, she knew skiing was his passion. Sadness ran through her that she couldn't share this passion with him. Maybe she should push herself. Try to do it, for his sake. At the very least it would show him how much he meant to her.

Her cell phone rang. The number on the screen made her catch her breath. Michael.

"Got a minute?" he asked.

"I do. I'm just driving home from work."

"I was hoping to catch you, since I haven't been able to talk to you for a couple of days."

"I'm sorry about that. It's been so busy at the shop."

"That's a good thing, right?" Michael said.

"Yes, very good. The word is out about the sheep, and women are getting excited about the spinning classes. I guess it's a good thing I told Mr. McCreedy I'd keep the sheep."

"I guess so. By the way, do you want to go check on them after dinner? Or better still, we could go out to dinner and then go? I have something to tell you."

Alarm shot through her. Normally a positive person by nature, she wasn't sure why she would automatically think there was a problem. But usually when someone couldn't say something over the phone . . .

"Sounds good. But let's save dinner for another time. I'm not all that hungry."

"You okay?"

Anna could hear faint music and people talking in the background. It sounded as though he was shopping somewhere. "Sure. It's just that I've been snacking on leftover Christmas goodies all day."

He chuckled low and soft in her ear. "Okay, Mountain Perks then. I'll pick you up around seven. Does that work?"

"See you then." Anna clicked off her cell phone and spotted Tess's car in the toy store parking lot. Maybe she'd get a chance to visit with her and Sophia, Ryan's daughter. That little girl would be her granddaughter if Tess and Ryan got married — that was something to think about.

Anna pulled her car into a parking space. Once out of her car, she walked to the door, and the person coming out the door practically ran into her.

It was Michael carrying a toy trike. A young man was with him.

"I'm so sorry. I wasn't watch — Anna! How great to run into you here. No pun intended."

She smiled. "Looks like your hands are full."

"Can you walk with us out to my car?"

"Aren't you a little big for that?" Anna meant it to sound teasing, but she had to swallow down her questions. Heather's little boy would be about the right size for the trike.

"I never got one as a toddler, so I decided it was time. Better late than never." He grinned. "Actually, this is for Heather De-Meritt's little boy, Charlie. We've sort of bonded, so I wanted to get him something."

Bonded. "That's nice," Anna said, not meaning a word of it. Trying to ignore the growing jealousy in her belly, she turned to the young man. "Hello."

"Hi." He extended his hand.

"I want to make the introductions," Michael interrupted. "Let me dump this trike first." He opened the trunk of his car, placed the trike inside, then turned to Anna. "Anna, I would like you to meet Christopher Conners . . . my son."

Anna gasped. Then she smiled and held out her hand. "Christopher, so very nice to meet you." She glanced at Michael. "Was this what you wanted to tell me at the coffee shop?"

He smiled and nodded. "Sure is."

The two men filled her in on Christopher's story. Anna welcomed him to town, then got into her car. She suggested they not meet for coffee so Michael could spend time with his son. Besides, she needed time to think. Obviously Michael had some sort of connection with Heather and her son. Anna didn't want to jump to any conclusions, but with the facts staring her full in the face, she struggled to let go of her fears.

She fought to keep thoughts of Joe's hurtful words far from her mind, telling her how bad she looked, how he couldn't be happy staying together, but lately, those words had bombarded her.

Had she been a fool for giving her heart
away . . . again?

CHAPTER EIGHT

As much as Anna loved the holidays, she was thankful they were over and she was back into her usual routine. The middle of January had practically sneaked up on her. The Valentine's Day dance was just around the corner. She rang up a customer's order with a slight sigh. Her body went through the motions, packaging the yarn, smiling and thanking customers for their business, while her mind tried to sort out what was going on with Michael.

They hadn't seen each other much over the past couple of weeks. Michael was busy with his son, but also she made up excuses when he tried to meet her. She'd been taking care of the sheep on her own. She knew she was acting like a schoolgirl, but she had to protect herself. She refused to play second fiddle to another woman ever again. If a man didn't love her and her alone, she wanted no part of it. She'd just give Michael some time and space to see what he wanted, and if it was Heather, she'd leave them alone.

After work Anna stopped by to see her mother. She stepped inside the house and was about to call, "Anybody home?" when she heard voices speaking in serious tones.

"I'm so sorry, Rose." An unfamiliar softness, a sort of pleading, laced Aunt Vi's tone.

Anna didn't mean to eavesdrop, but she wasn't sure how to interrupt.

"I don't understand," Anna's mother said, her voice quavering. "You had those dog tags all along? Why didn't you tell me?"

"You were married, so I wanted to protect you. Think what would have happened if you'd known he was alive. And you were pregnant with Anna."

"You weren't looking out for me." Rose raised her voice. "You wanted him for yourself. That's why you didn't tell me."

"It's true I thought I loved David and told him so, but you were married, Rose. What could you do about David then? I didn't tell you he came back because I thought it would cause you more pain."

"And this doesn't? Knowing my sister lied and kept it a secret all these years? You could have told me after Martin died, but you didn't. You knew how much I loved Da-

343

vid, and yet you let me believe he was dead. I suppose you didn't want another man in my life because you've never had one."

Anna wanted to leave, but her feet were rooted to the floor. Her heart pounded in her chest.

"Do you hear yourself? You were married! Would you have allowed David back into your life to break up your marriage?"

Anna didn't dare breathe till she heard her mother's response.

Her mother sighed. "No, of course not."

"I love you, Rose. You're my sister. And I'm so sorry I hurt you. I'll do anything to make it up to you."

"You can never make it up to me. I can't talk about this anymore, Violet. How can I ever trust you again?"

Slowly, silently, Anna eased back out of the house with a heavy heart.

The next morning as Anna sleepily poured herself a cup of coffee, the phone rang.

"Good morning, beautiful."

Anna smiled at Michael's greeting.

"Did you hear the news?"

"What news?" Surely her family's disagreement wasn't already on the gossip chain.

"RailAmerica has decided not to come

through Smitten."

"Oh no! The town has been counting on it." Anna inwardly said good-bye to all the would-be tourists she'd thought would visit her shop.

"I knew you'd be disappointed. But we knew bigger towns were bidding, so it was a long shot."

"Yeah."

"Say, would you like to go ice skating tonight in town? Might cheer you up."

She couldn't face him, not with so much on her mind. Not when she didn't know what his relationship was with Heather. "Oh, um, I don't know . . ."

"Anna, you haven't seemed yourself lately. Is something wrong?"

"Not that I know of."

"Great. I'll pick you up at seven."

Sighing, Anna hung up her phone as her head began to pound. It couldn't go on this way. She had to know the truth.

By six thirty her migraine had only intensified. Anna punched in Michael's number. "Michael." She adjusted the wet cloth over her eyes. "I'm afraid I won't be able to go ice skating tonight. I've come down with a migraine."

He didn't answer at first, then sighed. "Are you sure about this, Anna? I mean,

I'm sorry you have a headache, but you seem to be finding excuses a lot lately. Do you still want to see me? Are we still on for the dance?"

"Sure we are. I really do have a migraine."

"Okay, I'll talk to you later. Hope you feel better soon."

He didn't sound convinced, but there was nothing Anna could do about it. Maybe it was just as well.

Michael thought about checking on Anna the next morning, but decided to leave her alone for a while. She seemed to want some distance between them, so he'd give it to her. Maybe just check in a time or two before the dance. Maybe by then she'd have worked through whatever it was that was bothering her.

Christopher walked in, hair askew, T-shirt sagging over his pajama pants. He let out an enormous yawn.

"Well, you're a sight for sore eyes," Michael said with a laugh. "How about some cereal?"

"Sounds good."

They gathered some bowls and poured the snappy rice cereal into them. "So how are things going with you and Heather?" Michael grinned as he poured a little more

346

milk in his bowl.

"Going all right. She's a nice girl."

"Yes, she is." He looked at his son and wondered what all he'd missed in his life over the past five years. "Listen, Christopher, I know we've said our apologies, but I'm sorry I wasn't around home more when you were growing up. I was just set on making a good life for us."

"And you loved your job."

"Yeah, that too."

"I always thought you loved it more than me."

Michael's heart squeezed. "I never meant to make you feel that way. Forgive me."

"It's over and done," Christopher said. "I'm just thankful we're back on track."

"Me too." Michael whispered a prayer of thanks in his heart for the miracle of reconciliation with his son.

"So glad you could come over for dinner, Mom," Anna said as they settled in the family room with tea after dinner.

"It was nice of you to have me." Rose stirred some sugar into her tea.

Anna watched her and noticed the dark circles that underlined her eyes. A true indication that something bothered her. Anna knew it was that whole fiasco with

347

Aunt Violet. Should she bring it up? Now that Aunt Violet had revealed the secret after all these years, Anna thought maybe if *she* had told her mother it might not have been such a shock.

"Are you all right, Mother? I mean, you seem like something's bothering you."

"I don't need to bring you into my problems."

"You're my mother. I care about you and your problems."

Rose's gaze lingered on Anna's face. "You know what Violet did, don't you? How long have you known?"

No sense pretending now.

"A few weeks. The girls wanted to find out what happened to David for you."

"You should've told me."

"It was Aunt Vi's secret to reveal. Not mine."

Her mother's eyes filled with tears. "My own sister betrayed me and kept it secret for years. Oh, she's apologized, but sometimes 'I'm sorry' just doesn't fix it. Not when the hurt goes this deep. I just don't know how I can work through it." Rose's mouth looked pinched and her eyes were full of pain.

"Whatever she's done, I'm sure you'll work it out. You always do."

"I don't think so," Rose said. "Not this time."

By the look on her mother's face, Anna believed her.

"I told her I was sorry," Aunt Violet said, her voice breaking. She sat on Anna's sofa and dabbed her eyes. "I've tried everything to make amends, but she won't hear of it." She sniffled, then blew her nose loudly. "Well, I'm through."

An uncomfortable churning began in Anna's stomach. "Give it time, Aunt Vi."

"What's done is done. I can't undo it. I messed up. I'm sorry. But now it's time to move on — with or without my sister." Her tone took on a steely quality.

Anna gasped. "You don't mean that, Aunt Vi."

"I most certainly do." She stood up and gathered her purse. "I've done all that I can. If she won't receive my apology, so be it. There's nothing more I can say."

Anna saw her aunt to the door and shut it behind her. She'd known it was a mistake for Aunt Vi to tell her mom. They should've made a pact to let sleeping dogs lie. The churning in her stomach gathered momentum.

Lord, I can't fix this without you. Please find

a way to save our family.

Anna hadn't seen Michael in days. She told herself it was the way she wanted it, but the hollow place in her stomach told her otherwise. She busied herself with inventory checks behind the counter at Sit 'n Knit.

Zoe had dropped by and poured herself a cup of coffee. She glanced at the patrons and then spoke to Anna in a hushed voice. "Mom, are you and Michael all right?"

"This is not the place, Zoe." She made a note to buy more size thirteen wooden needles.

Zoe pressed her lips together. "I knew it. You haven't been going out like usual. Are you still going to the dance?"

"Yes, we're still going, but —"

"No buts, Mom. You have to go. It's the biggest dance of the year, and Sawyer and his wife will be there. Imagine," she said with stars in her eyes, "they'll celebrate their first anniversary in the town where they married. Isn't that romantic?"

"I suppose so."

"Anyway, Sawyer will be singing at the dance. How could you miss it?"

Anna sighed and glanced around to make sure no one was listening. The other ladies, fingers working skillfully through yarn, appeared engrossed in their own conversation.

"I don't know, Zoe. I'll most likely be there because I told him I would go, but I'm not sure I want to."

Zoe leaned farther into her mother's shoulder. "What is it, Mom? What did he do?"

"Just not sure about things, that's all." She couldn't admit her jealousy. She was the mom and Zoe was her daughter. Anna had to be strong. The very idea, at that precise moment, gave her the courage she needed. When she got to the dance, she would confront Michael about Heather and hear the truth. He might be all right with not dating exclusively, but she wasn't comfortable with it and would prefer not to date at all. She never should've gotten mixed up with him in the first place.

"Mom, did you hear me?"

"What? No."

"I said, he's a good man. Make sure you have a good reason to call it off."

Hearing the words *call it off* brought a pain to Anna's midsection. No, the ball would be in his court. This time she would confront him, no matter how much she hated confrontation, and she would hear the hard truth one way or the other.

■ ■ ■ ■

Braving the cold winds, Anna got out of her car and headed for the barn. She could hear the sheep bleating, no doubt complaining about the cold. Inside the barn was warm in comparison to the elements outside.

"Sorry I'm late, kids." Anna was scooping food into their trough when she heard a car pull up. Though Smitten had very little crime, she didn't like the idea of being out in a barn on an isolated property alone. She peeked through the window and relief washed over her. Michael.

He stepped inside and stomped his boots free of snow. "Hi," he said, the endearing grin in place. "They told me you were here, and I thought I'd pop in to help."

"Thanks." She glanced at him, taking in the warmth of his gaze.

"Looks like they're getting along okay out here," he said.

"Yes, it does. Thanks for letting them stay in your barn, Michael."

"Forget it. I'm enjoying them too. In fact, I've been thinking about something."

"What?"

"I was thinking that maybe come spring I'd look into starting a petting zoo out here."

"A petting zoo?"

"Yeah, kids love that sort of thing. Don't know if I'd need special permits and all that, so I'll have to check it out."

"That's nice." He was always thinking of others. That was one of the things she loved about him.

Loved. About. Him.

So there it was. She knew she cared about Michael, but love? She hadn't considered that until that very moment. There it was, tucked behind a corner of her heart that she hadn't dared explore. His actions toward her said he cared about her too, but what about Heather?

Would Michael's heart ever totally belong to Anna?

CHAPTER NINE

Today was the big day. Once Anna got home from the shop, she took a long bath and tried to relax from all the hustle and bustle of the day. Tonight would be a great night or a horrible one, depending on Michael's reaction to Anna's question about Heather.

After Anna slipped the black dress over her head, she put the finishing touches on her hair and makeup. She smiled at her reflection. It was good to feel at her best, regardless of Michael's answer. She'd come so far since the divorce. That assurance alone was worth something.

The doorbell rang, and she took a deep breath. As her dainty slippers hit the hardwood floor on her way to the door, she couldn't help feeling a bit like a princess. She couldn't remember the last time she had dressed up like this for a special occasion. But the real payoff came when she opened the front door.

Michael's eyes widened and sparkled at the sight of her. It made Anna's stomach leap.

"You look absolutely amazing," he said, his voice a little hoarse.

"Thank you. You look nice too," she said, meaning it. The way he looked in the black tux made her heart skip.

"So, shall we go?"

She grabbed her handbag. "Yes, let's." Anna followed him out the door and to the car.

Once they arrived at the Timber Lake Lodge parking lot, people in lovely evening wear were spilling out of their cars. Light perfume wafted along the night air like a scented ribbon dancing on a summer breeze.

Michael took her hand and escorted her into the banquet room. Most of Smitten had turned out for the gala event. It seemed there were tourists there too, so the place was packed. Red and pink dresses colored the room. Sawyer had already started to croon a song while people mingled at round tables and the punch line.

After the song, Michael and Anna picked up some appetizers, then sat down at a candlelit table.

"This is really nice, Anna. You ladies did a

fine job of decorating," Michael said.

"It was fun." Anna looked across the room. Her friends were laughing and enjoying the enchanted evening as much as she was. But behind them rose a commotion. Anna was pretty sure she heard Aunt Violet's voice.

"I've suffered enough with this through the years. I said I was sorry. What do you want from me, my dentures?"

"Oh dear, I'd better check on them," Anna said.

"Betrayed by my own sister!" Rose's voice jumped above the crowd.

By the time Anna got there, she could see fire in her mother's and aunt's eyes.

"Mother, Aunt Vi, could I talk to you for a minute?"

"No, you cannot," they said simultaneously.

"Obviously family means nothing anymore," Aunt Vi said, stomping across the floor in her flat shoes and long dress. She flew toward the door.

"What's a family without trust?" Rose called after her.

As much as it pained her to see her mother and aunt argue, her mother's words about trust cut her to the core. Zoe came over and steered her Grandma Rose off in another direction to talk, so Anna sat back down next to Michael and explained what was going on. His understanding soothed her nerves and gave her the resolve she needed.

"Michael," she began tentatively. "I've been meaning to ask you something."

"Ask me anything."

"Well, we've never said that we were dating exclusively, but . . . this is awkward."

He took her hand. "What are you asking, Anna?"

"Why do I, um, see you with Heather DeMeritt a lot?"

Michael shifted in his seat, looking uncomfortable, and Anna's heart sank. So it was true. He was seeing Heather. She struggled to breathe.

He held her gaze. "I do meet with Heather quite often, but not for what you think."

"Oh?" She held on to her flagging hope.

He sat there a moment, saying nothing. Then he sighed. "I had hoped not to tell anyone this, but I don't want to keep secrets from you."

She took encouragement from his words. "Yes?"

"You remember the Parakaleo Pal? The person who helps children and single moms?"

Realization dawned. "It's you?"

He nodded. "Heather works with single moms in the community. She sees who's in need and tells me so that I can get toys for the kids, grocery money to the mom, that sort of thing. I handle it through Heather so they don't know it's from me. You know, that whole "don't let your left hand know what your right hand is doing" thing."

Guilt tinged Anna's heart for not trusting him. She should've known the kind of man he was. She squeezed his hand. "That's so like you, Michael."

He grinned, a teasing light in his eyes. "So you thought I was seeing Heather? Anna, she's young enough to be my daughter."

It was going to be all right. More than all right. "You're a good-looking man. I can see how she'd be interested in you." Anna smiled back at him.

He glanced toward the entrance. "Well, my son might have something to say about that."

Anna followed his gaze and saw Christopher walking through the door with Heather on his arm.

"Christopher and Heather are dating?" Joy erupted in Anna's heart. Or was it relief?

"Yep. Getting along pretty well too. Listen, I told Christopher about the Parakaleo Pal thing, and now you know. But no one else does, and I'd like to keep it that way, okay?"

"Absolutely. Your secret is safe with me." She smiled.

"Want to dance?"

"Sure."

Michael swept Anna onto the dance floor. She nestled against his chest as Sawyer sang the song he'd introduced last year, "Smitten." Her heart had never been so light and carefree. Michael wasn't dating Heather. They were exclusive. She was exclusively his. And they shared a secret. A good secret. Magic was in the air.

"Anna," he whispered. "I've fallen in love with you."

Could this really be happening? Michael's words permeated every part of her being. He loved her. Michael Conners loved her.

"I love you too, Michael. And you know what? I've been keeping a secret from you too. Well, more like a surprise," she said. "Something fun."

He pulled his head back and searched her face. "Oh?" A glint of pleasure flickered in his eyes.

"Tomorrow. Can I meet you at the ski resort tomorrow after work?"

"Oh, a woman of mystery. I like that." He grinned and pulled her close again. "I can't wait."

As much as Anna didn't want to get involved, she had to stop by to see if her mom and her aunt were all right. She had a little time before meeting Michael at the ski resort. The air was fresh with the smell of winter and burning wood from a nearby home. Anna took a deep breath and knocked on the door.

Dressed in a bright red pullover and polyester tan pants, Aunt Violet opened her front door. "What are you doing here?" She didn't look all that happy to see Anna.

"May I come in?"

"Your mom isn't here."

"That's all right. I want to see you."

Aunt Violet stepped aside. "I figured the whole family would shun me." Tears filled her eyes.

Anna's heart squeezed. "Oh, Aunt Vi, we still love you." Anna hugged the older woman. "You did what you thought was right at the time."

They stepped away from the door and walked over to the living room sofa and sat down.

Aunt Vi twisted a handkerchief between her fingers. "I'm so sorry I hurt Rose. I was a foolish kid. She was married, and I thought . . . Well, it doesn't matter now. I've made a mess of things."

"Mom will come around. She's just hurting right now."

A pensive look settled on Aunt Vi's face. "She thinks I was trying to steal what was hers because I didn't have a man in my life. I thought I cared about David, but that was so long ago it feels like another lifetime. Being single works for me. I've managed just fine."

"Yes, you have."

They sat in the silence for a bit.

"I just wanted you to know I love you and that we'll get through this — though it may take some time," Anna said.

They talked a little longer, then Anna left, thanking God for giving her the strength to deal with the conflict and praying all the while he would make their family stronger because of it.

Anna's breath came out in cold puffs by the time she arrived at the foot of the bunny hill. Sunshine lingered, though twilight pushed it deeper into the horizon. Anna's spirits were high. The lodge was serving dinner; the air smelled of grilled steak and French fries.

She carefully skied over to the rope tow

and began her ascent up the hill — and promptly fell down with a plop. Heat climbed her cheeks as she struggled to her feet, but the skis beneath her would not hold still. A little kid came over and held out his hand. He managed to get her to her feet, but once he walked away she fell forward and went careening wildly down the hill.

She fell on her backside three-quarters of the way down the hill and slid the rest of the way, stopping inches from Michael's feet. Covered with snow, she took his outstretched hand and stood, struggling to keep her balance. Michael grinned and wrapped his arms tight around her.

"It means so much to me that you tried to do that. But just so you know, I love you even if you never ski with me."

"If it weren't for wanting to impress you, I'd probably never have gone beyond the coffee shop in the lodge."

His lips grazed her forehead. "And I love you for it." He gently let her go, making sure she was steady on her skis. Then a serious expression shadowed his face. He reached into his pocket.

Anna gasped when he pulled out a small black box. "Michael?"

He searched her face, then bent to one

knee. "Anna, you have been such a blessing from God. I never thought I'd find love again until I met you. I love you, Anna Thomas, and will till my last breath. Will you marry me?"

Tears filled her eyes. Michael was everything she could hope for in a man. He'd proven himself time and again.

"Yes," she said with a smile. *Don't fall. Don't fall.*

Michael took the glove off her hand, then pulled the ring out of the box and slipped it onto her finger. "With God's help, I will spend the rest of my life making you happy."

Tears spilled down her cheeks. "Now look. I'm crying, and my mascara is going to run."

He laughed. "Trust me, you've never looked more beautiful." He stood and embraced her once again, making her feel loved and protected.

"I do trust you," she said, meaning it. "And I love you more than you know."

Somehow they would make it. Michael had taught her to trust and to love again. Anna Thomas was smitten, and she knew with Michael by her side her life would never be the same.

LOVE BLOOMS

DENISE HUNTER

Chapter One

Clare Thomas smoothed out the hardwood mulch, spreading it under the newly planted hostas. Partridgeberry now carpeted her mother's flower bed with green, but soon it would bloom with fragrant white flowers, and its red fruit would add a splash of color come fall.

The realization that it looked ten times better than it had three hours ago soothed her wounded spirit.

Anna Thomas dumped the last load of mulch from the wheelbarrow. "That should do it." She blew her long bangs from her face, picked up the shovel, and spread the load with the vigor of someone half her age.

"It looks beautiful, girls." Clare's sister Tess set a tray of iced lemonade on the porch table. Her blue eyes were lit with a joy that only comes from new love.

Not that Clare knew anything about that.

"Thank goodness we're almost done." Her

younger sister, Zoe, pulled off her pink garden gloves and appraised the sky. "Looks like it's about to rain."

Clare breathed in the scent of loamy dirt and rain, hoping the organic fragrance would relieve her unrest. "Smells like it too."

"God's going to water my new plants," Anna said. "Isn't he thoughtful?"

Oh yeah, all was coming up roses now that everyone was in love. Everyone but her. Clare chided herself for the selfish thought. She was happy for her sisters, thrilled for her mom. Still, they all had romance and candlelit dinners and kisses, and she had . . .

Plants.

She set down the rake and frowned at the garden. This wasn't the way she'd imagined it. She was almost thirty, for pity's sake. Where were her husband, her two-point-five children, her devoted golden retriever? Okay, so she had the dog part covered, but still.

She hadn't even found love, much less a husband. Somehow her looming birthday hadn't seemed so terrible when she'd had a relationship in the works. Now there was a countdown clock ticking toward an unavoidable deadline. Was she headed toward an Aunt Violet/Aunt Petunia future?

Her mom nudged her. "What's wrong,

Miss Perfectionist? Did you miss a wilted leaf?"

Clare began gathering the empty plant containers. "I was thinking about Aunt Violet." Sort of true. "I wonder if she and Grandma Rose are getting along." Gardening enthusiasts, the two older women helped out at the nursery during the busy spring and summer, mostly giving advice to customers.

"I hope they're not at each other's throats," Anna said. "I shouldn't have pulled you away."

"Hopefully they're too busy to argue. Besides, I needed a break from all the tension." Clare intended to sit them down tomorrow and talk some sense into them. Their argument over Grandma's old beau, who had also been her sister Violet's secret crush, was getting old.

"Some break." Tess sipped her lemonade. "I hope Mr. Lewis finally gets you some help. You about worked yourself into the ground last year, literally."

"I forgot to tell you," Clare said after downing half the lemonade. "He said I could hire someone. I put up some notices around town. Just hope I can find time for the interviews and such. Memorial Day weekend is coming up, and after that it's a zoo."

Zoe sat next to Tess on the porch step. "Speaking of Memorial Day, can you ask Josh to bring his camping chairs?"

"Uh . . . Josh won't be coming." Clare dumped the containers in the trash bin, mentally dumping the remnants of any feelings she'd had toward Josh. The memory of their date two nights ago still left a sour taste in her mouth.

"Tell me you didn't break up with him," Zoe said.

She supposed she deserved that. "*He* did, actually." She eyed Zoe just as her sister opened her mouth. "And no, I do not need your help. That's how I got into this mess to begin with, if you recall."

Zoe's lips puckered in a rosy pout.

"Oh no," Anna said. "What happened, honey?"

Clare shrugged. "Nothing, Mom, really. We're just too different, I guess. No chemistry, no spark." No interest, especially on his part.

"Oh rats," Tess said. "I thought you liked him."

Their breakup, if you could call it that, had nothing to do with the fact that he'd called her boring. Just remembering it made heat flood to the back of her neck where her hair was gathered in a loose braid. She couldn't believe Josh Campbell, Mr. President of the high school chess team, had the nerve to call *her* boring.

Okay, so he hadn't used that exact word, but she could read between the lines. She'd been raised in a female household. Reading between the lines was necessary for survival.

So she liked her routines. So she liked to look before she leaped. That was just smart, sensible. *Not boring, Josh Campbell. You should learn the difference.*

Clare rolled the wheelbarrow up the board and into the truck bed, then checked her watch.

"Uh-oh. She's going to be late for her tea run," Tess said.

"Better hurry, Clare," Zoe said. "Nat will faint dead away if you fail to appear at 7:17 on the dot."

Clare frowned at her sisters. "What's that supposed to mean?"

"Oh, honey, they're only teasing," Anna said.

"We like that you're predictable," Tess said.

"I'm not predictable."

Zoe grinned and flipped her dark hair from her eyes. "Please. There's a picture of you by the word on Wikipedia. I just saw it yesterday."

"I go to the coffee shop at 7:17 because I get off work at 7:00. Besides, there's no line then. It just makes sense."

"And we love that you're so sensible, dear." Her mom rubbed Clare's rigid shoulders, but it failed to calm her. "It's a very comforting quality in a world of constant change."

Zoe stood, brushing off her jeans. "I have to run too. William's coming over in a bit, and I need to de-grime." She looked down at her hands. "So much for my manicure."

Clare shut the tailgate with more force than necessary, then turned to say good-bye.

"You're not mad, are you?" Tess asked, giving her the hand tools she'd gathered.

Clare stashed them in the pockets of her handy-dandy coveralls. "I'm just touchy today. No worries."

Her mom thanked her with a big hug and a kiss on the cheek.

"See you later," Zoe called as Clare pulled from the drive.

The first droplets of rain hit the windshield when she pulled onto Lookaway Lane. Within seconds the slow, fat drops turned into a hard, heavy downpour. She turned on her wipers, her sisters' words ringing in her ears, louder than the pattering on her roof.

She wasn't boring. Or predictable. Well, maybe a little predictable, but that didn't make her boring.

Did it?

Man bored to death by girlfriend. News at eleven.

She squashed the thought, though the mood persisted as she entered town. Tourists huddled under colorful canopies, waiting for the storm to pass. Judging by the gray abyss above, that wouldn't be anytime soon.

She parked in a parallel spot on Main Street and dashed in for her warm tea. Her cousin Natalie had it ready, and Clare was back out the door in sixty seconds flat. See? No line, no waiting. Sensible.

She put the truck in gear and headed toward the nursery. It was closed, but her own shed was full, and she couldn't let the tools sit in the rain all night.

When she passed the Wind Chill Creamery, her mind returned to Saturday night. Josh had ordered two medium razzmatazz cones.

"Oh, make mine vanilla," she'd told Bethany Hopkins, who was looking frazzled on their first open night of the season.

"You don't like razzmatazz?" Josh asked.

Truth be told, she'd never tried the multi-colored fruit-flavored ice cream. She shrugged. "I just prefer vanilla."

The other comments had come three licks into her cone, and the night had only gone downhill from there.

So she liked vanilla. That didn't make her boring. Maybe it was the whole sensible thing that made her come off as boring. Now that she thought about it, she recalled Josh saying something about taking a chance once in a while. He probably thought she wasn't spontaneous enough.

Her sisters obviously agreed. Maybe she *was* stuck in a rut. Well, she could be spontaneous if she wanted to be, take a chance now and again.

And she would. She nodded her head once, confirming the promise. That's what she'd do. Her next decision — completely and utterly spontaneous. No weighing it out, no pondering for days, and above all, no safe choice. It would be good for her. Healthy. And she'd be sure to let her sisters and Josh know about it. Not that she had anything to prove.

She turned onto the rutted shady lane, passing the old wooden sign that read THE

Red Barn Nursery and Greenhouse, Since 1973. Clare had started working there as a cashier during her high school summers and had learned everything there was to know about growing healthy trees and plants. When she graduated, Mr. Lewis, wanting to cut back his own hours, hired her full-time as manager.

Last year she'd talked him into staying open year-round. With the added tourists, she thought it was a feasible plan. They'd offered holiday plants and decorations, and Clare had started growing tropicals in the greenhouse. They'd made a nice profit selling them to the local flower shop, but the gift shop hadn't done as well as they'd have liked. Sure would've been nice if Smitten had gotten the train contract. She didn't want to go back to finding winter work.

The sun was long gone by the time Clare crested the hill, the night pressing in through the woods. She passed the deserted barn with all the artistically arranged potted trees and bushes and rounded the corner, pulling up to the old lopsided shed.

Thunder roared and rain pelted her as she dashed from the truck and lowered the tailgate. She guided the wheelbarrow down the plank and hurried toward the shed. The door opened with a loud squeak, and she pushed it inside.

A movement against the far wall caught her eye. The sight of a man hunkering in the shadows made her jump. Even in the dim light, she could see he was big. And hairy.

She grabbed for a tool and came up with the rake. Her heart thudded as loudly as the rain on the roof. "Who's there?"

The stranger stood slowly, unruffled.

She'd been right. He was every bit of six foot three and broad as a boxwood hedge. He remained by the wall, his body seemingly on full alert.

Clare raised the tool over her head. She wished she wasn't alone, wished she'd taken the time to lock up earlier, wished she was holding something more substantial than a rake.

"I said, who's there?" She heard the fear in her voice and knew he did too.

Thunder cracked.

Hairy Man stared back. "Name's Ethan Foster. Just taking shelter till the storm passes." His voice was deep as a country well. He nodded his chin toward the corner.

Her eyes darted to a motorcycle parked against the wall, then back to him. He had longish dark hair and a face that hadn't seen a razor in weeks.

Without taking her eyes from him, she reached for the string on the naked bulb. Sixty watts flooded the dank space. He was a little older than she'd first thought. Not some kid, but a man of thirty-three, thirty-five. He wore a black T-shirt and jeans that had seen better days.

She gripped the rake. The nursery was well off the road, not the most convenient place to seek shelter. "What are you doing all the way back here?"

Dark eyes stared back, calm and knowing. "Sorry I scared you. Looking for Thomas."

It was her last name, but all the better if he thought there was a man on the premises.

"About . . ."

He shifted. "A job."

Her heart started to settle to a dull throb. He seemed less threatening now that the light was on. She wasn't sure why; he hadn't shrunk. Maybe it was his gentle eyes.

She lowered the rake a smidge, loosened her grip. "I don't charge by the word, you know."

"Heard he was hiring. What is this place anyway?"

She knew he wasn't referring to the nursery. "Smitten is a honeymoon destination . . . home of country star Sawyer Smitten . . . Haven't you heard of it?" After Sawyer's wedding the year before, she didn't think there was a soul left in the country who didn't know about their little town.

"Not from the area. Thomas around? I could really use the work, and I heard he was hiring."

"We're closed for the night." She looked at his motorcycle. There was a big bundle on the back. Was he a drifter? Homeless? One thing was sure, Mr. Lewis would have her head if she let him bunk here tonight.

"You can't stay here."

"When will he be back?"

She sighed, lowered the rake to the ground, keeping hold of it — just in case — and stuck out a hand. "Clare Thomas."

His eyes flickered with comprehension. He reached across the space and wrapped his hand around hers. It was warm despite the spring chill. He squeezed her hand before releasing it. She missed the warmth immediately.

Great. Now she was going to have to turn him down. The rain let up, ushering in sudden silence.

"I'm a hard worker, good with my hands." He looked away as a flush crawled up his neck. A moment later he found her eyes again. "Good with plants. And I'm a fast learner."

Clare pushed her wet hair from her face, not letting go of the rake just yet. "Listen, I don't think this is going to work out."

"I have references."

From people she didn't know. "I don't think so. Sorry." Someone else would apply soon. She wasn't desperate enough to hire a stranger. A big, tall, hairy stranger.

"I'll work a day for free. Give me a chance."

Chance. She thought again about Josh and vanilla ice cream. About the vow she'd made only moments before to make her next decision spontaneously.

She looked him over, instantly regretting the promise. This wasn't a matter of her blue blouse versus the white one. She bit the inside of her cheek.

"Two days free."

She swallowed hard. Stupid economy. "The job's temporary. Probably only through July."

"Suits me fine."

"It doesn't pay much."

"Didn't expect it would."

Of course he didn't. Her pulse sped, not liking this spontaneity thing one bit.

I don't like it either, heart.

It felt wholly unnatural. Like when your

food comes up instead of going down.

"Tomorrow then?" he asked.

She stared at him, searching for a reason, any reason, to say no. Something besides his too-deep voice, his all-seeing eyes, and the memory of his warm hand.

But she came up empty, and he was waiting. "All right."

His lips lifted in something just short of a smile. "All right."

She cleared a space as he walked his bike past her, out the door, onto the wet gravel. He straddled the seat and started the engine.

She wondered where he was going. Night had fallen, and Timber Lake Lodge was likely full. She doubted he could afford it anyway. Carson's cabins were no cheaper, and besides, she couldn't picture the man under a down duvet or in a heart-shaped tub . . .

"What time?" he asked.

She stared at him blankly. "What?"

"In the morning."

She crossed her arms against the chill. "Oh. Eight, I guess."

He nodded once and let off the clutch, then sped down the dark gravel drive.

Well, Clare, there goes your spontaneous decision. I hope you don't live to regret it.

380

CHAPTER TWO

Ethan closed his Bible. He couldn't make his mind stick on the words tonight. Instead, he reviewed the confrontation with his new boss until he'd memorized every detail. Clare Thomas.

He flicked off his flashlight and slid deeper into the sleeping bag. Not even the cold was going to shatter his good mood. It had been a productive night. First he'd found a camping spot with a picnic table, a fire pit, and a grove of evergreens, complete with a soft bed of pine needles. Then he'd scored a job. Plus he'd discovered a coffee shop in town that opened early enough for a hot cup of coffee before he had to show up for work. A lucky night for sure.

He pictured Clare again, sopping wet in those baggy overalls, wielding a rake, and gave in to the grin he'd smothered earlier. A rake. Really? Did she think he couldn't see the fear sparking in her smoky blue eyes?

It hadn't been the best way to get a job, but it had worked. He closed his eyes, letting his body sink into the bag, and whispered a prayer of thanks. He'd found no work in the last three Vermont towns, and gas and food had dwindled his resources to nothing. Then he'd entered Smitten and had liked the cozy, small-town feel, the bustle of tourists.

What do you have in store for me here, God?

As he pillowed his head with his arm, the image of the long-legged Clare returned. She wasn't used to feeling threatened, but she'd faked courage pretty well. And she'd surprised him by giving him the job. That didn't happen often — people surprising him. She'd probably regretted her decision before the sound of his bike had faded in the distance.

But he'd prove her wrong. Just as he'd done with so many before her. Maybe he could even have an impact somehow. After all, that's why he was here.

Clare's alarm pierced the morning, startling her awake. Her arm ached. Her whole body ached. She shut off the annoying bleeping and fell back onto her pillow. Her pajama top stuck to her stomach. Her head throbbed.

Perfect.

She'd made it through the whole winter without so much as a sneeze, and now when the nursery was a zoo, when Mr. Lewis was out of town —

— when a new employee was starting!

She closed her eyes, hoping to shut out reality for a few minutes. She needed a little healthy denial. It worked for the mentally unstable. Some days she qualified.

Maybe she'd feel better in a few minutes. Maybe if she just rested a bit. Maybe . . .

A loud continuous chirping chafed the corners of her mind. *Hush, stupid martin.* Her eyes flew open. 7:42 a.m. She'd fallen back asleep!

Muscles protesting, Clare rolled from bed and dragged herself into the shower. Her skin crawled as she dried off and dressed. She pulled her damp hair into a low ponytail and topped off her morning rituals with two Tylenols.

Just before she pulled into the nursery drive, she glanced in her visor mirror. Her eyes looked glassy and her cheeks were flushed. Oh well. There was no help for it. The clock read 8:00 as she turned off the ignition.

Ethan Foster waited outside the red barn

in work boots and work clothes. He turned as she approached. "Morning."

The double-take made her head throb. She wouldn't have recognized him if not for those gentle eyes.

"You shaved." She cleared the croak from her voice as she unlocked the door and let him in.

The facial hair had hidden a square jaw-line, a cleft in his chin, a tiny scar by the corner of his lips.

The lights hurt her eyes when she flipped them on. Her limbs dragged as if working through molasses.

"This is the garden center. My Grandma Rose and Aunt Violet help out in here, plus a couple of part-time high school kids. You'll mostly be helping me out back."

He followed her to her office, where she checked her schedule.

"We have some deliveries today." She cleared the frog from her throat again, but that only made her cough.

"You okay?" he asked when her fit ended.

"Fine." She picked up the stack of invoices.

"You don't look fine."

"I'll find you a map for the deliveries, then we'll load the truck."

So much for sitting Grandma and Aunt

Rose down for a nice long chat. For once she didn't care about their ongoing war, as long as they handled the walk-ins.

Clare had Ethan pull the company truck around back while she set aside the bushes and trees Reese and Griffen Parker had purchased. They'd bought the old Halverson place after they'd married in the fall. Now that spring was here, a little landscaping was in order. They were taking the day off work to put the plants in the ground.

She helped Ethan load the bed. Her heart raced and her head pounded. No matter how hard she tried, she couldn't keep up. She wiped away the sweat that beaded on her forehead as he pulled away. She could only pray he'd follow her unloading instructions . . . and didn't have a secret history filled with dead bodies.

She couldn't believe she'd hired him without checking his references. She sent Reese a text while she caught her breath, letting her know who was doing the delivery.

Grandma and Aunt Violet arrived shortly after Ethan left. She waved hello and acted busy so they'd get to work right away. If they took one look in Clare's glassy eyes, they'd send her straight home.

The morning moved slowly. She heard Grandma and Violet advising customers, but they never spoke to each other. She had to do something soon. How could two sisters be so stubborn?

Aunt Violet came into the greenhouse at noon. "I'm headed home for lunch if you'd like to — oh dear, what's wrong?"

"What do you mean?" Clare brushed some dead fronds from a Boston fern.

"You're flushed." Her penciled-in eyebrow twitched. "Maybe it's something to do with that new young man you hired."

"Don't be silly."

"Where'd he come from anyway?"

"He's new to the area. Needed a job."

"Well, heaven knows you can use the help around here. Jim Lewis should've let you hire someone long ago."

"Clare, dear, do you want to grab a —" Grandma froze when she spotted Violet, her lips thinning. "Oh."

"Clare's going to lunch with *me.*"

"Maybe that's because she hasn't had a better offer."

"Oh, you think your offer is —"

"Ladies! I appreciate your offers — both of you. But I'm working through lunch today." The sooner to get home and fall into bed. "Why don't you keep each other company?"

"Ha! Fat chance," Violet said.

Grandma's chin lifted. She turned on her heel, her slim shoulders square and high.

"You two can't keep at it like this. You're sisters."

"She's the one who's making this difficult, not me," Violet said.

Clare covered the floor for Grandma and Rose while they took their lunches — separately. Aunt Violet returned just before Ethan. Two deliveries down, three to go. Clare met him out back.

"How'd it go?" She'd been nervous about sending Ethan on that run. Mr. Metcalf was so particular.

"You still here?"

"Was Mr. Metcalf satisfied with the trees?"

"Seemed to be."

Clare felt her cheeks warm more as he looked her over good. She didn't like the way he seemed to see right into her.

"You should go home."

She began loading Ellie Draper's annuals. A flat of violas and pansies. Larkspur. The amethyst petunias looked especially nice. Ellie would love those.

"I can finish here," Ethan said.

"You don't know what she wants."

He slid the flat of pansies deep into the bed. "Says right on the sheet."

"Well, you didn't talk to her, don't know

her or her garden space." She turned into him with a mature hosta.

He took it from her. "Suit yourself."

When he left, she prepared the next load, the fatigue getting the best of her. She was relieved when she finished deadheading the flowers. She had three minutes to grab some water and rest before she heard the truck rumble up to the yard.

Just two more, she promised her body, *then you can rest.*

A wave of dizziness flooded over her when she stood. She took a second, then left her office.

Ethan lowered the tailgate as she approached. "Nice lady."

"She owns the fudge shop in town."

He tossed her a grin. "Good thing I was nice. She was pleased with the flowers."

"Good."

They loaded six window planters for the Maple Valley Inn. Clare had arranged them herself. Despite her dragging body, she perked at the aesthetically pleasing mixture of annuals and greenery. The rustic green boxes matched the inn's canopies, and the purple petunias and pansies added a splash of color. She couldn't wait to see them up on the lodge-style inn.

She bent down for the large porch planter.

"Let me help."

They squatted opposite each other, getting under the ceramic planter. They lifted together, balancing the pot between them. As they set the planter on the tailgate, a wave of dizziness crashed over Clare, making her waver.

"You okay?"

"I'm fine."

Darkness closed in, fogging her sight until only two points of vision remained.

Panic welled up, loosening her tongue. "Ethan," she said. Or thought she did.

And then, darkness.

Ethan lowered Clare to the grass, her body as limp and light as a flower petal.

"Clare." He pulled off his gloves, brushed her bangs from her eyes, then set his hand on her forehead. Burning up, just as he thought. Her glassy blue eyes and flushed cheeks had given her away. She had no business being here, stubborn woman.

"Clare, wake up."

He was about to go for help when her eyelids fluttered.

Her blank stare slowly focused on him. "What — what am I —"

"You passed out."

She blinked, tried to sit up.

He stopped her. "Lie still."

"I just stood up too fast. I'm okay."

"You're sick as a dog. Oughta be home in bed."

She ran a hand over her face. Smoothed back her glossy brown hair. "I just need some Tylenol."

And her head examined. "There're only two deliveries left — I can handle it; you go home."

She sat up. "It's mulch and gravel — haven't done that yet. Won't take long."

Was she that stubborn or did she think him incompetent? He pulled out the big guns, eyeing her hard. "Don't make me get your grandma."

She narrowed her eyes at him, but they closed in a slow blink as if that was too much work. Sick or no, she was cute as a button.

He took her arm. "I'm taking you home. Ready to stand? Up you go."

She wobbled as she came to her feet but pulled from his grasp anyway. "I can do it. And I can drive myself."

"And pass out on the road? I don't think so. You should probably see a doctor."

"I just need rest."

He helped her to the truck, then retrieved her purse from the office. Her head fell against the seat back as she directed him to her house. In between directives, she talked him through the mulch and gravel deliveries, her speech slow and groggy.

Clare lived just outside town in a neighborhood with generous wooded lots. Her beige Craftsman featured a quaint porch edged with a proliferation of well-groomed flowering and climbing plants.

He shut off the truck and helped her into the house, where a lively golden retriever met them at the door.

"Down, Dixie. Thanks for the ride," she said, already on her way to her bedroom.

"I'll lock up," he muttered to himself.

Dixie followed Clare around the corner. He noticed the dog bowls in the kitchen. No telling when Clare would be up again. He topped off the water bowl and gave Dixie a pat when she returned to lap up the fresh water. Then, just like that, the dog was trotting back to Clare, tail wagging, nails clicking on the hardwood floors.

He turned the lock on the door and let himself out.

CHAPTER THREE

Clare woke to sunlight streaming through her lacy curtains.

She squinted at her nightstand. 8:39. Beside her clock, an empty bowl, a glass of water, a limp rag, a thermometer.

She had vague recollections of Grandma stopping by earlier — yesterday? — checking her temp, setting a cool cloth on her forehead. Staggering back and forth to the bathroom. Mom and Zoe coming in with soup. Tess with Tylenol and tea.

Good grief, how long had she been sick? She sat up and found her cell phone plugged in and charging. May 25 . . . Saturday? It was Wednesday when Ethan had practically carried her into her house.

She threw off the covers, startling Dixie, who was curled at her feet.

"Morning, sweetie." She took a moment to scratch behind the dog's ears in case she'd been worried, then headed to the shower on rickety legs.

Memorial Day weekend, one of their busiest. And Mr. Lewis was returning today! She rushed through her shower, dressed, and pulled her hair back. Then she remembered that her truck was still at the nursery. But when she glanced outside, she found it parked in the drive. Breathing a sigh of relief, she fed Dixie, then grabbed a granola bar and OJ on the way out.

She forced herself to keep to the speed limit on her way to work. The place was probably in ruins. She'd hired a stranger — a drifter, no less — and taken to her bed for three days! The man drove a motorcycle, no doubt had a wardrobe of black leather, probably had tattoos up and down his spine. What had she been thinking? Mr. Lewis would never leave the hiring to her again.

Worse, she'd had no time to train the new man. He didn't know how to deadhead the plants or tell a healthy tree from an unhealthy one. Plus she was supposed to approve an ad for today's newspaper, and Mulligan's Mulch had been scheduled to deliver a fresh truckload on Thursday. Ethan wouldn't have known how to handle any of that; how could he? He'd probably quit on day two, and Mr. Lewis, no doubt, had arrived home to a complete mess. Why had she made that stupid decision to be impulsive?

See? This was why sensible worked. This was why she didn't go off all willy-nilly, taking reckless risks.

God, please. Don't let Mr. Lewis fire me, because I don't know what else I'd do. It's not like I have other skills. And the nearest nursery is miles away, remember, God?

She forced down the granola bar, her hands shaking. When she pulled up the drive and down the lane, she found the parking area full, the grounds buzzing with life. She prayed the newspaper ad hadn't gone to print with something like *Free perennials!* instead of *Fresh perennials!* It had nearly happened two years ago.

Clare rushed through the barn. Rose was busy assisting Shelby Majors with a hanging planter of asylum and phlox. Aunt Violet was on the phone. Clare headed straight back to Mr. Lewis's office and tapped on the door.

"Come in."

"Mr. Lewis, I'm so sorry about —"

Ethan stood, removing his baseball cap.

Still here.

Mr. Lewis brushed a thin hand over his ruddy cheeks. "Clare, for heaven's sake. Whatever's the matter?"

"I —" She looked at Ethan. His expression gave away nothing. She faced Mr. Lewis. "I've been sick."

He patted her arm. "I know, your grandma filled me in. You should go home. You still look a little peaked."

"I'm fine. I — is everything okay here?" She looked back and forth between them.

"Everything's fine. Ethan was just filling me in on everything I missed. Good hire, by the way." He nodded toward Ethan. "Well done, Clare. I can always count on you to do the job right."

"Thank — thank you, Mr. Lewis."

She picked up the newspaper from the corner of his desk and opened it to the ad on the back of the Living section.

"The ad's perfect," her boss continued. "Rose said she was collecting a lot of coupons this morning. Sure you're up to working?"

Clare glanced through the open door into the store, where everything appeared to be running like clockwork. "I'm fine now. Just a quick virus, I guess."

"Your grandma was worried. She said you passed out on Wednesday." He forked his fingers through the dozen or so hairs left on top.

"Well, right as rain now." She looked at

Ethan. "I'm sure we have some deliveries to make. Ready to get to it?"

Moments later she and Ethan were headed toward the loading area. Everything was in its place. It was as if she'd never been gone.

"How did you do all this, know what to do?"

He shrugged. "Been around, worked a lot of jobs. You do the work of two people around here. You really feeling better?"

"Much."

"We're about out of hanging baskets. Design is where my skills end."

"And where mine begin. I'll get started on those if you can get the first delivery set to go."

"Already loaded, boss." He gave a crooked grin that made her heart stutter.

"All right then."

He placed his cap on his head and started for the truck. She watched him retreat, noticing his broad shoulders, his muscled arms, bronze already from the spring sun. The man might be a drifter, might look like a rebel, but he was capable enough, she'd give him that. He'd sure saved her rear end this week.

"Hey, Ethan."

He turned, the sun hitting his eyes, making them like caramel.

"Thanks."

He jerked his chin up and gave a hint of a smile.

CHAPTER FOUR

"I miss Grandma and Aunt Violet." Zoe fished a spoon from the silverware drawer and put it in her orange Jell-O. "It's been weeks since they've joined us."

Anna shooed Clare out of her way and lifted the CrockPot lid. "Church is like a war zone. Who to sit with? I hate it."

The savory smell of slow-cooked roast made Clare's mouth water. "If you think that's bad, try working with them. Smells good, Mom."

Zoe stole a forkful of roast and winged it to her mouth before Anna could swat her hand.

"I don't envy you." Tess poured lemonade at their mom's oak table.

"I've tried talking to your grandma, but the more I talk, the deeper in she digs."

"I've tried too," Clare said. "They're both stubborn."

Sunlight streamed in from the window

and a light breeze fluttered the quilted valance.

"How are the spinning classes going, Mom?" Tess asked.

"I can't believe how many have signed up. It's become my most popular class. And I'm actually enjoying the sheep."

"She named them and everything," Zoe said.

Anna set the roast on the table and touched Clare's cheeks. "You look so much better, sweetie. I didn't like seeing you all flushed and lifeless."

"Did McBad Boy really carry you into your house?" Zoe asked.

"Who?" Clare took a seat.

Tess added a sly grin. "That's what they're calling him."

"Word is he's a convict just released from prison," Zoe said.

"That's ridiculous."

Anna frowned as she took her seat. "What do you know about him, Clare? Where'd he come from?"

After a full week in her employ, Ethan was still a mystery. "I — I'm not sure. He doesn't talk about himself."

"You mean you hired him without a background check?" Zoe asked. "Without a healthy dose of truth serum or at least a lie detector test?"

Clare narrowed her eyes. "Obviously my intuition was spot-on. He happens to be the best decision I've ever made."

"Whoa-ho!" Zoe smiled.

"You know what I mean. Besides, he's no convict. He was even at church today; didn't you see him?"

"No . . .," Tess said. "But then, I wasn't looking for him."

Clare flicked her napkin at Tess. "Can we bless the food? It's getting cold."

They joined hands and Anna said grace, then they passed the dishes.

Clare took a bite of Tess's maple baked beans. "Mm. These are so good, Tess."

"Eat up, honey," their mom said. "That virus took a few pounds off, I think. You look a little gaunt."

"Thank you, Mother."

"I've been thinking about your birthday, Clare," Tess said. "It's only two months away."

"Don't remind me."

"Natalie said we could take over the coffee shop for a few hours. Does that sound good?"

"Thirty . . ." Clare blew on a forkful of broccoli. "I'm getting so old."

"Thirty's not so bad," Tess said.

Easy for her to say. She was halfway to Blissville with Ryan. Clare couldn't find Blissville with a pair of long-range binoculars.

"So back to McBad Boy . . ."

"She's a dog with a bone," Clare said.

"You're a free agent now that Josh is out of the picture," Zoe said. "And I'm determined to help find your true love, whether you want my assistance or not."

"And you thought a convict would be a good match for me?"

Zoe waved away the comment. "Oh, no one really believes that. He's probably just a loner. Hmm. Maybe I can get him to sign up for Cupid's Arrow."

Clare laughed. "Yeah. Don't think so." That's the last thing Clare imagined Ethan doing. And she had to admit, she'd been imagining him doing all kinds of things.

"Invite him to the picnic tomorrow," Zoe said. "We can vet him."

"He's my employee. Besides, he's just passing through."

"Where's he staying?" Tess asked.

"I'm not sure."

"You don't know very much about this man, Clare," Anna said. "I'm surprised you hired him."

Clare tipped her chin. "I can be spontane-ous."

Her first impulsive decision and it was a home run. Maybe she could practice being a little more fun, a little less predictable. Something had to give if she wanted to find a man before she turned into a lonely old spinster.

And maybe Ethan would make the perfect target practice. She could flirt and stuff. He didn't know her, and he wasn't sticking around. What could it hurt?

"Just be careful, dear. I don't want you getting hurt."

Sometimes it was like her mother could read Clare's mind. "I'm fine, Mom. Ethan's perfectly safe."

Zoe gave a wry smile. "Don't kid yourself. There is absolutely nothing safe about that man."

Two days later the unanswered questions were still haunting Clare as she rode with Ethan to the Carriage House Bed-and-Breakfast. The cab smelled like him now, a slightly piney, musky scent.

Smell aside, she was beginning to realize Ethan possessed some indefinable quality that made her aware of his presence. Some-times she knew he was nearby before she even saw him. Here in the confines of the cab, that quality was almost unnerving.

His weathered jacket lay on the seat beside her, brushing her thigh. The label had a name scrawled in faded ink. She squinted.

Luke Fletcher.

Clare frowned and looked out the passenger window as they passed a grove of Norway spruce. A borrowed jacket? From the thrift store? Or was Ethan Foster a borrowed name? It did sound kind of . . . planned.

Clare rolled her eyes at the thought. *Of course his name was planned, Clare. By his parents.*

Even so, a niggle of concern wormed through her. What did she really know about him? It was time for answers.

"So, Ethan . . . you never mentioned where you're from."

He spared her a glance as he turned onto Maple Street. "Originally from the South, here and there."

That was helpful. "You don't have an accent."

"Nope."

"Any family back home?"

"Just me."

She picked at the sleeve of her shirt. "Can't imagine that, surrounded as I am.

You haven't met my sisters. Tess is older, a real mother hen, and Zoe's the youngest."

He cocked a grin. "Guess that makes you the troubled middle child."

Was he flirting? The thought made her middle all warm and gushy, a feeling she hadn't enjoyed in a while. Nice. She'd have to return the favor.

Hmm.

She came up blank.

"Middle children are usually opposite of the oldest," she said. "Where did you fall in the birth order?" Not flirty, but she congratulated herself on the clever segue, and for her ability to think past his distracting grin.

"Only child."

"Oh. What with Mom and two sisters, there was never a dull moment in our house. Add Grandma, Aunt Violet, and Aunt Petunia to the mix, and it was an estrogen fest around our place."

"What about your dad?"

"He left my mom ten years ago — for another woman. Lives in Arizona now."

"Tough break."

Clare shrugged. "We tried to keep in contact, but he's not very responsive. I guess he traded in one family for another."

"His loss."

He turned onto Main Street. Spring had arrived in the village. Colorful pansies and petunias sprang from window boxes, and the newly planted maples along the sidewalk budded with fresh growth. Couples mingled, window shopping, holding hands. A couple on a park bench stole a kiss.

They passed Outdoor Adventures, and Reese turned from the picture window she was washing to smile and wave. Clare waved back. Marriage agreed with Reese, that was obvious. Soon Clare's mom and even probably her sisters would join the Parkers in blissful matrimony. Clare sighed.

"Everyone knows everyone around here."

And everyone's business, Clare thought, remembering the rumors circulating about Ethan.

"That's about the size of it. What brought you to Smitten?" *Have fun with it, Clare.* "I assume you're not on your honeymoon." She threw in a crooked little smile of her own, then wondered if she looked like a victim of Botox.

Ethan, braking for a group of pedestrians, missed it entirely, thank goodness.

"Just looking for work. When you came upon me in your tool shed, I thought you'd call the sheriff. Sure didn't think I had a shot at the job."

"I'm not usually so spontaneous."

"You don't say."

She gave him a look. "Do I detect a note of sarcasm?"

His eyes lit just before a grin tugged his lips. "Little bit."

That warm feeling invaded her belly again. She looked away, wishing she had some cute quip. Zoe made it look so easy. Clare remembered the name on the tag of his jacket, and Zoe's warning floated to the surface.

"So what's with your grandma and aunt?"

Clare sighed. "That. They're not usually like this."

"They had me relaying information between them last week. It's tense as all get-out in the nursery."

"I'm sorry. Don't let them drag you into it. I told them to pass notes if they had to, but I was not going to be in the middle."

"Must've been some argument."

Clare told a quick version of the story of David Hutchins. Finding his dog tags in the attic, Aunt Violet's secret that he'd survived the war, David's refusal to return to Smitten and be reunited with Grandma Rose. No sense hiding it — the story had circulated around town after the Valentine's Day dance. By the time Clare finished the story,

Ethan was pulling along the curb at the Carriage House.

He turned off the ignition. "Sounds like your whole family's in knots."

"Aunt Violet felt horrible at first when we found out what she did. I thought it was going to work itself out."

"But your grandma is taking too long to forgive — in Miss Violet's opinion — so now she's resentful."

"Basically." She spared him a smile. "Welcome to my world."

"How long's this been going on?"

Clare exited the cab and met him around back, where she lowered the tailgate. "Let's just say it's been a long, cold winter."

An hour later Ethan pulled up to Clare's house so she could let Dixie out.

"I don't know about you, but I'm thirsty. You can come in if you want."

They'd reached the porch steps when Ethan sighted a man on Clare's porch. He wore a dress shirt, a navy tie, and a frown. He tucked his hands in the pockets of his khaki trousers as he met them on the edge of the porch.

Clare's cheeks bloomed a pretty shade of pink. Her boyfriend?

"Hi, Josh."

"Clare." He bent in for a hug that connected only at the shoulder.

Not a boyfriend.

"I brought your sweater — I know it's your favorite." He grabbed it from the table he'd laid it on and handed it to her. "You left it at my place."

Ex-boyfriend then. He'd lay all the money in his wallet on it. Not that it was much.

"Oh. Thanks." She took the sweater.

Josh's neatly clipped hair shone with hair product and his smile revealed too-white teeth. Ethan supposed he was nice-looking enough, if you liked the pretty boy sort. Which Clare apparently did.

She flashed a look at Ethan. "Josh, this is Ethan. Ethan, Josh Campbell."

Josh's grip was firm as he looked between them. "Nice to meet you. You're the new guy at the Red Barn."

"Word gets around."

Clare's elfin chin inched up. "I hired him the night he arrived in town."

What was that all about? An awkward pause ensued.

"Well . . .," Josh said.

"Well." Clare's face went two shades deeper. "Thanks. For the sweater."

Josh nodded at them both. "Nice to meet you, Ethan. See you around, Clare."

Ethan watched him go as Clare fumbled with her key.

Josh slipped into a white Saab and pulled away without a second glance.

"Darn it." Two more tries and the knob twisted.

Dixie's full rear end was wagging as they slipped inside. "Come on, girl, let's go out."

Ethan followed her through the house. She stopped on the way through the kitchen and handed him a water bottle.

As soon as she opened the back door, Dixie shot out.

Ethan stepped out onto the stoop, stopping as he caught a view of Clare's backyard.

High leafy canopies draped over a garden the likes of which he'd never seen. Flowers and shrubs everywhere, but instead of looking like a nursery run amok, it looked like the garden of Eden.

"Wow." It wasn't a word he used much. Maybe never. But the sheer beauty of the — he hated to give it such a name — *yard* deserved it. Dixie meandered down one of the cobbled walkways, stopping to smell something. It seemed a crime for a dog to use the space as her own personal bathroom.

"Did you do this?"

Clare smiled, seeming more relaxed since they'd stepped outdoors, and no wonder. A person could rest in a place like this.

"I did."

A small gazebo sat off to the side. A waterfall splashed into a pool of water, fern fronds dipping down into it. A couple of benches beckoned visitors into the depths of the garden. It didn't look fake, like some landscaping he'd seen, but seemed like it was all part of God's natural creation. The woman was gifted. She was skilled at her nursery job and all, but this . . . this was art.

Clare sat on the stoop. "Sort of a perpetual part-time project."

Ethan joined her. "How long did it take?"

Clare shrugged. "It was just a lawn when I bought the place seven years ago. I've been adding to it since."

"You designed it?"

"Yep. Griffen Parker built the gazebo for me last year. You remember him — he was your first delivery. He made the one on the town square too."

Her talents were wasted at the nursery. Couldn't she see that? "Why don't you start a landscaping branch off the Red Barn's business — it's a natural fit."

Clare shrugged. "I asked Mr. Lewis about

that a long time ago, but he's not interested in expanding. I barely talked him into staying open year-round."

"You should start your own business then."

"I probably will . . . someday."

He wanted to push, but it was none of his business. Clare was none of his business. Best to keep things simple. He'd be moving along in a matter of weeks.

He was curious about her, though. Curious about the blush Josh had put on her cheeks. Curious about why she worked at a job so close to, but not quite in, her area of giftedness.

Let's just leave it right there, Foster. We all know what curiosity did to the cat.

Last thing he needed was an attachment to the pretty brunette. She'd already wiggled her way into his affections with her quick blush and penchant for doing things a certain way. He'd even found her little game of twenty questions amusing. It was killing her to not know more, but he'd fended off questions from people far more skilled at interrogation than Clare Thomas.

He wasn't quite sure why God had sent him here. Clare and her family were already Christians, apparently. But you never knew. Maybe he could help fix the rift between her grandma and aunt somehow.

Out in the garden, Dixie looked at Clare, head tilting, ears popping up as if just realizing they were there. She bounded toward her mistress, brushing plants on her way, then barreled into Clare with her big, furry body.

Caught off balance, Clare bumped into Ethan. She planted her palm on his thigh, steadying herself.

She laughed. "Dixie, down!"

The dog nuzzled her face. She turned toward Ethan to escape the sloppy kisses.

She opened her eyes and the laughter fell away. Blue irises with sparkling flecks of silver. She smelled like honeysuckle and fresh air. She had the perfect nose, a straight line tapering down to a cute nub, and below that a pair of perfectly kissable lips. A shallow dip in the top, full on the bottom.

Clare straightened. She snatched her hand from his leg as if it were a hot plate. "Sorry."

She pushed Dixie down. The blush bloomed on her cheeks again and she stood abruptly. "You need some manners, little girl."

Ethan pretended not to notice the breathy sound of her voice, the little wobble as she stood, or the shake in her hand as she reached for the door.

And as he drove back to the nursery, he pretended not to notice that he still felt the imprint of her hand on his leg.

Chapter Five

The next Saturday a ruckus from the direction of the garden drew Clare away from the hanging planter arrangements. The voices grew louder as she rounded the tool shed. Thank God there were no customers around.

"Well, I wasn't going to let you steer her wrong." Grandma's hands knotted into fists on her narrow hips.

"I think I'd know better than you about *violets,* Rose. They're my namesake!"

"Everyone knows African violets require a shallow pot."

"Says who?"

"Says me, that's who!"

"All right, you two!" Clare frowned at the both of them. "Sit!" She pointed to the park bench gracing the walkway between the cedar and tamarack saplings.

Grandma's lips thinned.

Aunt Violet's arms crossed over her ample

bosom. Her purple sleeves fluttered in the breeze.

"*Now.* I mean it, you two. I've had enough."

The women sank onto the wooden bench, hugging the ornamental arms at either end. Clare would never disrespect her elders, but someone had to talk some sense into them.

"This has gotten out of hand. You're sisters. You love each other."

"Humph," Grandma said.

"She corrected me in front of a customer." Aunt Violet pursed her lips, her bright orange-red lipstick puckering like a withered orange.

"Well, you were wrong!"

Clare knelt down between them and took their soft, wrinkled hands in her own. "That's not what this is about, and you know it."

She'd start with Grandma — the less stubborn of the two. At least, she'd always thought so. Lately she wasn't so sure.

"Grandma, you know Aunt Violet is sorry. Hasn't she already said so? She feels terrible, don't you, Aunt Violet?"

Her aunt looked the other way. "I refuse to say it again."

"You know how hurt Grandma was. She loved David. It was a shock to learn he'd survived the war, and that you knew and didn't tell her. You can understand that, right?"

"You're wasting your time, Clare," Aunt Violet said. "There's no pleasing her."

Grandma scowled at her sister. "You're all heart, Violet."

"I told one lie! And I did it for your own good. You were already married."

Grandma's blue eyes narrowed. "You wanted David for yourself! He was alive, and you kept it from me all these years! You let me think he was dead!"

Violet sprang to her feet, surprisingly quick for an eighty-year-old woman. "I said I was sorry!"

Grandma stood. "Well, excuse me if it takes more than two minutes to forgive a sixty-year sin committed against me by my own sister!"

Aunt Violet gasped as her penciled brows shot upward.

Grandma spun and walked away, her slim shoulders back.

"Seventy times seven, Rose! Seventy times seven!"

"Aunt Violet . . .," Clare chided, touching her aunt's fleshy arm. "She just needs time. Can't you be patient with her?"

"I can't believe you're taking her side."

Violet huffed off in the opposite direction, slamming the nursery's back door.

Clare let out a loud growl. "Why can't everyone just get along?"

A noise by the shed caught her attention. Ethan came out with a shovel, shutting the door behind him, a sheepish look on his handsome face.

She arched a brow. "Hiding?"

Ethan shrugged. "Went in for a shovel and got stuck."

"You could've come to my rescue, you know," Clare said.

"And get in the middle of that? No thanks." He approached with that slow swagger of his.

She stuffed her hands in her overall pockets. Ever since she'd touched Ethan the week before, she didn't quite trust herself. She found herself thinking about the strength of his thigh at the most inopportune moments. Like now. She cleared her throat.

"At least you tried." Standing in the shade of the shed, his eyes were deep brown, nearly black. He had a fringe of lashes that could make a woman jealous.

"For all the good it did. What's it going to take? They've never argued like this. They've always been so close."

He leaned on the shovel. "Maybe if you could get your grandma's beau to come back, it would fix things."

"No. He already refused — doesn't want to come between them, although it's a bit late for that. Besides, that would only make it worse. Stir up old feelings."

"Or it could give your grandma and this guy another chance."

"And what if Aunt Violet still cared for him? What if David developed feelings for her? It could be disastrous."

If she could just get Grandma to forgive Violet, it would be over. But first she'd have to get Violet to exhibit an ounce of remorse. She thought about Violet's stubborn scowl. Fat chance.

She stared at the nursery door her aunt had disappeared through. "I just want things to go back to normal. Back to the way they used to be before those dog tags were ever found."

Maybe her mom was right. Maybe some secrets were meant to stay that way. She sure wished this one had remained buried.

"That's not possible," Ethan said.

"It is if they can forgive and forget."

"In my experience when something major happens, things change. Either you let God use the circumstances to change you, or you become bitter. Your relatives are firmly grounded. I'm sure they'll come around, but their relationship might be different."

Clare squirmed. She didn't want things to be different. She liked their family dynamics. At least, she *had.* "I guess I never thought about it."

"It'll be all right. Just give it time." And then he was gone with his shovel to dig up two sugar maples for the Bourne family.

Clare returned to the hanging planter, adding yellow petunias to the purple violas. Everything was changing. Not only Grandma and Rose, but her sisters and her mother — her best friends. They were all in relationships, headed toward marriage, and where did that leave her? They wouldn't have time for her anymore.

Their Memorial Day picnic the week before had felt odd. Grandma and Aunt Violet had refused to attend, and Mom and her sisters were all paired up, leaving Clare and Aunt Petunia the odd ones out.

And now they'd decided to start bringing their men to Sunday dinner. The girl time she looked forward to was about to be flooded with testosterone. Clare half wished she'd come down sick again before tomorrow. Three couples . . . and her. She didn't fit into her own family anymore.

Too bad she wasn't still dating Josh. At least he'd have filled the chair next to her.

Outside, Ethan began whistling a tune while he dug up the trees. The melodic notes of an old hymn.

You could always ask him, Clare.

Yeah, right. She snorted. Her cheeks grew warm at the thought. Flirting was one thing, asking him out was another. First, she was his boss. Awkward. Second, he wasn't the mingling type. Despite her best efforts to draw him out, she could count the things she knew about him on one hand. Though her sisters would no doubt have better luck at that. No one was better at prying than Zoe. It went with her job, Clare supposed.

Hmm. She was actually entertaining the idea. Which only attested to the sheer dread she felt about being a fifth wheel.

Unfortunately, getting him there would mean asking him, a task that was only slightly less uncomfortable than, say, an FBI interrogation. After all, what was in it for him? Sure, he turned that crooked little smile on her here and there, but she had no grand notions the man was interested in her. Sensible Clare. Boring Clare.

The thought deflated her like a pricked balloon. She patted down the soil around the flowers. She was being ridiculous. She only wanted to fill a chair at a family dinner, not propose marriage.

Food!

He was a bachelor. Heaven knew when he'd last had a home-cooked meal. Grandma said food was the way to a man's heart. Well, she didn't want his heart, but she'd take his company.

Having decided to take the plunge, she waited for the right time. It came late in the day after the sun had sunk behind Sugarcreek Mountain, inviting twilight to come sit a spell.

While Ethan was returning tools to the shed, Clare gathered her courage around her like a shawl. *Be casual. Indifferent.*

He snapped the lock on the door and turned with a parting smile. "All locked up. See you Monday, boss." Then he was walking toward the parking lot.

"Wait!"

He turned.

Waiting. Just as she asked.

Clare's mind went blank. Why hadn't she planned this out? Because she was trying to be more spontaneous, that's why.

See where that gets you, Clare? Standing ankle-deep in a puddle of awkward silence.

"Uh . . ."

His brows inched higher.

"You like home-cooked food?"

Stupid. Of course he likes home-cooked food. Come on, Clare.

"I mean . . ." Casual. Indifferent. She shrugged, stuffing her hands in the back pockets of her overalls. "There's a dinner at my mom's tomorrow. We eat every Sunday." She winced. "I mean we eat *together* every Sunday. There'll be other people there too." Mom's finacé, Zoe's boyfriend, Tess's boyfriend . . . "So, you know, home-cooked food, if you're interested. One o'clock. Corner of Oak and Vine. If you want."

She tossed her hair over her shoulder the way she'd seen other women do. It flopped back in her face, covering her eyes. She swatted it away in time to see one of his brows disappear under his bangs.

"That sounds great."

"So you'll, uh, come?"

He backed away with a nod. "Sure. See you then. And thanks."

Clare didn't realize she'd been holding her breath until Ethan was zooming down the drive on his bike.

CHAPTER SIX

They sat outside on a covered porch facing the spacious backyard of Clare's mom's home. Anna, as he'd been asked to call her, seemed too young and energetic to have three grown daughters.

The men were friendly enough, including him in the conversation. They'd asked about his bike, then moved on to the Red Sox–Yankees game played the day before.

Ethan couldn't remember the last time he'd sat at table with family and friends. He didn't realize how much he'd missed the easy camaraderie, the give-and-take, the teasing.

He mostly watched and listened. That is, until Zoe pulled him in. He was just enjoying his first bite of crispy chicken, his guard down, when she struck.

"So, Ethan, tell us a little about yourself."

He took his time with the chicken, wiped his mouth with the paper napkin. "Not much to tell. Just passing through, really. Clare helped me out with a job."

He glanced her way, remembering how her cheeks had flushed when he'd arrived, when he'd seen the couples. He understood better than she realized the feeling of being an outsider.

"Have you worked at a nursery before?" Tess passed the beets.

"Not really. Clare's a good teacher, though." He nodded toward the yard, a shaded paradise, then smiled at Clare. "That has to be your handiwork out there."

"It is." Anna spooned out some home-made applesauce. "My yard would be a disaster without her."

"All our yards would be," Tess said.

"She's talented," Ethan said.

"Can you believe she found her niche while she was still in high school?" Anna asked. "Mr. Lewis hired her, and that was that. We should all be so blessed."

Working at the nursery hardly skimmed the surface of Clare's talents. Didn't they see her flair for vision and design?

"Tell us about your family." Zoe passed the basket of blueberry muffins to her boyfriend. "They must miss you, being on the road."

He wondered if Clare had put her sister

424

up to this. "My parents have passed, and I'm an only child."

"I'm so sorry," Tess said. "That must be hard."

"It was a long time ago."

"How long ago were you in the service?" Michael asked.

Ethan blinked at Anna's fiancé. He hadn't mentioned his time in the military.

"I passed you when you were unloading at the Maple Valley Inn," Michael said. "Saw the tattoo."

Clare's brows shot up.

Ethan took a drink of tea. Swallowed. Wiped his mouth. "Six years." He couldn't think of the army without remembering Fletch, so he tried not to remember it at all.

Clare touched his arm. "Michael served in the marines."

"He was a sergeant," Anna added.

A look passed between Ethan and Michael. War came with a backpack full of burdens that weren't as easily removed as the uniform. The man nodded. He understood.

Unfortunately, Zoe didn't. She continued to pepper him with questions until the meal was finished. Somehow he got through it.

By the time the dishes were stacked in the sink, the other men had left. Anna shooed

Ethan from the kitchen, refusing his offer to help.

"Well, thanks for the meal," he said, turning toward the women.

"You're welcome anytime," Anna said.

"I should go too," Clare said, grabbing her purse from the couch. "I need to let Dixie out."

He hadn't seen Clare's truck in the drive. "Need a ride?"

Zoe laughed. "Yeah, right. Like she'd be caught dead on the back of that thing."

Clare straightened to her full height. He could see the internal wrestling in her eyes. "Actually, that would be great. Thanks, Ethan."

Tess's mouth fell open. Anna blinked.

Ethan turned toward the door before they could see his smirk.

"I don't believe it," Zoe said.

"No way."

"Maybe she's running a fever again."

"Now stop it, girls."

If Clare heard them, she didn't comment. She passed out hugs and followed him out the door.

Clare stopped at the curb, eyeing the motorcycle. Ethan grabbed the helmet and put it on her head, strapping her in, then straddled the bike. He pulled something, turned the key.

She frowned. It seemed bigger up close.

He pressed a button with his thumb.

Bigger and louder.

He turned toward her, raising his brows.

She bit her lip. What had she gotten herself into? "I — uh, don't you need a helmet?" she yelled over the racket.

"It's six blocks, Clare."

Well, she knew that. She gave him a look.

He kicked up the stand, steadying it. The thing must weigh four hundred pounds, and he was balancing it between his thighs? They were going to go flying down the road with nary a restraint.

She glanced back at the house. Three heads peeked out the curtains. Why had she opened her big mouth?

"It's not too late to chicken out, boss."

"That's so not going to happen." She glanced back at the house and muttered, "Not with them watching."

"Throw your leg over and hang on tight. That's all there is to it." He kicked something down.

"Uh-huh." *Here goes nothing.* She clutched his shoulder and swung her leg over. The miniscule seat sat higher than his. She grabbed on to his shirt.

"Put your feet on the pegs and center your weight. Whatever you do, don't be moving around back there."

He didn't have to tell her twice.

"Okay, here we go," he said, then the bike surged forward.

Clare grabbed on tighter, squelching the scream that rose in her throat as they accelerated. The wind stung her eyes. *Please, God. If you let me live, I'll never do this again.*

Just when she thought it might be okay, they turned a corner. She leaned with him. A squeak escaped. A moment later the bike righted itself. She realized there were two more turns before she reached her house. Three if he turned into the drive.

Gravity clawed at her body as they turned again. She hung on tight. Forgot to breathe. And then they righted again.

A few short lifetimes later the bike slowed and he turned off the engine. Silence rang loudly in her ears.

She opened her eyes. Her face was pressed into his back, her arms wrapped around him, her purse practically in his lap. Her fists clenched against his stomach.

Ack! She let loose, peeled her body off him, snatched her purse. "Uh, sorry 'bout that."

"Not bad. A little practice and you'll get

the hang of those turns."

"I'm so not getting on this thing again."

He smiled over his shoulder. "Why not? Gives you a different perspective on things, doesn't it? Scenery looks different without a piece of glass in the way."

"I kind of had my eyes closed."

He laughed, a deep, throaty chuckle that warmed her insides. "You're funny, Clare."

Now that they weren't speeding through time and space, she wished she could've seen the looks on her family's faces as they'd darted away from the house. It almost would've been worth the ride. Almost.

"Ah, Clare? You going to dismount?"

"Oh. Oh, sorry." She removed the helmet, set it behind her, and, not wanting to maul him again, swung her leg over without a handhold.

Her knees quivered, her legs buckled. "Whoopsy."

He reached out to steady her, and she grabbed the lifeline.

"You're shaking."

She gave a breathy laugh. "Guess I am."

He was off the bike, grasping her elbow.

She waved him off. "I'm fine."

"Last time you said that, you hit the ground two seconds later."

She narrowed her eyes. "I had the flu."

"Don't argue, woman."

She rolled her eyes but let him walk her to the door. By the time they reached the porch, her legs were steady, though his touch made her arm hum with electricity.

"Thanks. I'll be fine. Guess I'm not Harley chick material."

"That was never in question."

She deflated a little as she fished for her keys. A little excitement had her quaking in her shoes. But at least he'd come today — gotten her through that one awkward meal. Now she only had, say, about a thousand more to go.

"Thanks for the invite. It was nice to have a home-cooked meal." To his credit, he said nothing about the odd combination of fried chicken, beets, applesauce, and muffins.

"Sorry about Zoe. She's a little, uh, curious."

"That's one word for it." His smile softened the words.

"You don't talk much about yourself."

He shrugged.

"Why not?"

Those brown eyes locked onto hers. Something passed between them, something indefinable. "What's the point? Sharing leads to relationships, and relationships complicate things."

"What kinds of things?"

Indecision flickered in his eyes as if weighing whether to answer. "I'm just passing through, you know."

Clare saw something else flicker in his eyes. A longing? Just as quickly it was gone. Didn't he have anyone in his life? A place to rest when he got tired of running?

"It must get lonely."

"Sometimes." His deep voice cut right through her.

She couldn't imagine going from town to town. No family, no connections. Who did he talk to? Who did he confide in? No one, that she could see.

Dixie barked behind the door. Clare unlocked it and let her out. The dog accepted their greetings and dashed down the steps to sniff out the front yard.

For all Ethan's talk about attachments, he seemed in no hurry to leave. Clare sank onto the top step and gestured toward the spot beside her.

He lowered his weight and his thigh brushed hers. She shifted away.

"Tell me about your ex-boyfriend."

Clare frowned at him. He'd met Josh right here on her porch, but she hadn't introduced him as her ex.

"My turn to interrogate," he said. "Turnabout's fair play."

She tried for a flirtatious smile. "I suppose you're right. But how did you know he was my ex?"

"I'm asking the questions."

"Tyrant."

"How'd you meet?"

She grimaced. "Through Zoe's matchmaking business — I know, I know. Lame."

"Not lame at all. How long did you date?"

"Five months."

"You broke up recently?"

"How did you know?"

He gave her a warning look.

"All right. Yes, three weeks ago."

He studied her. "Yet you don't have feelings for him."

"How do you —" She clamped her lips shut. It was disconcerting the way he read things. He was uncannily perceptive, and she wasn't sure she liked it.

He lifted his brows, waiting.

"I guess it wasn't that serious."

"Who broke up?"

"You mean you don't know?"

"That would be him then."

She flipped her hair back. "A first for me, actually."

"Do tell."

She shrugged. "Nothing to tell, really; I just don't drag things out if the guy's not right for me. But like I said, it wasn't serious with Josh and me."

That last night at the Creamery flooded through her mind, Josh's words buzzing in her ears like a pesky fly. Her face heated at the recollection. Why had he dated her so long if he felt that way? That only made her feel worse.

"Didn't mean to embarrass you."

"I'm not embarrassed."

"You're blushing."

"Well, you're bringing up bad memories."

"You said you weren't serious."

"We weren't."

Ethan's brows pulled together, forming twin commas at the bridge of his nose. He stared at her until the heat wave in her face flowed through the rest of her.

"Did he hurt you?"

"Josh? Good grief, no. Maybe he isn't Mr. Knight in Shining Armor, but he's harmless enough."

"Then why the 'bad memories'?"

He just wasn't going to let it go.

"He called me boring, okay? He thought I was as exciting as tree bark, and being with me put him to sleep faster than a prescription sedative."

Clare winced. Why had she admitted that to a man she barely knew? Told him something she'd been too embarrassed to tell her mom and her sisters? She looked away, squirming.

He'd gotten awfully quiet. He probably thought she was boring too. Maybe everyone thought she was. Maybe she was so boring she'd wither away in her quiet house, single and alone, her only joy in life doting on her sisters' grandkids.

A stupid lump knotted in her throat. Daggonit. She was going to make a real idiot of herself. She started to get up.

He grabbed her arm, his touch burning through her skin. His eyes bored into hers, gentle, searching. She wanted to close her own, shutter her thoughts, but she couldn't look away — he had that effect on her. Instead she swallowed against the hard lump.

His lips tilted sideways. "You're not boring, Clare. Not even close."

He was just being nice. Just sucking up to his boss. Whatever, he sounded sincere, and the words still soothed her.

"Thanks."

His head tipped back, his eyes narrowing. "That's what the bike ride was all about."

Her cheeks burned. Did the man have to

see everything? "No, it wasn't. Not at all. Maybe a little. Okay, yes."

He smiled, his eyes roaming her face.

There was something warm and pleasant about the way he was looking at her. Like he was . . . charmed by her or something.

Her. Boring Clare.

"The guy's an idiot," he said. "Just be yourself — that's who God made you to be."

He had a point. Though so far it hadn't gotten her to happily-ever-after. Not even close. Besides, God had made her aunts too, and they were spinsters. How had they ever come to peace with that?

Please, God, I hope that's not your plan for me. I love my family, but I want one of my own. A loving husband, children, devotions around the kitchen table, all of it. Send the man you have for me. Someone godly, who'll love me for who I am and be here through thick and thin.

She thought of the way she'd felt when Ethan had touched her. The hum of electricity between them.

And a little spark wouldn't hurt either, God.

"Why haven't you opened a landscape design business?" His question startled her from her prayer.

"That was random. Isn't the interrogation over?"

"Were you at lunch?"

She sighed. *Zoe.* "I've worked at the Red Barn for eons. I'm happy enough there for now. Besides, what do I know about starting a business? Mr. Lewis handles all the paperwork, the finances, the taxes. The thought of it all is enough to give me a headache. And starting a business is expensive. Like I said . . . someday."

She'd have to take out a loan, put everything on the line, and what if she failed? Just the thought of such a crazy venture sent a thread of anxiety worming through her limbs.

"You should. You're really good. I've seen a lot of beautiful property in my travels, but your yard outshines them all." He was studying her again. She felt his gaze, but she didn't want to think about this anymore. She'd answered enough questions for one day.

He seemed to sense her need for escape and slowly got to his feet. "Well, I should probably be going."

Clare stood, and Dixie came running, nudging her hand until she petted the dog. "All right. See you tomorrow, then."

"Thanks again for the meal."

"You're welcome anytime," she blurted, then bit her lip. Ethan did something to her insides, made her feel a way Josh never had. It was something she yearned for, with someone.

But not Ethan.

He stared down at her with those soulful eyes, making her legs feel weak and wobbly all over again. "Be careful what you ask for."

Before she could respond, he was striding toward his bike. Clare watched him go, his long legs eating up the distance, his longish hair fluttering against his collar, and wondered if playing with fire was the antidote for boredom.

CHAPTER SEVEN

Ethan turned the mower into the shed, shut it off, and left the barn. It had been years since he'd had a yard to mow. Not since his dad had that place on Harper Avenue. He'd had no idea when he'd enlisted and left home how long it would be before he had a place to call home. Actually, he still didn't know.

He found Clare in the greenhouse, repotting a begonia. She had a smudge of dirt on her cheek that was too cute to mention.

"All done. What's next, boss?"

She blew her bangs from her face. "Ever repotted plants?"

"Nope."

"Grab that petunia." Her hands wrist-deep in a pot, she nodded toward the plant and gave him instructions. "Gloves are on the shelf over there."

He began transferring the flower to a larger pot. Clare worked at double his speed, her gloved hands sure and efficient.

She held the pot while he pulled out the flower, roots and all, and transferred it. "You're a natural."

He'd thought about Clare a lot since their chat on Sunday. When he settled into his sleeping bag and closed his eyes, it was her face he saw. Her cloudy blue eyes, her silly sideways smile. He wanted to punch that ex-boyfriend of hers, making her feel bad about herself. *Boring* was the last word that came to mind when he thought of Clare.

In fact, last night he'd found himself wondering if this attraction was worth pursuing. He'd been on his own so long, the thought made him nervous, but he'd asked God about it just the same.

"Okay, guess what?" She patted down the soil around the begonia. "It's my turn to interrogate . . . so brace yourself."

Ethan scowled. "We each had a turn — game over."

She lifted a brow. "Chicken?"

Women. Always wanting to talk. "Fine. Take your best shot. But just remember." He pointed a gloved finger. "Your turn's coming."

"I have nothing to hide." She turned that funny lopsided smile on him.

"We'll see about that."

"What's your favorite place, of all the towns you've visited?"

Amateur. "Don't have one. Every one's pretty much like the next."

"Where do you sleep?"

"Campgrounds mostly."

She looked at him. "Here? Now? It can still get down in the forties at night."

He shrugged. "I stay warm enough."

"Rumor is you're staying at the old Patterson place, wash up in the Green River, and rummage through neighborhood garbage cans after dark."

He laughed. "I'm staying at the campground, using their facilities, and I haven't gotten desperate enough to Dumpster dive. Yet. Maybe you can spread that around for me."

"I can try, but it's not outrageous enough to get far." She spared him a smile, then grabbed another begonia.

He held up the petunia. "This look right?"

"Perfect. Only ninety-nine to go." Her cheeks bunched as she smiled, the splotch of dirt spreading.

He pulled off his glove, swiped his thumb across her cheek.

She froze in place.

Her skin was soft as silk. "You have some dirt . . ." He swiped again, telling himself the first one didn't get it all.

Those startled gray-blue eyes pulled at him. The color of storm clouds. He wondered what was going on behind the storm.

She looked away. "Occupational hazard," she said, wiping at the spot.

He chided himself for touching her. What was he thinking? She was his boss. Regardless of any attraction he might feel — okay, *did* feel — he shouldn't act on it. Flirting was one thing, but ties . . . was he ready for that?

He hoped the touch had at least ended the interrogation. But as it turned out, she was only reloading.

"Who's Luke Fletcher?"

The name stopped his hands. Where had she heard it? Her gaze was on him like a touch.

"His name is on your jacket label," she said. "I saw it in the truck a couple weeks ago."

Ah. "He was a friend."

"Was?"

That memory returned with a freshness that denied the passage of years, another sucker punch. He'd been stationed in Baghdad, eating in the mess hall when he'd received word. The food had churned in his stomach, then had come up an hour later.

"He died in Iraq. Grenade."

"I'm sorry." Her voice was soft and delicate, a flower petal. "Did you serve together?"

He loosened the petunia. "Grew up together. Learned to fly together. Enlisted together."

"Learned to fly?"

"Small aircraft. Cessnas, Pipers, et cetera. My dad taught us."

She smiled at him. "No kidding. Do you miss it?"

"Every day. There's something about loosening yourself from the ties of earth that's a real stress reliever." Sometimes he'd looked down and wondered if this was God's everyday view.

"I'm not sure how flying miles above the ground could relieve stress."

"You'll just have to trust me. There's nothing quite like it."

She shared a smile with him. "You still wear your friend's jacket — that's nice."

"His mom gave it to me." They'd been like brothers. Wearing it made him feel like a piece of Fletch was still with him. When he wore it, he wasn't alone. Or maybe that's just what he told himself.

"Does being on the go make it easier?"

It was the closest anyone had come to

understanding him. "Little bit. This was something me and Fletch planned to do together after our tours ended."

"What do you mean?"

"Traveling the country. We decided we'd try it for a year, meeting people, talking to them about God when opportunity arose. Sort of a ministry, I guess you could say."

She stared at him for a long minute. "That's an awesome idea."

"When he didn't make it, I decided to do it myself. Met a lot of people, led a few to the Lord. It's been rewarding overall."

"It's been well over a year, though, hasn't it?"

He shrugged. "Guess I just never found a reason to stop."

Though truth be told, "on the go" was wearing thin. Finding jobs had gotten harder. And lunch on Sunday had made him remember what he was missing.

Family. Relationships. And yes, home-cooked meals.

A couple hours with her family had him longing for something he hadn't had in years. In some ways, had never had. He admired the closeness Clare's family shared. He hardly remembered his own mom, and it had just been him and Dad most of his life.

Someday, though, he wanted something just like that. And a little part of him wondered, as he worked side by side with Clare, if she could be a part of it.

Clare loosened the petunia from its pot. Ethan had sure shed a new light on the drifter thing. Ministry. It made her respect him in a whole new way. Despite the good he did, he must feel lonely, traveling from town to town, no roots, no home, no loved ones.

She felt bad for asking about Fletch. She'd seen the hurt in the depths of Ethan's brown eyes. Fletch's death had left its mark. A part of her had wanted to reach out and comfort him.

But she remembered the way electricity thrummed through her veins at his touch. The way she felt when he was nearby — all jittery — and a thread of worry spread through her, making her heart race.

It wouldn't do to get attached. He was leaving soon, on to his next mission field, and while she did want a man, yearned for love, she didn't want a broken heart. And she was sure that's exactly where a relationship with Ethan Foster would lead.

CHAPTER EIGHT

June marched by, and pruning took over most of Clare's day. The nursery was burgeoning with flowers and customers, but the extra help allowed her more time in her own garden, doing what she loved best.

Planning for the bicentennial celebration ramped up, and the town vibrated with excitement about the coming parade and festivities. The celebration was all the more anticipated because of the hard work and faith that had transformed Smitten from a dying logging community to a thriving tourist destination. Railroad or not, they had much to celebrate.

Ethan had made himself indispensable at the nursery. Clare wondered how she'd gotten along without him. He'd taken over the deliveries completely. She was beginning to dread his leaving. How would she manage without him?

The feud between Grandma and Aunt

Violet dragged on, but Ethan mediated like a pro. He had a quiet way of cutting through the tension — even if the women still weren't talking except to bicker, Aunt Violet always getting in the last word.

Ethan was also full of ideas. He had come up with ways to improve traffic flow and a more efficient way to schedule deliveries. They were good ideas, but Clare hadn't made the changes yet. Maybe later, when they weren't so busy.

One quiet afternoon while they pruned suckers from the roses, he admitted to Clare that one of Pastor Walden's sermons had gotten him thinking about some changes he might need to make. He didn't expound, but Clare felt honored that he'd opened up enough to share his heart.

When she saw him talking privately with the pastor after church the following Sunday, Clare whispered a prayer of gratitude. It bolstered her faith to see God working in his life.

It also did her heart good to see Ethan in the pew with Aunt Violet or with Michael — their military history was a strong bond. Others from the community had taken him under their wing too. He'd met many members through the nursery, and Clare saw him talking with them before church in the parking lot. For a man short on words, he'd sure made friends quickly.

He'd been joining her family for lunch on Sundays, and Clare told herself that the ribbon of pleasure she felt at each appearance was relief at not having to be the fifth wheel. She told herself that providing a home-cooked meal for a homeless man was the Christian thing to do.

But inside she knew better. Knew that the flutter in her stomach was more than poor digestion, the thudding of her heart more than a circulatory issue. She liked Ethan. He made her feel things no one else had.

That was the direction of her thoughts the first Friday night in July. Her Lean Cuisine eaten, she settled onto the sofa and flipped on the TV, the night ahead stretching into the distance, long and lonely, like the Smitten railroad tracks.

Dixie plopped at her feet and laid her head on Clare's lap, her eyes questioning.

"You'll keep me company, won't you, girl?"

Her sisters and mother were out with their true loves having fun, she was sure. Candlelit dinners, music on the square, or a carriage ride through town. She hadn't asked. Maybe Clare should just rejoin Zoe's dating service and get it over with.

A jewelry store commercial came on. A couple, the man on one knee with a ginormous diamond. Clare turned off the TV. She had to get out of here. Meet people. Have a little fun. She was only twenty-nine, for pity's sake. Too young to sit home on a Friday night.

Dixie spun in two circles when Clare grabbed the leash off the hook. She locked up, gripping the leash tight lest Dixie drag her all the way to Burlington.

The temperature was balmy, the air still. Perfect for a nighttime stroll through the village. Maybe they'd stop at Wind Chill Creamery.

"How about some ice cream, girl?"

Dixie looked at her, eyes bright, ears perked. Bethany always gave Dixie a doggie cone.

The town looked beautiful. White lights twinkled from storefronts and spiraled up lampposts. Annuals of every color and variety burst from window boxes. Music floated from the town square, Grandma and her aunts harmonizing with their stringed instruments in a way they no longer could with words.

Couples crowded the brick sidewalks, browsing the gallery window, spilling from Sweet Surrender, waiting hand in hand to cross the street on their way to dinner in their sundresses and linen suits.

Clare sighed. Smitten really was the worst place for a single girl.

Despite her desire to do otherwise, her thoughts returned to Ethan. They were doing that a lot lately. She was both dreading and anticipating his nearing departure. Dreading because she'd miss him. And not only for his role at the nursery. He'd become a friend. She enjoyed her time with him.

A little too much. He hadn't touched her since the day he'd swiped dirt from her cheek. Sometimes she found herself wondering what it would be like to be in his arms, to be kissed by him. If one simple touch had made her knees buckle, how wonderful would his kiss be? She shouldn't indulge in the fantasy, she knew that.

The one touch should've served as a warning. Notification that he'd somehow wormed his way into her heart, filled a spot she desperately wanted filled.

But not with him.

He's all wrong for me, God. He'd make me fall for him, only to leave me.

Who was she kidding? She was already falling for him. But the only thing worse than being thirty and alone was being thirty, alone, and heartbroken.

He was too big a risk. Why did she have to fall for a man who didn't know the meaning of the words *home* or *family*? A man bent on a mission that she really couldn't criticize, not if it was God's will for his life.

If she were smart, she'd stay as far away as she could until he left. Send him on errands, deliveries. Because even though he may have let the people of Smitten in, he'd leave it all behind, just as he had the other towns.

And then where would she be?

Dixie surged forward, pulled hard on the leash.

Clare pulled back, to no avail. The eighty-pound dog dragged her through the crowd, making her bump pedestrians. "Sorry! Excuse me! Dixie, *stop.*"

But the dog rushed on, pulling Clare until they were under the green canopy of Outdoor Adventures.

Ethan stopped and turned when Dixie nudged his hand with her nose. "Hey, girl." He rubbed her head behind her ears.

Clare was breathing hard. Even so, her stomach fluttered at the sight of him. Blue T-shirt, fitted jeans, overgrown dark hair falling in his eyes. Sigh.

"She chased you halfway through town." Just in case he thought *she* was the one chasing him down.

Pedestrians jostled by until they moved aside.

"What are you doing in town?"

"What brings you out tonight?"

They spoke simultaneously, then laughed.

"We're going for ice cream," she said. "Aren't we, Dixie?"

"That's where I was headed."

Reese exited her outfitters store, locked up, and greeted them. "Hey, Clare. Heard from a little birdie you have a big birthday in a few weeks."

"Shh, I'm in denial."

Ethan's crooked smile beckoned. "The big 3-0?"

"Her sisters are throwing a big birthday bash at Mountain Perks."

"A *small, intimate* gathering," Clare said.

Reese winked. "With fifty of her closest friends."

Clare groaned.

"You should come, Ethan," Reese said.

"Sounds like fun," he said, not taking his eyes off Clare.

"Sounds like my worst nightmare."

Reese laughed, then waved, dashing home to her hubby. Her happily-ever-after.

Clare and Ethan began walking again, Dixie wagging contentedly beside them.

"It's just a number, boss."

"A big number."

He nudged her shoulder. "Not so big."

They walked in companionable silence for a moment, Clare admiring the sights and sounds of the village.

"I was just listening to your grandma and aunts playing on the square. They're pretty good."

"Grandma used to play for the Boston Symphony. Hard to believe they can make such beautiful music together when they're in such discord. I just don't know what we're going to do. How can they go on like this? They don't know what tomorrow will bring. What if something happens to one of them? It would be so awful."

"It'll work out."

"I have sensed a softening in Aunt Violet lately. Ugh! I had no idea they were so stubborn."

He smiled, his eyes dark in the shadows. "All you can do is pray for them, you know that."

They left Dixie leashed to the bike stand, waiting for her cone. The bell tinkled as they entered the creamery.

After they ordered, they carried their treats from the crowded shop and found an empty parlor table on the patio overlooking the square. Dixie downed her cone in one gulp, then stared at them with pitiful brown eyes.

Clare glanced at Ethan. She wasn't sure how this had happened. One minute she was determined to avoid him, the next she was having ice cream with him at a table for two under twinkling white lights.

He held up a spoonful. "Bite?"

Clare wrinkled her nose at Ethan's ice cream boat. "No thanks." Razzmatazz topped with hot fudge, strawberries, rainbow sprinkles, and whipped cream. It looked nasty, but you had to admire a guy secure enough to order sprinkles.

She thought of Josh's disapproval of her flavor choice and took a defiant, swiping lick of her vanilla. Wind Chill really did have the yummiest vanilla.

"I noticed we're fairly light on deliveries on Monday," he said. "How about if we start moving things to change the flow of traffic like I was talking about? We could work into the night if we had to."

Something about the idea made Clare uneasy. His idea was good, but changing everything . . . "Why don't we wait on that? I'll probably do it at the end of season when things slow down."

"It'll be easier if I'm there to help."

453

And he wouldn't be there in the fall — her brain made note of the mention just in case her heart had missed it. "I hate to shake things up midseason, you know? The customers are accustomed to the layout."

Ethan scooped up another bite. "They might like the change."

Clare gave him a look. "Or they might not," she said firmly.

Ethan studied her until her face grew warm. Maybe he just wanted to be there to see the plan implemented, but it really wasn't a good time.

"Whatever you say, boss."

Clare licked her dripping cone. Dixie, giving up on table scraps, lay down on the brick patio and heaved a sigh.

The creamery's bell rang as a couple exited the shop. Josh Campbell, razzmatazz cone in hand, scoped out the patio tables. He had a date, a pretty brunette she didn't recognize.

Clare ducked, glancing at Ethan.

He had followed her eyes and gave a sympathetic smile.

She licked her cone. It wasn't that she wanted to trade places with the woman. The breakup had been for the best.

Ethan narrowed his eyes, watching her closely.

"What, do I have ice cream on my nose?"

That little half smile. Mercy, he had it perfected. He leaned in, weight on his elbows, until she could smell his musky cologne. His bangs fell over his forehead, kissing the corners of his eyes.

"We could pretend we're on a date, if that would make you feel better," he said.

Her heart rate ramped at the thought. If this were a real date, she might lean a little closer. He might kiss her right here, over his razzmatazz sundae.

"Why — why would we do that?"

"So he realizes what an idiot he is."

She wasn't going to lie — it felt nice to hear that.

His gaze, as tangible as a touch, swept over her face, stopping on her lips.

She swallowed. She should say something, but she couldn't think with him looking at her like that.

"Or we could go on a real date," he said softly.

"A real . . ." She cleared her throat. "A real date?"

His lips twitched. "You know, where the guy asks in advance, the girl says yes, he picks her up . . . a real date."

She knew the kind. Imagined them on a moonlit boat ride on Timber Lake. Just him and her and his sexy, crooked grin. When they reached the middle, they'd set their oars down and listen to the sounds of nature, then he'd lean close and kiss her.

Bad, Clare. Bad idea. Awful, stupid, reckless idea.

"We could, I don't know, rent one of those bikes for two and ride over to the lake, have a picnic or something."

Or something. Have a kiss or two, fall in love — and she could love him. That was the problem. She could see herself falling so deeply for him, and it would be good . . . for a while. Where Josh's breakup had only bothered her, Ethan's would break her.

"What's the point?" she asked.

"The point?"

"The point of going out — you're leaving soon, as you said."

He blinked. Looked confused, endearingly so. He probably hadn't thought that far ahead. Well, she had, and she didn't like what she saw coming.

"I could stick around awhile," he finally said.

Stick around long enough to fall for him. And then what? Didn't sound like a safe plan to her. It sounded like the fast track to heartache. He'd move on to the next adventure, and she'd be left here to pick up the pieces. No thanks.

"I like you, Ethan, I do." She hesitated, weighing her words. "Maybe too much. But I think it's best if we keep things as they are — simple."

His eyes seemed to see right into her.

Well, look all you want, Ethan. I'm right about this. Save us both a bunch of heartache.

Finally he looked away. He nodded toward her dripping cone. "Might wanna lick that."

She caught the drips on her tongue, but suddenly the vanilla cone had lost all its appeal.

CHAPTER NINE

Ethan was halfway to the campground when he realized he'd left his jacket in the work truck. He thumped his palm on the handlebar grip. It wasn't cold yet, but it was supposed to get down into the forties tonight. A fire would warm his bones until bedtime, but it would be a long, cold night without his jacket.

He swung his bike around in the middle of the deserted country lane and headed back toward town. Night had fallen, and the nursery had long since closed.

After work he'd treated himself to a meal at the Country Cupboard Café. Of course, it wasn't like the homemade meals he'd had with the Thomas family . . .

He'd run into Miss Violet at the café, and they'd shared a table and talked. The woman was taking some steps in the right direction. Clare had been right about her softening toward her sister.

Clare. Things had been awkward since he'd asked her out two weeks ago. She'd thrown up a great big wall and wasn't letting him over. He was a risk, he got that.

But it was a risk for him too. This was the first time in years he'd met someone he was willing to take a chance on. Loving was always a risk — and Clare was someone he could love. He was halfway there already. His feelings had grown, date or no. He fell for her a little more every day, watching her patiently assist the customers, lovingly tend her plants, calmly mediate between her grandma and aunt.

But his job here was nearly over. He'd stay for Clare's birthday, the bicentennial, but he couldn't see himself staying much beyond. The past two weeks had been difficult enough.

Besides, he didn't know how long it would take to find work. He'd learned to stretch his money as far as he could. *Where to next, God? Providence? Hartford? Boston?*

The pause brought no answer, no quiet whisper to his heart or strong feeling about his next move. None of the towns even sounded intriguing. In fact, packing up, scoping out another new town, begging for work . . . none of that sounded appealing either.

What was wrong with him? He was usually eager to hit the road after a couple months in one place. Ready to shake the dust of the town from his feet, ready to meet new people, see where God was working and join him there.

Was it Smitten, or was it Clare? Maybe it was both. Maybe he was smitten *with* Clare. And maybe the fact that he didn't want to leave meant it was past time he did.

Is that it, God? Am I through in Smitten? I don't feel like I did anything worthwhile here.

But in his heart, he knew what his reluctance to leave meant. He missed having a place to call home. People to call friends. He thought of Aunt Violet, Michael, Griffen Parker. Good people, all of them. People he wouldn't mind being neighbors with.

But then there was Clare. He could always stay awhile, see if she'd come around. He'd been wrestling with his nomad lifestyle, had even spoken to Pastor Walden about it. Maybe God was telling him it was time. Maybe if he stayed, he could make Clare see that he was more than a drifter. That he was someone worth taking a chance on.

He turned into the gravel lane, passing the old Red Barn sign, then accelerated up the hill through the woods. When he reached the lot, he spotted Clare's truck. He'd never known her to stay this late. Maybe she'd decided to start moving things around.

Not likely.

Maybe someone had picked her up. Maybe her car hadn't started. Or maybe something had happened. She could've fallen or hit her head. He was being paranoid, but he was going to check just the same. Better safe than sorry.

He retrieved his jacket from the truck, tossed it across his bike, and followed the cobbled path. The air smelled like a blend of pine sap, lilacs, and mulch. A fragrance he'd come to associate with this place. He drew in a lungful as he neared the barn. The windows showed a darkened interior.

The shed door was closed, the lock fastened. No sign of life in the gardens either.

Farther down the path, past the towering pines, the greenhouse glowed dimly, the windows fogged. He followed the walkway, his heart kicking up into his throat. Clare babied the tropicals. They were expensive and fetched a good price at the local flower shop. But why would she be checking on them this late?

He entered the steamy greenhouse, the scent of sweet flowers and loamy earth assaulting him. The air, thick with humidity, was warmer.

He looked down the narrow aisle. "Clare?"

He advanced down the row. Flowering plants of all kinds burgeoned from upper and lower shelves, blocking his vision. Tropicals, orchids, all kinds of plants that would die under his care. Under Clare's touch, the exotic petals bloomed in vibrant colors, and lush foliage overflowed from plastic green pots.

"Clare?"

Why didn't she answer? He reached the end of the row and turned down the next. He spotted her halfway down, swaying, her hips sashaying back and forth. Wires from her earbuds led down to one of her overall pockets. In between her bebopping, she checked the soil of a flowering plant, then belted out the chorus of some country tune.

He'd never heard the song, but he knew off-key when he heard it. His lips twitched.

"Clare," he called as he advanced, not wanting to startle her. She must have that thing up loud. She stopped singing long enough to examine a ruffled yellow flower, frowning at the petal.

Too much water. Clare removed the planter tray from the hibiscus pot and turned to dump it.

A man stood in her path.

She screeched. The tray went flying, the water with it.

She pulled her earbuds out and pressed her hand to her chest, her heart thudding violently against her palm.

She closed her eyes. "Ethan. Good grief, you scared me silly."

"Sorry." His hands squeezed her upper arms. "I'm sorry. I tried to get your attention, but —" He gestured toward the wires dangling from her pocket.

Her heart slowed as the past several seconds rewound to include her little talent show. Great.

She shrugged out of his grip. "What are you doing here?" So what if she sounded perturbed.

He had the grace to look chagrined. "Left something here, saw your truck." He started to say something else, then closed his mouth.

"So you thought you'd sneak up on me and scare the tar out of me for fun?" A bit of humor had crept into her voice.

He shrugged, his eyes puppy-dog wide. "I was bored."

Despite herself, she smiled. "Next time find your own entertainment."

"I don't know. That was pretty entertaining."

She shot him a look. A familiar tune swelled from her earbuds, a gentle guitar riff, the warm sound of a fiddle. "Oh, you have to hear this."

She put the bud up to Ethan's ear. "It's Sawyer Smitten's latest hit — he's a hometown boy." The song was popular nationwide, but in Smitten it had become their love anthem, playing in the coffee shop, in the bookstore. Even her grandma and aunts played it on the square.

"Have you heard it?"

He shook his head, listening, as Sawyer began singing, his voice soft and mellow.

I was a man without a place
To call my own
Before you came
You were everything I longed for
Everything I need,
You gave

As the fiddle swelled, Ethan's eyes locked with hers, flashed with something. She got the message loud and clear. He could've written the words himself.

Her arm suddenly weighted, she lowered the earbud before Sawyer could start crooning about how smitten he was. Her breath had stopped, stuffed in her lungs despite the oxygen-rich environment.

Ethan took a step closer.

She couldn't look away. Her heart rustled, a dry leaf trapped against the lonely corners of her chest. His eyes said so much, and she was suddenly hungry to hear it all. They slid down to her lips an instant before he touched her face. Just a whisper of a touch.

The nerves sparked to life beneath his thumb, sending fire through her limbs. He threaded his fingers through her hair, wakening every cell. A wanting kindled inside, so strong and undeniable she was helpless against its power.

"Clare," he whispered just before his lips took hers.

His touch was soft and warm, his lips lingering over hers in a way that made her impatient. Her hands trailed up his chest, around his neck, found home in the softness of his hair.

He deepened the kiss, and her knees buckled. His arm came around her, pulling her closer, just in time. She sank into his weight.

This was it. The way kisses were supposed to feel. Have mercy. How had she lived without it so long?

Her hands found the scruff of his jaw and delighted in the roughness against her palm.

She inhaled him, piney, musky, all man.

Ethan. He'd managed to reach into her deepest places, warm her through. She wanted to stay right here in his arms. Her body had found its home.

Home.

Something about the word tugged at her. Tried to steal her from the rapture that had swept her away. She resisted the pull. Surrendered to Ethan's touch, to the blissful current coursing through her veins, to the heady emotions swelling inside.

Home.

That word again, a pesky fly. She tried to shoo it away, but it returned, bringing other words.

Missionary. Drifter. Tent.

Risky.

The reason she'd turned him down. Why she'd put distance between them. And now she was kissing him — feeling things for him.

She pushed at his chest and a whimper escaped her lips.

His eyes were dark with wanting, shadowed with something vulnerable that tore through her. Those feelings stirring inside her were returned. She felt heady with the knowledge.

Space. She needed space. She stepped away.

He reached toward her. "Clare . . ."

"No, don't."

His hand hung there a minute, then fell to his side.

She tried to formulate words. Nothing coherent emerged. She couldn't think when he was looking at her like that.

"Let's give this a shot," he said.

Desire to do just that coursed through her, so strong, the pull almost sucked her under. Despite the need, maybe because of it, she shook her head.

"I care for you. I think you care for me too."

Was it the passionate kiss that gave it away? She choked back a crazed bubble of laughter. He was going to think she was insane.

His brows drew tight. "I'm not just a drifter, Clare. There's more to me than that."

"I know that."

"Then give us a chance."

Chance. The perfect word for it. "I can't. I'm sorry, I just . . . it's not going to work." Her throat ached at the words, at the look in his eyes. She hated that she was hurting him. Wanted to reach out and smooth the frown between his eyes.

She balled her hands into fists, crossed her arms before she started something she couldn't finish.

The look in his eyes changed, the hurt morphing into something else. Something shifted. A shadow flickered in his jaw, his lips thinned. He straightened, pocketed his hands. The cord of tension running between them seemed to tighten unbearably.

"For someone who wants love," he said softly, "you sure know how to run from it."

She frowned. "I don't." That was ridiculous. He'd known her a grand total of two months. Sixty days. "I do want love."

"You might have to leave your comfort zone to get it, honey."

The words chafed. "You don't know what you're talking about."

"How many men have you broken up with, Clare?"

She sucked in a breath, her own feelings shifting. "That's not fair. They weren't right for me. And Josh broke up with *me*, remember?"

"Because he thought you were boring? You're not boring, Clare. You're just scared."

No. That wasn't true. He was wrong. She wanted to be loved, yearned for it, even. Clare shook her head.

"Scared of following your dreams, scared of seeing where this might go, scared of doing anything that might shake your world up a little. Shoot, you can't even make a simple change around here without —"

"I said I'd do it later."

"Later, when? You won't do it because you're afraid of change."

She didn't want to talk about this anymore. "The kiss was a mistake." Maybe hiring him had been too.

"You like the safe little world you've created for yourself. Well, keep it up and you're going to find tomorrow and every day after that a carbon copy of today." He paused. "But at least you'll be comfortable."

The words traveled to her core and scored a bull's-eye. Her eyes burned. That was so unfair. She'd thought the distance she'd put between them had protected her heart, but it hadn't. There was only one way to do that.

"You need to leave, Ethan. Just go away, and while you're at it, don't come back."

He flinched. The look in his eyes softened a moment. Long enough to make her regret her words. Too short to take them back.

"Whatever you say, boss." He turned to go.

She heard his footfalls on the pavers. Heard the squeak of the door opening, the

469

clicking as it closed. Then she heard the quiet, lonely sound of her heart breaking in two.

CHAPTER TEN

Clare forced down her last bite of birthday cake and settled back on the patio chair. The party had flowed outside the coffee shop, her friends and family enjoying the mild July night. Music flowed from the speakers, laughter from nearby tables. Her favorite flowers, Coral Fay peonies, were clustered in iridescent vases at the center of each table, sweetening the night air.

The party was finally winding down. Across the table William wiped a crumb from Zoe's lip, then bent down for a playful nip. She never would've put those two together in a million years, but look at them. So in love.

Next to them, Ryan curled his arm around Tess's shoulders and whispered something in her ear that solicited a secret little smile. At least something good had come from the dog tag mystery. Their search for the truth had led Tess to Ryan's attic and straight into his arms, and Clare couldn't deny the couple was meant to be.

Across the room Anna and Michael served the last slices of cake. It was nice seeing her mom learn to trust again with someone patient enough to earn it. She couldn't think of anyone who deserved a happily-ever-after more than her mom.

Clare looked away, their shared smiles rewarding and painful at the same time. Griffen and Reese huddled at the next table, Natalie and Carson served coffee together, Shelby and Nick Majors laughed at something his daughter, Willow, said.

Was she the only one alone? No, she thought, spying Grandma cleaning up the wrapping paper over in the corner. Not the only one. Clare watched her, working diligently, holding her back as she bent over to retrieve a bow. She wondered how hard it had been for Grandma since Grandpa had passed, how lonely. Surely being single would feel even lonelier after being married so many years. Rose had found love twice and had lost it both times.

Her eyes continued to sweep the room and found Aunt Petunia chatting with little Sophia. Aunt Violet had left town on some kind of bicentennial business. She'd hoped to return in time for the party but had called to say she'd been delayed. Between Aunt Violet's and Ethan's departures, the nursery had been a madhouse the past three days. Clare had dropped into bed exhausted each night, glad for the oblivion of sleep.

Ethan. She sucked in a quiet breath. She'd been trying so hard not to think of him. Especially today. It only made her feel hollow inside. She'd told him to leave, and he had. Why wouldn't he, when she'd given him no reason to stay?

The backs of her eyes burned.

She stood quickly, making Zoe jump.

Clare grabbed her mug. "I'm going inside for a refill."

"I'll get it," Tess said, already halfway out of her chair.

"That's okay. I need to use the ladies' room anyway."

The inside of Mountain Perks was blessedly quiet. Only the trickle of music and chatter coming through the walls broke the silence. She just needed a few minutes alone, then she'd go back outside and face her thirtieth birthday again.

Knowing Nat wouldn't mind, she entered her cousin's office and tugged on the lamp chain. She sank into the plush chair that faced an antique desk. Nat's desk sported neat piles of paper, a top-of-the-line computer, and a photo of her with Carson and Mia on their wedding day.

Her thoughts returned to Ethan. Despite her efforts to forget him, he was there all day, his words eating at her while she pruned, while she shoveled, while she loaded. At first she'd refuted them. He was wrong, hadn't known her long enough to see so deeply inside her. Sure, they'd spent hours together, but if it were true, she'd know it. Her sisters would know it, and goodness knew, if they knew it they would've told her, especially Zoe. No, Ethan didn't have a clue. He'd been hurt and had lashed out, just as she had when she'd told him to leave.

That reasoning had worked for the first day and even the second. But the third day, as she'd been going through her daily routine exactly the same as she had every day for as long as she could remember, a finger of doubt had tapped her softly on the shoulder.

Is it true, God? Am I really afraid of change?

Was she so snug in her comfort zone that she ran from love, something she desperately wanted? She couldn't deny that she'd seen Ethan as a risk. Was that the same thing? Or was that just being smart?

A light knock sounded on the door, and

her mother entered. She looked beautiful in a shimmery silver top. The color made her gray eyes pop.

"Everything okay, honey?" Anna asked.

Clare smiled. "Just needed a few minutes."

Her mom stepped inside and perched on the edge of the desk. "There're a ton of people out there."

"Nat was nice to let us have the place for the night. Hope we didn't scare away all her business."

"She was happy to do it. She loves you. We all do."

Anna had seen right through the smiles. "I know that, Mom."

She tucked her sideswept bangs behind her ears and studied Clare. "You miss him."

Clare didn't want to go there. "Well. The nursery's been busy, and with Aunt Violet gone too, it's been a little crazy."

Anna's smile didn't reach her eyes. "That's not what I mean."

Clare knew exactly what her mother meant. And doggonit, she was right. Clare didn't like it, but she wasn't going to lie to herself. "A little bit."

"I think maybe a lot. I can't believe he just left like that, without notice or good-byes or anything. I didn't think he was that kind of person."

So Clare hadn't exactly doled out the details to her family. She hadn't seen them since Sunday, and she'd done nothing but work and sleep. And fret.

Clare cleared her throat. "I, uh, kind of told him to go."

Anna's brows rose. "Oh."

The confession made those last moments with Ethan replay in Clare's mind. The kiss, the things he'd said, the way he'd flinched when she'd told him to leave. That one was the killer.

"Mom . . . do you think I'm afraid of change?"

"Afraid of —" Her mother tilted her head, squinted at Clare. Slowly her face softened in a sympathetic smile. "Well, honey . . . I think you're the only one who can answer that."

"I do like my routines."

"True."

He'd also said she was scared of following her dreams. It was true her real passion was designing gardens, not growing them. But she'd always told herself she'd start her own business someday. Did she mean it . . . or was that just something she told herself?

"Do you think I'm boring?"

Anna's delicate brows lowered. "Did he say that?"

"No. Josh Campbell did."

Her mother's pink lips pressed together. "I've never heard anything so ridiculous. You have a whole town that loves you, Clare. If he's too blind to see how special you are, it's his loss."

Clare smiled at the mother tiger response. "Thanks, Mom."

"About Ethan, honey . . . why don't you call him? Straighten out your differences? There was something special about him."

She'd never agreed with anything so strongly. "That's the thing, Mom. He doesn't have a cell phone. I don't know where he went, wouldn't even know where to look."

It was all so final. She'd gotten up the nerve to drive by the campground last night. Lloyd Draper said he'd left early Tuesday morning, the day after their kiss, and hadn't said where he was headed. Desperate, Clare had even gotten on the computer to see if he had a Facebook or Twitter account.

"I'm sorry to hear that. I thought he'd be good for you."

"He's basically homeless, Mom."

"Technically, yes, but for a good cause, wouldn't you say? He's got a lot of love to give, and the way he looked at you . . . well, I can certainly see when someone's smitten with my daughter. A mom can dream, can't she?"

So could her daughter. In fact, that's all she'd done. Dream about designing, dream about love. Dreams got you nowhere without a plan of action. Unfortunately, with no way to reach Ethan, that particular dream was a dead-end street.

Grandma Rose poked her head into the office. "I'm heading home, girls."

Clare stood and embraced her. "Thanks for your help, Grandma."

She framed Clare's face. "Oh, to be thirty again — so young!" She kissed Clare on the cheek. "Happy birthday, sweetie." Her blue eyes looked tired, the sparkle missing.

"Thanks, Grandma."

"I'll walk you out, Mom," Anna said. She turned to Clare at the door. "You coming?"

"In a minute. I'm going to get a refill."

After they left, Clare helped herself to half a cup. The look in her grandma's eyes haunted her. Rose was a good woman, had such a servant's heart. She deserved to love and be loved, and for the first time since they'd discovered David was still alive, Clare wished he'd agreed to return to Smitten.

Maybe the reunion wouldn't be magical, maybe whatever they'd had all those years ago would have evaporated. But maybe not.

478

Maybe they would find love again, and Grandma could spend the rest of her years being cherished like she deserved.

True, it might cause more friction between her and Aunt Violet, but wasn't the potential payoff worth the risk? She didn't use to think so.

It didn't really matter, though. David had already refused to come back.

Clare sipped her coffee, watching through the window as Grandma eased into the driver's side, her silvery hair glowing under the lamplight. But what if they hadn't tried hard enough? What if David just needed a little more persuasion? What if . . .

Clare's eyes swept the party stragglers and settled on Zoe. Making up her mind, she dumped the remainder of her coffee and made a beeline for her sister.

Half an hour later she was entering her house, a scrap of napkin wadded in her hand. She checked her watch. It wasn't too late, she didn't think.

She picked up the phone, surprised at the way her hand shook. Looking at the scrawled number, she punched it in and waited as it rang once.

Twice. Three times.

Maybe it was too late. How would she persuade a tired and cranky old man to

479

drive seven hundred miles to see a woman he'd known sixty years ago?

"Hello?" It was a woman's voice.

"May I speak with David, please?"

"I'm sorry, he's not in. May I take a message?"

"Um . . . I'm calling from Vermont. My grandmother is a friend of his." Well. They were a long time ago.

"Oh, right. He's, ah, out of town right now. I'm not sure when he'll be back."

"Oh. I see. Well, I'll try another day. Thanks anyway."

They said good-bye and Clare set the receiver down, the rush of adrenaline draining, leaving her weak and shaky. It wasn't a no. He was just gone — for an indefinite amount of time. Well, she wouldn't give up. She'd call back until she reached him. One way or another, she had to know she'd done all she could for Grandma.

CHAPTER ELEVEN

"Here they come," Clare said.

The parade rounded the bend and headed toward the train depot. A celebratory song floated from the instruments of the Smitten High School band, the engine of the parade. Behind them, flags spun in synchronized rhythm, their twirlers proudly high-stepping.

The whole family, except Aunt Violet, who was readying for her speech, clustered closer to the curb for a better view.

Howard and Carson Smitten, descendants of the town's founders, carried the first banner. HAPPY 200TH BIRTHDAY, SMITTEN! it read in large block letters. The crowd cheered as they passed.

"Look at the loggers," Mom said. Men from the community had dressed in vintage clothing, axes resting on their shoulders. Behind them, a team of horses pulled a wagon full of logs.

Several floats followed, each by a different

community group, representing significant events in Smitten's history. The fire of 1872 when the chapel burnt down and the town came together to rebuild. The railroad coming through Smitten in 1935. The opening of Sugarcreek Ski Resort in 1971.

Clare was impressed. She'd known Aunt Violet and the celebration committee had worked long and hard, but she'd never seen a parade that told a story like this one, taking the viewers from the first days of the fledgling community to the most recent.

"Look," Grandma said awhile later. "There's Mia!" Nat's little girl led her Sunday school class, waving to the crowd. They all wore lavender wreaths, symbolizing the faith that had helped transform the town so recently.

Another float, decorated in red and white with hundreds of flowers, served as the parade caboose. A bride and groom, played by Julia and Zac, waved from beneath an ivy-covered arch. The float's banner read SMITTEN: THE ROMANCE CAPITAL OF THE WORLD!

A thunderous applause went up as the final float passed. Smitten had come such a long way in two hundred years. Clare was moved, reminded how proud she was of the heritage they all shared.

"Wow, that was wonderful!" Mom said.

"They outdid themselves," Michael said.

Tess took Ryan's arm. "Let's head over to the depot."

They milled in with the crowd heading toward the depot's natural stage where Aunt Violet would say a few words. Clare whispered a prayer for her aunt. She'd been a nervous wreck this morning over the speech.

The crowd gathered on the depot lawn, drawing close to the redbrick building.

"I wonder why they're doing this at the depot," Grandma said. "The square has a bigger lawn."

"Guess they figured we may as well use it for something," Zoe said, "after we spent all that time sprucing it up."

"It's kind of sad — a reminder of what could've been," Aunt Petunia said.

"The railroad would've helped," Grandma said, "but we'll survive. The parade was the perfect reminder of all the difficulties we've come through."

The depot looked beautiful with its new canopies, freshly painted green doors, and restored trusses. Clare took a minute to admire the landscaping she'd worked so hard on. Peonies and pansies dotted the beds with color. A cobbled walkway meandered through the perennials, merging with ivy as old as the building itself, which crept up the brick walls.

They pushed close to the stage, waiting for the others who'd be walking in from the start of the parade route. Her sisters began talking among themselves, but Clare found herself retreating inside, something she'd done a lot lately.

She found herself thinking of Ethan — something else she'd done a lot lately. She wished he'd been here to see the parade. She would've enjoyed sharing their rich heritage with him. She knew he would've appreciated the deep community roots, having none of his own.

God, be with Ethan wherever he is. Keep him safe on that crazy bike of his, use him for your glory, and . . .

Clare's thoughts tangled like a wad of yarn. *I don't know what else to say, Lord. I miss him. Let him know somehow I'm sorry.*

He'd offered her himself, and she'd not only rejected him, she'd sent him away. All because she hadn't liked hearing the truth. Her gut churned with regret.

Thank you, Lord, for never turning me away. For never getting scared, for never lashing out when I hurt you, for always being there with arms wide open, ready to take me back. Help me to love better next time. Fearlessly.

Love. Was that what she'd felt for Ethan? Why his kiss had frightened her so, why his absence made her feel hollow inside? She was beginning to think so. Beginning to see that sometimes taking no risk was the biggest risk of all.

She'd lost the only man she'd ever loved. It was too late to change things with Ethan. She'd resigned herself to that. But she'd made other changes in the week since her birthday. She'd changed things around at the nursery as Ethan had suggested, recruiting her family to help after closing. The new flow plan was an improvement, and the customers had complimented her on it.

She was even making plans toward starting her own garden design business. She was still afraid — that hadn't changed. But she was moving forward anyway, asking God to help her be brave, trusting him to help her.

She'd looked into purchasing the old Victorian on the edge of town near Tess's bookstore. The downstairs would make a perfect office space and the upstairs a nice living quarters. The yard, now just a boring patch of lawn, offered a clean slate to showcase her God-given talent.

Lead me, Lord. I don't want to hold back out

of fear, but I don't want to jump ahead of you either.

"May I have your attention?" William Singer, their city manager, spoke into the mike, and the crowd slowly hushed.

"Doesn't he look handsome?" Zoe said. "I love him in blue."

Aunt Violet and her committee stood behind him against the brick wall. Her aunt looked nice in a lime-green blouse and white capris. Clare could do without the bright red lipstick, but she wouldn't be Aunt Violet without her clashing lip color.

"Thank you all for coming out on what has turned out to be a glorious day," William said. "The Celebration Committee has worked hard to bring Smitten's unique heritage to life, and God has given us the perfect day in which to enjoy it. Let's show them our gratitude."

A boisterous round of applause followed. Behind her, Zoe let out one of her earsplitting whistles.

"Now, I know you're all eager to fill up on tasty treats and spend your quarters on the dunk tank . . ." He shot Pastor Walden a grin, and Pastor, wearing Hawaiian trunks and a T-shirt, pretended to bite his stubby nails.

The crowd chuckled.

"But, first, an important word from your Bicentennial Committee Chairperson. Please welcome Violet Garner."

The crowd applauded, giving Aunt Violet her due. Even Grandma, standing beside Clare, clapped enthusiastically.

Aunt Violet shuffled her papers on the podium as the crowd hushed. Her hands shook as she lifted her reading glasses from the chain on her neck, perching them on her nose.

"Good afternoon, friends." She cleared the tremble from her voice and continued, "We gather today on this momentous occasion to celebrate this town's great and long heritage. Whether you're a native of our community or are visiting for the first time, we invite you to celebrate our special town, born two hundred years ago, withstanding difficult times, and thriving today as a beacon of hope and love.

"The survival of Smitten has taken the effort of many people over many years. Common folk, like you and me, working together to provide a safe and peaceful place to raise families and a productive place to learn and grow."

Aunt Violet paused, finding her family in the crowd before returning to her notes. "One such man was born right here in

Smitten almost seventy-nine years ago. A man of honor, he went off to fight for our country, making all of us proud, the way so many of our young people have."

Clare glanced at Grandma, whose brows puckered in a frown. Where was Aunt Violet going with this?

"Unlike our other fine Smitten veterans, this young man didn't return from the battlefield. The community was informed he'd become, like so many others, a casualty of war.

"A mistake had been made, though. A mistake with repercussions that would ripple across the generations. Our veteran hadn't died at all but had been imprisoned until two years after the war's end. When he returned, it was only to find his family moved and his first love married to another.

"Distraught and disillusioned, our young man of Smitten went off to find his own way in the world. He took a menial job with Central Vermont Railway, worked hard, taking night courses, and after many years, against all odds, reached the level of corporate leadership.

"Meanwhile, the people of Smitten went on believing that the young man had died. Years went by . . . and then the veteran's dog tags were mysteriously found in an attic. The mystery stirred up a tale of betrayal and deceit.

"But it also stirred up the truth." Violet looked up from her notes. "And as you are about to see, sometimes the truth changes everything.

"Please welcome to the stage an honorable Smitten veteran, and the retired president of RailAmerica, David Hutchins."

CHAPTER TWELVE

Grandma Rose palmed her chest and drew in a deep breath.

The crowd applauded as David Hutchins appeared, rising up from the side stairs, tall and slender in a crisp gray suit. He had white hair and a sure gait. He crossed the stage to the podium.

Grandma's face had gone pale. Clare put an arm around her trim waist, as did Anna from her other side.

"You okay, Grandma?"

"Davy. Oh, Davy," Grandma whispered as the crowd hushed.

His gray eyes pierced the crowd. "Thank you. It's so good to be back home among friends. Smitten is the kind of place that always lives inside you no matter how far away you go.

"I don't have any notes or a fine speech to deliver, but I do have good news for this special town, these special people. Violet

Garner has been in contact with me over the past several weeks. She went to great lengths to persuade me to return, and when I heard the full set of circumstances, I knew I had to come home.

"The reason for my return is twofold, but it's the second reason that involves all of you. I've been in contact with the fine people at RailAmerica. I've told them about a charming village in the shadow of Sugar-creek Mountain, a place where community and tourism walk hand in hand, a place where lovers reunite. A place more people need to know about. I encouraged them to revisit the idea of a partnership with this special town."

He stopped, smoothing his red tie.

"And it's with great pleasure that I announce a new contract with RailAmerica and the town of Smitten. The deal has been struck and the papers have been signed. Welcome back to the Central Vermont rail system, Smitten."

A stunned silence followed, then a loud cheer rose and whistles pierced the air, the noise building into a thunderous applause.

"Oh my goodness!" Anna said.

Tess turned to them, hugging Grandma. "Can you believe it? Aunt Violet did all this?"

"I suppose she did," Grandma said, still staring trance-like at David.

"It's about time," Zoe said.

Once the hubbub died down, William wrapped up with some final words and the crowd began dispersing. The atmosphere had gone from nostalgic to jubilant in the space of five minutes.

Clare looked toward the stage where David mingled with Violet and the committee. "Come on, Grandma, let's go see him."

"Oh dear." Grandma couldn't seem to take her eyes off him, but her feet seemed rooted to the ground.

"What's wrong, Mom?" Anna asked.

"I'm just — I don't know — so *old.* I was eighteen years old the last time he saw me, and look at him — he's so handsome."

"Grandma, you look beautiful!" Tess said, and the others nodded.

"I can't wait until he sees you," Clare said.

Grandma pursed her lips. "I hope he's terribly near-sighted."

"Oh, stop it." Zoe took her arm and led her toward the side of the stage. "He's here, isn't he? How romantic is that?"

They reached the steps as the committee was descending.

When David reached the bottom, his eyes were only for Grandma. "Rose," he whispered. "I'd know those beautiful blue eyes anywhere."

Grandma's eyes filled with tears. "Davy."

The girls retreated a few steps, pulling Violet with them, casting glances back at the reunion.

"I can't believe you're here," Grandma said.

"I can't believe you're as beautiful as ever."

Grandma gave a watery laugh. "Oh, you rascal . . . you always did know how to charm the ladies."

David reached out for Grandma's hand. "I never forgot you, Rose."

"So much has happened . . ."

"We have plenty of time to catch up." He shook his head. "No one could replace you in my heart. I've missed you so much."

Clare turned away from the private moment, her heart aching at the devotion in David's eyes.

Anna dabbed her eyes. "Oh, it's so beautiful."

"How'd you pull that off, Aunt Violet?" Zoe asked. "The railway, talking him into returning . . ."

Violet blinked back tears, her mascara already smudging. "The railway deal's been in the works for weeks, but we didn't know for sure it would go through, so I didn't want to say anything."

Clare glanced back at Grandma and David. "And that . . . how did you manage that?"

"That took some doing." Aunt Violet dabbed at her eyes with a tissue Anna produced. "He was convinced his return would only stir up more trouble between Rose and me. That's where I went last week — to convince him to come home."

"Aunt Vi!" Anna said. "You went all the way to North Carolina alone?"

"Oh no, dear." She looked at Clare sheepishly. "Ethan gave me a ride."

"Ethan?" Clare asked, her heart going into overdrive. That's where he'd gone?

"Not on his bike!" Zoe said.

Aunt Violet laughed. "I'm not that crazy. He left that in my garage and drove my Buick."

Clare's thoughts skidded to a stop. If he'd left his bike in Aunt Violet's garage, he had to come back for it. She grabbed her aunt's arm. "Where is he? Is he still here?"

"I'm not sure, dear. I was so worked up over that speech —"

She had to try to find him. "I have to go." She took off across the lawn.

"Good luck, sweetie!" her mom called.

Clare dodged the people who milled around chatting. She had to get to her car, parked way over on Maple. She headed west.

Or would it be quicker to go straight to Aunt Violet's? The roads were blocked for the festivities. Yes, quicker to go straight there. She changed her course, thinking it through, already huffing.

Aunt Violet had returned last night. Ethan would've dropped her at her house and taken his bike then. Her heart dropped and her pace slowed. She passed through another cluster of people on the lawn. Why would he have stayed? He was probably halfway to Virginia by now. Or Ohio or Maryland.

Clare slowed to a stop, realization sinking in. She was no better off than she'd been five minutes ago when she'd thought he was gone for good.

He was gone. Again. This time the realization made her eyes sting, made tears well up, blurring her vision. She caught her breath, that familiar empty feeling swelling inside. She'd lost her chance, not once but twice. He'd been so close. If only she'd known.

She swallowed against the lump in her throat. If she was no worse off than she'd been five minutes ago, then why did it feel like the bottom had just fallen out of her world?

Her vision cleared as she blinked back the tears, and a man's form came into focus. A familiar form, rising from a park bench, his eyes on her. Hope sucked the breath from her lungs.

Ethan.

Her lips parted. Her feet moved toward him of their own volition. He looked so good. He wore a black T-shirt, jeans, and a hesitant expression that tugged at her heart. No wonder he was uncertain. She'd not only fired him, she'd sent him away. She'd thought she'd never see him again. Never see those deep brown eyes, that overgrown hair, that scruffy jaw.

He met her halfway, stopping an arm's length away.

"You're still here," she said. "I was afraid . . ." *I'd lost you for good. That my stupid pride had scared you away. That I was going to live the rest of my life wondering what might have been.*

He glanced toward the depot, and she took the opportunity to reacquaint herself with his face. With the fringe of lashes that tangled at the corners of his eyes, the sun-kissed cheeks, that little scar by the corner of his mouth.

He looked back to her and she pulled her eyes from his lips, feeling heat flood her face.

"So that's pretty cool, huh?" he said.

She didn't know if he was referring to the railroad deal or Grandma and David. It didn't matter. "Very cool. Thank you for your part in it."

He shrugged. "Didn't really do anything. It was all your aunt's doing. I hope she and your grandma work everything out."

"They will." She was more certain of that than ever.

They were talking about everything but what mattered. She could stand here making conversation, or she could be brave and say what she thought she'd never have the chance to say.

"I'm sorry I sent you away. I didn't mean it." Her eyes burned.

He stepped closer, his eyes softening. "I'm sorry too, for what I said."

She shook her head. "You were right. I was afraid."

He brushed her cheek with his thumb as if needing to remember how she felt. "Was?"

His touch was driving her to distraction. "I've done a lot of thinking since you've been gone, made some changes. I moved everything around at the nursery like you suggested, and I'm looking into starting my own business, and . . ." She didn't know quite how to say the rest.

"And . . . ?"

"And . . ." She swallowed hard. *Now or never, Clare.* "I'm thinking I might, you know, open my heart a little, give love a chance."

His hand moved down to her chin and he tipped her face upward. "Have anyone in particular in mind?"

Her smile wobbled. "Actually, I do. He's kind of a big risk, lives in a tent."

"Really? I heard he rented a place over on Lookaway Lane."

Her mouth parted. Wasn't he full of surprises. "Really?"

"Smitten is a mission field too." Ethan took her face in his hands. "I have an interview over at the airport next week."

She smiled. "You're going to fly again."

"If I get the job."

Her breath caught at the look in his eyes. They were saying all the things she longed to hear.

"I missed you, Clare."

She knew the feeling. The past two weeks had felt like a year. "Don't you ever go away again."

"Never," he whispered, drawing near.

She breathed him in, pine and leather. Ethan. His kiss was warm and slow, calling up wispy dreams of happily-ever-after. He pulled her closer, and she went willingly, at home in his embrace. He was the risk she'd been afraid to take, but the real risk had been in letting him go.

He broke the kiss, leaned his forehead against hers. "I love you, honey — in case I neglected to mention it earlier."

She relished the words she'd longed to hear, the term of endearment, the feel of his arms around her. "I love you too."

Somewhere in the distance a band struck up a festive tune. Children frolicked and neighbors caught up with one another. But then he kissed her again, and the sounds faded away as other senses took over.

A moment later he leaned back, his arms still around her. "I'm sorry I missed your big birthday bash."

Clare gave a wry laugh. "I was miserable — worst birthday ever."

"Turning thirty that rough?"

She swatted his shoulder. "I was missing you, you big oaf."

His lips twitched, his eyes twinkled. "That so?"

"You don't have to enjoy it so much," Clare said, pulling a pout. She didn't even want to think about that night again, or the last two weeks, for that matter.

"I'll make it up to you . . . dinner somewhere nice, over in Stowe. Soft music, candlelight, maybe a little dancing . . ." He swayed in time to the band.

Clare relented. How could she help it when he was looking at her like he was thoroughly charmed by her? "It's a start."

His eyes went all gentle. "I like the sound of that, Clare Thomas."

"It does have a nice ring, doesn't it?"

He was staring right into her, reminding her of the first time they'd met in a dank tool shed on that rainy spring night. It had bothered her then, that intense look, made her feel exposed. But now it only made her feel loved, cherished. There was something beautiful about being seen, right down into the darkest corners where all the secrets hid, and loved anyway. She supposed that's just the way God intended it . . . just the way a girl should feel when she was completely smitten.

READING GROUP GUIDE

1. Which heroine did you most relate to: Tess, Zoe, Anna, or Clare? Why?

2. We women can be so insecure. We wish we were thinner, blonder, and prettier. Instead of focusing on what you *don't* like about yourself, what *do* you like?

3. Tess mothered her sisters and everyone else but left little time for herself. What one thing can you start doing for yourself today?

4. Have you ever had anyone in your life who was a manipulator like Ryan's sister-in-law? How did you handle that person?

5. Zoe didn't want to go to college, though everyone else wanted it for her. Have you ever gone against the grain because you knew something wasn't right for you? Was

it the right decision?

6. William carries a sea turtle with him to remind him that home is where you make it. Have you ever carried something special to remind you of something? Do you think William really wanted a place to call home and not just a reminder of it?

7. William is a born worrier. Zoe takes life as it comes. Do you have a friend in your life who complements your weakness? How so?

8. Betrayal in Anna Thomas's life created a fear in her of trusting others. She finally had to let that go and trust God, the only One who never fails. Have you ever struggled with that? If so, what did you do about it?

9. Michael let his life get out of balance with his job eating up much of his family time. That created relationship problems between him and his son. What are some ways we can keep life in balance?

10. Anna didn't like confrontation for any reason. Sometimes in life, however, there is no avoiding it. When you're being

confronted or you're the one doing the confronting, how do you handle it?

11. When Ethan confronted Clare about her fear of change, she rejected the truth and became defensive, making a decision she soon regretted. Share a time when you've found yourself in a similar situation.

12. Clare discovered that dreams without a plan of action get you nowhere. Is there some dream you've had on the back burner for too long? Is it time for you to make a plan of action?

13. After losing Ethan, Clare realized that "sometimes taking no risk is the biggest risk of all." Have you discovered this to be true in your own life? Share a time when you avoided a risk only to realize it was a mistake.

ACKNOWLEDGMENTS

What a joy it's been to work on our second Smitten novel! The idea for *Secretly Smitten* was conceived in a beautiful Indiana log cabin (we pretended it was Vermont) and met with much enthusiasm by our wonderful editors.

As with every book, *Secretly Smitten* is the result of a lot of hard work done by many people. We are so blessed to work with Thomas Nelson. They've been supportive of the Smitten series right from the start, and their enthusiasm has been contagious. Thanks to the entire fiction team led by Publisher Daisy Hutton: Ami McConnell, Natalie Hanemann, Katie Bond, Kristen Vasgaard, Ruthie Dean, Laura Dickerson, Becky Monds, Kerri Potts, Jodi Hughes, and Amanda Bostic. Love you all!

A special thanks to our editors: Ami McConnell and LB Norton. Their expertise is truly astounding; we're so glad you have our backs!

Our agents Karen Solem and Lee Hough have been a huge help with this work and many others. Thanks, friends!

We're thankful for our families, our back-bones, as we juggle life and career.

Thanks to you, our reader — none of this would happen without you! We hope you enjoyed coming along on our journey back to Smitten.

Our biggest thank-you goes to God, who brought the four of us together in a bond of unbreakable friendship. We're all so different, and yet one, in our love for Christ and for one another.

ABOUT THE AUTHORS

RITA finalist **Colleen Coble** is the author of several best-selling romantic suspense series, including the Mercy Falls series, the Lonestar series, and the Rock Harbor series.

Christy Award finalist and two-time winner of the ACFW Book of the Year award, **Kristin Billerbeck** has appeared on the *Today Show* and has been featured in the *New York Times*. Her books include *A Billion Reasons Why* and *What a Girl Wants*.

Diann Hunt has lived in Indiana forever, been happily married forever, loves her family, chocolate, her friends, her dog, and, well, chocolate.

Denise Hunter is the award-winning and best-selling author of several novels, including *A Cowboy's Touch* and *Sweetwater Gap*. She and her husband are raising three boys in Indiana.

CPSIA information can be obtained
at www.ICGtesting.com
Printed in the USA
FFOW02n0952230813
1643FF